THE EYES
OF VENICE

Alessandro Barbero

THE EYES OF VENICE

*Translated from the Italian
by Gregory Conti*

Europa
editions

Europa Editions
214 West 29th Street
New York, N.Y. 10001
www.europaeditions.com
info@europaeditions.com

Library of Congress Cataloging in Publication Data is available
ISBN 978-1-60945-082-3

Barbero, Alessandro
The Eyes of Venice

Book design by Emanuele Ragnisco
www.mekkanografici.com

Cover image: Canaletto, *La Punta della Dogana*, 1726-28.
Oil on canvas (cm 46 × 62).
Photo © Ali Meyer/CORBIS

Prepress by Grafica Punto Print – Rome

Printed in the USA

THE EYES
OF VENICE

1.

The sun had been shining all day, but now the breeze off the lagoon had turned cold and the sky over Venice was growing turbulent. Matteo, standing on the main scaffold of the building under construction, wiped away the sweat with his sopping shirtsleeve for the hundredth time. In the summer the work day started early and never seemed to end. He looked at the sun to see how long it would be till sunset. None of the churches had sounded vespers yet, not even the Frari, which for a while now, because of some obsession or other of the bell-ringer, had taken to sounding it before all the others. Then he looked down at his men as they worked, pausing a moment over each one. Anybody else standing where he was, 65 feet above ground, would have avoided looking down for fear of vertigo, but Matteo had been a mason his whole life and was equally at ease on a scaffold as he was on the ground.

Beneath him, at the height of the second floor, three laborers were working quickly, unloading bricks from a nearly empty basket. Down on the ground, in the little square now covered in shade, a barefoot boy was stirring a tub of cement with a wooden stick, waiting for them to tell him to bring it up to them. Big and husky, used to thinking calmly about his business and staying on top of things, Matteo wondered if he shouldn't hire another laborer, or maybe two. If the owner really wanted the job done in a year, with the crew he had now he might not be able to deliver on time. But the mason wasn't sure if Senator Lippomano, despite his sumptuous garments and the proud crest with the rampant lion emblazoned on the cabin of his gondola, had enough cash to pay for the entire job. The hassle he had given him before paying for last month's work bothered him. No need to rush, Matteo thought, there's plenty of time to hire more workers, and relying on the rich is always risky business.

Making his way down to the lower level of the scaffold, the planks vibrating perilously under his weight, he told one of the laborers to go down and get another basket of bricks, gave a pat on the back to the last of the three, his son Michele, and then went down a few more steps before jumping directly into the court. The building was coming along nicely; even the architect who'd designed it on commission from the senator would have to admit that—and God knows Matteo had spent most of his working life fighting with architects. If they'd taken a brick in hand just once, instead of spending all their time sitting at a desk with a ruler and a quill pen, they wouldn't make such impractical demands! Among his fellow masons, it was common knowledge that once, a long, long time ago, buildings and churches were built by master craftsmen, without all the drawings and no need for a diploma, and, take a look around, all the buildings that were built back then are still standing. But as everybody knows, the world gets crazier all the time.

Sighing, because at the end of a day's work even a giant like himself began to feel tired, Matteo went to take a sip of wine from the flask they kept cool in the well bucket, right in the center of the square. The boy who'd been mixing the cement had left the tub and was now helping the laborer carry up the bricks, carefully piled in the wicker basket. Matteo had hired him the week before, when the other boy had quit; the pay was too low, he said, I can make more somewhere else, and if not I'll go to sea. The master mason shrugged, he knew it was hard to live on today's wages but he had a family to support. One ducat a month was all he could afford to pay, along with meals and a place to sleep on the floor in the entryway to his house. But at least there was always plenty to eat, thank God, nobody who worked for him ever had to climb up on the scaffold on an empty stomach. But he couldn't work without an apprentice and luckily he'd happened upon this lost Albanian. There were a lot of them in the city, and they worked hard and you had to pay them as much as anyone else, but this one here was still a kid, just arrived in Venice, and alone, as far as he could tell. Matteo liked him right off the bat, and so did his wife. Well yes, keep him, Zanetta had told him. They'd made an agreement: room and board until the end of the year, and that's it, just like a shop apprentice. Then, if you learn the job, you'll get paid. In the hope that Lippomano keeps paying every month, because if he doesn't cough up the zecchini the rest of us will starve to death. Now the boy was there on the job, climbing the scaffold, struggling to keep his hold on the handle of the overloaded basket. Zorze, his name was. He's going to make a good mason, Matteo thought, gazing at his skinny legs that now, however, were starting to thicken at the calves.

Then all of sudden the kid slipped. The heavy basket turned over on him, and he fell off the scaffold with a piercing scream. Bricks came pouring down after and on top of him, and a second later he was sprawled motionless on the pavement. "Virgin Mary!" everyone cried out. Matteo ran and in a minute he was kneeling next to him, while Michele and the other mason came scrambling down, making the scaffold tremble. Only the last laborer, the one who'd been carrying the basket together with Zorze, was still frozen in his tracks with his hands over his mouth. They could see right away there was nothing to do. The boy's bones were broken internally, and a lot of the bricks had come crashing down on him, hitting him in the chest and the head. Blood was seeping through his blond hair, his head was moving slowly, his glassy eyes rolling back, like the eyes of a cat that's just been clubbed to death.

"Virgin Mary," Matteo said again, afraid to touch him with his oversized hands. They all looked at each other.

"Should we take him home?" Michele said, in shock.

"I don't know," murmured Matteo. As always happened to him when things went wrong, the pain he felt inside was muffled by a smoldering rage. Why me? Damn work—and damn life . . .

"By now there's no use, look at him," said the last laborer, who meanwhile had come down off the scaffold, white as a sheet. And then everybody realized it was useless, the boy's eyes had turned into opaque glass, and his body had stopped moving. Michele knelt over him, touching him awkwardly, his pulse, his chest. He couldn't feel anything.

"He's gone, poor lad," he mumbled, and made the sign of the cross.

All the others did the same.

"What do we do now?" Michele asked. He hadn't yet turned twenty, and although his father had let him get married, he was still used to obeying him in everything. This time, however, even the master mason seemed baffled.

"Poor lad," he said again, tears welling in his eyes. Just then, the bell tower of the Frari began ringing out vespers, and Matteo pulled himself together. "The first thing we need to do is tell the owner. Then we'll take him home. By now it's late, we'll think about the burial tomorrow."

While Michele ran home to tell the women, one of the two laborers was sent to look for Senator Lippomano. Matteo staggered back over to the well, grabbed the flask and took another long swig, then he noticed the remaining laborer staring at him, curled up under the scaffold, and he motioned for him to come and take a drink. This is the last thing we needed, he thought, and he felt as though his head were spinning more than it should have been. What the hell, he thought, it's not my fault. I treated him good.

Just then Michele came back, with his mother and his wife. Their house was nearby, on a little square identical to the one where they were working, looking out on the Giudecca Canal. The two women knelt next to the dead boy, crying uncontrollably. Even though he'd only been living with them for a few days, everyone liked Zorze, so blond the way he was, and with that funny way of talking, the half-mastered Venetian dialect that sounded so strange with his hard pronunciation.

"Fate!" Zanetta declared finally, after the two of them had wailed for a while, as was the custom. And both of them turned to thinking about practical things. In such cases it was the women who took the situation in hand, heaven forbid that they should have to wait for the men. Michele, who was clinging to his wife Bianca and trembling a little, was sent off with one of the laborers to look for a stretcher to transport the body, and a sheet to cover it. Then Zanetta went over to Matteo, looked with a sigh at the empty flask left on the ground next to the bucket, and shot him a glance of disapproval. Her husband, embarrassed, wiped his mouth with the back of his hand.

"How did it happen?" the woman asked, breaking the silence.

"I don't know!" the mason exclaimed. "He was climbing up the scaffold with a load of bricks, together with Teta. I don't know, he slipped. And . . . "

The woman didn't speak. Only she knew that ever since her son had started getting up on the scaffold with his father, she waited every evening with a foreboding disquiet for them to return home, expecting each time that instead of the two of them a boy would appear at the door, sent to call her because there had been an accident. For some reason, as long as it was only her husband who went off to work she'd never been afraid. But now that her son was working too, she shuddered to think of it. He was the only child she had left, the other two boys had been taken from her by the plague of 1576, the one everybody remembered with dread, because it had killed half of Venice. He was the only one left, the youngest, and after that she hadn't had any more. In the meantime, how many years had gone by? Twelve? Yes, twelve, her baby boy had become an adult, and gone off to the building sites with his father. Oh life, Zanetta thought.

The sound of hurrying footsteps gave her a start. A man dressed in black velvet with a shiny gold chain around his neck came rushing into the square: his magnificence, Sir Girolamo Lippomano. Bianca, who was standing closer to him, had already launched into an embarrassed curtsey, and Zanetta hurried to do the same, as Matteo went over to him and bowed awkwardly. The Senator ignored the two women, nodded abruptly to the mason and planted himself before the corpse of the young boy, still lying on the ground. He winced and then looked up at the scaffolding on the side of the building under construction. Girolamo Lippomano looked to be around fifty. He had a high, hairless forehead grooved with wrinkles, a few gray hairs cut very short and a well-trimmed beard that was beginning to turn white. A longtime member of the Senate, elected several times to the office of Savio Grande and recently named Procurator of Saint Mark, he was one of the Republic's most highly respected diplomats. He'd begun his diplomatic career as ambassador to Turin and to Naples, and then rose to ever more important posts, as ambassador to the King of Poland and even to the King of France. From these prestigious courts he sent back reports with top-secret information that only he knew how to procure. His colleagues, who governed Venice with an iron fist and were never surprised by anything, held him in the highest esteem. After taking a long look at the unfinished building, Sir Girolamo turned to look at the corpse, taking a step backwards, and winced again. He didn't even think to doff his beret; but he did make a quick sign of the cross, and then ordered Matteo to come closer.

"Who was he?" he asked brusquely. Matteo shrugged.

"An apprentice. I'd only just taken him on."

"And where was he from?"

"From Albania," he said.

Lippomano winced again.

"We'll have to find one of their priests," Matteo said. The Senator gave him a cold look.

"What for? He's already dead; he doesn't need to go to confession anymore. Take him under the portico of the Ducal Palace and leave him there, the city gravediggers will bury him."

Matteo hesitated. He wasn't accustomed to disobeying his superiors, but this time he couldn't keep quiet.

"Illustrious Sir, that's not good enough. He has to be blessed by one of their priests. Otherwise his soul will never rest in peace."

Lippomano stared at him with sudden attention, then shrugged.

"Do what you want. Just don't come asking me for any money."

Michele and the laborer arrived with the stretcher. On seeing the Senator they both bowed, then they set the stretcher down next to the dead body and, grabbing him by the armpits and knees, loaded him onto it. He wasn't very heavy. The laborer had a bundle tied around his neck that, unraveled, turned out to be an old sheet from the house. They covered the boy with it, making the sign of the cross on his forehead.

"Where will you take him?" the Senator asked.

"I thought we'd take him back to my house," Matteo said.

"Bravo," replied Sir Girolamo, disinterested.

Matteo turned to the others.

"Okay, take him home. I'll be there soon."

The two laborers lifted the stretcher and set it on their shoulders. Michele, Bianca, and Zanetta bowed one more time and then headed off behind the body. Lippomano waited until he was alone with Matteo, then he pulled an embroidered handkerchief out of his cuff and dried the sweat from his high forehead. The sky had partly clouded over, but the wind had died down, and the air was heavy with humidity. Matteo, in shirtsleeves and canvas shoes, with no socks and his beret in hand, figured the Senator was feeling the heat. Too bad for him that the laws of the Republic are so severe and so rigorous with regard to the decorum of the nobles, who aren't allowed to go out dressed as they wish, but always in black, or in purple if they are magistrates in the exercise of their official duties, because all of them, from the first to the last, represent the Serene Republic. But the rest of us, Matteo thought, can go around barefoot with rags on our backs, and it doesn't matter at all to anyone, not even if we die in a corner of the street.

"Listen, Matteo, I've got something to tell you," Lippomano said.

"At your orders."

"Tell me, how far along are you with the work?"

The tone with which the Senator had posed the question put Matteo on guard.

"As I told you, your Excellency," he began prudently, "it'll take all of a year and a half, but I'll be able to hand over the completed building next year in time for the holidays. If you'd rather I finished sooner then . . ."

Matteo interrupted himself; something told him that this was not the right time to be asking Lippomano for more money. In fact, Sir Girolamo was staring at him with an unpleasant look, playing with the gold chain he wore on his chest. He had thin fingers, with manicured nails.

"No," he said abruptly. "Instead, let's suspend the work. I'm going away, I don't know yet when, maybe as early as this winter. I'll be away for at least two years. And I don't want the work going forward when I'm not here to be in charge."

Matteo already felt a little dizzy and this unexpected blow knocked him back.

"But Illustrious Sir . . . " was all he could muster.

"No buts!" Lippomano cut him off, with the tone of someone who is used to being in command and not being contradicted. "Even as it is I can't understand how this building is costing me so much. Imagine if I weren't here to keep an eye on things. I know what you people are like."

Disheartened, Matteo didn't answer.

"So we're agreed then," the Senator concluded. "You'll come to my house tomorrow and we'll settle the accounts. Good-bye, Matteo."

"Your servant, Excellency," the mason muttered. As the other man walked off, Matteo stood there with his cap in hand, so confused he didn't know if it was morning or evening. Then he remembered the flask and looked over toward the well, but Zanetta, who never left anything out of place, must have taken it home with her. Matteo spit and after taking a good look around, he cursed, but under his breath. Even the walls had ears, and if they got an anonymous complaint about his behavior, the Holy Office of the Inquisition wouldn't think twice about hauling in some poor guy for a couple of lashes. Matteo remembered full well that it had not always been that way. When he was young people were not so afraid, and no one thought there was anything terrible about a curse spoken in anger. But times had changed and not so much for the better. We don't even have the satisfaction of cursing anymore. What a world, he thought bitterly, as he went on his way home.

When he got there he discovered they'd been waiting for him to eat dinner. He washed his hands in the bucket, sat down at the table on the only good chair, with arms; Michele sat in the other chair, at his right side. The laborers took their places on two stools. By contract, the workers ate with them and Matteo deducted the meals from their pay. Zanetta and

Bianca served the soup, then Zanetta sat down on the edge of the fireplace with her bowl on her knees, while Bianca went on working, stoking the fire, fetching a bucket of cool water from the well. Finally, she served herself a bowl of soup, took her place standing next to her mother-in-law, and started eating. When he finished his first bowl of soup, Matteo had her serve him another ladleful, grabbed the big loaf of stale bread and cut off a slice with the knife he carried in his belt, dipped it in the soup and started chewing. Nobody talked. The dead body had been laid on the floor in one of the two bedrooms, the one where the younger couple slept.

"But tonight, we'll take him in there, right?" Bianca whispered, nodding her head toward the kitchen. Having the dead body in the house made her skin creep. Michele wanted to say yes but out of habit he waited for his father to speak.

"Sure," Matteo finally said, as he went on chewing. Then, feeling the anger burning in his belly, he told them the news from Lippomano.

Bad things never happen one at a time, Zanetta thought, but she didn't say it.

"What good news!" she said instead.

Everyone stopped eating, and in the eyes of the two laborers you could clearly see the fear that this soup would be their last. There wasn't much work to be had in Venice in those days.

"Just like that, he says he's going away?" Michele enquired, curious. His father just shrugged but his mother chimed in again.

"He must have some new ambassadorship. You're too young to remember, but years ago he was always away."

"But it's been a long while now that he hasn't been away," Matteo intervened gloomily.

"Yes, and what's more, I hear he's been saying that he's had enough of traveling," Zanetta added, recalling the chat she'd had with one of Lippomano's household servants, a childhood friend of hers she met sometimes at the fish market.

"Give me something to drink for once," Matteo said, and right away, Bianca, who had also been sitting on the step next to the fire, got up, went to get the flask, and filled his glass. Matteo drank and then leaned his elbows on the table. "It's all very clear, couldn't be any clearer," he blurted out angrily. "The guy is hard up for money. I figured that out last month, when I had to work so hard to get him to pay up. He may not be going away at all. It's just an excuse to close down the job."

"And in the meantime he leaves you without any work," Zanetta protested.

"Come on now, people like us who are good at what we do, can always find work," Michele declared cheerfully. Bianca looked for his eyes and found them. He smiled at her, and she could feel the knot in her stomach start to loosen. Before they were married, he'd said to her once, you'll see, with a guy like me, one way or another, you won't go hungry. Now, every once in while they jokingly reminded each other of that, especially in bed, as the old people snored. Michele was only a kid and didn't know anything about life, but since she was a kid too, she trusted him blindly. Matteo and Zanetta looked for each other's eyes too, but they'd been through a lot together. There wasn't a whole lot of trust left in their eyes.

It was getting dark, and Bianca got busy arranging for some candlelight. The flame from the candle, flickering on the table, gave everybody the impression that the rest of the house was even darker.

"Come on, let's wash the dishes and go to bed," Zanetta sighed, getting up from her corner. "The rest of you carry that poor lad in here."

As the women cleaned up, the men took the table off the sawhorses, put it back up against the wall along with the chairs and stools, and carried the stretcher with the dead body into the kitchen, depositing it on the straw pallet where the boy had slept until the night before. It wasn't long before the men, with their twelve hours of work weighing on them, were sleeping like rocks. Zanetta and Bianca stayed up to keep watch over the boy, because it's not right to leave a dead person alone on the first night. The candle lit the room dimly, and the two women sat there next to each other in silence until Bianca finally gave in and dozed off, and Zanetta was left alone to keep vigil through the night.

2.

When they woke up the next morning, a thick gray fog was looming over Venice. The two men emerged from bed soaked in sweat, even though they'd slept naked, or almost, under the linen sheets; all that was left from Zanetta's trousseau. When Michele came out of the bedroom, he shot a glance at the dead body lying in the corner, covered by his patched-up sheet, and without thinking about it he sniffed the air. Maybe you could already smell the odor? No, thank God, but it wouldn't be long, with that heat. In the kitchen, the two women, already busy and cheeks flushed, their eyes still puffy with sleep, were preparing the first soup of the day, a clean rag tied around their heads to hold back the sweat when they got near the fire. Michele walked barefoot out into the square; his father, bear-chested, was washing himself at the well.

"You go see about the burial," he told Michele when he saw him coming, moving aside to leave him the bucket. "I don't have time."

Michele plunged his hands into the water and washed his face, enjoying the pleasure of the cool rivulets slithering down his neck.

"Okay," he said. "But where is it that I have to go?"

"To the Albanian School, I'd say. If they don't know what to do, I sure as hell don't. You have to look for the Church of San Maurizio. It seems to me it's behind Saint Mark's, but ask your mother, she knows better than I do."

Michele had never heard of that church, but he knew very

well what a school was. Just about everybody in Venice was enrolled in a School, even he and his parents. Theirs was the closest one to their house, under the protection of the glorious virgin Saint Agnes, although the ceremonies were held in the church of Saint Barnabas, two bridges farther down. When he turned sixteen, his father took him to the church, made him kneel in front of the altar of the saint, paid his forty soldi enrollment fee and had him write his name in the *madrègola*, as the book was known where the names of all the members of the confraternity were recorded. Because the School, you understand, was certainly not a place for learning how to read and write, as he used to believe. That'll be the day, Matteo laughed, when everybody wants to waste their time on things like that. Working people have more important things to think about. You enrolled in the School and paid the annual dues because when you got sick the confraternity provided assistance, if you lost your job they gave you charity; and when you died they took care of your funeral. It was important to know that you wouldn't end up being buried all alone like a dog but that they would accompany you with lighted candles, and the banner of the School at the head of the procession. That's how Matteo had explained it to Michele. He, Michele, wasn't so inclined to worry about that far off day, but he obeyed like he always did, despite thinking to himself that his parents had some very strange preoccupations.

He went back into the house, where the two women had put the table back on the horses and ladled out the soup. Bianca looked at him with satisfaction as he started to eat. She had only just embarked on her vocation as a wife, but she was learning fast and she liked making her husband feel good. Then Matteo came in, noisily took his seat at the table, looked at his plate and scowled.

"What's wrong?" Zanetta rushed to ask.

"With this heat . . . Give me a glass of wine then."

Zanetta made a face but didn't say anything. Knowing her husband's weakness, when she got up she had already put the wine bottle to cool in a bucket of water. She went to get it and poured him a glass. Matteo gulped it down, sighed with satisfaction and cut himself a slice of bread.

"Another one; this red stuff is the best soup of all."

Zanetta filled his glass again, and the mason dipped his bread in the wine and began chewing it with pleasure.

"So then, what have you decided?" the woman asked a couple of minutes later, and when her husband looked quizzical she gestured toward the dead body.

"Ah! Michele's going to the Albanians, they'll know what to do."

"Where's the church of San Maurizio?" the boy asked his mother, wiping his plate clean with a piece of bread.

"It's easy, from Rialto you go to the right toward the Riva del Ferro and down the Calle dei Fabbri, but not as far as Saint Mark's square, and if you can't find it, ask somebody."

"Okay, I'm off then," Michele concluded, getting up from the table. He caught his wife's eye and shot her a half smile: come on outside and say good-bye the way a good wife does. She responded with a smile of her own, left the beans she'd been shucking, dried her hands on her apron, and followed him out the door. Between the front door and the square, in a corner where no one could see them, they gave each other a fleeting wet kiss.

"I love you so much," he whispered in her ear. She smiled happily, and then hurried back inside, so the in-laws wouldn't think something was amiss.

Michele set off at a fast pace. It was a long way to the Rialto—the only bridge over the Grand Canal. If he had taken a boat over to the other side he would have been there in a minute, but it didn't even cross his mind to throw away a soldo like that. In those days only rich people took the ferry and the boatmen complained that they didn't have enough work. Lean years, leaner than anyone could remember, except maybe during the reign of Doge Loredan, when Michele was just a baby. His mother told him that Loredan used to be called the Famine Doge, and at his funeral the people pelted his coffin with loaves of the millet bread they'd been forced to eat to survive; bread that was fit for pigs but not for human beings.

Michele went up the canal as far as the Frari, and then over to Campo San Polo, where he realized that he was sweating and slowed his pace because a half hour more or less wasn't going to change anything. He was in shirtsleeves and wearing no socks but the humidity was suffocating, so much so that he took off his cap and stuck it in his belt. The people out on the streets were all busy working. Every minute or so he passed a loaded pull-cart or a porter with a sack on his back. In front of a bakery, a long line of women waited for their turn to bake their own bread; it was Saturday and everyone wanted to have fresh-baked bread for Sunday. It wasn't often that Michele left his neighborhood. Even the building contracts his father worked on were almost always in their area. There were far too many masons in Venice to think you could find work where people didn't know you. Now the young man was having a grand old time discovering new streets and squares, but then he remembered the reason for this walk through the city and quickly made the sign of the cross.

At the Rialto the market was so big and crowded he could hardly make his way through it. Michele didn't dare use his elbows to clear a path through the women bargaining over prices, expectant mothers weighed down by their protruding bellies, the well-nourished, florid-cheeked cooks in the employ of noble families, and every now and again a young wife or servant girl with her shirt unlaced at the bosom and the sleeves rolled up to beat the heat. Out of habit, Michele always gave those young women a smug look. Before he was married, he and his friends would often go wandering the streets in their free time and they'd given them a lot more than looks! There was no lack of loud-voiced comments always uttered in the hope that the girl was willing, and always disappointed. Once, on a Sunday night, after they had been drinking, somebody proposed that they go to a certain street to lay in wait for a girl who came there every night to sell herself, and convince her, nicely or not so nicely, to show them a good time. Michele had hesitated at first and then said no, I'm not coming. He'd felt ashamed of himself all night long for acting like a coward, but then the next day his friends told him he'd been smarter than the others. The girl never showed up but in her absence a police patrol came by and they all risked getting arrested. Michele smiled at the memory. He still felt a little ashamed of himself, even if he wasn't sure anymore for what. Anyway, now he was a married man and boyhood pranks like that were something he'd never do again.

The Rialto bridge was all but closed to traffic due to construction. A few months ago they had started demolishing the old wooden structure and it was said that they were going to replace it with a new one made completely out of marble, but in the meantime the only way to cross the Grand Canal was a gangway that could be used by only one person at a time. There was a huge crowd waiting to cross and the people were protesting. Why in the world did they have to replace the old bridge when it worked just fine, and even worse, why spend all that money just to create all that inconvenience for people who had work to do! On the other side of the bridge it was just as hard to make your way through the fruit and vegetable stands and the fish counters and the hordes of customers, but finally Michele was able to turn down the street with all the blacksmith shops all lined up in a row. There was much less traffic and he could get back to walking at a decent pace. He had to stop a couple of times and ask his way because he really didn't know that part of the city very well, but he finally came to the rear of a tall, crooked bell tower and walked around it into the empty square of the church of San Maurizio. In one corner, next to the church, there was a low building with a small door that looked like it might be the home of the School. Michele went over to it, put his hand on the knocker, and knocked.

The door was opened directly by the chaplain, one of those Greek Orthodox priests with a threatening beard and a big cross hanging around his neck. Michele explained in a few words the story of the dead boy. The priest scratched his head, puzzled.

"But was the poor soul enrolled in the School?" he finally asked. Michele shrugged.

"How could he have been enrolled, he'd only just arrived in Venice."

"And what did you say his name was?" the priest insisted.

"Zorze. That's all I know," Michele said, apologetically.

The bearded man let out a long sigh.

"Wait here and we'll see. We've certainly got no obligation, you know."

He vanished into the building then he came out again, went over to the front of another house and called out. A window opened, a woman looked out, and the priest spoke to her briefly in his mother tongue. The woman disappeared and a minute later a man came to the window, an old man with thinning gray hair. The two men, one down in the square and the other in the window, talked for a while. Then the old man withdrew from the window and after what seemed to Michele like a rather long time, he reappeared at the door.

Together, the two men walked over to him. "Tell him again what happened," said the priest. Michele repeated his story. The old man scratched his head, just like the other man had done. He wasn't happy either. But on the other hand, Michele thought, what was there to be happy about?

"But are you sure he was Albanian?" the old man finally said. His accent was a bit thicker than the priest's, as though he hadn't ever really gotten used to speaking Venetian.

"Absolutely certain," Michele reassured him. The two men looked at each other and conferred a bit in their language, completely ignoring the young man who was still there and who couldn't understand a word they said. Then the priest told him that everything was fine, they would take care of the funeral.

"But only out of charity, eh? We're not obliged, but for one of ours, when we can, we do it willingly. We'll send a gravedigger to get him this evening."

Michele explained the way to his house from the church of St. Agnes, and went on his way content with how things had gone. At least that problem was taken care of. After all, it's Saturday, he mused, tomorrow we don't work, and tonight, without the dead body in the house, Bianca won't be so sad the way she was last night.

He was so enthused by the idea that he didn't notice that he had gone the wrong way. When he realized it, he was in a square he'd never seen before and there was nobody he could ask, so he followed his instinct and entered a portico he figured would take him back to the Rialto. Instead, to his great surprise, he found himself looking up at the façade of Saint Mark's. Curiosity drew his gaze down to the water where a group of bannered masts announced the presence of some large vessels, and he struggled to make his way through the usual crowd gathered between the Ducal Palace and the monastery of Saint Zachary. When he got down to the water he saw that two galleys were docked nearby, in a fluttering of multicolored flags and pennants. Both of them were loading trunks and barrels transported from the dock by their tenders. Michele stood there for a while, his eyes wide with wonder, observing the operation. The galleys were huge and utterly

gorgeous, with a brand new coat of red paint, and their ver-
milion oars raised and fastened in their oarlocks, like the paws
of some fabulous beast. Two oarsmen, in canvas trousers,
patched shirts, and regulation red caps, were standing next to
him holding a barrel, waiting for their turn to load it on the
tender. Curious, Michele started up a conversation.

"Where are you sailing to?"

One of the two looked at him and batted his eyes as though
he didn't understand; fair-haired and blue-eyed, he must have
been a Slavonian.

"Who knows?" the other one replied. "Nobody ever tells
us where we're going. But there are rumors that we're headed
for Candia," he added, using the Venetian name for Crete.
Then he stared at Michele and asked him point blank:

"Do you by chance want to sign on for the voyage?"

Michele started.

"Me? No way!" he said. "It's got to be a pretty hard life,"
he added. The other man spat.

"No worse than a working stiff landlubber's. Your wages
are paid, and anybody who signs on now gets a five zecchini
premium from the *sopracomito*. I'll bet you've never in your life
set eyes on five zecchini."

"So you're looking for people?" Michele asked, his curiosity piqued.

"Hey, we're always looking for people," the other man
replied. But he didn't add anything else and kept on studying
Michele. He must have got it into his head that if he were the
one to take him to the sopracomito, there would probably be
a zecchino in it for him too.

"Well?" he asked again, when he saw Michele had taken to
looking at the galley closest to them, where men were rolling
barrels along the deck, making them disappear down into the
hold.

"Well, what?" Michele replied.

"Are you sure you're not interested? The sopracomito set up the counter yesterday for new recruits and he'll keep it there for a week. We need more than fifty men."

"Me no, I'm not interested" Michele said sharply. He was almost offended that they considered him a man who would sell himself to a galley and live like a slave for starvation wages; he who was the son of a master mason, enrolled in a guild.

"As you wish," the other man said, disappointed. Then his partner gave him an elbow in the ribs and they left, because the tender was waiting for them. Michele stood there a while watching, then he realized that his father might be expecting him at the work site, and he went on his way. The last time his father had sent him on an errand and he hadn't come back till evening, Matteo had given him enough belt lashes that he still hadn't forgotten it, even though it was two or three years ago.

The mason had left home to go do the accounts with the owner. Ever since the Ca' Lippomano in the Santa Sofia neighborhood had been burned in a fire, a good many years ago, each of the Lippomano cousins lived on his own, and given that most of them were men of the church—bishops in Padua or Verona—they didn't need a building in the city to serve as their headquarters. Sir Girolamo was the first to have decided to build one, but it just might be that his reach was longer than his grasp, the mason was thinking, ruminating bitterly. Doing the accounts with his clients had never been the most pleasant part of his work. Standing on the scaffold, come rain or come shine, working with an axe or a saw or the trowel, giving orders to the laborers, and watching a new building grow taller day by day in the care of his hands, all those things he liked and then some. But having to talk about figures and money with the owners was a whole different story. To get his courage up before their meeting, he stopped in a tavern for a glass of wine, and since he was already there he stayed for another, and finally he stepped up out of the pleasant, damp shade of the tavern into the sweltering hot street.

On his return from his last ambassadorship, in a faraway country whose name Matteo had never been able to recall, Senator Lippomano had bought a house near the church of the Carmines. When the mason arrived, Lippomano was waiting for him in his study, sitting at a table covered with a large Turkish carpet and cluttered with papers, wearing a pair of eyeglasses that squeezed his nose.

"Oh, Matteo, come here," he said flatly. Matteo was dressed in clean clothes, but he still moved awkwardly, afraid of mussing the furniture. He took off his cap and took a firm stance in the center of the room. The Senator stared at him coldly, through the shiny lenses of his glasses.

"So, let's see what you've got."

Matteo laid out his papers on the table. He didn't know how to read or write, but he had learned how to tabulate accounts, even though he kept everything in his head anyway. The columns of strokes and crosses that he toiled over were only a visual aid. He leaned forward and began to explain, pointing with his index finger. Sir Girolamo had drawn back as soon as he'd gotten a whiff of his breath, but he was listening carefully, occasionally interjecting a question. When Matteo had finished, he began to reexamine the entire account, checking one item at a time, and contesting all of them. The mason had had troublesome clients before and he didn't let himself get rattled. The wine gave him courage. It'll take a lot more than this! he thought, you're not the one who's going to get the better of me. They had long arguments over the prices of cement and bricks, the wages of the apprentice and the laborers. The Senator felt they were overpaid.

"You've gotten used to treating yourselves too well!" he said venomously, removing his glasses. Matteo, his gaze darkening, reminded him of the price of bread. "You think I don't

know what it costs?" Lippomano shot back. "The wheat supply from the East has dried up, that dog of a Turk is keeping it
all for himself. We've all got to make sacrifices, but you people
don't want to understand that!"

Matteo shrugged; the way he saw it he'd already made his
share of sacrifices. By now even eating meat on Sunday had
become an exception to the rule. The Senator put his glasses
back on, and went back to examining the figures he'd transcribed into his ledger as Matteo had gone through them.

"So according to you I owe you fifty zecchini?" he said in
the end, with a sour smile.

"Fifty-two, Excellency."

Lippomano pursed his lips and fell silent.

Then he said, "Not on your life." The tone was intended to
be harsh but his voice cracked in the middle of the sentence.
Matteo was so surprised he didn't know what to say. "But the
figures . . ." he stammered.

"What figures?" Lippomano retorted, sounding more confident. "Your figures make me laugh!" Tapping his finger on
the papers he went back to contesting every item. Everything
had been overpaid, and the quantities for all the supplies were
wrong too. Too much lumber, for example. Who ever heard of
using so many oak beams? And wasn't there too much cement
for the number of bricks they'd laid? The mason, whose head
had already been filling with blood, couldn't contain himself
any longer.

"Who is building this house, me or you?"

Lippomano blanched.

"How dare you, you scoundrel!" he exclaimed. Matteo,
beside himself, gritted his teeth, leaned forward, and showed
him his fist.

"Mind your words, or you'll be sorry!" he growled.

In his fifty years of life nothing like that had ever happened
to the Senator, and he couldn't believe it was happening now.

A vulgar, uncultured lout, a manual laborer paid so much per day, instead of kissing his hand to thank him for the work he gave him, allowed himself to speak to him in that insolent tone and to threaten him, yes, to threaten him, in his own home! For a second, his astonishment, anger, and even fear, stifled his voice in his throat. "Out of here," he finally screamed, jumping to his feet. "Get out! And come back when you're sober again and have put your accounts in order, you thief!"

"Thief? You're the thief, if you don't pay up! Thief, cuckold, and varmint!" shouted the mason, blind with rage. "You're all the same, you nobles, capable only of sucking the blood of the poor! Oh, the time will come when we'll make you pay! God will come, or the devil, or the Turk, and then you'll see, you dogs, you're nothing but dogs!" He spat on the floor with contempt, swept up his papers in one hand, and rushed out of the study in a fury. Lippomano, ashen, stood there for a moment, his clenched fists resting on the scarlet carpet; then, as his color came back, he shook his head slowly, staring hatefully at the empty doorway.

"You'll pay for this," he vowed.

That evening Matteo came back home with a contorted face, his eyes wide open, and his breath smelling more than ever of wine. He'd spent the whole day wondering around looking for work, but none of his contacts knew of anything. Even beyond the neighborhood, all the way to Canareggio, he hadn't found a single construction site in need of a new crew. There had already been plenty of other times when Matteo had been out of work between one contract and another; it was normal in his trade, or better, in all the trades. No artisan was lucky enough to have work every day, except the ship's carpenters and the caulkers who by law had the right to draw their pay at the Arsenal every blessed day if they didn't have work in their shop. But he had never been afraid; sooner or later, God would see to it that work came his way, and a little money to tide them over during the wait had never been lacking.

This time, however, if Lippomano didn't pay, he would run out of money very soon. At the mere thought of going back to the Senator, hat in hand, to beg him at least for an advance, Matteo could feel his stomach turn. With clients from the nobility, repeated requests for payment were the rule, and even bowing and scraping to get what was rightfully owed to you, but as he rushed down the stairs Matteo had sworn to himself that he would never stoop so low with that one there. But the master mason was no fool. He knew damn well that it was easier to swear such oaths than it was to maintain them, and that if he didn't come up with another contract, in just a few days wine would be giving him the courage to retrace his steps and swallow his pride. Assuming that, in the meantime, the Senator had not already denounced him. Matteo couldn't remember what he had actually said in that instant of blind rage, but he knew he'd said enough to merit a fine that would leave him breathless and maybe even a few lashes with the rope, just to teach him to bite his tongue the next time he spoke with a patrician. That's why the mason was so agitated when he got back home empty-handed. He didn't say a word at dinner, and when Michele, naively, asked him if they were going back to work on Monday he answered him so harshly that Bianca's eyes filled with tears, and everyone finished eating in silence.

But Michele didn't let it get him down. He had a thick skin when it came to his father's heavy silences and his unpredictably gruff demeanor. He didn't notice how much their quarreling made his mother suffer and, like any twenty-year-old, he thought much more about himself and his own woman than he did the elder couple. The important moments of his day had been his expedition to San Maurizio Square and, later on, the arrival of the gravedigger from the School, who, with two assistants, had carried off the body of the dead boy. Matteo wasn't there and he, Michele, had been the man of the house. He'd discussed things with the Albanians and worked everything out, and he was still proud and excited about that.

As the summer evening wore on, Matteo dozed at the table and the two women sewed in the last light of day, sitting on the front doorstep. Michele waited impatiently for darkness to fall so it would be time to go to bed. Finally, realizing that she couldn't see well enough anymore to thread her needle, Zanetta decided it was too late, went over to rouse her husband, took him in arm, led him off to their bedroom, and closed the door. The young couple heard her muttering Hail Marys, Our Fathers, and Glory Bes, then the sound of those two big bodies getting settled on the mattress, and after a while the both of them snoring, Matteo's sibilant and Zanetta's sonorous and coarse.

Michele had gone out to sit on the step beside his wife.

"It's time to go in," he whispered, putting his arm around her shoulders.

Bianca didn't need to be told twice. After barring the door, they undressed in silence, smiling at each other in the shadows, hung their clothes on the hook nailed to the wall, and slid down onto the bed, already fondling each other. They were both inexperienced, the first times they'd hurt themselves, and even now Michele almost always unintentionally hurt Bianca. Sometimes Zanetta woke up and listened through the wall, smiling tenderly as she recognized the fear, shame, and awkwardness that had been hers many years ago. Every night, though, Bianca noticed that Michele's hands were getting more familiar, and that her body was finding it easier to relax under their touch, but at the beginning she still closed up as if they were the hands of a stranger.

"Not so rough," she murmured when he squeezed her breast too hard. But then she took Michele's hand, which had quickly pulled away, and put it back where it was. He squeezed again, but more gently, and kissed her on the neck. She wriggled onto her side, and looked for his mouth.

"Come on," she whispered after a while, turning on to her back and pulling him down on top of her.

As the two old people snored on the other side of the wall, Bianca opened her legs and felt Michele slide into her, almost without hurting her, and she bit down on the sheet to keep from screaming. For an instant she closed her eyes but then she reopened them and saw Michele's staring joyously into hers, his mouth gaping for breath as he strained, and she smiled at him, ecstatic. He smiled too, stopping for a moment, then he plunged his face into her hair and started moving again.

"And if a baby comes?" he murmured in her ear. Up to then they'd done everything possible not to have any, given that times were so tough. When they got married her mother had taught her what to do, and told her not to tell anyone, not even her confessor. This time, though, she realized she didn't care anymore.

"Let it come," she whispered, her eyes shining brightly.

At that very moment Sir Girolamo Lippomano was sitting as his desk, writing a letter in the candlelight. "Most Excellent Lords," he began, "knowing from my own experience that there is no affront to the honor of this Most Serene Dominion that is too small to be made known and punished in the interest of the public good, I hereby bring to your attention that today, in my own home . . ." There followed the detailed account of how Matteo the mason, come to bring him the accounts that he, Lippomano, had found to be falsified, had permitted himself to insult him and threaten him, directing his anger not only at him but at the entire order of the nobility who so wisely and paternally governed the Republic. "And no one could fail to see," Lippomano concluded after chewing a bit on his pen, "how such an insult cannot be tolerated, not so much for me, who as a good Christian am ready lovingly to forgive, but in my capacity as a Senator and Procurator of St. Mark, such that every shameful attack and threat made against me can be said to have been made against this Most Serene Republic." After rereading the letter, Lippomano folded it, closed it with sealing wax, and wrote on the back the most feared address in Venice: "To their Lordships the Heads of the Most Excellent Council of Ten."

3

B loody Venice!"
The exclamation startled the innkeeper, who was dozing behind the bar, now and again shooing off the flies that kept buzzing around his head. He peered out into the semi-darkness of the cellar, wrapped in silence. At a table where four or five shirtsleeved men sat drinking, the biggest of them slammed his fist down on the table, hard enough to shake the pitcher and tinted glasses.

"Bloody Venice!" Matteo said again. "And there's not a man who can gainsay me! You sure can't call this a life the way they make us live here!"

"I'm the one who can gainsay you, my dear sir," the innkeeper said, striding slowly over to the table. "Here in my place we don't talk that way."

The occupants of the table, like Matteo all masons and also like him unemployed, glared at the innkeeper. They'd been drinking for a while now and some of them were starting to see double. If Matteo had made a move, they would have been up and fighting in no time. But the innkeeper knew how to handle himself; he had to face situations like that every day. Before Matteo could respond, he had already reached the table, and he bent down over them, resting his meaty hands right in the middle of it.

"Come on now, don't be making trouble for me. Whoever wants to can walk in here at any time," he said, in a confidential tone. Then he picked up the empty pitcher.

"Good, huh?" he said, clicking his tongue. "Could you use some more?"

The tension eased visibly. In their hearts, really, more than one of the masons were happy that the tavern-keeper had come over to interrupt Matteo. That kind of talk could get you into serious trouble.

"Come on, wine makes all your worries go away," one of them chimed in. The others smiled, only Matteo looked gloomy.

"Good thing you want wine and not water," the innkeeper joked. "I couldn't give you water if I wanted to, the well is dry."

They all started talking about the drought. In Venice, drinking water was always in short supply, but that summer was the worst in a long time. The water sellers, who brought it in barrels from the mainland and sold it in buckets on the streets, had raised their prices.

"Won't be long till water costs as much as wine," one of them laughed.

The tavern-keeper had just come back with a pitcher of white when a man looked in the doorway and called him. Recognizing him, the tavern-keeper wiped his hands on his apron, and hurried up the five or six steps to street level.

"You came at just the right time," he said, turning back toward the table. "They're here to deliver the water for the well."

Out on the street there was a cart pulled by two porters with four casks of water on it. The man who had called the innkeeper had a piece of paper in his hand.

"Where's the well?" he asked.

"This way, out in the courtyard," the innkeeper replied. With one of the keys he kept on his belt he opened the gate and led the way. In the courtyard there was just enough room for a toolshed, a fig tree, and the well.

The man looked around, carefully eyed the piece of paper, then said softly:

"So, it says here two barrels. But if we want to do like we did the last time. . ."

The innkeeper hesitated.

"Like we did the last time is too much."

"Water is more expensive this year. I'm already giving you a deal by charging you last year's price."

The innkeeper shrugged.

"Okay," he said. He untied the purse from his belt, felt around inside it, pulled out some coins, and counted them into the palm of his hand.

"Here you go."

The other man counted them too and then made them disappear.

"Hey, bring them on in, all four barrels."

The porters slid the cart staves down to the ground and set up a ramp to roll the barrels down. The innkeeper stayed to watch the operation. He wanted to be sure that all the water ended up in the well. When the barrels were empty, the man leaned against the side of the cart, took out a pen and ink, wrote something on the paper and handed it to the innkeeper.

"Sign the receipt."

This task was a lot harder for the innkeeper than if they'd asked him to help unload the barrels, but he applied himself seriously and in a few minutes he'd finished, scribbling a sort of signature at the bottom of the page. The man stuck it in his cap and the cart started back on its way, creaking. The innkeeper stood there watching it go down the street, then he sighed and went back down into the cellar.

"So, now you've got water, you can start watering down your wine again," one of the masons joked on seeing the innkeeper come back in.

"No danger of that, with what it costs me," the innkeeper shot back with a wry smile.

Matteo, who had kept drinking the whole time without even raising his eyes from the table, shook himself to attention.

"But doesn't the Senate supply the water? You don't have to pay for it!"

"Bravo! You don't have to pay for it, because you don't need very much, but in my business we go through lots of it! If I settled for what I can get for free, I'd have to close down the establishment. So you have to make arrangements."

"See what I mean? It's always the same crap," Matteo commented, his voice shaking. "We're governed by thieves."

"Oh, let's not start that again," the innkeeper said, and to cut it short he went back behind the bar.

"No," Matteo stuck to his guns. "You can't deny it. They're all thieves, and those damned cuckolds of the nobility are the biggest thieves of all. I know whereof I speak."

"It's true," agreed another mason, who had also drunk his fair share.

"Yes, it's true, but that's the way it is everywhere," said a third, slightly more sober.

"Oh no," Matteo raised his voice, and hit the table again with his fist. "No, Venice is the worst! We poor people are being murdered here, we can starve to death and their lordships couldn't care less!"

"We've got to put a stop to it," another observed. "There are lots of us and only a few of them."

This time the whole table voiced their approval.

"Alright, that's enough. All of you get out of here," the innkeeper yelled, alarmed. "Let's go, outside, all of you, make your speeches outside, you dogs." But the last words were muttered under his breath.

The men slowly got up from the table.

"Let's go see what our old ladies have managed to put in the soup tonight," one of them said.

"Turnips! What do you think they put in it?" another replied.

"You're damn right we've got to put a stop to this."

Outside, the group broke up and each of them went home. Back inside, a man who had been sitting quietly by himself in a corner a ways back from the window, diligently draining his mug, got up as soon as they left, paid his bill, and went quickly up the steps.

In the blinding heat of the afternoon, two gentlemen stepped out of a gondola in front of Saint Zachary's and made their way toward a side entrance to the Ducal Palace. The older of the two, who had a slight limp and was holding onto the arm of the younger man, was wearing the purple robes of a magistrate and had a thick white beard. The other was dressed in black velvet with a large starched white collar, loosened a bit against the heat. The gondolier, in red and silver livery, stood leaning on his pole, as if he expected one of the two to come back right away. When the two men arrived at the door to the Palace the halberdier on guard recognized Sir Alvise Bernardo, a member of the Council of Ten, and stood aside. Struggling a bit, the old man extricated himself from his son's arm and smiled at him.

"I told you we'd make it. My leg is feeling better. Go now."

"Don't you want me to wait for you?" the young man said deferentially.

Sir Alvise shook his head.

"We'll be here till late. Go home to your wife, she's the one who needs you now."

Lorenzo Bernardo made a slight bow and then turned back toward the gondola. A passing flight of seagulls let out a loud scream and dived down at him, almost hitting his head, because a sailor on the deck of a boat at anchor just off shore had thrown some leftover food into the water. The birds swooped down, skimming over the sparkling surface of the water, and then those that managed to grab a beakful of food rose back up, flapping their wings and screeching in victory as they headed toward St. George's Island while their unlucky mates dispersed in disappointment. Sir Lorenzo shielded his eyes with the palm of his hand against the dazzling light reflecting off the lagoon, and jumped into the gondola without taking the hand proffered respectfully by the gondolier.

"Take me home"

Sir Alvise was already climbing one of the thousand dark stairways of the palace, assisted by an usher. The gout attack that had kept him in bed for the last fifteen days had finally passed, but he didn't dare force his leg for fear of the excruciating pain that could easily strike again without warning. They finally came to the room where the Council meetings were held, and the usher held the door for him. Almost all the others were already there: the Doge, the Most Serene Lords, and the Ten; fifteen or so patricians in resplendent purple. Sir Alvise identified a free place in the last row and headed for it, forcing two colleagues to get to their feet to let him pass. Worn out, he let himself fall onto the bench, dabbing the sweat off his brow.

One of the three Heads of the Council whose turn it was to preside that day stood at the pulpit at the end of the room, holding a bunch of papers. Sitting at a little desk in a corner, the secretary was stirring the inkwell with a piece of wood to check the thickness of the ink. He was the only one in the room dressed in black. Speaking in a monotone, the president announced the items on the agenda for the meeting. It was so long that some of the backbenchers began shifting in their seats.

"We won't finish in time for dinner," one sorrowful voice moaned. Somebody laughed. The discussion began, punctuated by sudden spikes in volume, especially when someone got contradicted and gave a heated rebuttal. In most cases, those who rose to speak had no personal interest to defend, and were even less concerned with the interests of the State, but just wanted to hear the sound of their own voices and force the others to listen to them and acknowledge that their opinions were important. For Sir Alvise, who had already sat many times among the Ten in the past, there was nothing new; on the contrary, he found it boring.

As always happened, after a while the discussion lost sight of the agenda, and got entangled in the pursuit of other concerns, age-old rivalries, and political animosities. The issues to be discussed today all involved, in one way or another, security measures that the Council was called upon to adopt in order to resolve some unpleasant situation, in response to a report from a neighborhood policeman, a gentleman sopracomito of a galley, a magistrate on the mainland or in the Overseas Dominions, but even that did not prevent the arguments from going continually off course. For some unknown reason, they kept drifting away from the Venetian neighborhoods of Castello and Dorsoduro, or the hinterlands of Verona and Vicenza, or the islands of Zakinthos and Corfu, and veered off north and west, toward the far-off Atlantic, where the unknown English heretics were engaged in a fight to the death with the feared and hated Spanish. On that late afternoon of July 1588, the patricians packed into that undersized chamber knew that the Spanish galleons had set sail from their ports to seal off the English channel, and they knew that the heretic queen Elizabeth had put to sea everything that could float in her little lost island, to resist the invincible armada, and that was all they could talk about.

Sir Lunardo Michiel, whom they all knew as the confidant of the apostolic delegate and a faithful servant of the pope, was moved to declare, on more than one occasion, and always totally off the point, that at a time when his majesty King Phillip was embroiled in a struggle to the death to defend Christianity, Venice could not lower its guard nor permit itself to be indulgent with its enemies. Most of those present found these arguments absurd and the familiarity that men such as Michiel maintained with Rome dangerous, but that certainly did not mean that they were anxious to lower their guard, then or ever. The Ten had never hesitated to condemn to death and if necessary even secretly murder whoever might represent the smallest threat to the security of the Republic, and they were committed to keep doing that without the least concern for the pope or that bigot King Phillip, or the heretic Elizabeth.

It was already late, and several measures had already been approved, almost all of them unanimously, when the President introduced the complaint filed by Sir Girolamo Lippomano. After reading the letter, he leafed through the file and found two reports by informants containing information on the life, habits, and declarations of the mason Matteo, from the *sestiere* of Dorsoduro, parish of St. Agnes. Regarding his life and habits nothing need be said, but his declarations, especially as they emerged in the second report, provoked an agitated buzzing. Pronounced in a tavern on a holiday, those declarations could have been passed off as the result of some bad wine, but the man had repeated them again and again over the next few days, and what's more, to people who listened and voiced their approval. The words he had been heard to utter resounded through the room like stones: the patricians are all thieves, the poor are being murdered, and "we've got to put an end to this." Among the purple-clad gentlemen sitting on the benches, almost all of them were following the report attentively, some shaking their heads as if to say: what can you expect from these people?

Sir Lunardo Michiel was ostentatiously admiring his fingernails, when the President pulled out one last sheet of paper. It was a complaint from the pastor of the parish of St. Agnes, who yesterday morning had found scribbled with charcoal on the wall of the parish house the following words: MAD VENEZIA REASON YOU HAVE UNDONE. While the priest was trying to muster the courage to decide what to do and struggling to fill out his complaint, an effort that had cost him the whole day and the following night, another hand had completed the text. That morning, the pastor reported in a desolated addendum, some more words had appeared: FOR THE POOR. The president reread the whole text, pronouncing each word clearly and distinctly, and then fell silent.

"Mad Venice reason you have undone" repeated one of the Ten, with a pensive air.

"Yes, but only for the poor," another completed the phrase.

Several hands shot up. The President motioned to Sir Lunardo Michiel that he could speak.

"At a time like this, when all the forces of Christendom are straining in agony for the triumph of goodness," Sir Lunardo began. Sir Alvise Bernardo lifted his eyes heavenward, then he caught the eye of his neighbor and like him, sighed and shrugged his shoulders. There was nothing to do except resign oneself. Somewhere in the rules of the Council of Ten there was some provision about the use of an hourglass to measure each speaker's time, but it was one of the rules that were never applied anymore, assuming they ever had been.

Sir Lunardo went on and on, even though everyone had figured out right from the start where he was going to end up—at a request for an exemplary punishment. That the writing on the wall had shown up in the very same parish where the mason had been making such statements, and that two different people, both of them able to write! (Michiel was scandalized), had embraced those statements and turned them into that subversive text, was a glaringly obvious sign of what could be expected if such thoughtlessness and impunity were allowed to prosper in any of the city's neighborhoods. Sir

Lunardo specified that he was leaving to his colleagues the choice of which measure to take, as long as they were rapid and decisive; then he sat down, satisfied with himself.

The next speaker avoided mentioning King Phillip and the supreme hour, but agreed that the case had to be resolved, and in the most drastic manner. Sir Alvise Bernardo listened unhappily, not knowing even himself exactly why, trying to figure out in the meantime if the sudden shooting pain in his leg was the product of his uncomfortable seat on the bench or a foreboding of the feared return of his gout. If it had been up to him, he would have summoned the mason and put the fear of God into him, and then he would have sent him home. A man forewarned is a man forearmed, and might be a better asset for maintaining social tranquility than a man silenced by force. But listening to the speakers who followed him, Sir Alvise realized that things were going well beyond that. When all of those who had raised their hands had expressed their opinions, the President, after conferring rapidly off the record with the secretary, formulated the resolution to be put to a vote, and read it to the assembly. Following a summary reference to the complaints filed against the mason, he continued: "therefore, it is proposed that said Matteo be arrested and condemned to having his tongue cut out, in order to warn the public and set an example for the wicked."

A murmur of consent spread through the room. Before putting the motion to a vote, the President asked if anyone else wished to speak. Sir Alvise squirmed on the bench. He wasn't accostumed to speaking in the Council, even less when the decision was already so sure. More than that, his leg was really starting to hurt. Nevertheless, almost without realizing it, he raised his hand. The President concealed his surprise and gestured to him courteously that he could speak.

"My dear sirs," Sir Alvise began, "it seems to me that we are exaggerating, and that this poor man does not deserve this.

Isn't it a bit too much too cut out his tongue? I say it would be sufficient to summon him and interrogate him. Let him see the instruments," he added. He knew they would all understand what he meant. In a criminal interrogation, the prosecution had the right, or better the duty, to torture the defendant. Otherwise all the criminals would get off by denying their guilt. But often the mere sight of the torture chamber and the interrogator with all of his tools at the ready was enough to loosen their tongues and make the defendants listen to reason. Sir Alvise would have liked to go on but he could see that his colleagues were listening impatiently. The man was already lost. "Think about it," he concluded, severely, and sat down.

The secretary had the ballot box ready, with the two compartments in which to insert, hidden from view, the little balls expressing the vote, now made of cloth rather than lead as they used to be, so they would not make noise when they fell into the box and so not reveal on which side they had been inserted. One after another, the Ten passed in front of the President's pulpit and deposited their votes in the box. Then they removed the cover and counted the votes: twelve in the white compartment of votes in favor, none in the green one of votes opposed. One vote was missing, an abstention, that would be recorded as an "insincere" vote. As the President announced the outcome, Sir Lunardo Michiel looked at Sir Alvise Bernardo with a smirk of contempt.

Matteo and Michele were at the Rialto to sell a load of bricks. After closing down the construction site at the Lippomano house and firing all the laborers, the mason had no choice but to sell the leftover materials. He hoped to make enough from the sale to live on until he landed another contract and, with a little luck, an advance.

The buyer was a fellow mason who Matteo had known for a long time, and who had enough patrons that he was still working, even in this year of famine. He hardly looked at the bricks that Matteo, soaking with sweat, had carried there on a cart as a sample of the lot. Then, not looking Matteo in the eye, he made an offer. It was low, and Matteo's blood rose. On their way there they had stopped at a tavern to drink, and in that heat the white wine went down nicely. Michele looked at his father with pity and was suddenly aware that he was an old man, his cheeks and nose red from wine, and his five-day beard forming what looked like a veil of dirt on his cheeks. As long as he could remember, Matteo had always shaved only on Sunday, but now that his beard had turned white, it made him look seedier during the week.

"Let it be, father," he said suddenly, taking a step toward the two men. Both of them turned to look at him.

"The price is fine," he added. He was irritated with his father, who was always making trouble over nothing. Matteo kept looking at him, furrowing his brow, then the other man burst out laughing.

"Bravo, kid!" he exclaimed. "You've got better sense than your father!" As Michele blushed, the other man patted Matteo on the back. "Come on, Matteo, that's all I can afford. The next time it'll be me who's in your place and you'll remember." The mason shook his head, undecided. Then he shot a sideward glance at his son, shrugged, spat in his hand, and held it out to his colleague. In turn, the other spat in his hand and shook Matteo's vigorously.

"Come on, let's drink on it," he said.

They were about to set off, and Michele had already raised the cart staves, when all of a sudden a man dressed in black was standing in his way. He was accompanied by four halberdiers, and all around them the Rialto crowd had scattered as though in a dream.

"One minute, gentlemen," said the man in black. "An inspection. Show us if you are carrying arms."

Being stopped by a patrol for an inspection wasn't such a rare event, especially there at the Rialto, where the whole world passed through the market. The buyer of the bricks immediately spread his arms and one of the halberdiers started patting him down. The others moved toward Matteo and Michele. But Matteo was out of patience. He cursed vehemently and took a step back.

"Keep your hands off me, eh!" He protested, in a threatening tone. The officer looked at him coldly. "Are you the mason Matteo, who lives in St. Agnes?"

"So what if I am?" Matteo challenged him.

The officer nodded at the halberdiers, but before they could get to him, Matteo had already thrown a powerful punch. The officer groaned and fell back, his nose broken and spouting blood. Michele, without thinking twice, turned the cart over in front of the halberdiers, took his father by the arm and started running. A second later, however, the soldiers were on him and one of them struck Matteo on the back with the handle of his halberd. The mason grunted with pain and anger and tried to turn around but the other man hit him again and Matteo staggered, lost his balance, and fell into the putrid water of the Grand Canal. As he was falling he cried out and he was swallowing water before he knew what was happening to him. The canal was deep at that point. Matteo flailed, trying to stay afloat, but the soldier, beside himself with rage, hit him again in the face with the wooden handle, and Matteo sank below the surface.

The man in black, who was holding a blood-soaked handkerchief pressed against his face, shouted something. The halberdiers all turned to face him. He was shouting that they should pull Matteo out of the water, but by now he had vanished. Michele, kneeling on the shore, stretched out his arms frantically, but there was no longer a hand that could grab on to his. Finally, the boy stood up, stunned, looked around as though to search for help, and saw that the man in black was shouting new orders and pointing at him. The soldiers were coming at him and Michele took off. He slipped into an arcade and ran desperately through the shadows.

Behind him he could hear the heavy footsteps of the soldiers and the metallic banging of their halberds against the low ceiling. He came out the other end of the arcade onto another canal and ran along the shore before crossing a random bridge. He didn't know the neighborhood but in that labyrinth of alleyways, totally empty at that hour, he had some hope of losing them. The footsteps and the gruff voices of the soldiers were still echoing behind him, but farther away. Michele kept on running for a while, not knowing where he was going. Then he stopped for a minute to catch his breath, pressing his body flat against a wall. He couldn't hear anything anymore, and thought he was finally safe, but then he heard the rushing footsteps again, up close, and he started running again. He went up and over a bridge in a flash, bumped into a man who first turned to curse him and then, seeing the soldiers closing in, yelled out, "There, he went that way!" Michele knew that if he came across other people he was lost. Sooner or later, acting on some sort of automatic reflex, someone who saw him being chased by soldiers would jump in his way to stop him. His only hope lay in the fact that the soldiers, weighed down by their helmets and halberds, couldn't run as fast as him, and he was gaining ground again. He ran blindly into another arcade and then, before he even realized it, came out into the broad daylight again. In front of him was the promenade of the Riva degli Schiavoni, teeming with people, and in the distance he could see the shimmering water of the lagoon. I'm done for! Michele thought to himself, his heart beating wildly.

4.

For a second he had the impulse to turn back. But the voices of the halberdiers were already echoing at the far end of the arcade. There was nothing to do but throw himself into the crowd, but he had to control himself to keep from running so nobody would notice that they were chasing him. Desperate, Michele looked around to choose a direction. One of the two galleys that he'd seen a few days ago anchored in front of Saint Zachary's was still there, on the verge of setting sail, its enormous oars sticking out like the legs of a centipede. Over there the crowd was even thicker: women hugging their departing men, porters loading the last supplies onto the galley's tender boats. Instinctively, Michele headed that way, forcing himself to walk at an almost normal pace. An instant later he was in the midst of the crowd, terrified by the thought of a brutal hand suddenly grabbing him from behind, or even worse a blow from a halberd handle between his shoulder blades. But he didn't dare turn to look, for fear the soldiers would recognize him. When he got down to the dock he saw that one of the sailors loading the tender was the same guy he had talked to a few days ago, and without hesitation he walked right up to him. The other guy didn't recognize him.

"Don't you remember?" Michele muttered. He spoke softly, afraid he'd be heard by the soldiers, who at that very moment were making their way through the crowd, brutally swinging their halberds and provoking a hubbub of protest, but not knowing where to look. Luckily, the man now recognized him.

"You've change your mind?" he asked with a greedy smile. Michele hurriedly nodded yes.

"Have you still got room?"

"There's always room at the oars, my friend. Figure it this way. We're leaving with just two men per bench. We'll be going to Dalmatia to pick up the thirds. Come on, hop on, I'll take you to the parone. The *sopracomito* will be pleased."

Michele, who had never in his life set foot on a galley, didn't understand half of that old-salt lingo, but he sloughed it off and jumped onto the tender, which a minute later started rowing away from the dock. Suddenly he felt like he was sticking out like a sore thumb, standing up in that boat in the middle of the shimmering water. With a smile he nodded at the red cap the oarsman was wearing, and held out his hand.

"Will they give me one of those too? Let me try it on!"

It was a risky move, because if the other guy was grumpy he could have punched him in the face. But instead he was happy, thinking about his percentage, and let it slide. Michele pushed the cap well down on his head, and then he turned for the first time and looked back at the shore. The halberd blades, held high to keep from injuring someone, were moving here and there above the heads of the crowd, but they weren't coming towards him. The officer had issued forth from the arcade now as well, still holding the bloody handkerchief to his face, and he was scanning the crowd too, not knowing where to search. His gaze crossed paths with the tender rowing out to the galley, but looked right past it without stopping. I made it, Michele thought, with a wave of relief, and in that instant the tender lurched under him and he would have fallen down if he hadn't grabbed onto the oarsman's arm.

"Never been on the water, eh?" the man observed with a grin. Then he took his cap back. "You'll learn all right. And anyway, you row sitting down."

The tender passed in front of the bow of the galley, where

its mighty bronze-tipped wooden ram hung over the water, and sidled up to the partly submerged ladder. The two rowers passed their oars to some other galleymen there to greet the tender who pulled them up on board, and with the same system they loaded the supplies. Then everyone climbed up the ladder and the tender was hoisted on board with a tackle. The galley was rocking slightly and Michele was having trouble keeping his feet. He was struck by the odor of fresh paint, but above all by the huge crowd on the deck, where a remarkable number of oarsmen and sailors were moving around, each tending to his own task, in spaces so cramped it seemed they were bound to elbow and step on each other all the time. It looked to Michele like he was the only one without a place, and he looked questioningly at the oarsman who had brought him aboard.

"Wait there," the man told him, nodding toward the powerful cannon dominating the galley's prow. On either side of that bronze monster there were two smaller cannons, and there was a little free space between their carriages. Michele wriggled his way in between two gun barrels and sat down on a wooden crate, which, as he would later discover, held the cannonballs. He stayed there a long time, while the galley pulled away from the shore and crossed the lagoon, with the salty water splashing over him at every plunge of the bow. In no time at all everyone on board was soaking wet, except for the sopracomito and his officers, sheltered behind a curtain in the stern cabin. The galley's deck, because of the weight of the cargo and ballast packed into the hold, was just a few palms above the water's surface, and the movement of the oars, twenty-five per side, was raising clouds of spray. Michele was enchanted by the synchronicity with which the oarsmen, obeying an officer's whistle, maneuvered the oars, inhaling and exhaling all together in a sort of collective rhythmic breathing. The strangeness of everything he was seeing delayed his awareness of what had happened to him that morning. It took a while before it came crashing back into his mind, with lacerating pain and a profound sense of shame, that his father was probably dead, and in what a terrible way!, and that he had been unable to save him. Not only, but the last conscious feeling he had had for his father, before the soldiers had stopped him in his tracks, had been irritation, for the way he had lost his temper negotiating the price of the bricks. And now he was running away like a desperado, not knowing if he'd ever see his wife and mother again.

With the nausea of seasickness welling up from his stomach to his throat, he didn't even think to sharpen his gaze to take a last look at the bell tower of St. Mark's glittering in the sunlight. Later on, when he realized he'd missed it, they were already in the open sea, after crossing, without stopping, the gap between the twin castles of the Lido, rife with cannons. The oarsmen, their heads even with the bridge and an amazing quantity of boxes and bundles crammed between their legs, were rowing in silence, straining with the effort. Michele saw that there were two on each bench, even though there was room for three. Only the first benches, near the stern, were completely manned. He also saw that where there were only two rowers their faces looked contorted with fatigue, and that they certainly wouldn't be able to maintain that pace for long.

Luckily, a northerly wind was blowing, and as soon as the galley reached the open sea the order came to hoist the sails on the mainmast and foremast. The oarsmen took a rest and sat watching the sailors whose turn had finally come to do a little work. There were about fifteen of them aboard in all, barely enough to maneuver the thick ropes of hemp that governed the sails. The sailors were busy for a while working the winches, then they pulled two ropes along the entire length of the galley and the oarsmen took them in hand. At the sound of a whistle blow they all started pulling together, straining under the weight, and the yard that held the immense mainsail, almost as long as the galley itself, began to rise, swaying back and forth, accompanied by the profanity coming from the men whose hands were being chafed. The hull rolled frightfully as a hundred men all pulled together, and the great fustian sheet, known as the bastard, rose, swelling in the wind. It took a quarter of an hour for the yard to reach the right height so the sailors who'd shinnied up the shrouds could block the sheaves. At that point the ship was able to maneuver and it took off, driven by the favorable wind, while the oarsmen, soaked in sweat, caught their breath.

Michele was trying to get over a stomachache brought on by the galley's bouncing on the waves, when the oarsman who had brought him aboard came to call him. He had an officer with him, a man with red hair, dressed in a worn-out vest of black fustian.

"Here he is," the oarsman said, showing him Michele. The lad got to his feet, staggered and leaned against one of the cannons.

"Ever been to sea?" the officer asked. Then, seeing from Michele's ashen face that the answer was obvious, he shrugged his shoulders and addressed the oarsman. "A fine purchase you talked me into. Give us a look at you. Take off your shirt." His tone was brisk but not hostile, and Michele hurriedly pulled off his soaking wet shirt. The officer, who was the crew chief, known as the parone on Venetian galleys, looked him over carefully and felt his muscles.

"Not bad," he sighed. "Could have been worse. What kind of work did you do?"

"I'm a mason," said the lad.

"Not bad," the red-haired man said again. "Alright, come on, let's go sign you up."

The officer and the oarsman headed off toward the stern, and Michele followed them, treading carefully on the narrow passageway of varnished wood. The galley was at most seventeen feet wide, and most of that width was occupied by the rowers' benches, crammed with men in red caps. The only way to move up and down the deck was that gangway, maybe four feet wide, a sort of lane that ran the whole length of the ship, and that Michele would soon learn to call, as they all did, the *corsia*. But when the sailors had to move up and down the ship, they ran barefoot, jumping between the heads of the rowers, the oarlocks, and the platforms sticking out between one oarlock and the next, where the harquebusiers rested their guns during battle. The three traveled the whole length of the ship from stem to stern, and Michele nearly lost his balance more than once. He envied the two men walking in front of him, who were obviously used to the rolling of the ship and walked swiftly as though they were on dry land.

In the stern cabin, the sopracomito of the galley was sitting on a folding chair, together with two other young noblemen dressed like him in black, with wide lace collars and gold chains around their necks, drinking white wine in crystal glasses. But Michele was not taken all the way back there. At the entrance to the cabin there was a wobbly table, and sitting at the table was a scrivener, intent on checking figures in a blotter, held together by a piece of string, and transcribing them into a volume bound in red leather.

"Don Muzio, here's a new one," said the parone.

The scrivener looked up. Although he was young, he was almost bald, with a goatee and bright, shifting eyes behind a pair of shining spectacles.

"Last minute embarkation, eh?" he commented. He looked in a drawer for a printed sheet and gestured to Michele to come close.

"So, name?"

"Michele, son of the mason Matteo," Michele answered automatically; and he immediately felt like an idiot; why give his real name? It would have been so easy to lie! For now he was safe, but what if the police came looking for him? The Signory, as everybody knew, had sharp eyes and long arms . . .

"Sestiere and parish," the scrivener continued.

"Dorsoduro, parish of St. Agnes," Michele said, incapable of inventing a false address.

"Age?"

"Nineteen."

"Okay," muttered the scrivener, completing the form. "So then, your salary is ten lire a month for the first four months, then eight a month as long as we remain at sea. But it's already late in the year. If all goes well we'll be back to lay up earlier than that. I'll credit you for four months as an advance, that's forty lire, is that clear?

Michele, who hadn't understood a thing, nodded.

"Now, let's see. Have you got any baggage?"

Michele spread his arms.

"I came away with nothing."

The scrivener gave him a curious look and Michele felt himself blush under his penetrating gaze.

"Alright," the scrivener said after a long silence. "Then we'll give you a cap and two shirts, a cloth nightshirt and an overcoat; it gets cold at night on the water. In all that comes to . . ." he figured in his head, "eighteen lire, which I'll mark down as a debit. That leaves you a credit of twenty-two lire, clear?"

Michele had no idea how much clothes cost because his mother had always taken care of those things, and he wasn't able to figure out if the prices asked for those clothes were too high. But even if he had known he certainly couldn't have objected. The rules were set by the government and he was already lucky that none of the eighteen lire ended up in the scrivener's pocket.

"Now comes the best part," the scrivener went on, smiling.

"His lordship wants to get this voyage done in a hurry and he's decided to give a bonus of five zecchini, so I'll mark that down for you as well. Have no fear," he added, on seeing Michele staring blankly at the figures accumulating in the spaces of the printed form, "later I'll write it all down in the book. Everything is in order, okay?" he repeated, closing for a moment the bound volume that he kept there on the table to show the lion of St. Mark painted on its red cover. "These are public records and anyone can check them."

At this point the man who had accompanied Michele on board stepped forward, his cap in hand and a greedy look in his eye.

"I'm the one that brought him on board, sir," he said. The scrivener looked up at the parone, who had remained standing nearby, and the red-haired man nodded.

"Well," said the scrivener. "Then I'll give you one zecchino in cash." He unlatched the purse he kept tied to his belt, took out a gold coin, and showed it to Michele. "Have you got a purse?" Michele nodded and showed him the little purse that he kept on his belt too.

"You'd do better to keep it tied around your neck. Show him," he said to the oarsman, who promptly opened his shirt to reveal a minuscule leather bag.

"So then," the scrivener went on, "one zecchino in cash and the other four credit. If you need money, come to me and I'll give you some, but it's better for you not to keep too much in your purse, here on board. You know how to write?"

Michele shook his head.

"Then put an X here," the scrivener said calmly. He would have been surprised and even annoyed if an oarsman were not illiterate. Usually the only people on the galley who knew how to read and write were himself and the sopracomito, and surely that meant something. Michele gripped the quill pen awkwardly and scratched out an X.

The scrivener opened a hatch and went down into the hold and came back up a minute later carrying a hefty bundle.

"There you go, now you're fully equipped," he said, handing it over to Michele.

"Come on, now we'll find you a place to sit," the parone ordered, and he started down the *corsia*. Michele made to follow him but the man who'd brought him aboard grabbed him by the arm.

"Hey, aren't you forgetting something?" he snarled. Michele looked at him, dumbfounded. "That one's for me," he said, pointing at the purse where the lad had put the coin.

"What?" Michele said, incredulous.

"Don't pretend you don't understand! Hand over the zecchino!" the man whispered in his ear, squeezing his arm so tight it hurt. Michele looked around. The scrivener, sitting just a few feet away, had gone back to leafing through his blotter, the parone was intent on inspecting the benches. With tears in his eyes from pain and fear, Michele opened his purse and took out the gold coin. The oarsmen grabbed it and made it vanish into the little leather sack he kept around his neck.

"Good, now we're friends! And remember that if you need protection, I'm the one to call on, and no one else. Look for the wolf, that's what they call me here. I'm up at bench twenty-four. Hang in there, buddy!"

Jumping nimbly along the oarlocks, the man went off toward the bow. Just then the parone called Michele.

"Hey you, the new one, come here a minute!"

The officer was standing near a bench on the starboard side of the ship. Another officer had joined him, he too dressed very simply in black fustian, like a well-paid craftsman. It was clear there was a big difference between them and the noblemen who were drinking in the stern cabin. The parone pointed to the two oarsmen on the bench, who were looking up at him curiously, and Michele could hear him say to his colleague:

"What do you think? This looks like the weakest pair to me."

The other man shrugged his shoulders.

"They all seem weak to me. These days they're all a bunch of pansies. Nothing like the rowers we used to get in the old days."

"No two ways about it," the parone agreed. "Today's young people are worthless. They're too used to the good life, I'm telling you, not like in our day."

Then he turned to Michele.

"For now, your place is here. On bench six. Can you remember that? Let me hear you."

Michele, ever obedient, repeated:

"Bench six, sir."

"Good, go down to the end. You others make room for him. No, not there, you're the third! You got it? You count starting from the *corsia*. Your place is on the water side."

Michele edged his way between the legs of his bench mates and the canvas sacks piled on the floor of the deck and sat down. The bench was covered in leather and even though it was wet, the contact wasn't unpleasant. On his left, at shoulder height, was the wooden mounting of the oarlock and right below it the water. If he looked straight in front of himself he could see the backs of the rowers sitting on the benches ahead of his, then the curtain that kept the stern cabin dry, emblazoned with the red lion of St. Mark. The play of the oars was conceived in such a way that the rowers sat with their backs turned in the direction in which they pushed the galley. He turned to his side and saw his two bench mates looking at him. He had no idea how he should behave toward them.

"I'm Michele," he said, with a timid smile. He was relieved to see them smile back. They were lads his age, maybe even a little younger, one of them didn't even have a beard. Their names were Marco and Giulio and they were from Chioggia.

"It's terrible there, no work at all," they told him, drawing out the vowels in their singsong Chioggian accent. His being from Venice seemed to make them uneasy.

"Have you rowed before?"

Both of them shook their heads, this was their first time out. But they'd been aboard for a week and the sopracomito had made the crew practice every day.

"It's not hard to learn. It's just that it kills your back. And look what it does to your hands!"

They showed them their hands, full of red blisters, not yet turned into calluses.

"The others say you get used to it. Let's hope so!"

"But what work did you do back on land?"

They were bakers' apprentices, both let go by a baker who'd gone bankrupt. They couldn't find any other jobs, and their families couldn't support them. Even when they were working they were poor.

I was a mason, Michele wanted to say, but his voice cracked in the middle of the sentence, and he turned away so they wouldn't see the tears in his eyes. Come on, he told himself, a man doesn't cry.

He started studying the enormous oar, painted red, that occupied the space in front of all three of them with the end reaching almost to the beginning of the *corsia*. It was so large around that you couldn't get a grip on it so in front of each of them there was an iron handle screwed into the oar. As he was thinking apprehensively about the hard labor he had to look forward to, Michele realized that he was famished. All he'd had to eat that morning was a piece of bread and that was hours ago.

"Listen," he said to Marco who was sitting next to him, "when do we eat?"

Marco looked up at the sun, high in the sky.

"It's noon, it looks like. It won't be long now."

Indeed, a kind of activity was spreading through the galley that was different from the background buzz of nonstop conversation that had struck Michele when he first came aboard. That space measuring one hundred thirty by seventeen feet was packed with one hundred and fifty men, and since they had come out of the lagoon and the galley had been sailing along powered by the sails, the oarsmen had had nothing to do. So they talked. Now, however, the buzzing had become more intense and hopeful. Michele turned around and saw a big pot making its way down the *corsia*, carried in the straining hands of two sailors, and the oarsmen seated on their benches were stretching out their bowls to be filled with soup. Michele suddenly realized that he didn't have a bowl. Consumed by the overwhelming anxiety that he was going to be left hungry, he interrogated his bench mates in a tremulous voice. Laughing, the lads told him to look in his bundle. He turned it in his hands and saw that it was rolled up inside a big woolen overcoat, knotted at the sleeves, and inside, along with a red cloth nightshirt, two linen shirts, and the famous red cap, he found a bowl and a spoon. He plumped the red cap down on his head with satisfaction and waited for his rations.

5

Rations were composed of a fava bean soup, thick and plentiful, and a portion of sea biscuit so hard it was impossible to chew it without first soaking it in the soup to soften it. Water was available from a cask under the bench with a tin cup chained to it, from which the three drank in turns.

"Well, life on a galley isn't all that bad," joked Michele. At his age and with a full stomach it was hard to be a pessimist.

"Not so fast!" interjected a sarcastic voice from behind. The lad turned and saw an elderly man, with a graying mustache on a wrinkled face. Lurking among the wrinkles, his eyes shone with malice.

"Now the water's fresh and the casks are new. Wait and see how it tastes in a month or two, when the casks are rotten. And at the start of the voyage the soup is always thick and rich, because the parone figures you new guys have to get used to things a little at a time. But then it gets runnier and runnier, because they realize that the bags of fava beans are emptying too fast, and it'll end up that they give it to us only when we're in port, with the excuse that at sea it's too hard to cook. Anyway, here's to your health!"

The old man raised his hand, and Michele saw that it was holding a cup full of wine.

"But we didn't get any wine," he protested. The old rower grinned.

"If you don't buy it, sure you don't get any. There, next to the kitchen, two benches behind us, there's the guy that runs the tavern. Go back there, pay, and he'll fill your cup. Otherwise, water."

For Michele, life on the galley was a constant surprise. Without thinking, his fingers tapped the purse he kept on his belt and he decided that he'd have to tie it around his neck as soon as possible, even if all he had in it was a few coins, everything he owned when he'd left the house that morning.

"Anyway, I thought it would be a lot harder than this. But there's no rowing at all!" he said, naively. This time the old man roared with laughter, and so did the rower sitting next to him on the bench, a gaunt, spindly type with a few straggly, greasy hairs sticking out from under his cap.

"Get a load of this guy! He's living in the land of plenty! He thinks he can fill his belly without working. Up to now you've had it easy, we've had the wind at our backs, and as long as we're undermanned they don't want to wear us out, but when we've got a full crew you'll see how they make us sweat. No, get ready, we're going to start right now," he added, all full of himself. All the rowers had raised their heads, because a whistle blow had reached their ears from the *corsia;* immediately they sprang into action, putting their bowls and spoons back in their bundles, after carefully licking them clean. The officer who together with the red-haired man had chosen the bench for Michele was now pacing up and down the *corsia*, his whistle around his neck. When they were all ready and gripping their handles, he blew on the whistle again: four short blasts, one after the other.

"That's the *comito*. He's a two-faced scoundrel, be on your guard with him. When he blows four times it means all the benches have to row," Michele's bench mate whispered to him. Michele told himself he would be able to learn this too, and he got ready to imitate the movements of his mates. But he noticed right away that each of the three, because of his position with respect to the oar, was forced to move differently. Giulio, who was closest to the *corsia*, had to pull the oar in a wider rotation, so each time he had to get to his feet and push forward, planting his foot on the bench in front of him, then, with the oar immersed in the water, he pulled backwards until he was sitting down again. Marco, in the middle, stopped short of putting his foot on the bench in front, but he leaned it against a footrest nailed to the floor and pushed against it to pull backward. Michele had to make an even shorter movement. All he had to do was stand up and sit down again, pulling the oar to his chest. As grueling as it was, so much so that he was covered with sweat in just a few seconds, he realized right away that the other two were laboring even more than he, and that it was especially tough for Giulio. He also noticed that it was absolutely indispensable that all the oarsmen on the galley rowed in unison, because even the smallest error would have caused Giulio to kick the guy in front of him or hit him with the tip of the oar, or be hit by the guy behind him. But keeping to the rhythm was easy, because the comito, standing at the midpoint of the *corsia*, sounded it with whistle blows, and the thud of the oarsmen banging back down on the benches all together marked it even better, along with the collective puff that came blasting forth from all of their throats.

Giulio was the more robust of the two Chioggians, but Michele could hear that even his breathing was becoming more labored. Turning toward him he saw that the lad had closed his eyes and was gritting his teeth with exertion. He felt bad for him and wanted to offer to change places but he had enough good sense to understand that it wasn't possible right then and that it might not be possible later, given the determination with which the officers had chosen the place for him that morning. Oarsmen were not asked to take the initiative. They were supposed to work together like the gears of a machine, and that's what they were paid to do. So Michele concentrated on his work, feeling all the muscles and joints of his body protesting against that unremitting strain, the sweat streaming down under his shirt, the salty spray of sea water washing over him with every turn of the oar, although with all that body heat the water actually felt good.

They kept on like that for an hour or an hour and a half, when a long, sharp whistle came from the *corsia*. Somebody shouted, "It was about time!" and everybody let go of their oars. Giulio had already dunked the cup in the water barrel. He emptied it in an instant, drew another cup and then a third, and finally, on his last legs, handed it to Marco. The lad downed three cups and passed it to Michele. It seemed to Michele that he'd never felt a thirst like that. The cup held a pint of water, but he gulped it down instantly, and the second one too. He was about to fill it a third time when Marco and Giulio yelled at him.

"Hey, that's it! The *terzicchio* only gets two cups! What are you thinking? It's got to last us till tomorrow!"

Michele was about to yell back at them, but he saw the mean looks on their faces and their closed fists, and he realized he had no desire to fight.

"I didn't know," he muttered, handing back the cup.

Just then the comito whistled again, one long blow followed by one short one. With a buzzing of protest, the rowers sitting in the front of the ship, behind the three lads, started rowing.

"It's the bow third's turn," Marco explained. "When he whistles twice, it's our turn."

Relieved, Michele collapsed onto the bench and closed his eyes. The rhythmic sound of the rowing, cadenced by the whistle, blended with the swishing of the oars and the waves. The galley sped along, leaving behind Venice and the little house in St. Agnes square, where at that hour Zanetta and Bianca were crying for his father and wondering, desperately, where in the world he had gone. For the second time that day he felt like crying, but he got a hold of himself. I'll see them again, he told himself, I swear I will. When he reopened his eyes, two dark shadows made him look up. The parone and the comito were standing there looking at him.

"He's right," the comito said, without Michele having any idea who he was talking about. "You," he added, nodding toward Michele, "come here a minute, we're going to move you." Michele squirmed his way to the end of the bench and stepped out into the *corsia*.

"You sit here," the parone said, pointing to Giulio's place. And you two slide down a place. From now on, you're the *pianiero* on this bench, understand? It's a big responsibility. You're the one who sets the pace. Understand?" he repeated, staring into his eyes.

"Yessir," Michele said, looking into the eyes of the red-haired man. He cursed to himself. He had just figured out that that was the most exhausting place of the three, and now it was all his. But it gave him a certain satisfaction to know that the officers had noticed that he was stronger than the other two. And now he'd be entitled to another cup of water.

"There's a good lad," the parone said. Then the two officers went away.

Michele turned to his two mates to see how they'd taken it, and luckily he saw that both of them seemed relieved. An hour later, when it was their turn to row again, Michele was able to confirm that his new place was really much more fatiguing. He had to grit his teeth and at the end of their turn when the comito's whistle let everyone fall back down exhausted on the bench, the three cups of water weren't nearly enough to make up for the sweat he'd lost.

Rowing in thirds, with only part of the crew working and the others at rest, the galley couldn't go very fast but on the other hand they could keep it up all day long and, as Michele would soon learn, even at night. But for now the sopracomito, despite wanting to hurry, couldn't afford to exaggerate, not with only two rowers on almost all the benches, and a lot of them city boys who had never rowed before. When the galley, sailing along without ever losing sight of the coast, came abreast of Caorle, the sun had set a while ago and it was almost dark. The comito, after consulting with the sopracomito in the stern cabin, ordered the helmsman to head toward the shore. A buzz of satisfaction spread through the benches. They had already taken turns eating their evening rations, a bowl of sea biscuit, submerged in water with a tablespoon of olive oil, and this maneuver meant they would be sleeping in peace, at anchor near the beach.

"Are we going into the harbor?" the comito asked, back in the cabin.

"No," the sopracomito replied, after thinking a minute. "Let's not waste time. Let's sleep outside and get back underway first thing in the morning. Is there a good place to anchor?" he asked, turning to the pilot, an old seaman, barefoot and toothless, who was standing next to him respectfully, cap in hand.

"Oh, yes there is, Excellency. Right in front of the town there are some shoals, but as soon as you're past them it's fine, you can anchor wherever you please."

So the galley passed slowly in front of the bell tower of Caorle, keeping a wide berth to avoid the shallows, and then moved in closer to the sandy shore. The seamen, working fast and sure-handed, took down the mainmast and laid it along the *corsia*, to make the ship more stable.

"Now we sleep," said Giulio.

"What? Here?" Michele asked. When he'd been in the stern cabin talking with the scrivener, he'd looked into an open hatch and noticed that under the *corsia* there was pretty big hold that a man had to scrunch up his shoulders to get into, and he had imagined that they'd be sleeping down there, even if the space was occupied in large part by chests and barrels.

"Can't we go below?" he asked. Raucous laughter rang out from the bench behind them. He turned around; the two veteran oarsmen were laughing at him.

"There's no room for us below," the old man said. "That's where they keep the cargo. It's worth a lot more than we are."

But how can so many of us all sleep up here?" Michele objected. The old man chuckled.

"Why, do you think it's crowded? Just wait until we've filled all the benches, and the bachelors have come aboard."

"And who would these bachelors be?" Michele asked. By now he'd understood that the galley had a language all its own, and that landlubbers like him had to learn it in a hurry if they wanted to get along.

"You'll see, at our first stop we'll take a good number of them aboard. Didn't you see that down below it's full of weapons? Who do you think they're for?"

Actually, down in the hold, Michele had got a glimpse of bundles of swords and halberds, and a good supply of harquebuses, all carefully stacked.

"If you run into pirates, you'll have a fight on your hands, my friend," the old oarsman went on smugly. "And don't be thinking they'll be handing you a harquebus! Or do you know how to shoot?"

Michele admitted that he'd never held a weapon in his life.

"You see? That's why as soon as he can the sopracomito is going to sign up some bachelors. They're Slavonians and Albanians who know how to use a sword and a harquebus, and if need be they can lend a hand with the sails as well. A galley can't go to sea without having some of them aboard. If there's extra room in the hold then it's them who sleeps below, understand?"

As they were talking, a gang of sailors and rowers directed by the comito had brought up an enormous tarp from the hold and were unfolding it, starting from the stern, fixing the edges to the oarlocks with sturdy wooden pegs. A little at a time, the tarp unfolded until it pretty much covered the entire length of the galley, and everybody settled in under it for the night—some stretching out on the benches, others curling up on the floor. Michele had the impression that the bench, seeing as it was covered in leather, would make for a more comfortable bed.

"I'll take the bench," he said, trying to adopt an imposing tone. After all, he was the pianiero, the one who worked the hardest, and he was also the strongest. The two from Chioggia, who had already spent several nights on board, let him have the place without discussion, knowing full well that the places underneath were better sheltered from the cold night air. Michele spread out his overcoat on the bench, made a bundle out of his shirts and put it under his head like a pillow, and then he lay down. The bench was narrow, but it was roomy enough, especially considering how tired he was, and as soon as he put his head down he could feel his eyes closing . . .

Michele woke up suddenly in the darkness.

"This'd be the time to take advantage," he'd heard a voice whisper behind him.

"Take advantage of what?"

Trying not to let himself be noticed, Michele shifted on the bench so he could see who was talking, and opened his eyes.

"That the bachelors aren't on board yet, but their weapons are" said the first voice, which belonged to the guy with the greasy hair.

"To do what?" said the old man.

"Goldarnit! To take the galley, and the ten thousand zecchini."

The dialogue was so intriguing that Michele's eyes sprang wide open and he noticed that underneath him the two Chioggians were awake and listening.

"Don't let me hear that kind of talk, even as a joke, you hear me?" the old man said harshly. "And besides, those guys in front of us are wide awake and listening. Isn't that right, lads?"

Michele raised himself up on an elbow.

"What ten thousand zecchini?"

The old man sighed.

"Oh, what the heck, the whole galley knows it, except for you. Where do you think we're headed?"

Michele didn't know, but one of the two lads beneath him responded promptly:

"To Candia."

It wasn't an unusual destination for a galley. Ever since the Turks had taken control of Cyprus, some years ago, Crete was Venice's largest remaining possession, the most important colony in its Overseas Dominions.

"There, exactly. And why are we going there?" Since nobody answered, the old oarsman went on:

"The sopracomito is carrying a sack of gold coins for the government of Candia. All the money they use there has to be brought there from Venice; there's no mint there on the island. They say he's carrying ten thousand of them."

The idea of those ten thousand zecchini, only one of which would be enough for him to live on for a month, fired Michele's imagination. With a gush of pride he thought that he already had four zecchini, credited to him in the scrivener's book. Then he remembered where the fifth had gone, and turned gloomy.

"That's exactly what I'm saying," said the other oarsman. "So now, tell me, how hard would it be to take those weapons, throw the officers and the sailors overboard, and take the galley and all those glittering zecchini? All we need to do is make sure we're all together."

At that, the old man raised his voice.

"And I say, and I'm saying it loud so everyone can hear, that

I don't want to hear talk of such things, or I'll go and tell the sopracomito."

The other man cursed.

"You don't know what you're talking about," the old man continued. "Now listen to me and I'll tell you a great little story. One time, quite a few years ago, at the time of the war against the Turks, a ship left Venice with the governor of Dalmatia on his way to Zara, and carrying a sack of *scudi*, much bigger than this one. There were eighty thousand scudi in it, God as my witness."

He fell silent for a minute, to let the others appreciate the size of that figure.

"The ship had a crew of convicts, chained to their benches," he then went on. "One of them told his mates that once they were out to sea they could kill the governor and take off with the ship and the money. They couldn't figure out if he was joking or serious. He was a Turk who had turned Christian, and then he'd been sentenced to a galley for theft. One after another, three of the men he'd talked to about his plan went to denounce him. A fourth kept quiet, and for that he was sentenced to six more years on the galley."

"And the first?" Michele asked, breathless.

"He was hanged, naturally."

"And how do you know about all this?"

"I was the one who didn't denounce him," said the old man. "My sentence was about to run out and I didn't want any trouble. Oh, sure, the six years went by fast. And galley life, like you were saying this morning, lad, isn't so bad. You see? I like it so much that after they set me free I kept on doing the same work. Alright now, that's enough, let's go to sleep."

The man stopped talking and curled up on his bench. Michele stayed awake for a little while, thinking, despite himself, about those ten thousand gold coins sitting in a sack in the sopracomito's quarters. Ten thousand zecchini!, he thought.

And all we needed was for Senator Lippomano to pay my father the fifty he owed him, and we'd still be back home, all of us, and none of this would have happened . . . His heart swollen, Michele tossed and turned on the bench, unable to sleep. Underneath him, Marco and Giulio, lying on top of each other in the tiny space between the bench and the footrest, were whispering to each other, but so softly that, even pricking up his ears, he couldn't make out what they were saying to each other.

6.

The next morning at dawn, Michele woke up stiff and sore. Tripping over themselves and cursing, the rowers assigned to the task were rolling up the enormous tarp that had sheltered the galley during the night, and, as soon as he came out from under the overcoat he'd wrapped himself in, Michele started shivering; the air was freezing cold. He shook his head and ruffled his hair back to life to get his mind working again. He recited a prayer under his breath, like his mother had taught him, drank a cup of water, and looked toward the bow to see if the kitchen had started preparing rations. But the battered, rusty metal stove he'd seen them cooking the soup on yesterday looked cold and abandoned. Most of the oarsmen had pulled out a piece of bread left over from yesterday's ration and were chewing on it voraciously. Michele turned to his bench mates:

"Are they going to give us something to eat or what?"

Giulio looked at him with a sympathetic air.

"Not in the morning! Only at noon and in the evening."

Michele, his prayer long forgotten, muttered a blasphemous curse, like his father had taught him.

"But I'm starving!"

The others gave him a roguish grin.

"You got some money?"

Michele reached for his purse. Yes, it was still there, tied to his belt. I've got to remember to tie it around my neck, he thought.

"A little," he replied prudently.

"Well then, go to the tavern and buy yourself something to eat."

On the bench beyond the stove he could see a man pouring wine into the tin cups of two or three early morning customers. Giulio explained that the man, as was the custom on all galleys, had been granted a license by the sopracomito to keep a tavern on board, in exchange for a handsome sum of money. Michele jumped up onto the *corsia* and started walking toward the bow, fingering the few coins he had left in his purse. I'll need to ask the scrivener for an advance, he thought. But he'd taken just a few steps when he saw the officers come out of the cabin and start down the *corsia* and the comito pulled out his whistle to blow a long deafening squeal. At that signal, everyone stopped eating and, amid a buzz of protest, started preparing themselves to get to work. Michele stayed up on the *corsia* a minute too long; the comito was already just a step away and gave him a shove.

"Go to your bench, now! Move it, goldbricker!"

Humiliated, Michele turned back and slouched down on the bench, grabbed the oar handle and breathed deeply. A second later, the comito's whistle began setting the pace for the rowing. Leaving behind the shoals and the bell tower of Caorle, the galley headed for the open sea. For a few minutes, the comito kept them going at a fast clip, to show his lordship, as everyone respectfully referred to the sopracomito, that the crew was well awake. The sopracomito, a very young nobleman, pink-skinned and beardless, made an appearance on the *corsia*, contemplating with pleasure the fatigue of those men over whom, when at sea, he had life and death authority, as though he were a judge of the Republic. Then, luckily, he went back inside the cabin to have breakfast, and the comito immediately slowed the pace. After a half hour or so, he gave the signal to row in thirds. The first turn belonged to the rowers at the stern, but after another half hour the officer blew the change of shift and on all the benches around Michele's the oarsmen slumped down on their seats, gasping for breath and soaked with sweat.

"The sopracomito is young, eh?" Michele observed, after they'd had a drink of water.

The Chioggians were too tired to answer him, but the bench behind him was in the mood to chat. So Michele learned that the sopracomito was a Loredan, and that, consequently, the galley was called the *Loredana*.

"But its real name," said the old man solemnly, "is *Christ Resurrected*. The owners call it the *Loredana* because on their papers it takes the name of the sopracomito. When he changes, so does the name. It's five years now that I've been rowing on this galley. When I came on board the first time it was called the *Contarina*, then up until last year, the *Giustiniana*, and now they've given it to this young shaver here. But everyone from the old crew calls it *Christ Resurrected*."

"Why?" Michele asked, naively. The old man looked at him severely.

"The first time you go ashore take a look at the stern. The image of Christ is carved on it. You understand what I mean? Sopracomitos come and go, but He stays."

All of them made the sign of the cross.

At midmorning the comito decided there was enough wind to hoist the sails. During the whole operation, the galley rolled and tossed dreadfully, taking on a great deal of water. Michele had been seasick the whole day before and had vomited overboard twice. Now he realized that all that rolling on an empty stomach had got his bowels in an uproar.

"Hey," he whispered to Giulio, "what if you have to take a shit?"

"Wait till evening and do it on land, no?"

"But I can't hold it!" Michele exclaimed.

Giulio looked at him with commiseration.

"Then go up to the bow. In front of the cannon, there's a hole in the deck."

Slipping and sliding on the wet boards, Michele made his way up the galley to the bow. When he got to the cannon, he looked around. Down on their haunches in a minuscule space alongside the barrel, the four artillerymen were playing cards.

"What are you looking for?" one of them asked him.

Michele explained.

"Another rookie," the man sighed. "Go over there, and be careful not to fall overboard or you'll end up under the oars and there won't be anything left to scoop up."

The hole, as Giulio had called it, was a board with a hole in it, sticking out over the parapet, tilted just enough so that whatever came out of the hole ended up in the water. You had to squat and hold on tight to the board because if the galley suddenly lurched you could easily end up in the water. Michele managed, as God willed, to do what he had to, and he headed back to his bench feeling depleted and spent.

The favorable wind didn't last long, and the *Loredana* dragged along pitifully on its oars down the Istrian and Dalmatian coast, anchoring each night near the shore. After eight days of sailing it docked at Zara, and the crew again felt the stone pavement of a city under their feet. Michele had discovered that the fatigue was bearable and that his brick-and-cement-worn hands had formed new calluses without getting too sore. So he was convinced that he had become a man of the sea, and he went ashore with pride together with his mates in search of a tavern, after asking the scrivener for an advance and solemnly placing a pile of coins in the little sack hanging from his neck.

The galley stayed three days in Zara, and in those three days it embarked more than a hundred oarsmen and bachelors. The sopracomito had set up a counter on the dock, and the scrivener sat there all day long, inscribing in his books the names of those who came to enlist. They were all Slavonians, with thick blond mustaches, sunburned faces, and a ring in one ear—fisherman out of work or with too many mouths to feed. They stood in line patiently in front of the counter, bundles under their arms. Michele could see by the ease with which they settled into their places on the benches and made room for their things that they were men accustomed to this work. Many of them even brought their own cask of wine with them, and managed to find room for it in spaces that already seemed jam-packed.

But Michele also noticed that the scrivener counted out their pay in advance, in so many gold coins, and realized that in Zara the sopracomito couldn't abuse his power the way he'd done in Venice unless he wanted to risk having the galley set sail without three rowers on every bench. One by one, as they came on board, the oarsmen were assigned to their benches by the comito, and they almost always were given the first place, the most exhausting one. The bachelors were assigned to benches too, in pairs, and they arranged their bundles, swords, and harquebuses between the legs of the rowers. Day by day, the ship at anchor in the quadrangle of the harbor got heavier and heavier with the weight of all those men and their baggage, and with each passing night it got harder to find room to sleep. The distribution of rations took longer every time, hours, and Michele noticed that the soup, as the old man had predicted, was starting to get thinner.

Finally, at the end of the three days, the officers decided there were enough hands on the galley, and on the evening of the fourth day, the *Loredana* weighed anchor. There was a light wind blowing in from the south, but after consulting the pilot the sopracomito decided it wasn't strong enough to keep them from leaving port.

"Let's see what these new guys are worth!" he said, cleaning his teeth with an ivory toothpick.

Michele quickly realized that rowing against the wind was tremendously tiring, but now the galley had three men per bench and it moved along, albeit slowly. It was so fully loaded that the parapets were practically even with the water.

"Just a little more and we'll go under," said the parone to one of the nobles from the stern cabin, who was inspecting the benches with him, assessing the strength of the rowers and shifting those who'd been assigned the wrong position and were straining too hard or too little. "These Slavs have their own habits. They carry three or four changes of clothes, wine, and there's no way to get them to change. Have you ever seen a galley from the west?"

The nobleman from the stern cabin, a boy of less than sixteen, who was there to learn the trade, shook his head.

"Their crews are all slaves or convicts, chained to their oars. They sure don't let them carry all that baggage—a red shirt, a blanket, and that's it! When they put their shoulders into it the galley flies through the water. Yessir, let me tell you, it flies. A whole different story from ours."

The noble from the stern cabin raised his eyebrows. In Venice, to assert that a western galley, and therefore Spanish or even worse Genoan, could perform better than a Venetian galley would have been a risky proposition, bordering on treason. But out at sea, as he had already understood, the rules were different.

With all the benches rowing, the galley left the harbor and was moving down the moonlit coast. The profile of the mountains behind Zara stood out against the sky, but none of the oarsmen had time to raise his head to look at the view. Bent over their oars, they moved like machines, soaked with sweat and with the water that sprayed into the air with every turn of the oar. After an hour the comito gave the signal to row in thirds, and most of the rowers, huffing with fatigue, got ready to sleep for an hour or two, until it was their turn. Luckily, the southerly wind had died down and the galley moved smoothly through the water, in the silence broken only by the comito's whistle and the rhythmic swishing of the oars.

It was the next evening that the incident occurred. The *Loredana* had anchored next to a sandy island, bristling with umbrella pine trees, to take on supplies of water and firewood. The sopracomito had decided not to spend the night there, but to get back underway as soon as everyone was back on board, and continue under sail to take advantage of the favorable wind. A detail equipped with axes was sent ashore to gather firewood and another to fill the water barrels from the nearest stream. According to the pilot, there was a fishing village but it was on the other side of the island and it wasn't worth going all that way. Michele was part of the water detail, a dozen men in all. In the distance, off in the woods, he could hear the monotonous beat of the woodchoppers chopping up some dead pine that had been struck by lightning.

They had filled the first two barrels when the parone came ashore. His feet sinking into the gray sand, he came over to them, looked into the stream of muddy water that emptied into the sea and frowned. Then he went over to one of the full barrels, stuck his cupped hand in, and drank a sip of water. He spit it out immediately, cursing loudly.

"What a bunch of animals! Didn't you taste it before you started filling the barrels? No, eh? I should make you drink it all! It's salty! You don't take water that's so close to the sea, you make the effort to go upstream. Come on, move it, or we'll be here all night!"

He looked around at saw Michele.

"You, go on up ahead and try to find a place where the water is clear. We'll follow with the barrels."

While the other oarsmen, swearing profusely, emptied out the barrels and loaded them on their shoulders, Michele scrambled up the dunes, happy to have gotten off the detail. He followed the streambed up into the pine trees, from where it flowed down between two sandy banks that made the water turbid. It was obvious that he'd have to get pretty far away from the beach to find water that was clearer, and Michele went off into the woods. After a while he came to a heap of stones and, climbing up the rocks like a goat, he discovered that the stream widened out there into a large, transparent pool. He tasted it. It was good. He was about to call the others, who, under the weight of the barrels, had to be well behind him, when a blast from a cannon suddenly fractured the silence. It came from the sea; it had to have come from the cannon on the *Loredana*.

Surprised, Michele froze for a second, not knowing what to do. Then he started running. He knew that the firing of the cannon was the signal to call everyone back on board, and he thought the galley was going to set sail without him, leaving him alone on that desert island. He kept on running for a while as fast as he could, and then pulled up suddenly. A second blast from the cannon reverberated through the evening calm. Scared to be all alone and without a clue as to what was going on, he started running again, but without realizing that he'd taken another direction, and then the woods grew thicker and blocked his path. He knew he must be very close to the water, he could smell the salt air and at times he could hear the waves breaking, but he couldn't find a way out. Then, out of nowhere, he heard some voices yelling, and a series of shots rang out in rapid succession, which must have been the harquebusiers.

His first thought was that the galley had been attacked by pirates, and when he heard footsteps running through the underbrush very close by, he dove to ground instinctively.

Then he heard some agitated talking, and he recognized the voices of the two Chioggians, Marco and Giulio. Relieved, he got back on his feet and tried to make his way toward them, through the bushes.

"They got me, I'm not going to make it!" he heard Marco cry, his voice breaking with anxiety.

"Come on, if we stay here, they'll catch us."

Night was falling fast, and there in the middle of the pine trees you could hardly see anymore. Michele was about to cry out, when he heard the two lads screaming in terror, and a confused exchange of other angry voices. Instinct told him it was better to hold his tongue. He cautiously took a few more steps and, sticking his head into the bushes and thorns, he saw a clearing up ahead. There, so close he could almost have touched them, Marco and Giulio were lying on their backs, flailing away with their arms and legs, trying to defend themselves barehanded against three bachelors who were beating them with the butts of their harquebuses. A bit further behind them, the comito, panting, his unsheathed sword in hand, was looking on at the mismatch, making no attempt to intervene. Almost immediately the two lads stopped yelling and fighting back, but the men, from the way they were dressed and the way they were cursing, all Slavonian bachelors, went on hitting them before they too finally stopped.

"Are they gone?" the comito asked cautiously. One of the soldiers bent down over the two bodies shiny with blood.

"Gone," he grunted.

The comito stepped forward, put his still unsheathed sword under his arm and picked something up off the ground.

"Here's the sack. Heavy, huh?"

The men looked at it in silence. Michele, unseen, held his breath.

"Listen up, boys," the comito said. "Are you thinking what I'm thinking?"

Nobody spoke.

"There are ten thousand zecchini in here. Nobody knows we found the these two thieves. We could just as easily not have found them. It's dark now."

The silence grew longer, loaded with tension.

"Alright, if you're not interested, then we won't even talk about it," the comito said. At that point the three harquebusiers all spoke at the same time.

"No, no! What are you saying? Let's talk about it!"

"Here's what we'll do," replied the comito. "Now, we bury them, but good and deep, so you can't tell a thing, and we bury the gold too. Then we go back to the galley. By now it's nighttime, nobody will ever find them. I'll tell the sopracomito the best thing to do is to go to the village and give the alarm. They'll go looking for two live thieves, and no one will ever know they're dead, and that they're buried here guarding the treasure. Nobody except us. Have I made myself clear?"

The men all nodded slowly.

"On with it, then. Let's dig. Not here, though. Over there in the middle of the thorns bushes, where it's harder to get to. Go to it."

Michele, terrified, realized that the men were dragging the bodies right in his direction. He got down on his belly in the bushes and slid backwards, tearing his skin on the thorns and biting his lip to keep from making noise.

"Here, this'll do fine."

The men dug in the sand for a long time, using their hands, swords, and pieces of wood from the underbrush. It was a hellish job and all four of them cursed as they worked.

"No, we've got to dig deeper," the comito said at a certain point.

"Dogs will come through here anyway and dig them up," said another.

"That doesn't matter," the comito retorted. "There's nothing around here, who do you think is going to come here and see them? Weeks'll go by before they're discovered."

"Yeah, but then they'll find the gold too!"

"But we're certainly not going to put the coins here together with them. Are you kidding? When they find the bodies they'll dig all around here too. No, after we've got these guys taken care of we'll go a good piece farther into the woods, and we'll make another hole for the coins."

It was pitch black when they finished. Michele had tried several times to sneak off but every time he moved he caused a sand slide or made a dead limb snap, and immediately went stiff. Even after the men had finished burying the two lads and passed in front of him to look for a hiding place for the zecchini he lay still, flat on the ground, holding his breath as they went by. They hadn't gone very far when he heard the comito's voice say:

"Okay, right here is good."

Then curiosity won out and Michele moved slowly through the dark to get a better look. The four men were digging at the foot of the contorted trunk of an old scraggly pine tree, with an unmistakable profile.

"That'll do," said the comito. "The dogs aren't going to come looking around here. They could care less about gold."

The others laughed. Just then the galley's cannon fired another blast.

"They're calling us. Let's go."

But just as they started to go, a brusque movement gave Michele's hiding place away.

"Hey! There's somebody here! Who goes there?"

Instead of going flat on the ground, Michele let panic get the better of him and started running. In the black of the night he was nothing more than a shadow slipping off into the woods.

"There really is somebody! Let's get him!"

But Michele had a good lead on them, and while the others were still in the middle of the thorn bushes he'd already jumped up onto the dunes and beat it out of there. Breathing heavily he made it to the mouth of the stream, where the galley was still at anchor. The men who had gone ashore to search for the thieves came running from all directions, summoned by the blast from the cannon.

"Ah, so here you are!" said the parone, overseeing the loading of the water barrels. "What happened to you?"

"I got lost," Michele answered, panting. "But what happened?"

"Ah, so you don't know then? Two oarsmen stole the sack of zecchini from the sopracomito's cabin and ran off! The whole crew went ashore to search for them, but I don't think they ever caught up with them. Serious business, my friend!"

Just then the comito and the three bachelors appeared from behind the dunes.

"Find anything?"

"Nothing. Devil knows where they went to!"

On seeing Michele, the comito looked him over attentively. The lad was soaked with sweat, and his chest was still rising and falling from his breathless run.

"Aren't you the bench mate of those two guys?"

"So what? I didn't have anything to do with it," Michele replied.

"I think we're going to have to do some more talking, you and I," said the comito, menacingly. "Move it, climb on board."

Sopracomito Loredan was pacing up and down the *corsia*, his hands in his hair. He was pale as a dead man and all of his arrogance had vanished. The nobles from the stern cabin were all standing in a corner, their eyes cast downward, not saying a word. The comito went to make his report.

"We weren't able to find them, your lordship. It seems they've dissolved into thin air."

The sopracomito let out a moan. Despite his expensive garb, the lace and the gold chain, he was only a frightened young lad.

"I'll be put under investigation!" he muttered.

At the least, the comito thought, and grinned to himself, knowing well how merciless the Republic could be with those who disappointed it.

"And now what do we do?" Loredan asked, in a querulous tone.

"Excellency, I'd go to wait for them at the village on the other side of the island. If they want to get off the island, they'll have to go there."

The sopracomito grabbed onto that strand of hope.

"You're right! Let's go, right away."

He called for the pilot, who screwed up his mouth and shuffled his feet, and finally admitted, yes, they could try to make their way around the island, but after having already rounded the cape, making their way back amid the shoals would be no joke. But, if your lordship should order it . . .

"Of course, I order it! Go, unfurl the sails, and rowers to their positions!"

A few minutes later, the galley was under sail again, making its way along the coast of the island, propelled by the breeze. Michele was sitting on his bench, where he was now alone, and he was still shaking, thinking about the scene he had observed, and the secret that he knew. Should he go to the sopracomito and tell him everything? A voice inside him told him that would be the only way to keep out of trouble. But he had no confidence in the sopracomito. The one who was really in command, on board, was the comito, and how could he possibly go and accuse him? That man would have shut him up, one way or another. First, he would ask him to explain why he hadn't revealed everything right away, as soon as he was back on board. Why he hadn't done that, he didn't even know himself, but now it seemed to him that he had put himself in a trap. If he talked, they wouldn't believe him. They would torture him to make him confess, at the least, that he'd been an accomplice of those two poor guys from Chioggia, and when you're torturing someone it's easy to kill them and make it look like an accident.

He was deeply immersed in those thoughts when the parone called him to the *corsia*.

"Tell me something, lad," he whispered to Michele, when he had climbed up there. "There's something I don't quite understand. When the comito asked if you were the bench mate of those two rascals, you answered right away. But how did you know that they were the ones who stole the gold?"

Michele felt his head spinning. He looked at the parone with panic on his face and didn't say a thing.

"Was it that you'd heard them talking about what they were going to do? Be careful, because that's more than enough to get you hanged. If they told you something you'd better say so right away, so we can get you out of this."

The words were threatening, but the officer's gaze was questioning and even a little sad, as though he was displeased to see that Michele had got himself into trouble and was trying to help him find a way out. Michele was tempted to tell him everything, but just then the comito popped into view out of the darkness, and Michele flinched and fell silent. The parone saw his reaction and knitted his eyebrows.

"So," the comito exclaimed, "we need to add a rower here. Go find one, because in a while we'll be rounding the cape and we'll have to start rowing," he ordered the parone. The red-haired man exchanged an intense look with Michele and then walked off. The comito came over to Michele and lowered his voice.

"Listen to me, and listen good," he whispered menacingly. "I don't know what you saw, but whatever you saw, keep your mouth shut. You hear me? Going against me will only make things worse for you. And if you keep quiet there'll be something in it for you too."

He stopped there because the parone was coming back, followed by a well-built Slavonian with a load of bundles.

"Here!" said the parone, he'll be the *pianiero* and you the *postizzo*. Then as soon as we can we'll get you a *terzicchio*." The Slavonian took possession of the first position, Michele moved obediently into the middle position, and the officers left, after each of them had launched him a meaningful look.

That night a meeting was held in the stern cabin. The sopracomito, in shirt sleeves, lay on the bed and a servant was wetting his forehead with rose water.

"They must have had some accomplices!" Loredan repeated feverishly. "We'll flush them out! We'll put the whole crew on the rope and pulley!"

"The whole crew would be a little tough," the parone observed, tight-lipped. The sopracomito sprang into sitting position.

"Well then, everyone on the benches near theirs! It's not possible that they don't know anything! The one that shared the bench with those two scoundrels! At least that one I want to wind up until his arms are out of their sockets, then we'll see if he doesn't confess!"

The parone was about to say something, but couldn't figure out how, and he clicked his tongue, unhappy. But to his astonishment he heard the comito suddenly intervene.

"That one doesn't know anything. He's just a kid."

"The two thieves were just kids too!" he screamed.

"Yes, Excellency, but that one there doesn't know a thing, believe me. It's no use wasting your time. But we're still in time to pick up those other two tomorrow morning, if they make it to the village."

The parone looked at him, puzzled. It was the first time he'd ever heard the comito speak on someone's behalf, instead of abusing his power to make people fear him. The red-haired man could sense that there was something strange going on, and when the sopracomito, exhausted, dismissed them, saying he wanted to go to sleep, he stood in the dark for a good long while, thinking.

7

The stop in the village yielded nothing. After waiting there for three days, sending ashore teams of bachelors to search the area, and terrorizing the fishermen with threats of atrocious punishments, they had to face reality: the thieves had disappeared, and the ten thousand zecchini with them. As the *Loredana*'s voyage toward Crete continued the tension was palpable. The sopracomito never came out of the stern cabin and it was said that he had taken sick. The officers looked at one another with suspicion and did the same with the crew. The oarsmen kept quiet because no one wanted to be singled out. To everyone's great surprise, the investigation went no further than a thorough interrogation of the officers and crew, but the fear that the storm had only been postponed induced everyone to lay low. Michele could feel his skin creep under the hostile glare of the comito and the questioning look of the parone, and he concentrated on rowing hard, also because they were still missing a third on his bench and the work was twice as grueling.

During quiet times, however, and especially when he was eating his rations, he tried to reflect about what had happened, and figure out how to turn it to his advantage. As long as he was on the galley he had to keep his mouth shut; that much was clear. But afterwards? Come autumn, the *Loredana* would be going back to Venice to unrig, and the crew would be laid off. At that point the comito would have no more authority over him. Until that time, the ten thousand zecchini would be safe, buried on the island, whose profile and position Michele had committed to memory, to be sure he could find it again. Certainly, the comito and his accomplices would go back there to look for the treasure after the unrigging of the galley. So there were two possibilities, Michele reasoned. He could escape before then, get to the island first, dig up the money and vanish forever. He would be rich and he'd be able to send for Bianca and have her join him anywhere in the world. During those moments when he let himself daydream, Michele imagined he could actually pull it off. But all he had to do was meet the suspicious gaze of the comito, who never took his eyes off him, to realize that he was deluding himself, and that if he tried it he would end up buried on the island too. What's more, the gold was money stolen from the Republic, and Most Serene Venice had a long memory. With a touch of regret, Michele realized that the safest alternative was another: wait until the galley returned home to unrig and rush to denounce what he'd seen. The magistrate would put the comito under surveillance and send someone to dig up the treasure, and Michele would be pardoned and maybe even rewarded. Ten thousand zecchini was certainly enough to compensate for his broken nose at the hands of the police. Cheer up, Michele told himself, all you have to do is make it to the end of your contract without making any false steps.

After a few days sailing, the galley came within sight of Corfu. The green outline of the island stood out against the clear sky, and Michele, who had never gone anywhere before this voyage, opened his eyes wide and turned toward the bow to look out. The forts that protected the entrance to the harbor had recently been restored and they shone in the sunlight, but the rural villages scattered on the side of the mountain were half-destroyed and in ruins. As they came closer to the roads, the whistle sounded the signal for rowing in thirds, the galley slowed, and Michele, who could now take a rest, was able to look around at ease.

"What's the name of this place?" he asked his bench mate, but the Slavonian just shrugged.

"Corfu," said the old man behind them. "And it was a wonderful place in my day. Then the Turks came and burned it all down."

An enormous building outside the walls of the city attracted their attention. The stucco was full of cracks and the windows had no panes. Grass was growing up through its displaced stones and yet, somehow, it looked as though it was still under construction. Having worked as a mason since he was a child, Michele's expert eye understood immediately that one entire wing was still unfinished.

"The military hospital," the old man said, and then he spat. "They built it during the time of the war with the Turks; they spent so much money! They wanted to build the biggest hospital in Italy. It was never used."

"Did the Turks burn it down?" Michele asked, ingenuously.

"Oh come now!" said the old man with contempt. "Can't you see it's still there? They never even finished it, there was nothing to steal. They stuck their noses in and they left. Then the war ended and nobody cared about the hospital anymore. That's the way things go with us, dear friend."

When the galley entered the harbor and the sopracomito went ashore everyone held their breath, waiting to see if he would come back aboard accompanied by a police captain and some officers, to open a new investigation. Instead he came back alone and went straight into the cabin, and right afterwards permission was given to the crew to go ashore, just like any normal layover. Michele told himself he'd better be careful and keep on the lookout. The comito couldn't be certain that it was actually him who had seen the murder of the two lads and the burial of the gold, but his suspicion was obvious. If he wanted to get rid of him it would be on land, and not on the galley, that he would look for the chance. Michele wasn't even able to recognize the bachelors that had done the deed. It had been too dark that night and besides they were all people he'd never met, so he didn't even know who he had to look out for.

But as the stream of oarsmen on liberty flowed down onto the dock and dispersed into small groups on the streets of the city, curiosity made him forget all his worries. On the one hand, Corfu seemed very familiar to him, on the other it was a new and unknown world, where everything amazed him. The houses were built in the Italian manner, and you could make yourself understood anywhere speaking Italian, but the local people were dressed so strangely that he would have taken them for Turks if his mates hadn't laughingly assured him that they were Greeks.

"And are they Christians?" he inquired, incredulous.

"Sort of," they replied.

"But I wouldn't trust them too much," another added.

It took him a while to notice another oddity: there were no women on the streets. The stuccoed houses had their windows closed and the shutters open. Sometimes you could see through a front door into a courtyard shaded by a fig tree, but there was no sign of a woman anywhere.

"They keep them shut inside!" one of his mates explained, laughing. "That's their way. They don't trust them."

"And they're right not to" another added. "When a Greek woman sees a man, she goes into heat. There's nothing they won't do."

At a certain point, coming into a small square, Michele happened upon the scrivener from the galley. He was alone, sitting outside a tavern, sipping white wine on a bench in the shade of a climbing vine, and his eyes shone in the sunlight. When he saw Michele he motioned for him to join him.

"Come on and have a drink with me!"

Michele wasn't thirsty, but the scrivener was his superior, and he couldn't say no.

"So, tell me, how are things going? You like life on the galley?" the scrivener asked cordially, after ordering up another mug of wine.

"It's not bad," Michele answered, prudently. He had already noticed when he first came on board that the scrivener had a strange way of talking that was all his own, and he had wondered where he was from. And this time, after taking a drink, he found the courage to ask him.

"But, excuse me, you're not from Venice, are you?"

The scrivener chuckled.

"Not by a long shot! I'm from Naples, my friend!"

Michele had heard talk of it.

"What kind of a place is it?"

"A beautiful place, lad. A very beautiful place. Who knows if one day I'll go back there. By the way, my name is Muzio, Don Muzio Apricola. Come on now, drink up? Barman, another mug for my friend here!"

They drank some more. The scrivener's precociously bald pate pearled with sweat, his eyes shone brightly, open and cordial, behind his spectacles. A few days ago, the sopracomito had called him into the cabin to check on Michele's vital statistics, and then he'd ordered him to keep an eye on him and try to get him to talk. Obviously, Loredan knew nothing of what had happened on the island, but Michele was still the bench-mate of the two thieves. The comito had advised against torturing him, and his lordship had learned he could trust blindly in the experience of his second in command, but he still had a flea in his ear. So the scrivener had waited for his chance to come along and now that it had he was determined to take advantage of it.

"Well then, tell me, what do you think about those two who ran off with the sack of zecchini? Lucky them, eh?" he exclaimed, winking.

Michele sensed danger and kept quiet, limiting himself to a shrug of the shoulders.

"You knew them well, didn't you?" the Neapolitan went on. "Maybe you knew them even before coming aboard, eh?"

"No, I didn't," Michele answered, briskly. The scrivener sighed and changed the subject.

"And who have you got left back home? Don't you have a girl that you miss?"

As always when he thought of Bianca, Michele teared up, and the wine he had drunk didn't help. Seeing him look away, the scrivener was moved and for a moment he forgot his motive for having asked him to join him.

"Come on, out with it! What's her name? I'll bet she's beautiful, huh?"

Michele, screwing up his courage, talked a little about his wife, and his family, taking care, however, not to let anything out about the circumstances in which his father had died and he had decided to go to sea.

"Listen," said the scrivener, suddenly struck by an idea, "would you like to write home?"

"Would I?" Michele said.

"Well then, let's do it. That's my department. Come on, let's go back on board and I'll write it for you. Your wife can surely find someone who can read it to her."

"But sending it will cost a fortune, won't it?" Michele objected. The Neapolitan shook his head, smiling.

"We'll send it with the sopracomito's packet. She'll only have to give the tip to the postman."

The scrivener was pleased. Partly because he had been drinking too, he liked the lad, and giving him a hand cost him nothing; and partly because he hoped that as Michele dictated the letter he might let slip something interesting that he could report to the sopracomito. He paid the bill for both of them and together they walked off back to the ship.

"Well!" said Don Muzio when he was installed behind his counter. In front of him were a sheet of paper, a quill pen, an ink bottle, a candle, and some sealing wax. "How would you like to begin?"

"I don't know," Michele admitted, embarrassed. The scrivener smiled indulgently.

"Don't worry, I'll help you. So, 'My dearest wife'?"

Michele nodded vigorously. The other started writing.

"What would you like to tell her?" he asked. Michele scratched his head. He wanted to say a lot of things, but he couldn't tell them to the scrivener.

"Does she know you've gone to sea?"

"No," Michele acknowledged, relieved. "Let's tell her that."

The scrivener started getting suspicious, but he didn't say anything.

"So, 'I'm writing to tell you that I'm in port in Corfu on the galley *Loredana*, where I signed on after . . .' Oh yeah, after what?"

"Where I've signed on to the crew," Michele cut him off. "Don Muzio, let's not overdo it. She's already going to have a hard enough time getting someone to read it to her. The important thing is that she knows I'm well."

Just then they heard the cackle of a hen that had laid an egg. The scrivener stood up and went to inspect the cage near the hatch leading to the hold, where four frightened hens had managed to survive all the way from Venice. He rummaged in the straw and pulled out an egg.

"This is supposed to be his lordship's," he said with a wink, "but nobody'll notice, and you keep quiet, okay?"

He poked a hole in the shell and sucked it dry and then went back to his seat.

"What else do you want to tell her? No, wait, I'll tell you. If she wants to write back she'll need to know where to address the letter. We're going to Candia, we need to tell her to address it there."

Michele was amazed as he followed the quick, nimble gestures of the hand wielding the quill pen. The scrivener finished the sentence and looked at him.

"Don't you want to tell her when you're coming home? By November, if all goes well, we'll be going back to Venice to unrig."

Michele nodded.

"There we are!" said the scrivener, after he finished writing. "It's short, so she won't have any trouble getting someone to read it to her." With rapid movements born of long habit, he folded the page twice, and sealed it.

"Now the address: 'For Bianca, wife of the mason Michele, parish of St. Agnes.' What else do you want to put?"

"We live on a square that's so small it doesn't even have a name," Michele confessed. "Behind the dock of the ferry to the Giudecca."

"Let's put that, then," Don Muzio said, figuring out how to make it all fit on the now minuscule twice-folded page. "That's done, now I'll stick it in the packet for the courier."

Looking at the lad who was smiling happily, the scrivener told himself that this one had nothing to do with the robbery. Good for him that they hadn't put him on the rope and pulley, he thought. And so much the worse for his lordship . . .

After the layover in Corfu the galley continued its voyage toward Crete. The weather was beautiful, in contrast to the mood of those two hundred and fifty men crammed on board. There was almost no wind, so they couldn't use the sails, and they spent all day long rowing in thirds, to keep from wearing out the crew. The whistle never stopped blowing and it seemed to Michele that time was standing still. Whether he was rowing or dozing during his turn to rest, the rhythm of the rowing

kept pulsing in his veins, obsessive and relentless. The sailors
had very little to do, even though, to keep them busy, the officers ordered them to mend the sails, check the ropes, polish
the cannons. The bachelors loafed the whole day through,
hunkered down wherever they could find a little room. In the
stern cabin, the sopracomito had gone back to drinking with
his fellow noblemen, as though nothing had happened, his eyes
bloodshot.

One morning at dawn, abreast of Morea, the foretopman
spotted a sail that could be barely made out on the horizon.
The comito and a few sailors went up to the bow and leaned
out over the gilded ram, sharpening their gaze, but the ship
was still too far away for them to figure out what it was. The
comito, leaving his whistle with a sailor, went to talk with
Loredan and the two of them decided to raise the sails to take
advantage of a breath of wind while continuing to row in
thirds. After a couple of hours the distance from the unknown
vessel had diminished, and the men with sharper eyes started
making their wagers. It wasn't a galley, they all agreed on that,
because it had only one sail. One of them hazarded that it was
a corsair galliot, but others objected that they were rarely
sighted in those waters, so the question remained open.

The sopracomito had come out to see too, and after standing silently for a few minutes, he gestured to the comito that he
wanted to talk.

"What do you think, could it really be a corsair?"

The comito shrugged.

"I doubt it, Excellency."

The other man frowned and spat. The comito noticed that
despite the early morning hour he'd been drinking.

"But if it really were a corsair!" the sopracomito sighed.
"Maybe even loaded with loot! Then we would have solved
everything, eh?"

Even though Loredan wouldn't lower himself to confide in

his inferiors, the comito knew that he was terrorized by the prospect of what would happen to him when he arrived in Candia without the money. Surely, he would be put on trial, and even if he were cleared, his career was as good as over. For a young patrician on his first time away from home in service to the Republic, a catastrophe of that nature had no remedy. And if, as was highly likely, his father had invested heavily, with both recommendations and money, to get him the command of the galley and help him to outfit it, even his return home had to be looking like a nightmare. For the whole time since the robbery, the comito, who had his reasons to be on guard, had been observing him on the sly, asking himself what he would do. And now he was beginning to get an idea.

"Ah, to be sure," he said cautiously.

"And if it's not a corsair, who could it be?" the sopracomito continued. The comito stretched out his arms.

"A brigantine or a merchant tartan. Full of olive oil, maybe, or cheese. We see them often around these parts."

The sopracomito didn't seem enthused at the idea. He played with his peach fuzz beard that barely concealed the pimples of adolescence.

"Anyway, let's try and catch her," he decided. "Are we gaining on her?"

"Little by little."

"And how long will it take to reach her?"

"At this rate, six or seven hours."

The sopracomito looked up at the sky, where the sun was getting higher. Summer was drawing to an end, but the days were still long. Six or seven hours, though, seemed like an eternity.

"We need to go faster. No more rowing in thirds, get them all rowing."

The comito knitted his brow.

"With your lordship's permission, it's not yet time for that. People will wear themselves out and when the time comes they'll be exhausted. And then there's another thing. That one there is going down along the coast, just like us. By this time they've sighted us for sure, and they're wondering who we are and what our intentions are. If they notice that we've picked up speed they might get scared and head toward land, and in that case they could reach Modone before we catch them. But if we keep on gaining on them a little at a time, and maybe at a certain point we tack toward land, they won't notice a thing. On the contrary, if we're lucky they'll think we want to go into the harbor. When we get closer we have the men row amain and we'll get between them and the coast, and then they'll have no escape, even if we have to wait until tomorrow to take them."

The sopracomito was listening openmouthed.

"Well, yes, that appears to be a good idea," he deigned to admit. "Proceed," he ordered. As he went back to his place on the *corsia*, the comito looked back and saw that his lordship was once again seated inside his cabin, intent on pouring himself a drink.

Several hours later the mysterious ship was close enough to allow the lookout to identify it beyond doubt. It was a merchant felucca, probably loaded with goods, judging from how low it sat in the water. The light wind was pushing it slowly south, while the galley, with two-thirds of its benches rowing, was gaining ground. The comito had directed it gradually closer to the coast, so that if the felucca had suddenly decided to change direction and sail toward a harbor, the galley would be able to cut it off. On the bow of the *Loredana* a handful of sailors kept watch continuously, talking animatedly. The comito, his whistle entrusted to an aid, came and went from the stern cabin, from which the sopracomito had never exited.

"I could be wrong," one of the sailors said, "but those guys are Turks."

Despite their best efforts, no one else was able to discern how the people on board were dressed. The felucca itself could have been Greek or Sicilian, there was nothing in the hull or the sail that betrayed its origin, and merchant ships rarely flew a flag.

"Turks, huh?" the comito said, and nothing more. But he cursed to himself. If it had been a corsair, Turk or Spaniard, it made no difference, they could have taken it and seized all its loot, and nobody would have protested. But if they were peaceful merchants, that was a different story. Let's hope the young shaver back there clearly understands the difference, and doesn't get us into trouble, the comito pondered uneasily.

The sopracomito came up from the stern cabin. He'd been drinking again and his walk was more like a stagger. He ordered a chair for himself and sat there, fanning himself with his handkerchief, until another of the sailors said:

"Yes, they're Turks all right."

Everyone turned to the sopracomito. If the felucca was Turkish, there was no reason to keep chasing her. Venice had been at peace with the Great Lord for fifteen years now, a peace paid dearly with many sacrifices that nobody had any desire to jeopardize. Incidents with corsairs were inevitable, and in such cases the authorities on both sides tried to avoid scandals, but warships and commercial vessels followed the rules scrupulously.

"How long will it take to catch her?" the sopracomito asked, his voice pasty.

The comito wrinkled his brow.

"Rowing like we are now, maybe an hour," he replied.

"Full speed ahead, then, let's take her before she can get away," the sopracomito ordered unexpectedly. The sailors standing near him looked at each other, but nobody dared object. They looked at the comito and saw that he was biting his lip. Up to then he had done more or less whatever he wanted, without Loredan ever noticing, but open contradiction was altogether different.

"Take her?" he said finally, summoning his courage. The sopracomito turned abruptly and glared at him darkly.

"Yes, take her! And see what they've got on board!" he exclaimed.

The comito bowed his head, went to get his whistle and gave the signal to row at full strength. The galley lurched forward and accelerated until it was flying across the surface of the water. The sopracomito, straddling his chair, stared out at the oil-smooth sea and the far off white speck of the felucca.

The parone came up to join the group of sailors standing on the prow arguing vivaciously, though they kept their voices low. After a while, the scrivener joined them as well, nodded forcefully on hearing what they were saying, and then he and the parone went to the comito. He listened to them while continuing to whistle, and then shook his head. Don Muzio spread his arms, and they both went back to where they were. They argued a bit more with the others, and then the parone scratched his head and went with his cap in hand to plant himself in front of the sopracomito.

"What is it?" the sopracomito asked brusquely.

"Excellency, the men are worried. We don't want to get involved in an incident with these Turks. Isn't it better to leave them alone?"

Loredan glared at him with contempt.

"Leave these things to those who know better!" he berated him. The red-haired man pursed his lips, then he bowed and went back to his companions.

"Nothing doing," he said. "I don't know what's got into his head, but he's not going to listen to anybody."

His words were greeted with a murmur of disappointment and apprehension.

"God help us," one of them said, and they all made the sign of the cross.

The felucca was much closer by now and everyone could

see that the people on board were in Turkish dress. Standing
on the stern of the small boat, a crowd of sailors were peering
in the direction of the galley. The sopracomito, his agitation
out of control, got up from his seat.

"Bombardiers!" he shouted. "Fire a warning shot!"

The parone and the scrivener looked at each other, both
ashen and speechless. Even among the oarsmen, all rowing
with their backs to the bow and not able to see what was happening, word had already spread that they were chasing a
Turkish boat, but the comito forced them to maintain such a
fast pace that nobody had the breath to comment. But among
the sailors gathered at the prow alarm was starting to give way
to the excitement of the chase. After all, the sopracomito must
know what he was doing, and it wasn't their business to worry
about it. The chief bombardier and his assistants got busy
preparing the cannon. They opened the chest of powder and
the one with the cannonballs, loaded the piece, and waited.
The sopracomito, after taking two or three steps back and
forth in agitation, shouted, "Fire!"

The piece fired, making the ship shake and rolled back to
the mainmast, where a pile of mattresses and ropes were barely
able to absorb the impact of those two tons of bronze. The ball
flew through the air and fell into the sea, raising a splash far
from the felucca. Everyone waited anxiously to see what the
Turks would do, then the lookouts all shouted in unison:
"She's lowering! She's lowering!"

On the felucca the sail was slowly going limp.

8

S oon thereafter, the galley was side by side with the felucca and the boarding ramps were holding the two hulls close together. On the Turkish vessel the crew had gathered together as far as they could get from the galley—a dozen men, frightened and half naked—with rags wrapped around their heads in lieu of a turban. At the stern, under a minuscule canopy, surrounded by crates of goods and canvas sacks, three men in elegant caftans, wearing enormous yellow turbans on their heads, were huddled together on a carpet, their eyes wide with amazement. Loredan climbed on board, accompanied by the comito, together with a team of soldiers with swords drawn and harquebuses pointed, and looked all around him with menacing glare. The captain of the felucca broke off from the crew and came over to greet him with an unctuous smile.

"Master," he said, using the pidgin Italian that was the lingua franca of sailors throughout the Mediterranean basin, "how can we be of service?"

The comito, using the same jargon, asked him who he was and where he came from. It turned out that his name was Veli *rais*, that he was the owner of the felucca, and that they were transporting some merchants and their goods from Ragusa to Salonika. After relating all of this with repeated bows, the captain ventured to ask why it was that the galley had stopped them, given that for all he knew the Most Serene Republic was at peace with the Great Lord. But the Venetians had already stopped listening to him. With avid grins they turned to the merchants, who had listened to everything, trembling.

"Judeans!" the sopracomito remarked, indicating the yellow turbans.

"Sure looks like it," the comito sniggered.

Loredan went over to plant himself in front of the three merchants, and since one of them, who was elderly, took a long time getting to his feet, he kicked him.

"So, Judeans, what are you carrying?"

The youngest of the three bowed all the way to the floor, and replied, not in lingua franca but in quite correct Italian. They were merchants from Salonika returning from Ragusa, where they had sold pepper and cinnamon and bought hemp and canvas.

"Show it to us!" the sopracomito ordered. The Jew called one of the sailors, had him open one of the crates and pulled out a piece of canvas. Although his face was white with fear, the tone of his voice conveyed the habit of a merchant proud to display his goods.

"How much is the whole load worth?"

The Jew's jaw dropped.

"Very little, Excellency, very little!" he then warranted, his voice breaking.

"Which means how much?" the sopracomito insisted, in a strident tone.

"A hun . . . a hundred ducats, Excellency."

"He's lying!" hissed the comito. Loredan raised his gloved hand and slapped the merchant across the face. The man staggered, not so much from the force of the blow as astonishment. A murmur spread among the soldiers and the sailors.

"You think it's worth more?" the sopracomito asked his subordinate, in a huff. The comito examined the goods quickly and counted the crates.

"There's enough here for five or six hundred zecchini," he surmised.

The sopracomito frowned.

"It's still not nearly enough," he muttered.

The comito pondered.

"Excellency," he then said, lowering his voice, "if these Judeans sold spices in Ragusa, they must have taken in much more than that. They're taking this stuff back with them so as not to make the return trip empty, but they made their money in Ragusa."

"And so?" the sopracomito asked, just beginning to understand. "Go on!"

"And so there must be money on board. Lots of money."

"The felucca is small, it couldn't have transported much merchandise," Loredan objected.

"But spices are worth more than gold," the comito rebutted.

The two stared into each other's eyes. The sopracomito's were still bloodshot and turbid from wine, while the comito's were bright with cunning, but greed prevailed in both.

"Order the soldiers to tie up the Turks," Loredan whispered

Under the watchful eyes of the three merchants, who didn't miss a move, the comito ordered the harquebusiers to keep their guns trained on the sailors, then two bachelors came back from the galley with ropes and began tying the sailors' hands behind their backs. The captain stepped forward to protest, but was brutally thrown back among the others and tied up just like them. The merchants threw themselves on their knees and began begging for mercy, but Loredan paid no attention. The oldest of the three pulled out a purse from under his caftan, untied it, and showed the sopracomito the coins it contained.

"Accept our money and let us go, sir!" he implored. Loredan, his mouth agape with greed, grabbed the purse, then he turned to the others.

"Yours too! Now!"

The merchants obeyed. The two Venetians went under the

canopy and there, out of sight, they quickly counted the money. There were several hundred zecchini in all.

"It's way too little," the comito said, determined. "Hey, you!" he intimated to the youngest of the merchants. The man came over to him, hesitant. The sopracomito did not intervene.

"Where's the money?" the comito asked brutally. Then, when the other nodded toward the purses, he pressed him:

"Don't give me a hard time! This is small change. Where's the take from the spices you sold?"

The Jew, ashen as a dead man, spread his arms.

"Ah, so you don't want to talk?" the comito threatened. "Come here!" he exclaimed, gesturing to the soldiers. The harquebusiers, who had finished tying up the sailors, approached. Strip this rascal naked, and get me a rope!"

The Jew was stripped and when he was down to his undergarments, they tied his hands behind his back. Then a sailor from the galley shinnied up the felucca's mast and passed the rope through the pulley that was used for raising the sail. The other two merchants started crying. At an order from the comito, the man was hoisted up with a jerk, and remained suspended by his wrists, with his arms stretched to the breaking point in that unnatural position.

"Please, sirs!" he screamed.

"Where's the money?" the comito asked.

"There is no money! We've already given you everything! Oh, please, for the love of Christ, sirs!"

"Let Christ be alone, Judean!" the comito yelled. "Give him a yank!"

The rope was lowered abruptly and then tightened again before the suspended man could touch the ground with his feet.

"Aaah! Please, stop! I can't take anymore! Oh, please, sirs, have mercy! Be good! I can't take anymore!"

"Pull him higher, and let him drop again" the comito ordered. The victim's cries shredded the silence.

"Where's the money?" the comito repeated, relentlessly. The man screamed and begged for mercy, then, after another tug on the rope, he couldn't manage to say anything intelligible and nothing came out of his throat but an animal-like howl.

"Sir, I beg you! The money is here," suddenly exclaimed one of the merchants, who had watched the torture crying and pulling on his beard, under the constant surveillance of the soldiers. The sopracomito and the comito were on him instantly.

"Where?"

The Jew pulled back the carpet to uncover a hatch. On an imperious nod from the sopracomito, the soldiers opened it and pulled out a large sack. The two officers went over to it and ran their hands over it.

"Ah, yes indeed!" the comito said. "These are zecchini, if I'm not mistaken. How much is in here?"

"Fifteen thousand ducats, Excellency," the merchant confessed. "For the love of God, let him down."

The suspended man was still screaming, his eyeballs popping out. He had pissed himself and the urine was dripping from his pants.

"Huh? Oh, yeah. Let him down," the comito said, distractedly.

"Fifteen thousand ducats," Loredan muttered, ecstatic. All of a sudden the nightmare that had kept him from sleeping for days and days evaporated. The money that the Republic had entrusted to him was found. He would not have to confess that he'd allowed it to be stolen. He wouldn't be dragged in front of a judge.

"Later, we'll divide it up, isn't that right, your Lordship?" the comito whispered to him, in a tone that was respectful, yes, but also a bit too peremptory. Loredon was astonished. Up until a minute ago, the scoundrel would never have dared speak to him that way. He would have liked to give him a good hard kick, but he realized that he really couldn't. From that moment on, they were no longer a superior and his subordinate, but two accomplices.

"Of course," he said, haughtily.

"First, though," the comito continued, "we've got to get rid of these people. No witnesses, eh?"

The sopracomito, although his head was still spinning from the wine and from the emotion provoked by his sudden salvation, realized that something was wrong.

"But our crew saw the whole thing."

"That's why we've got to divide the take, Excellency. There's enough to go around. Ten thousand zecchini for your lordship, two thousand for me, five hundred each for the parone, the scrivener and the nobles in the stern cabin, three each for the soldiers and the sailors, and two apiece for the oarsmen," he calculated, fast and smooth. "Nobody will be able to complain. We'll say it was a pirate boat, and that they were in cahoots with the two thieves, and that we found the stolen money on board, and nobody will blow the whistle."

The sopracomito nodded, completely overmastered.

"As far as the Judeans and the Turks are concerned," he comito continued, "we've got to get rid of them. To begin with, order the men to strip and tie up the merchants too."

The sopracomito called the soldiers, and a minute later the Jews were being pushed into the heap of sailors, wearing only their shirts and with their hands tied behind their backs.

"Now, push them overboard" the comito ordered. The soldiers looked at each other.

"What are you waiting for? They're pirates, don't you understand that? They're the ones who stole his lordship's money. We're doing justice here. Then we'll divide up their loot. There's enough for everyone. Three zecchini a head!"

The soldiers stood there speechless for a minute and then one of the harquebusiers, who had still not drawn his sword, unsheathed it clamorously.

"All of them into the sea!" the comito yelled. The soldiers heaved into the prisoners. With a frightful scream they tried to escape the blades spinning in the air, spurting blood every time they sliced into a naked body. The prisoners jammed up against one another, but since they were already amassed near the edge of the felucca, they started dropping into the water. Hacking away with their swords and hitting them with the butts of their harquebuses, the soldiers attacked them until they had all fallen, screaming, into the sea. In the meantime, the comito had called a team of sailors, armed with axes.

"Break up this boat and send it to the bottom!"

The sailors went to work, and before long water was seeping in through the sheathing of the felucca. All around the little boat, the men overboard with their hands tied were writhing desperately, trying not to drown, but one after the other they went under and never came up again. Their terrible screaming waned.

"Let's get out of here," the comito said. In a rush, the soldiers and sailors jumped aboard the galley, abandoning the felucca, which was slowly breaking up, the stern already half submerged. The sopracomito personally carried the sack of gold aboard the galley. The comito was the last to leave, after taking a last look around. Two or three Turks were still flailing among the waves, but the sinking ship would certainly take them down with it.

"To the oars!" ordered the comito. "Let's get out of here!" He grabbed the whistle he carried around his neck, and an instant later the galley was slipping through the water, leaving behind the scene of the tragedy.

The whole night long, the *Loredana* ran south, pushed by a steadily stronger wind and the toil of the oarsmen. It wasn't until several hours had gone by that the comito suspended the full-force rowing and let a third of the oarsmen rest, and only in the middle of the night, when the wind had become a gale and filled the sails to bursting, did he decide that it was useless to keep them rowing, and all the oarsmen, exhausted, stretched out on their benches, trying to get some sleep. But the ship was rolling so drastically under the blows from the waves and was taking on so much water that only the saltiest veterans among them managed to get to sleep. Everywhere, an unrelieved buzzing indicated that the crew was commenting on the day's events, which they had all witnessed despite not budging from their benches. The officers had informed them that the sunken felucca was a corsair raider, that on board they had recovered the money stolen by the two fugitives, and that every oarsmen would be given two gold ducats as compensation for their participation in the capture, but even though this last news had been welcomed with satisfaction, the prevailing tone of the oarsmen's comments was perplexity.

"Those guys were not corsairs," said a one-eyed oarsman on the bench in front of Michele's. "I've seen a lot of corsairs in my life, and I'm telling you, those guys were not corsairs."

"The sopracomito wanted to get back his ten thousand zecchini," his neighbor confirmed. "Poor guys, they were in the wrong place at the wrong time. If they hadn't had that money aboard, they would have let them go. But, instead, they're all on the bottom, and nobody's left to tell the tale."

"As long as nobody survived," One-eye shot back. "Otherwise, we'll really be in trouble."

"Why?" asked Michele.

"Why? Listen to the lad! You think the Turks will let something like this go unanswered? No sir! Where was that felucca headed?"

"To Salonika," someone said.

"There you go!" One-eye went on. "In a few days, people in Salonika will start wondering why the felucca hasn't arrived yet. Then, when it's clear that it's never going to arrive, they'll write to all the ports and watchtowers along the coast to find out if they saw anything. They'll know where they last touched land, and let's hope there wasn't some lookout in a tower today with good enough sight to notice what happened."

For a while the men discussed the chances that someone could have seen something from land. It didn't seem possible to Michele, but everybody else wasn't so sure.

"Sails can be seen, my friend. First there's one, then two, then the two come together, and then there's only one left. What do you think that means?"

"But nobody will ever be able to tell that it was us," Michele exclaimed. It didn't seem fair to him. Sure, he knew better than all the others that the money taken on board the felucca was not the money stolen by the two Chioggians, but he didn't feel guilty at all. He had looked on at the boarding of the felucca without imagining what was going to happen. When the Jew was strung up he was shocked and frightened, like most of the oarsmen, although there were some who found it amusing. As for the drowning of the prisoners, he had heard their screams with shivers down his spine but without understanding, and had realized what had happened only after it was over, when the galley was already under way and news of the slaughter spread through the benches.

"Let's hope so," One-eye said, shaking his head. "If someone were saved, however, I wouldn't swear that they won't be able to follow the trail back to us."

"But even if someone managed to make it to shore, who knows where we'll be by then!" another objected.

"Yes, but the Turks have long memories. Sooner or later they'll send a protest to Venice, and there they know which galleys were at sea when it happened."

A heavy silence fell on the benches.

"Well, maybe," the greasy-haired guy with a grin said, "but I can't see how anybody could have been saved."

"You'd better be right," One-eye insisted. "If not, you know what's in store for us if the Turks get their hands on us."

"What?" Michele asked.

That was all One-eye needed to hear.

"The pole!" he said, with the voice of doom.

A chill enveloped his listeners.

"You people don't know what the pole is," he continued, "but I do. Many years ago, during the war, I was a slave in Constantinople."

Everyone looked at him with respect.

"Three years I spent there, and then there was an exchange, and I was freed."

"You must have been through a lot," someone said. One-eye shrugged.

"Oh, it wasn't all that bad. You can get used to anything. But when I saw them give the pole to that Franciscan, well, days went by before I could sleep like I used to."

"Tell us about it!"

One-eye couldn't have asked for more.

"It's simple. The Turks were at war with Venice, and the Venetian ambassador, the bailo, was under house arrest. They had nailed his windows shut and boarded up the balconies to keep him from communicating with the outside, and a guard of janissaries was stationed in the entryway. This Franciscan brother was living in the monastery in Pera, and he traveled a lot, and in the end the Turks got suspicious. When he came back from one of his trips they searched him and they found some secret letters from the Venetian Senate to the bailo. Well, that rankled them, because they trust the Franciscans, they always speak well of them, and they leave them alone. But the discovery that this one had taken advantage of them and was spying really got their dander up. They searched his cell at the monastery, and they found some more letters and a secret code and, to make a long story short, they sentenced him to the pole. All of Pera turned out to watch him go by that morning. You know, in Pera there are more Christians than Turks. It's as though there were one of our cities inside Constantinople. All of our merchants stay there, and there are more taverns there than in Venice."

His audience waited with bated breath.

"They had him pass down the main street, with the pole on his back, naked, with nothing but a rag wrapped around his hips, so he looked like Our Lord at Calvary. He passed in front of the bailo's house, and everyone inside looked out at him through the spaces between the boards. Then he came to the front of the Franciscan monastery, and they took him inside, right in the middle of the church, as an affront to Christianity. Then they tied his hands behind his back, made him lie flat on the ground, and impaled him."

Somebody let out a sigh.

"They have experts that know how to do it perfectly," the storyteller continued, "they impale a man without killing him. You know, the end of the pole is sharpened to a point, it goes in the hole, then you have to push a little at a time, softly. Oh how he screamed! Some of the women fainted. Then they pulled him to his feet and left him planted there in the middle of the church, and they ordered the brothers not to close the doors, so that everyone could see him. At that point, I left, and then I wasn't able to go back again. I had too much work to do. All I remember is that rag he had around his waist, all stained with blood, and the blood dripping down the pole. They told me that he stayed alive for two days, but he stopped screaming. Then the second night, two janissary cadets went into the church, drunk, because the Turks are not supposed to drink, their religion prohibits it, but when they come to Pera, they drink, and how! They had bows and quivers around their necks, and they used him for target practice. They planted two arrows in his body and he died. The next morning some sailors went in, took him down off the pole, and carried him off to throw him into the sea, and that's how he was buried."

"Amen," someone said. The rest sat there in silence, aghast.

"That's all there is to it, my friends!" the oarsman concluded. "So let's hope they never come to find out what happened, and that they don't get their hands on us, because I'm not sure they'd care about distinguishing between the officers and the crew."

"But that's not fair!" Michele exclaimed. "The sopracomito is the only one to blame, and he took the ten thousand zecchini while we've been promised two apiece!"

"That's the way the world works, lad," One-eye opined, and he spat. The wind was howling and the waves were beating against the sides of the galley. Soaking wet and numb with cold, the men wrapped themselves up in their overcoats, hoping to get some sleep.

9.

By the time the *Loredana* entered the port of Candia, which the Greeks call Iraklion, the sopracomito and the comito had perfected the official version of the boarding of the felucca and what followed. During their layover on the island to track down the thieves, they had managed to extort a lead from an informer which enabled them to intercept the boat the thieves had escaped on. There was only one thing left to worry about—passing off the ten thousand zecchini they had taken form the merchants as the zecchini that had been consigned to them on their departure—and it was not a simple matter. To be sure, one zecchino is the same as any other. The only thing that changes is the name of the doge that coined it. And since the coin never loses its validity, in a sack of that size you can find a lot of different doges, and nobody would dream of questioning that. But when the Republic transfers funds, the sack is sealed, and that means big trouble if on delivery the seal with the lion of St. Mark is discovered to have been broken. At the least, the coins will be recounted, one by one, and the carrier will be asked to account for the broken seal. The sopracomito had resigned himself to the counting of the coins, even though it would take an entire day, but here he was going have to come up with an explanation for why the seal had not only been broken but had completely disappeared, along with the original sack. Before entering port, the sopracomito had held a conference on this topic with the comito who, as usual, had advised him well. They should say that rats on the felucca had gnawed so many holes in the sack that it broke open and the thieves had put the coins in another sack. Since the money was intact the government offices in Candia wouldn't have any reason to question the story.

The thoughts of the sailors, soldiers, and oarsmen were of a totally different tenor. After divvying up the loot, each of them had more money in his purse than he could ever have imagined, and the dominant thought in all their heads was how they were going to spend it. Candia was a big city, a port where all kinds of ships docked, and where you could find anything you wanted. On the evening they arrived, knowing that once they entered the port it would be impossible to keep the men from going ashore, Loredan had the galley anchor outside the harbor, and the next morning he went ashore on the tender, hugging the sack of zecchini to his chest. The comito had advised him to be prepared for any eventuality, including the most calamitous one of having to beat a hasty retreat, though God only knew what they would have done in that case. When he presented himself at the office of the Governor, the sopracomito was pale as a ghost, but he explained that away as a symptom of some intestinal weakness he'd come down with during the voyage and that he was now getting over. Luckily, it all went down as smooth as olive oil. His explanation of what happened was accepted and the inevitable recounting of the money confirmed that it was all there, so the sopracomito was sent back to his galley with permission to remain in port for a week to rest his crew, before being assigned a new mission.

That same evening, the *Loredana* made a triumphant entrance into the port of Candia, and the crew pressed together at the top of the gangplank, anticipating a night of celebrations, with the exception of a detail of sour-faced sailors and soldiers, chosen by lot to keep guard on board. For one and all, the program was first and foremost to go drinking, given that the wine of Crete was famous and so much better than what the sopracomito parsimoniously distributed to them on holidays. After which, opinion was evenly divided between those who planned to wager on dice and cards those gold coins that seemed to be burning their fingers, in the hope of turning them into a fortune, and those who preferred to spend them in exchange for some contact with some female flesh. Every time a ship came into port, but especially if it was a galley, crammed with more men than one could imagine, all the taverns and brothels of Iraklion readied themselves for a sleepless night. The innkeepers got out their casks of good wine and those of watered down wine to serve to customers who were already drunk. The madams made sure their girls were made up and perfumed to a T, and pimps and bouncers ran their thumbs up and down the blades of their knives because you never knew what might happen.

Michele hadn't gotten close to the two rowers who were put next to him after the disappearance of Marco and Giulio. They were both Slavonians who spoke very little Italian, and who always had something to discuss in their own language, so he had hardly even learned their names. It ended up that the three rowers from the bench behind his convinced him to go ashore with them. They weren't yet sure where, but first of all to drink, damn it, and then they'd take it from there. They wandered around for a bit on the streets near the harbor. It was a moonlit night, with a breeze blowing off the water to ease the suffocating heat, and from all the taverns you could hear the intense buzzing of the customers and the tinkling of their glasses. The first and second taverns they tried to go into were so full they couldn't find a place to sit. Then the old man, who knew the city well, led them through a labyrinth of dark alleyways that took them away from the harbor.

"There it is!" he said finally, pointing to a half-open door at the far end of a quiet square. A leafy branch hanging above the door indicated that they served wine there. They pushed open the door and went down a few steps into a cellar illuminated by some oil lamps. It was already pretty crowded there too but they still managed to find a place. Before sitting down, however, the old man went up to the bar in the back of the room. It was the darkest corner of all, where the innkeeper could go about his business without being seen by his customers. Instead of the owner though, there was a buxom woman behind the bar who knitted her brow on seeing the four of them coming right at her, and then opened up into a big smile when she recognized the old man.

"Well, look who's here! Zuan Dolce, it's been such a long time. I had no idea you were in Candia!" From the way she spoke Venetian, you could tell she was Italian, and more than that, no Greek would have let his wife serve at the bar. Even in Candia, Michele had already noticed, no women showed their faces in public.

"We came into port this evening," the old man replied. Then he gave her a hug, and after drying her hands on her apron, she brought them a pitcher of wine and five glasses and sat with them at a nearby table. After some small talk and a first round of white wine, the old man broached the subject that was on everybody's mind.

"Tell me now, where can we go to have some fun tonight, eh? I've been gone too long, I need to get up to date."

The woman laughed.

"That depends on what you have in mind! You got any money?"

The old man showed her the leather purse around his neck, caressing it meaningfully. The woman laughed again.

"Good, then all you have to do is tell me what you'd like! If you want to gamble, go to the Cat Eater's place, right behind us, there's always someone there who's interested in a game. But if you want another kind of amusement, I've still got the room upstairs, and it won't take me long to get a girl in there."

"Only one?" asked the greasy-haired guy, with a lascivious smile. The woman spread her arms.

"You see how crowded we are tonight! More than one will be tough. But don't worry; I can get you one that'll be enough for all of you."

The men were getting excited. Michele looked at their faces shiny with sweat, their lecherous eyes, and he realized that all he felt was irritation. I don't have to go if I don't want to, he thought. But how would that look? They'd all take me for a pansy.

"Italian?" asked the third oarsman.

"Greek," the woman answered. "But you'll be licking your chops!"

"Come on then, send for her," Dolce decided. "Then we'll still have time to roll some dice if we want."

The woman got up, went behind the bar and refilled the pitcher, then disappeared into the dark interior of the house. The four of them kept drinking long enough to empty the second pitcher, not talking very much. Each of them preferred to be alone with his desire, anticipating the satisfaction that wouldn't be long in coming. It was a little long in coming, however, and the men started getting restless, but the hostess, having returned a while ago to her place, kept reassuring them with gestures that were all too explicit. Finally, coming from inside the house, which must have had a back entrance, they could hear the sound of clogs, followed by the heavy step of a man, and a young girl came in the room, accompanied by a mustachioed Greek. The man spoke briefly with the hostess, gave a suspicious look at the four sitting at the table, then nodded and disappeared. The hostess took the girl by the shoulders and led her over to the men.

"Here she is, her name is Melissa. Come on, aren't you going to offer her a drink? The room upstairs is ready, if you want to take her up there, make yourself at home."

Zuan Dolce took the girl by the hand and sat her down on his knee. She was very young and scared, with a black braid, shiny with oil, wrapped around her head, and a blouse fastened tight under her throat, with just a hint of two small breasts underneath it.

"Come on, drink," said the old man, filling her glass. The little girl obeyed. Michele met her glance and something he couldn't figure out made him feel a sharp sense of shame. But he forced himself to erase that feminine sentiment. He was a man, let there be no doubt about it.

So, who's going up first?" the old man asked abruptly. The others looked at each other.

"You go, Zuan Dolce," the third oarsman said. Michele and the greasy-haired guy assented. The old man opened his toothless mouth in a ravenous smile, rubbed his chin to make sure it was nice and smooth, since earlier that day, in anticipation of liberty, everyone on board had shaved. Then he got up and walked toward the door. The girl followed him docilely, and Michele accompanied her with his eyes until she was out of sight. The sound of her wooden heels lingered for a moment as they clip-clopped up the stairs. Then he heard a door close, and then nothing.

At that very moment, on one of the docks in the port of Iraklion, the comito of the *Loredana* was speaking in hushed tones with another of the oarsmen; and the subject of that conversation, being held out of earshot of indiscreet ears, was none other than Michele. Ever since that horrible night when he had killed the two boys and buried the sack of zecchini, the comito had suspected that Michele had seen something. But his suspicion wasn't strong enough for him to act drastically. Upon their arrival in Candia, however, he had learned something new that compelled him to make a decision. In the course of its voyage, the galley had lost a lot of time owing to the various incidents, and that very day a frigate that had left

Venice ten days after the *Loredana,* had entered the harbor. It was carrying, among other things, a list of exiles—outlaws banned from all the dominions of St. Mark, under pain of death if they should ever be captured—and the governor had notified the list to Sopracomito Loredan, in accordance with procedure.

In itself, this fact was anything but extraordinary: banishment was the sentence handed out for all sorts of crimes. The courts of the Republic—in Venice, in the hinterland, and in the Overseas Dominions—worked fast. Every month they pronounced dozens of sentences, which were then notified from port to port, striking, with no discrimination, patricians and plebeians alike. The sopracomito had scanned the list and handed it over to the comito without comment. It was clear that he was still unable to think about anything other than the affair of the ten thousand zecchini, which had all gone miraculously smoothly, and the names of the banished meant nothing to him. But the comito had been struck by one name that did mean something to him, and back on board the galley, a quick check in Don Muzio's registry had confirmed that Michele, son of the mason Matteo, from the parish of St. Agnes, condemned to banishment for infidelity, was in fact the *pianiero* of the sixth starboard bench, the lad who, that famous night on the island, had come back on board in a rush, his eyes full of fear.

At that point, the comito found himself in a dilemma that he was forced to resolve. Even if his superior, with his usual insouciance, hadn't noticed anything, sooner or later the lad would be identified and arrested. The time limit granted by the court for leaving the dominion of St. Mark had expired. The fact that the sentence had not been notified personally to the interested party was not an excuse. After all, it was his fault if he had gone on the lam rather than let himself be arrested and tried! Captured, thrown in prison, threatened with the gallows; if the lad knew something he would certainly talk. In the face of this peril, the comito thought, the hope that his instinct was wrong and that Michele had actually not seen anything was no longer enough. Something had to be done, and fast.

So that night the comito summoned a rower that he had occasion to make use of in affairs that had to be kept hidden, and as they walked innocently along the dock taking the fresh air, he explained to him what he had in mind.

"You're the right man to do the job," he concluded. "Aren't you the one who recruited him?"

The oarsman, who was none other than Lupo, grinned in affirmation.

"That ingrate. I promised to protect him, but he never came to look for me."

"Protect him, my arse!" the comito sniggered, "you're going to do him in! I don't want him to come back on board tonight, you understand?"

"It sure won't be easy to find him tonight," Lupo objected. "Better to wait until he goes ashore tomorrow night. I can follow him and do the job nice and clean."

The comito shrugged, less than pleased.

"It's up to you. If you don't find him tonight, so be it. But you look for him just the same."

"Candia is a big place."

"But the streets that lead to the harbor are no more than a handful. Lupo, listen to me now, this is a job that needs to be done fast, five zecchini extra if you do him in tonight."

The oarsman's eyes gleamed with greed.

"All right," he said, "I can see I won't get any sleep tonight. But your lordship knows that I'm your servant."

"All right. And be careful. I don't want any trouble."

Lupo laughed.

"Certain things you don't have to tell me!"

The old man came back down the stairs whistling.

"So, whose turn is it?"

The greasy-haired guy looked around to see if anyone wanted to object to his being the next in line. Since the other two lowered their eyes, he got up, licking his lips, tightened his belt flamboyantly, and started up the stairs.

Zuan Dolce chugged a glass of wine and banged it back down on the table.

"What satisfaction," he exclaimed. "We lead a hard life, but it's still worth living, my friends!"

The other oarsman laughed.

"So how is she?"

"You'll see!" the old man said with a wink. "And you? Ready to quench your desire?" he continued, turning to Michele.

Michele said nothing, and drank.

"The lad's shy," the other one chuckled.

They kept on teasing him for a while, but with no results to speak of. It didn't last long anyway because they soon heard the door open and close again, and steps coming down the stairs. The greasy-haired guy appeared in the doorway, reeling.

"That was quick!" the old man joked.

Greasy-hair sat down with a thud.

"That one knows what she's doing!" he burst out.

"I'm going, then," said the third one; and he headed off.

"There won't be much left for you," greasy-hair laughed to Michele. The lad said nothing and drank some more.

"Get ready, because with that one it's bang-bang and you're gone," the old man advised him; and both men laughed.

They waited a while.

"Oh! The guy is holding out! I didn't think he'd last this long," Zuan Dolce said.

"Said and done," greasy-hair replied, because the door upstairs opened and closed for the third time.

"Now it's your turn! Go, lad!" the old man encouraged him.

Michele put his empty glass down on the table.

"I don't feel like it," he said.

The two men were incredulous.

"What is it, what's wrong?" asked the third oarsman, who had now arrived, buttoning up his pants.

"The lad here, says he doesn't want to go upstairs," greasy-hair said mockingly.

"You don't know what you're missing!" said the latest arrival. "She's up there waiting for you with her legs spread," he said with a vulgar gesture.

"I'm not going. I don't feel like it," Michele said again stubbornly. He'd been drinking constantly, to give himself the courage to not go up those stairs, and to face the ridicule of his companions.

"But what's the problem, are you a man or not?" the third one said, surprised. But he was even more surprised when Michele stood up and leaned heavily against the table. "If you want, I'll show you right now, outside." Michele shot back.

"Hey, hey, cool off!" said Zuan Dolce, alarmed. "Tonight is no time to be fighting! We've just begun to enjoy ourselves. You don't want to go up? Fine, that's your business! You let him be, he's just a lad," he said to the third one.

They settled up the bill with the hostess and went out into the street. Greasy-hair asked what they wanted to do.

"Let's roll some dice," the old man said. "You heard the lady. There's the tavern run by the guy from Vicenza right behind this place, I remember it. There's always somebody willing to play there."

"I'd rather not," said Michele, determined. The others looked at him, this time frankly irritated.

"What, you afraid to lose? Don't worry, haven't you ever heard of beginner's luck?"

"I don't feel like it tonight. I'd rather go back and get some sleep."

"Ah, so now I get it! You've got a girl stowed away some-where and now you're going to look her up," Greasy-hair laughed.

Zuan Dolce stared at Michele. Then he burst out laughing too.

"What do you mean?! He's just dying to get some sleep. Go back and sleep, lad, if that's what you need. By now the rest of us can get by with no sleep at all, but when you're young it's different. Go back and go to sleep," he repeated.

Michele took his leave from his three companions, had them show him which direction to take to get back to the har-bor, and started off down the deserted streets.

When the comito left, Lupo took a quick look around and identified a dark corner under the cornices of the last houses overlooking the harbor. From there he could keep watch on the movements of the soldiers, sailors, and oarsmen between the ships anchored offshore and the streets flanking the har-bor. The five zecchini reward was appealing but getting the job done would be anything but easy. If he waited until tomorrow he could talk to the kid aboard the galley and invent some excuse to convince him to go ashore together the next night, without anyone thinking something was up. Afterwards, when Michele's failure to return to the ship raised the alarm, it would be hard to follow the trail back to him. Nobody knew how long the *Loredana* would be staying in port, and with a little luck several days would go by before the boy's absence was noticed. Even though the nights were getting cooler, a lot of the men, as long as they had the opportunity, preferred to sleep on land, wrapped up in their overcoats in some sheltered cor-ner instead of in the crowded confines of the galley.

It might not be until the day of their departure, when the parone called the roll, that they would notice that Michele was missing, and even then they would think that he had simply deserted. The scrivener would note the fact in his log, and he would divvy up the boy's credit with Lupo, falsifying the accounts so that it would appear that the account had already been settled, and nobody would ever worry about Michele again. But doing him in tonight, Lupo pondered, was a different deal altogether. The kid had surely gone ashore with some companions, and it was very unlikely that he'd come back to the ship on his own. And Lupo was too prudent to take any risks. The observation point that he'd chosen, however, gave him an idea. With a little luck, he could see Michele approaching and attract his attention by calling to him from the shadows, without the others being able to identify who had called him. All the better, he said to himself with a chuckle, if they were all drunk, as they surely would be. If he could swing it so that Michele came over to him in that dark corner, and the others went back on board without waiting for him, he'd be more than halfway home. So he sat there on his haunches, being careful to stay out of the light, and prepared himself for a long wait. In another era he would have smoked a cigarette, but at that time tobacco had still not been brought to Europe from America. Lupo took a bone toothpick out of his pocket, and started picking his teeth. That was a good way to pass the time too.

As the night wore on, people started coming back to the ship. His toothpick still in his mouth, Lupo sharpened his gaze and got ready for action. The wind had come up, and a bank of clouds were floating through the sky, now and again covering the moon, but the oarsman had a sharp eye. Group after group emerged from the alleyways, reeling more or less, depending on how much wine they'd guzzled, and made their way toward the ships at anchor. Many of them, once they got to the water's edge, took a look around, picked out a sheltered spot, and lay down to sleep. If Michele should also decide to sleep on shore, it would be possible to cut his throat in the middle of the night, but with the risk that someone else would be awake and would notice, and in any case with the certainty that the murder would be discovered the next day and the hunt for the murderer would begin. No, Lupo said to himself, I need to intercept him before he goes aboard or goes to sleep, and convince him to come with me, then I know damn well how to make him disappear in a way that nobody will notice for a while.

Then, he froze, his teeth clamped down on the toothpick. He couldn't believe his luck: it was Michele alright, and he was alone.

He had come from an unexpected direction, almost from behind, and now he was passing by no more than a few steps away. For a second, Lupo's hunter's instinct made him want to pull out his knife, run up to him, knife him right then and there, and run away. But he held back, realizing that it was unwise. Instead, he got to his feet without making any noise, and whistled softly. Luckily, there was no one on the dock at that moment, and Michele couldn't help but hear him. But he kept on walking, and Lupo realized with vexation that Michele was too drunk or too absorbed in his own thoughts to pay any attention to what he heard. An irrational rage against this victim who refused to cooperate made him clench his teeth. I'll show you, he thought with hate. Then, without chancing to move out of the shadows, he called out in a quiet voice:

"Hey! Kid!"

This time Michele heard. He stopped and looked around. Lupo chanced a quick move out of the shadows.

"Over here. Come here a minute."

Michele hesitated and Lupo realized that, unless Michele was completely drunk, there was no reason why he should accept such a dangerous invitation. So he came out into the open and smiled at him.

"Don't be afraid, it's your old friend Lupo," he said.

Michele glared at him, but then his knitted brow relaxed. Instinctively he'd never liked the guy, and after being forced to pay him a kickback when he joined the crew, he'd decided never to have anything more to do with him. But anyway, he wasn't a stranger.

"What do you want?" he asked.

"I got to talk to you. It's a big deal," Lupo improvised. He had no idea what he was going to say next, but the important thing was for the kid to come over to him, let him take him under his arm, and lead him away. He knew well that the backside of that last row of houses overlooked a drainage ditch where the water was so thick and fetid that you couldn't see any farther than the palm of your hand. When they found him, they'd think he'd fallen into it drunk, and that he'd drowned in those five feet of water.

Michele had too many big things weighing on his mind not to believe what this guy was saying to him. He was alarmed, but his curiosity was stronger, and his anxiety too, rather than hold him back, was pushing him to accept the invitation. He didn't know what it was Lupo wanted to talk to him about—if it was his escape from Venice, of which he'd been an unwitting observer, or maybe the murder of Marco and Giulio and the burial of the ten thousand zecchini, or maybe, who knows, the massacre on the Turkish felucca, but whatever it was about, for his own survival, Michele needed to know.

"Come here," the murderer said again, waving him over, and Michele started walking toward him.

10

In Venice, Bianca and Zanetta had been through some hellish days. They were expecting Matteo and Michele to come home for lunch, and instead some police officers arrived, accompanying a gentleman who said he was a captain in service to the Lord Heads of the Council. He inquired if the mason Matteo lived there, and, as the two women blanched and asked what had happened, ordered his men to search the house and those around it. The people came out of their houses to protest and right there, in front of all their neighbors, the captain informed them that the mason had died while resisting arrest and that his son was wanted, "and heaven help anyone who harbors him," he admonished severely, looking straight at the people gathered round who stopped protesting.

In the following days both of them were summoned to the palace to be interrogated by a magistrate, who advised them that to avoid worse trouble they should denounce Michele if he came back home, and sent them away, more dead than alive. They had to arrange to bury Matteo, whom the soldiers had fished out of the canal after hours of searching, swollen beyond recognition. Zanetta went to the priors of the confraternity to ask them to take care of the funeral, only to hear them respond that in such a case they had no responsibility to intervene. Matteo, they said, died under arrest and the burial of criminals was someone else's responsibility. Zanetta went to beg for the help of the confraternity of Mercy, which assisted those condemned to death, but there too, they didn't want to hear about it. They accompanied the condemned to the gallows and tried to convert them so they could have an edifying death, and then they buried them, but this was an entirely different case and had nothing to do with them. In the end, Zanetta managed to get help from the pastor of St. Agnes, and the body was carried off without any ceremony to the pauper's field.

When Matteo was buried, the two women, the old wife and mother and the young wife and daughter-in-law, woke up as though from a dream. For several days they had been entirely occupied by that sad duty, and hadn't had time to think of anything else, not even of what to eat. Even the torment of not knowing what had happened to Michele was attenuated by the necessity of running here and there, of humiliating themselves and begging for help, of talking with all those supercilious, patronizing strangers. But when they were alone in the empty house, they discovered how impossible it was to forget the absence of the two men; and not only because of the constant pain. There was nothing in the house—no flour, no wine, no bags of rice or fava beans, which in good times were heaped under the bed in the older couple's bedroom. Matteo had been out of work for too long, and they'd used up everything. Lately, they had been living day to day, eating whatever the mason managed to bring in by selling the leftover materials from the work site. Zanetta and Bianca embraced.

"What are we going to do?" the girl sighed, her voice a thin thread.

"Come on now," her mother-in-law responded, in a voice meant to sound tough. "We're not dead yet."

She went in to her room, opened the trunk which held both of their trousseaus, pulled out a pillowcase from the pile of linen, took it into the kitchen, and undid the seam with a pair of scissors. Six gold coins fell out, six shiny zecchini. Bianca's eyes opened wide.

"Even he didn't know I had them," Zanetta said, with a sigh.

"My mother gave them to me when I got married. I thought I'd never need to touch them. Such is life!"

She pushed one toward Bianca and then sewed the others back inside the seam.

"Now, listen to me good. I don't want anyone to know we have them. Otherwise someone will come into the house looking for them. Go to the Rialto to change it, but don't get cheated. Ask in two different shops and see how much they'll give you. The last time I changed a zecchino I got six lire, but these days everyone says they're worth more."

"But I don't know what to do!" Bianca said, her eyes wide with alarm. Zanetta looked at her severely.

"It's time you learned," she replied.

When Bianca came back, worn out from rushing, with her purse full of silver coins, Zanetta had just about finished washing the kitchen floor; the house was spotless.

"Well done," the mother-in-law said, after counting the coins. "I knew gold was worth more these days. Now," she went on, drying her forehead with the back of her hand, "let's go buy a sack of flour and then go to bake some bread, if we want to eat."

An hour later the two women were dragging the sack back to the house. Both of them strained under the effort, and they staggered their way along. At a certain point Bianca lost her grip and had to lean up against a wall to keep from falling.

"Stupid! Be careful!" Zanetta reprimanded her harshly. Then she went over to her and scrutinized her face.

"What's the matter? Don't tell me you're expecting!"

Bianca found the strength to smile. "Oh no, don't worry. That's all we need! I'm just very tired, that's all."

Zanetta fell silent.

"You haven't eaten anything since this morning. What do you say? Shall we go to the tavern and get something?"

Bianca looked at her gratefully but shook her head.

"No! We've got to save. I can do it. Come on, let's pull it home."

Zanetta didn't say anything but it was clear she was pleased.

At home they made the dough for seven big loaves of bread, made a cross on them so they would rise well, arranged them on a board, and took them to the bakery. It was Saturday and a long line of women were waiting their turn to bake their bread for the week.

"We'll be here all afternoon," Zanetta muttered.

The smell of fresh-baked bread filled the piazza, and Bianca felt faint from hunger. The women in line were from the neighborhood, they all knew each other by sight, and a couple of them lived on their same square. At first, nobody knew what to say, and the group that had been rattling with chatter up to a minute ago was suddenly overcome by an unnatural silence. Then, though, one of their neighbors, Caterina, came over to them and mumbled a few words of comfort. She was a cooper's wife and her windows looked out on the street right in front of Zanetta's, so in the summertime the two women chatted from window to window while they were working in their kitchens. The other women started talking again; first one comment and then another drew a reply from Zanetta, and after a while the tension dissolved. But nobody dared mention Matteo or Michele. How strange, Bianca thought. Usually, when someone dies, people talk about him every day, for months on end, whenever they meet up with his family. Now it's as though Matteo hadn't died. And Michele . . .

Her eyes filled with tears. Michele was not dead, and she was not a widow. He was hiding out somewhere, and he would be back soon, she was certain of that. But not knowing where he was, and how long she would have to wait, was even more anguishing than being widowed. Zanetta had aged suddenly, the few dark hairs she had left had gone white, yet the old woman knew that you always have to keep going, no matter what happens to you. But if you don't even know what it is that's happened to you, it's even harder, Bianca thought.

When it was their turn, the two women slipped off the cloth that was covering their loaves and the baker's boy slid them into the oven one by one. After a short wait the two of them were on their way back home, with their board loaded with seven fuming loaves of bread, slightly charred from the ashes. When they got home they sat down and greedily ate their first meal of the day.

On Monday morning Bianca went looking for work. Before getting married she had worked as a laundress, and even in the few months she'd lived with Michele in her in-laws' house until they could find a house of their own, she'd continued working whenever she had the chance, to contribute to the family finances. So she knew which doors to knock on. She came back home carrying a heavy bundle of dirty laundry on her head, and that same afternoon she was at the washtubs, in an alley a few streets away from the house, with her sleeves rolled up and her arms immersed in water. She went back there every day from then on, and in the evening, after work, she took down the dry laundry from the clothesline and made the rounds of her customers' houses to deliver it and get paid, getting back home after dark. Zanetta went with her to the washtubs right from the start, even though Bianca insisted that it wasn't necessary. Zanetta stood there at the ready and did what she could to help her whenever she needed a hand; otherwise she sat on the edge of the stone platform and talked, partly with Bianca and partly to herself. The topic she talked most about was Michele, but choosing her words well because there were other women there, whom they hardly knew, and she didn't want to talk about their business in front of strangers. Where Michele had gone was a mystery that neither of them could solve. He was hiding out, sure enough, because if they'd captured him they would have found out about it; but where? Except for a few, who had gone elsewhere to seek their fortune, all of his friends lived in the parish, and Bianca didn't believe he would hide out with one of them without trying in some way to let her know.

"He'll have gone to sea," Zanetta said one day, with a dreamy air. Bianca, who was vigorously rubbing a shirt against the stone, stopped and dried her sweat with her apron. Even though summer was on the wane and the water at the washtubs was getting cooler every day, the exertion still made her sweat. With a grimace she felt the painful muscles in her back and rubbed her hands over her kidneys, letting out a long sigh.

"Gone to sea! What are you saying?" she protested.

"Yes!" replied the old woman. "Where else could he be?"

"Venice is big!" Bianca said, scornfully. Tired as she was at that moment, she was almost resentful toward her husband who was hiding out God-knows-where, and had left her alone.

"No, I'm telling you, he's gone to sea," Zanetta went on, paying her no heed. Then, on seeing that the sun was already going down and that there was still a big pile of laundry to do, she said, "Come on, let me give you a hand." Bianca accepted the offer, and the two of them went back to work.

As much as Zanetta tried to help, however, Bianca had to do most of the work. What they earned amounted to one person's wages, or maybe a little more, and it had to feed the two of them, and, unlike some of the women they met at the washtubs, they weren't used to eating just bread every day. Zanetta went home before Bianca, put some soup on the fire, cooked some rice or vegetables, occasionally a plate of sardines, and the money Bianca earned disappeared in a hurry. For her part, Bianca came home every night after twelve or thirteen hours' work, and she couldn't take it anymore. She needed to eat well; she hadn't even finished growing yet. Zanetta noticed tenderly that some of her blouses were tight on her. She ate and then collapsed on the bed, and her mother-in-law, who like all old people slept very little, stayed up well into the night, fantasizing.

Zanetta didn't know what she could possibly do to cut down on their expenses. Their only luxury, aside from eating and soap for washing, was the candle they lit every Sunday for Michele's return at the altar in the church of the Madonne delle Grazie in San Barnaba, and they certainly couldn't give that up. Better to skip a meal. They had promised not to dig anymore into the little treasure hidden in the pillowcase, but it wasn't long before they had to change another zecchino. Bread was expensive, and there was a lot of competition for work—some hard up Friulian women newly arrived in the neighborhood would take care of a basket of laundry for ten cents less than the going rate. Used to leaving everything up to her mother-in-law, Bianca didn't notice, but Zanetta was finally forced to admit it: they were spending more than they were earning. She started going with Bianca even for pickups and deliveries, helping her carry the baskets and bundles, so they could wash more stuff, but she tired quickly, her bones ached, and what she did didn't amount to all that much. I don't know how long we can go on like this, she thought, but she didn't want to say anything to Bianca.

Autumn arrived, and with it the cold, and new expenses. They bought a load of firewood from the Istrian who made the rounds of the neighborhood every year at that time, delivering it on a boat from a warehouse behind the Arsenal. Zanetta knew how much they needed to buy to heat the house all winter, she'd always been the one in charge of that, and this time she decided to buy a little less. The men weren't there anymore, they used less wood for cooking, and if it got cold in the house, the two of them would wear two pairs of stockings instead of one. But after paying the Istrian she sat for a long time in silence, so long that even Bianca noticed, and asked her what was bothering her. The old woman didn't want to talk about it.

Late one afternoon, at dusk, Bianca was home alone. Her mother-in-law, as she did every evening, had gone to vespers, and she was going to stay on afterwards in the church to pray. Bianca had come home earlier than usual, but instead of going with her to church she had stayed home to get warm. Since the onset of cold weather, the work at the washtubs with cold water had gotten harder. She'd also gotten her period that day and she wasn't feeling well, and she had a bucket full of bloody rags that she was ashamed to wash in public. So she set about doing it at home, in front of the hearth where the soup was cooking, carrying in some water from the well. She was hanging the rags on a clothesline outside the front door when an old woman she didn't know came up and asked her if she was Bianca, the wife of the mason Michele. Bianca, astounded, said yes she was.

"Can I speak with you?" the woman asked.

Bianca invited her into the house, drying her hands on her apron. The two of them sat down on the stools.

"You look a little pale. Work is tiring, eh?"

Actually, Bianca was pale because she'd been losing a lot of blood in those days and she had circles under her eyes because she had a constant pain in her gut that wouldn't let her sleep, but she didn't say anything and just shrugged her shoulders.

"Have you had any news about your husband?" the old woman asked suddenly.

Bianca shook her head and blushed.

"Did you know him?" she asked, warily. The old woman's mouth opened in a toothless grin, and Bianca noticed only then, with a feeling of disgust, that her lips were painted a bright red.

"I know everybody," she said. "And the rent, have you paid it yet?"

Bianca felt like she was going from one surprise to another and she didn't know how to react to this stranger who was so obviously sticking her nose into their private affairs. She should have thrown her out, but she was used to keeping quiet and obeying older women, and behaving otherwise would have been too much for her.

"Why the rent," she said faintly.

The old woman looked her triumphantly.

"St. Martin's Day is just around the corner, dear! You know that's when the rent is due. You'll have to pay it too if you want to stay in this house. But isn't it too big for just the two of you? What a useless expense!"

Bianca thought she understood.

"You want to rent a room? We've talked about that a lot. Wait until my mother-in-law gets back."

The woman laughed.

"But what are you thinking? No, it's just the opposite, dear. You see, I have a house not far from here, where I put up some good girls who work. They give me part of what they earn, and they get a safe place to live."

Bianca and Zanetta had never thought of moving. It would have been like admitting that Michele was not going to be back any day now, and that their life from before was over for good. Renting out a room to a tenant was something they'd considered often. After all, since they'd been on their own they'd been sleeping in the same bed, not to feel lonely. They hadn't done it yet only because they hadn't found the right person— they would have gladly taken a woman, the prospect of a man was a little scary. Now, though, listening to the old lady, Bianca told herself that maybe that was the solution: rent out a room somewhere else, spending half of what they were spending there, that was the way they could survive. And if Michele came back, well, he'd just have to get over it if he didn't find the old house full of memories.

"If there were room for me and my mother-in-law," she said slowly, "I'd consider it."

But the woman laughed again, and shook her head.

"No, dear, there's no room for your mother-in-law. She's not right for the kind of work my girls do."

For some reason, Bianca was afraid, even though she still didn't understand. The woman's tone of voice scared her.

"But why not, what kind of work do they do?" she asked, her voice shaking.

The woman told her. Bianca looked at her, her eyes wide with astonishment.

"You'd be just right, dear, take it from me, I know how to size a girl up," the old lady continued, examining her with an expert eye. "And tell me, don't you miss your husband? How long has it been since you've had a little fun?"

Bianca could feel the blood rising to her head. She wanted to scream at that woman to leave, and she had already opened her mouth, but suddenly she felt something inside her snap. Who do I think I am? she said to herself, crushed by the humiliation. All the others that this has happened to never believed it could ever happen to them. But by now what else can I expect from life? Michele is not coming back, it's useless to delude myself. The woman looked at her and knew exactly what she was going through her mind. She had had other conversations like this, with woman reduced to misery, and she also knew that half the cases ended up going one way and half the other; she'd gotten used to it. Seeing the soup on the fire, when she'd entered the house, had seemed like a bad sign to her. I made a mistake, she'd said to herself, I should have waited a little longer. When the house is cold and there's nothing but bread to eat it's more likely to go the right way.

But what if Michele does come back? Bianca suddenly thought. She didn't know it, but it was the smell of the soup wafting over from the hearth that had brought to mind the many nights when Matteo, Michele, and the workers came home to eat, and there was a soup on the fire like that one. The only difference was that the pot was full and it was enough for only one night, while now they made half a pot and it lasted two days! And if he comes back? She missed her husband's body, and how. His, not someone else's. She tried to imagine herself in bed with some other man, with the hands of another man touching her, and she felt sick.

"Thank you," she said, making an effort to be polite. "I'd rather not."

The old lady was irritated.

"You're a stupid girl! You'll come looking for me, I can tell you that."

She looked at Bianca with regret. She was well-built. She would have earned her a lot of money. Oh well, she thought, it'll go better the next time.

"You know where to find me," she told her in a sweet voice. "Good-bye, dear, and good luck."

As soon as the madam was gone, Bianca recited an incantation and took a rag to wipe clean the stool where she had been sitting. When Zanetta came in, she was stirring the soup.

"It's so cold out!" her mother-in-law lamented, taking off her shawl. Then, when she saw Bianca's face, she exclaimed, "What's the matter with you? You look like you're dead!"

"Nothing. You know I've got my period," the young one lied.

"Still? But it's been a week, my darling, they never end. It's a great liberation, when you can put that all behind you, take it from me, I didn't stop till I was fifty. Come on, let's set up the table and eat."

While they were eating, Bianca mustered up her courage and asked:

"St. Martin's Day is coming up soon, isn't it?"

Zanetta, who was noisily slurping up a spoonful of soup, stopped and looked at her, astounded.

"Sure," she said, still not understanding.

Bianca swallowed hard; she wasn't used to taking the initiative.

"And the rent?"

Instinctively, Zanetta was about to tell her to be quiet and not get involved in things that were none of her business. Then, all of a sudden, she realized she was tired. Maybe it was time for her to stop trying to carry the whole burden by herself. If Michele were there he would be the head of the family.

"The rent will have to be paid," she admitted.

"And how much is it?" Bianca insisted, amazed at her own audacity.

"How much, how much! It's twelve ducats a year, that's how much," her mother-in-law burst out, and then, to Bianca's immense surprise, she broke down crying. "And I have no idea how we'll ever pay it," she added, weeping. Bianca hesitated, and then she got up and came to embrace her.

"Come on, now," she said. "We'll find a way, you'll see." She was tired, distressed, bewildered from all of the uncommon things that had happened to her that day, and in her head she kept hearing over and over again the sinister things that the other old lady had said to her no more than an hour ago: "You'll come looking for me, I can tell you that . . . "

11

When Bianca woke up the next morning, Zanetta was already standing over the fire preparing the soup.

"Listen," her mother-in-law said in a decisive tone, "I spent the whole night thinking. We can't go on this way. You can't work for the both of us. You barely make enough to maintain yourself, and I can't really help you anymore. It's not a job for me anymore, with my back. I'm going into the hospital."

Bianca tried to discuss it, but Zanetta wouldn't budge.

"It's the only thing to do, I'm telling you. Today, let's get my things together and go over to the Derelicts. They're nice; they'll take me in and there'll be some work there that I can do. And we'll find a place where you can go into service, that way you won't be alone."

There really wasn't anything else they could do. Bianca understood that. So, after eating for the last time the soup she had prepared so many times for her husband and her children, Zanetta gathered up in two big bundles her linens, her skirt, jacket, and shoes that she wore on feast days, wrapped in a handkerchief her earrings and gold chain and put them in the purse tied to her belt, then took one last look around the family home, sighed, and made the sign of the cross.

"Come on, let's go," she said, holding back the tears. They loaded the bundles on their backs and, faltering under the weight, left on their way through the city.

The hospital of Saints John and Paul, popularly known as "the Derelicts," had as its mission not to care for the sick but to house widows and orphans who were unable to earn a living: abandoned wives with small children, prostitutes who no longer wanted to live that life and whom no one would accept in service, widows without means, too old or sick to work. It took them a long time to get there, crossing San Trovaso and San Barnaba, Santa Margherita and San Pantaleon, the Calegheri and San Polo, Sant'Aponal and the Rialto bridge, Saint Bartholomew and Saint John Chrysostom, and the Miracles. When they came out into the piazza of Saints John and Paul, they put their bundles down on the ground and sat down for a minute to catch their breath. From atop his marble pedestal, a warrior on horseback glared down at them with a disdainful air. All morning long the wind had been blowing, carrying in brief showers off the lagoon, but now it was starting to rain steadily. "Courage," Zanetta sighed, taking up her load again and heading off toward the hospital entrance.

The priest they spoke with was very old, his face covered with wrinkles. Bianca figured he must be at least seventy. He obviously couldn't see well because he came close to them and scrutinized their faces carefully. Then he limped all around them, looking them up and down, front and back, and he even stretched out his hand to feel the fabric of Zanetta's shawl. He had received them coldly and had hardly said a word, after they had explained their reason for coming. But after studying them attentively, he planted himself in front of them and smiled, and the two women realized that there was goodness in him, even if he was reluctant to let it show.

"Well then," he said, addressing Zanetta. "There's a place for you. It's a life we have to take as the Lord gives it, right? Dedicating yourself to work, as long as you can, and to prayer."

The old woman nodded, solemnly.

"For you," the priest said, referring to Bianca, "we'll have to think on it. We can always find you a house that needs a servant girl."

The two women loaded their bundles on their necks and followed the priest up the staircase to the first floor, where the wards were located. As they passed by, a woman who was washing the floor moved aside and bowed to the priest. She was still young, but her face was puffy and wore the signs of life, and she had a perpetual expression of alarm in her eyes. Bianca recalled the old lady from the day before and what she had come to propose to her, and she felt her blood boil again. Not me, she swore to herself.

In the ward, a group of old women were sitting on stools, spinning wool. They all said hello with respectful familiarity, and scrutinized the two newcomers with unconcealed curiosity. The priest assigned a bed to Zanetta then looked at the two bundles they had placed on the floor.

"Don't you have a trunk?" he asked, knitting his brow.

"My trousseau chest," the woman replied, and looked away. "I didn't know if I could bring it with me. And anyway it's too heavy for the two of us."

"That means I'll have to send someone to get it, you're going to need a trunk," said the priest. "And everything that might be useful here. A chair, some dishes. I'll send a cart."

Bianca could see the tension easing in Zanetta's face at the thought of her things joining her. How egotistical old people are, she thought. And me?

The priest turned to her.

"So, you understand. Tomorrow a man will come with a cart. You can close up the house and come back here with him. We'll find you a place."

"Thank you," Bianca muttered, and kneeled to kiss his hands. She felt herself shaking inside as though she had a fever, and she couldn't tell if it was because of hope or fear of the unknown life that awaited her.

Two days later, Bianca started as a servant girl in the home of Lady Faustina, in the San Simeon Grande neighborhood. Her new mistress was an aging widow, heavyset, imperious, who made her living by skillfully managing the rents from houses and shops that she inherited from her husband. She received Bianca, warily studying her for a long time, and then gestured her assent to the scrivener from the Derelicts, who had accompanied her.

"Very well, I'll take her," she said, as though she were concluding a purchase. Bianca knew that before her another girl recommended by the priest had worked there but then she got pregnant and had gone back to her hometown.

"You'll just have to make the best of it," the priest had sighed, describing her future mistress to her and the house where she would be working; and Bianca made the best of it. The work was no harder than what she did at home, especially since the men's disappearance had obliged her to work outside the house as well. The difficulty lay only in the fact of not working for her own family but for a stranger, not sleeping in her own bed but on a pallet in a closet, not eating the warm leftovers of her husband but the cold ones of her mistress. In the first few days she never went out of the house. Lady Faustina went to the market to do the shopping by herself and didn't want to leave the house empty. When she came back, she checked in minute detail how much bread, wine, and cheese were left in the kitchen. On Sundays, Bianca accompanied her mistress to mass, sitting in the back pews, and then afterwards waited for her outside while milady Faustina commented with her women friends on the neighborhood news. As they were walking home, the mistress asked her if she wanted to go visit Zanetta at the hospital. Bianca, who was learning to live a new life and didn't know any of the rules, hadn't even thought of it, but milady said that she had nothing against it as long as she came back in time for vespers. So Bianca went to Saints John and Paul, embraced Zanetta, and stayed with her, talking some and crying some, until the setting sun reminded her that it was time to go home.

The days passed and Bianca slowly got used to her new life. Bad thoughts continually crossed her mind but luckily she didn't have time to dwell on them; there was too much work to do, from the moment she got up, before dawn, and got the fire going, stirring the embers, to when the mistress checked to see that the front door was locked and sent her to bed. Milady Faustina was not mean, but she was a tyrant. She liked to be in command, and to stand there and watch as the young girl obeyed her. As long as her husband was alive, she had ruled tyrannically over him, as well as their two live-in servants, a man and a woman. Now that she was alone, and one servant girl was enough, all of her voluptuous taste for command was taken out on Bianca. What gave her the most pleasure was obliging the girl to ask for things so that she could then deign to grant them. She would purposely give her too little bread so she could hear herself be asked for more, and when they were both in the same room, Bianca had to ask her permission even to interrupt the work she was doing and go piss in the urinal. She ought to buy herself a slave, the girl thought, resentfully.

And then one day, several weeks after her entry into service, something strange happened. She was washing vegetables in the kitchen when she heard a knock on the front door. She went to answer and opened the door to a gentleman in rather dusty clothes, and boots on his feet, who was surprised to see her.

"Well!" the gentleman said, examining her without compunction. "And who might you be?"

"Bianca, sir," she replied, blushing.

"New, eh? Tell me, is milady Faustina at home?"

"Yes, sir."

"Go tell her that Signor Fabio is here."

Bianca obeyed and milady Faustina, to her great surprise,

went into agitation. She ordered her to show the man in, bring him some wine and then to come back to the bedroom to help her put her makeup on. She became impatient with her for no reason, but she didn't slap her across the face as she had already done on more than one occasion. On the contrary, she changed her mood right away and a strange smile appeared on her painted face.

"Now go out," she told her.

"But what do you mean out?" Bianca stammered.

"Go buy twenty cents' worth of peppered bread. But don't go to the shop here on the corner. Go to the Rialto, you understand? It's much better there. Here," she added, handing her some money. "Don't lose it and don't let them cheat you. When you come back, if the door is closed, wait outside, understand?"

On her way to the Rialto, Bianca had time to think about that extraordinary event, and figure out what must be behind it. When she got home the front door, as she expected, was closed. She stood there uncertain, a little scared of standing there like that, outside in the middle of the street, without knowing how long it would be. Then she remembered that in the back of the house, on a little alleyway so narrow it was hard for even one person to get by, there was a small door into the garden that didn't close well. Curiosity pushed her to go around the house and try the back door. Indeed, although the door was latched, there was still a narrow opening through which a thin girl like Bianca could get in. Skinning her forearms and tearing her skirt—though she would only notice later that evening, when she undressed to go to bed—she found herself in the garden. The windows on the first floor were too high to look into, but the well was right under them and Bianca, seeing as she'd come that far, gave in to her curiosity and carefully climbed on top of it. Standing on tip toe, she managed to see over the windowsill of a bedroom, and noticed with satisfaction that it was the bedroom of milady Faustina.

Sharpening her gaze, she could see through the rather opaque, bubbled glass, two naked bodies moving about on the bed. With a start, she noticed that the man was on the bottom and that the woman on top was straddling him, with her big breasts bouncing up and down. She knew it couldn't be anyone other than milady Faustina, but just the same she was astonished on recognizing in all its nudity the fleshy body that she had dressed and undressed every day. Ashamed and at the same time fixed there by a desire that she couldn't remember ever having felt, not even when she waited under the sheets for Michele to lie down beside her, she saw the two bodies thrashing around grotesquely, and heard through the thin glass the words that their two mouths were saying just a few feet away from her.

"Is this how you like it?"

"Ride, bitch, ride . . ."

"Go! Go! Go!"

"Give it to me, give it all to me, now!"

Then a loud, drawn-out moan, and milady Faustina shook her whole body one last time, and then let herself go, lying down on top of the man with all of her not inconsiderable weight. A minute later the man, his eyes cloudy, sat up, pushing her laboriously to one side, and started looking for something. And Bianca jumped down as fast as she could from the well, ran to the little door, went back out to the street, and sat on the front doorstep, just in time before the key turned in the lock and Signor Fabio, redressed and dusted off, came walking out with a satisfied air.

"Come on, why are you sitting there daydreaming? Come inside, no?" milady Faustina ordered harshly.

From that day on, the mistress started sending Bianca around town on all sorts of errands, almost always in far off corners of the city, and always with the order to wait outside if she found the door closed on her return. One time she had to take a pair of gloves to a friend of milady Faustina, another time she had to go to the pharmacist's with a prescription for a plaster and wait for it to be prepared, or go buy some trifle, which, however, was sold only in a certain shop on the other side of town. On her return, after hours of walking, Bianca almost always found the door closed, and sat down on the step to wait. But it was wintertime, the cold seeped into her bones, and so she would start walking up and down the street, to warm herself up. When it rained, she took shelter under a nearby balcony, and waited there until the door finally opened to let Signor Fabio come out and her go in.

But the worst thing was not the cold or the rain, but the glances of the men who saw her waiting like that on the street, or aimlessly walking back and forth. Under their gazes Bianca would turn flaming red, and when one of them whistled or called out some heavy compliment, she felt like she would die of shame. The streets of Venice were full of women who went out alone to take care of their business, but waiting out in the open like that for no apparent reason, maybe leaning your back against the wall when you got tired, was something else entirely. The insolent curiosity that she could read in the eyes of those men, and also the contempt or the pity she saw in those of other women, scared her to the point that she no longer dared hold her head up high. When she heard someone approaching, she would curl up even more with her eyes staring at the ground, until she heard the footsteps going away.

One Sunday, at the Derelicts, she told Zanetta about how she was treated. The old woman was horrified on hearing that Bianca was forced to roam the streets for hours, shut out of the house, and even more so on seeing that after confessing it to her the girl had tears in her eyes.

"I wish I'd never gone to that house," she whimpered. "I wish I could stay here with you," she added, looking around the room. The other women, who had come over to sit next to them to spin their yarn and listen to her stories of the outside world, nodded with comprehension. They were happy there. They had some work to do, they were fed, kept warm and well clothed, and they prayed a lot.

"We can ask Father Anzolo," one of them said.

"She's too young, and she's not even sick. They'd never take her," another objected.

"But Father Anzolo is such a good-hearted man!" the first insisted.

"And now that those two other poor souls have died . . ." a third added.

All in all, the old women decided that it couldn't hurt to ask. It turned out that Father Anzolo was the priest, white-haired and wrinkled, who had accepted Zanetta some time ago. He listened to Bianca's story knitting his brow, and he too was scandalized by what she was forced to do. An honest girl couldn't be made to live such a life.

"For tonight, you can stay here if you want," he said. "There's room on the beds," he added, pointing toward the half dozen large beds where two or if need be three women could sleep together. "Then tomorrow we'll see."

So that evening Bianca ate soup at the common table, and then said the rosary together with the other women, the old widows and some younger women, and she slept in the bed with Zanetta, along with another old woman with snow white hair and a lost look in her eyes, who never said a word and fell right to sleep murmuring a prayer. The next morning at dawn she got up with the others, prayed in the freezing cold chapel asking for God's help with all of her strength, and went to work. But she had been spinning for just a couple of hours when a manservant came to call her.

Father Anzolo was waiting for her in his office together with two elderly men, with dour faces.

"Here she is," he said. Evidently he had already told them the whole story.

"Well then," said the first of the two, while Bianca looked embarrassed, wringing her hands on her apron. "Are you sure you want to stay here?"

Bianca was already less enthusiastic than yesterday about life there in the home, but she was afraid they would send her back to milady Faustina, who by this time must be madder than a hornet about her not returning to the house.

"Yes," she said, her eyes on the ground.

The man sighed.

"Listen to me now. Don't you have a contract with milady Faustina?"

"I don't know," Bianca said, not understanding.

"When we sent you to her, didn't the mistress have you sign a paper?"

"No, sir!" Bianca replied, thrusting her eyes open wide.

"You see?" the man said, turning to the other one. Father Anzolo nodded energetically.

"Blessed women," the second gentleman commented, and this time all three of them nodded gravely.

"And hasn't she paid you up to now?" the first man continued.

"No, sir!" Bianca said again, amazed. A voice inside her was telling her that maybe she should have thought about this before. How was it that she was always more naïve than anyone else?

"When I entered into service with her she told me we'd work out an agreement," she defended herself.

The three men looked at each other, and one of them said something in Latin, and the other two nodded again.

"You can go, girl," the first man said.

Bianca went back down to the other women, who were waiting for her full of curiosity.

"I don't know anything!" she said, shrugging her shoulders, and she told them about the interrogation she'd been subjected to. But she hadn't even finished when Father Anzolo came into the ward smiling.

"It's all right," he said, "those gentlemen said you can stay."

Milady Faustina came to reclaim her three days later. In her heart Bianca had always known it would happen. When the priest came up to call her she blanched, but she followed him obediently to the parlor, where the mistress was pacing back and forth with an offended air.

"You were wrong not to come back," she said to her, as soon as she saw her.

Before Bianca could respond Father Anzolo intervened, asking milady Faustina if it seemed right to her that a young girl was shut out of the house for hours and forced to roam the streets.

"I had my reasons," the mistress said, stiff. "And a servant in my house has to do what I say."

The priest rebutted her so severely that milady Faustina blushed and was speechless for a minute. Then, however, she answered back in turn, raising her voice, and a minute later the two of them were so hot under the collar that Bianca looked at them with her mouth agape, expecting that any minute now they'd start hitting each other. In the end, however, Father Anzolo got control of himself.

"Until you promise not to treat her like that anymore we can't send her back to you," he said, in a conciliatory tone. But Faustina was too riled up to contain herself.

"Send her back to me? Well, don't worry about that, I don't want her anymore. I wouldn't take her back even if she shit gold!" she exclaimed. Then she left, slamming the door behind her.

Bianca breathed a sigh of relief, and went back up to the

ward, while the priest went on muttering something about women. But that wasn't the end of it. A few days later, the mistress was back in the parlor at the Derelicts, and was demanding to speak to Bianca. The priest asked her what she wanted this time, and Faustina, in a contemptuous tone, asserted that when the girl had left her house she had a handkerchief with her that belonged to Faustina. Worried, Father Anzolo went up to call Bianca and brought her down.

"Is what your mistress says true?" he asked severely.

Bianca, her face glowing red, said that it was not true. The mistress had given her the handkerchief as a present. She did not add that this extraordinary event had taken place on the very day that, for the last time, milady Faustina had forced her to stay out of the house for the whole afternoon, not opening the door until after dark. That night the mistress was in an excellent mood, she had caressed her and made her a gift of the handkerchief. She hadn't thought about it again, and that Sunday when she left the house she had no idea she would not be coming back. That evening she had shown the handkerchief to Zanetta and the others, and the women had told her to keep it and not worry about it.

"All lies, I want my handkerchief back, and I want to denounce this thief," milady Faustina exclaimed in anger, and she stretched out her hands toward Bianca. The priest stiffened, placing himself between her and the girl. "If you have something to say against this woman, you'll have to speak to the rectors of the hospital," he said coldly. But Faustina pushed him aside, grabbed the handkerchief that Bianca was holding in her hands, and after a brief struggle, took it away from her.

"Thief!" she exclaimed triumphantly, as she made her way out.

The same day, Father Anzolo sent someone to Faustina's house to pick up Bianca's things. The man sent on the errand came back saying that the mistress had done everything but attack him physically. She had yelled the whole time that the servant was hers, she had eaten and slept at her expense, she was still in her debt, and that the story was not over yet.

"She'll come back here to kiss my hands again and beg me to take her back, you'll see!" she'd screamed after him.

A few days went by and the priest sent for Bianca.

"Your mistress is here again and wants to see you," he said wearily. Bianca went downstairs reluctantly and found that this time milady Faustina was not alone. She was in the company of Signor Fabio.

"Oh, here's our Bianca," the young man greeted her with unexpected warmth. "Tell me now, isn't it true that you're going to return to your mistress? We'll forget the whole thing, and we'll all be happy together."

Bianca shook her head.

"No, sir, I'm not coming back there ever again."

"What a shame," the man said, wiping the smile off his face. And he left without another word. Milady Faustina, on the other hand, stayed there to talk vehemently with Bianca, swearing that from now on she would treat her well and that she would never shut her out of the house again. Father Anzolo listened impassively; there was something in all of that that seemed fishy to him, but he couldn't say exactly what. Why, for example, had the woman come back accompanied by a man, and why had the man left just as he had come without accomplishing anything? No, thought Father Anzolo, who had seen a lot of strange things in his long life, I don't like what's going on here. He was still ruminating, when he happened to look out the window and exclaimed, turning to Bianca:

"Get back upstairs, fast!"

12.

The door burst open and Fabio erupted into the room, accompanied by three men. With a cackle of triumph milady Faustina stretched out her hands toward the girl, but the priest got between them again, shouting:

"Go, run! Upstairs!"

Instinct saved Bianca. Even before she understood what was happening, she had already disappeared up the stairs. On the first step she lost a slipper but instead of stopping to pick it up she kicked off the other one too and kept on running barefoot. Cursing, Fabio brutally pushed Father Anzolo out of the way, but when he got to the bottom of the stair he realized that the three men were not following him. He was about to curse again, but changed his mind, and shrugged his shoulders with a smile. The other three were right. Spiriting the girl away from the parlor, practically on the street, was one thing, but invading the hospital and chasing her through the wards was another, and, if someone called for help, they risked getting trapped inside. The men stared at the priest and slowly backed their way to the door; the incursion had failed.

"Too bad, milady," Fabio said to Faustina, with a brief bow. "This bird has flown."

This time it was Faustina who swore horribly.

"You coward!" she screamed in Fabio's face. "Cowards, all of you!" she repeated looking at his lackeys, who were already at the door. "And you're supposed to be men!" And she stormed out, shaking her head, as the three of them contritely made room for her to pass. After her, they all left. Fabio was the last one out. The priest, gasping for breath, was left alone.

Father Anzolo and the women spent the rest of the day discussing how they could keep Bianca safe in case milady Faustina went back on the attack. The priest was determined to report what had happened, but it was unlikely that the police would do anything. After all, what had really happened? Some men had come into the parlor and then they went away again.

"Before anyone worries about something like this, my dears . . ." Father Anzolo said, and the old women all nodded.

In any case, one thing was evident: Faustina, unused to seeing herself opposed, had lost her head. Bianca couldn't stay there, she had to leave.

"There's my sister," one woman said suddenly. It was the one Bianca had noticed the very first day on the stairs, with her face swollen from all the pain she had suffered and her gaze perennially frightened.

"But yes," the woman insisted. "You know her, Daniela, she always comes to visit me. She's married but she doesn't want to live with her husband. She lives in the court of Ca' Trevisan, in the home of a widow, and there are some other women there too who don't have husbands."

She interrupted herself, turned red, and fell silent. Father Anzolo reflected. There were a lot of situations like that in a big city like Venice, and priests looked on them with suspicion. But he knew Daniela, she was a girl who broke her back working so as not to end up like her sister.

"What kind of work do you know how to do?" he asked Bianca.

"Washerwoman," she responded immediately.

The priest thought for a moment, his wrinkled face tense with concentration.

"Let's try it," he said.

So Bianca went to live at the home of widow Margherita, who had inherited from her husband three rooms on the top floor of Palazzo Trevisan in the St. Mark's area, and to maintain herself, in addition to her work as a seamstress, she rented out beds to women. The house was already overcrowded, and for Bianca they had to put a pallet on the floor near the fireplace. Besides the widow's daughter, Camilla, also a seamstress, and Daniela, who made her living selling fruit at the market, there were two other washerwomen, both immigrants and both separated from their husbands, the Slavonian Marta and the Friulian Lucrezia. Along with the six women there were two children because Marta had a five-year-old son and they were also raising an orphan from the Mount of Piety, a baby girl of eight months. Camilla, who had lost a baby the year before, was nursing her, and the orphanage paid a small sum to compensate her.

Bianca started going to the washtubs with the other two, and earned enough to eat and sleep. When they got up, at dawn, Daniela had already gone out a while ago to go and set up her stand at the market, and when they came back home they found the widow and her daughter sewing on a bench near the only window of the big room, while the soup cooked on the fire. Marta's little boy played in the courtyard or wherever, and he fell asleep holding on to his mother's hand. Then they lit a tallow candle and the two seamstresses continued working until late, while the other women took turns washing the dishes, changing the baby's diapers and rocking her to sleep.

During those long dark nights, with the only light in the kitchen coming from the flame of that candle in the corner, the women told Bianca their stories. She could see they were used to doing it every time a new woman entered the house, and they had a natural way of telling things that, in the beginning, they were probably ashamed even to reveal to their confessor.

"I got married when I was fourteen, and I didn't know anything about anything. Poor youth!" Lucrezia sighed. "But I didn't want him, that one there. How I cried when my father told me I had to marry him. He was revolting; all you had to do was look at him to see he wasn't a man. But he paid well." At that point the storyteller paused to see what effect her words were having on Bianca.

"What do you mean, he paid?" the girl asked, surprised.

"Just that, he paid!" the Friulian continued, satisfied. "I got married and my father didn't give me any dowry at all, on the contrary, that other one paid for it all. I didn't want that disgusting man but my father wouldn't hear of it. He was a man without the fear of God. I don't know where his soul is now, I mean it, I have no idea. He was like that his whole life. He'd come home at night and say dirty words that I can't repeat. He beat us mercilessly. When my mother told him I was right not to want to marry that man, he beat her so bad she was in bed for two months. I told him that rather than get married I'd drown myself and what do you think he did?"

"He beat you," Daniela said, joking.

"Exactly!" Lucrezia confirmed, without understanding. "And how he beat me, God help us."

Lucrezia fell silent and dried a tear from her eye.

"And then?" Bianca insisted.

"Eh! I married him. What else could I do? My father had the priest come to the house, and he told me that if I didn't say yes he would beat me again, and then he would throw me out of the house and I wouldn't be his daughter anymore. We ate lunch and then the priest married us. I cried the whole time and afterwards I told everybody about it, the neighbors and my girlfriends, that that marriage wasn't valid, that they'd made me say yes but I didn't want to. That night he came to sleep at our house. And I got a needle and thread from my mother and sewed my nightgown between my legs so he wouldn't be able to take me. He was so angry! But he was afraid to yell, because he was in my father's house, and that night I never gave in, and he couldn't do anything."

"And how did it end up?" Bianca wanted to know, fascinated.

"How do you think it ended up!? The next day my father took the nightgown and hid it, and he told me that if I didn't go to bed with my husband he would nail me to the front door, and that night he forced me to take off all my clothes and then he shut me in the room with him. I cried but I didn't dare scream, for fear of my father who was in the next room, and he took me. Lie still, he said, and I'll give you a nice present. I called on the devil to take me away and I told him he wasn't my husband."

Bianca had stopped breathing.

"And then?"

"And then he took me to live with him, at his mother's house. That . . . I don't even know what to call him, believe me. He'd always say to me: you know how much I paid your old man for you? Four hundred ducats!"

The women blurted out exclamations of surprise.

"You never told us that before," Margherita observed, dryly.

"Yes, indeed, that's just the way it is!" Lucrezia replied. "Four hundred ducats, cold cash. I saw him count it out with my own eyes! And then, after a few months at his house, when I had finally resigned myself to spending the night with him, even though I never stopped thinking that he was not my husband, but I never told him that for fear that he'd beat me, well, one day he comes to me and says: today a gentleman is coming to the house and you have to be nice to him."

"Oh, come on!" Bianca exclaimed, covering her mouth with her hand.

"Oh yes, my dear," Lucrezia repeated, sadly. "You understand how it was? He had spent his money and now he wanted to get it back. I was the one who had to get it back by working. And his mother was in on it too. She explained to me that that gentleman was an important man, that he liked the way I looked, and that he paid well."

"And did you do it?"

"After a while I ran away," Lucrezia cut it short, avoiding the question. "I went back to my father."

"Well then, you're a fool!" Daniela exclaimed.

"And where was I supposed to go?" the washerwoman defended herself. "I asked him if he still had the money the man had given him, but he had drunk it all, or he had spent it on whores. So I ran away again, and then I found my way here. Providence guided me."

Just then the baby woke up, and Lucrezia got up to go rock her. In the minuscule light of the candle, Margherita and her daughter continued sewing. Marta caressed the head of her boy, sleeping on her lap.

"What a story, eh, women?" she said after a moment of silence. The others nodded. "When I got married I didn't know anything either. I didn't even know if I liked him or not. I married him because my cousins told me I had to," Marta continued in her broken Venetian. "But the first night I was so scared! I didn't know what was going on. I ran away. I climbed into my cousin's bed and I told her I wanted to sleep with her and not with that man. Everyone yelled at me but they didn't beat me. They kept trying to convince me for two or three days, and I wouldn't give in. So they went to the priest and told him he needed to do an exorcism to convince me to go to bed with my husband."

"I know a woman who wanted more than anything to go to bed with her husband," the widow interrupted her, laughing, "but he couldn't get it up. It just sat there, limp as a sausage. The priest explained everything to her, how she should touch it and kiss it, to make it hard, and she got down to work, but nothing happened! In the end they went to a medicine woman and she taught her an incantation."

"Which one?" Daniela prodded her, amused.

"There were two of them. You could put the blade of a plow under the bed. That would make him get hard like iron! But where are you going to find a plow in Venice? That's an incantation that works for peasants. So they tried another way. You have to take the wedding ring of a newly married virgin, immerse it in holy water, and then he has to piss through the ring. That breaks the spell."

"And did it work?"

"It worked and how!" the widow laughed. "Now those two have six kids!"

"But with me the exorcism didn't work at all," Marta timidly went back to her story, without protesting at the interruption. "I was still afraid. My cousins explained to me that if I wanted to have a baby I had to go to bed with him. I didn't believe it. Sure, I wanted a baby but I didn't want to do that thing. I asked my neighbors, and all of them told me that my cousins were right. So I resigned myself. It's better that I don't think about that night. But he's what came out of it," she concluded with pride, caressing the hair of her sleeping boy.

"And where is your husband now?" asked Bianca, who hadn't missed a word.

"Who knows?" Marta said. "We didn't get along at all. In the end he went to sea and didn't come back, and I don't want him to."

Bianca sighed to herself, but the others didn't notice.

"My story is still the worst," Daniela exclaimed. The other women, who already knew it, nodded with an air of compunction. Daniela, her eyes suddenly shiny, turned to Bianca.

"You don't know it yet, my story, but it's quickly told. A schoolmaster lived near our house. His name was Master

Ambrogio. He liked me, and always gave me little presents. With one pretext or another, he was always at our house. When I turned fourteen, he started talking to my father about wanting to marry me, and said that he liked me so much he would take me without a dowry."

"Like me," chimed in Lucrezia, who had come back with the baby in her arms and was trying to sing her to sleep.

"Yes, but he didn't pay, he just offered to take me without a dowry. My father didn't have a dime. My sister had already run away from home, and he thought he was doing the right thing. I accepted to make him happy."

"But what was it that bothered you? Was he old?" Bianca asked.

"Yes, he was old, but that wasn't it." Daniela answered. The atmosphere in the room seemed to suddenly grow cold. "It's that I hadn't been a virgin anymore for a while. He had already taken me when I was seven, one time when I had gone over to his house. And then he'd continued to take me whenever he had the chance."

This time it was Camilla who broke the silence that followed the girl's last words.

"So you see, we're just a bunch of hard luck girls! Now I'll tell you my story, so you'll have heard about all of us," she went on, looking at Bianca. "And you'll know that men are capable of anything. My dear, I'd been married for three years and was expecting my first child. My husband was a good man, but a little odd. He always wanted to read the Bible and he had learned Latin so he could do it. The one day he ran off without saying a thing to anyone. When I think of how desperate I was! We didn't hear from him for a year. I thought he was dead. I prayed constantly for some news about him . . . Then one day a letter arrived, addressed to his father. It said how sorry he was for the pain he had caused him and me too. My dearest and most tenderly loved wife, it said, I still remember it by heart. But he had been thinking about it for several years."

"But what did he do?" asked Bianca, amazed.

"He became a Jew! He went to Salonika, in the empire of the Turk. There, he says, there's a city where all the inhabitants are Judeans, and he studied their laws and now he calls himself Abram Israel, and he says by a miracle of their God he learned to read their language in a week!"

"Oh, dear Jesus, please help us!" whispered Bianca, incredulous. And for a second a wild idea crossed her mind: could it be that Michele too had run off to become a Jew? No, she thought, that's not possible. But then where is he? Silently she started to cry.

"There, there," the widow said to her, wrapping her arms maternally around her shoulders. "Don't think that all men are like that. You'd like yours to come back, wouldn't you?"

"Oh, yes," Bianca sobbed.

"There," said the widow, dryly. "I'd like to have mine back too. But I know I can't, because I buried him," she added, making the sign of the cross, immediately imitated by all the others. "Yours, on the other hand, one day or another, will come back. You'll see."

"But if I don't even know where he is?" Bianca exclaimed, through her tears. The widow rubbed the tip of her nose, pensive.

"If you want, there is a way," she finally said. "There's no guarantee it will work, so don't get your hopes up. But I've seen it work other times."

Bianca stared at her with her mouth open, and the others too were suddenly attentive.

"But don't tell anyone!"

They all assented, excitedly.

"All right, here's what you do. You take a pail of water," the widow said. And as she said it, she got up, went over to get a tin basin out of the corner, and filled it with water from the pitcher.

"Now, pay attention. You have to stick your finger into your thingy . . . Yes, that's exactly what I mean," she added, because Bianca was blushing. "Come on, we won't look. Stick it way down deep, and then stir the water with it."

Bianca did it, clumsily.

"Good! Now, stir hard, mix the water with your finger. And repeat after me: for this water from the well, for this water from my bucket, with San Giuliano and San Rocco the pilgrim and the Three Kings, let me see where my mule has gone, where my boat has gone, let me see where my man has gone, let me see so I can find him."

Bianca, her heart in her mouth, was on her knees in front of the basin, repeating the incantation.

"Now, look!" the widow commanded. "What do you see?"

Bianca opened her eyes wide. It seemed like she couldn't see a thing, but maybe it was her, she thought, maybe she didn't know how to look the right way. What was that reflection? Could it be the sea?

"He's gone to sea," she murmured. The women around her drew a breath and held it.

"I knew it," said Marta.

"Where he is bound for?" the widow insisted. "Come on, look hard!"

The flame of the candle, reflected in the water, was projecting mind-boggling images.

"He's in the land of the Turk!" exclaimed Bianca, positive. The others couldn't hold back exclamations of surprise.

"See?" the widow said, triumphant. "It worked! And don't you worry, he's alive, just like I said. And he's going to come back a rich man!"

"Do you really think so?" Bianca murmured.

"Certainly! If not, why would he have gone so far away?

Come on, one day soon you'll see him walking down these streets with his pockets full of gold. You're a lucky one, take it from me! And now, that's enough, women, it's late, let's all go to bed!"

13.

It was a hard winter in Venice. Two consecutive years of poor harvests had left the granaries empty. The Signory bought grain in the Levant, from the immense landed estates of the Turkish pashas. The Sultan, concerned about ensuring the grain supply for Constantinople had prohibited the export of grain from his empire, but luckily the pashas didn't want to give up their profits. Their mercenary bent was also shared by the Grand Vizier, who had personally promulgated the prohibition on behalf of the Sultan. A multitude of small private vessels— xebecs, feluccas, and caramusals—shuttled between the Turkish ports of Volos and Salonica, smuggling grain to the Venetian islands of Crete and Zante, where it was loaded onto ships and taken to Venice. It was a dangerous business but highly profitable for the owners of the boats, and by the time it arrived in the granaries of the Ducal Palace and the Arsenal, the grain's price had risen beyond belief, but it was there. The government distributed it at a controlled price. It lost money but managed to avoid rousing the rabble, which was the most important thing of all.

The city was teeming with beggars, and almost every morning the body of someone dead from cold and hunger was found on the new Rialto bridge or under the portico of the Ducal Palace, where the poor huddled in search of shelter. One day it was an unemployed immigrant fired from the store where he'd been in service, another day it was the mother of a family who'd been abandoned by her man and ended up on the street. But even people who did have jobs found it hard to get enough to eat. The monasteries distributed soup every day, and in line with the desperate poor there were also hardworking, honest craftsmen. Bianca and the other women who lived at Margherita's went all together each noon to the monastery of the Celestines, the closest one to their house. The neighborhood was densely populated, and standing in line in the cold was interminable, but at least the soup was hot, thick, and plentiful. In the evening, what they had earned from working all day was enough to pay for dinner; so they made it from day to day, waiting for better times.

One day Bianca came home, panting under the weight of the pannier of laundry she was carrying on her back, and when Margherita opened the door for her she could see she was trembling. Bianca had lost a lot of weight in those months, the skin on her cheekbones had lost its sheen, turned sallow, but the widow had never seen her so shaken.

"What's wrong? What happened?"

It came out that Bianca, she didn't know how, had lost some pieces of laundry at the washtubs or on the street. She noticed it when she had made a delivery to the house of a merchant, whose laundry she did every week. Together with the servant girls she had counted and recounted, and then she had gone back to the tubs to look, but it all came to no avail. Some pieces were missing, and she would have to pay for them. Bianca was desperate.

"I don't have any money left! What am I going to do?" she kept repeating, through her tears.

The women came together for a consultation. The only thing that Bianca still owned, beyond the clothes on her back, was the earrings from her wedding.

"You'll have to pawn them," they all agreed. There wasn't one among them who hadn't gone, at one time or another in her life, to pawn earrings or a necklace, a belt or a purse, at the

Mount of Piety. Daniela examined the earrings closely under the candlelight.

"These will get you two or three ducats," she decreed. Bianca was despondent at the idea of separating herself from her earrings. They were her last reminder of Michele, but she understood that there was nothing else she could do.

"Maybe it would be better to sell them," she said bravely. "If I pawn them, where will I find the money to redeem them? In a year and a half they'll sell them and that'll be the end of that!"

"A year and a half is a long time!" Lucrezia objected. "Maybe your man will come back in the meantime!"

Bianca smiled and shook her head as tears streamed down her cheeks.

"If he comes back, I don't want him to have to repay for my earrings! No, it's better to sell them, they'll give me more for them, don't you think?"

"Double," Daniela said, with the air of an expert.

"Listen to me," the widow intervened. "Selling them is not the thing to do. I know what you should do. In the ghetto there's a Jewish lady who gives pledge loans. You should go to her."

"A Jew?" Bianca exclaimed, frightened.

"But the Jews are required to sell the pledge after a year, that's worse than the Mount!" Daniela protested. "What a great deal!"

The widow shook her head.

"But this one is a good person. If she knows that you're a woman in trouble, at the end of the year she'll renew the contract without asking you for a thing. She's done it for me too."

"A Jew? I don't believe it!" Lucrezia objected.

"You'd better believe me!" the widow simmered. "She's a good woman, even if she's Jewish. She's a widow too, without a man, and she knows what it means. Go to her," she said, turning to Bianca. "Go to the Ghetto Nuovo and ask for Lady Regina Calimani. Tell her the whole story and tell her I sent you. She remembers me. You'll see, this is the right advice I'm giving you."

So the next day at the first light of dawn, Bianca wrapped her earrings up in a rag and went out on the street. The Ghetto Nuovo wasn't far away and when she got there the guards had just opened the great iron door that shut the Jews inside their neighborhood at night and kept Christians out. Once she was inside that labyrinth of alleyways, shops and overcrowded apartment buildings, she had no trouble finding her destination. Everybody seemed to know Lady Regina. The Calimanis' house was a rundown building, with a leafy tree and a well in the courtyard. A servant girl accompanied Bianca up to the first floor, where the woman of the house was sitting in a well-heated room, behind a table piled high with papers. She was an old woman and very fat, who had difficulty breathing and looked sympathetically at the young woman who was standing there respectfully before her. Bianca had never in her life been to the ghetto and at first she was frightened, she kept her distance from people and avoided touching the walls, as though she were afraid she'd catch the plague. But the goodwill that shone in the old woman's eyes reassured her, so she unfolded her bundle, letting the earrings roll out onto the table, and asked how much she could have. Lady Regina took them, gave them a quick look, and then weighed them on a minuscule goldsmith's scale.

"Are you really hard up?" she asked, instead of quoting a figure. Bianca blushed.

"A little," she said.

"Your husband isn't working?" the woman insisted, looking at the ring on her finger.

"He's gone to sea," Bianca said. Ever since that night that the widow had taught her the incantation of the basin, she was convinced that it was really true, even though she hadn't had any news of Michele since the day he disappeared. The Jewish woman nodded.

"I know. It's tough to try to manage on your own. Let's say thirty lire."

Bianca made a quick calculation: that came to more than three ducats.

"I thank you," she said, tearing up.

The woman shrugged her shoulders.

"If you knew," she said vaguely, and then she stopped. They heard a noise from the floor above them, as though something had fallen on the floor. Lady Regina seemed alarmed.

"Beatrice, come here a minute, if you can!" she called out. The servant girl, who was in the kitchen, came up the stairs in a hurry and looked in, cleaning her hands on her apron.

"Go upstairs and check if Rabbi Salomon is all right. I heard him moving around up there," the mistress said. The servant girl vanished.

"My father-in-law. That God should take him with him when his day comes," Lady Regina explained. "He's over eighty years old, and he's become like a child. What can you do!" she concluded. Then she added something in a language Bianca couldn't understand.

"So," she said after a minute or two, getting back to Bianca. "Let's put it in writing. And you, look, there's a chair there. Have a seat."

Bianca hesitated a minute, and then sat down on the edge of the chair the woman had pointed to. Not only did the woman inspire confidence, but the room was totally similar to any other room that she had happened to see in Venetian houses. Nothing prompted her to think that it was the home of Jews. What she had never had occasion to see, on the other hand, was a woman writing with such nonchalance. In her fat, ring-adorned fingers the quill seemed to fly. In just a few minutes the contract was drafted.

"What's your name?"

"Bianca."

"And then?"

"My father's name was Francesco da Vicenza."

"The woman wrote another line.

"And your husband?"

"Michele, son of the mason Matteo."

"Do you know how to write your signature?"

Bianca shook her head.

"Put an X here. Wait, I'll hold your hand steady. It's not hard, you'll see. Ready?"

Bianca obediently grasped the pen and marked an X, guided by the old woman's firm hand.

"There we go! And now let's count out your thirty lire."

Lady Regina opened a drawer and started pulling out silver and copper coins, making two separate piles. She counted and recounted them, and then said to Bianca.

"Let me have your handkerchief. Or do you have a purse?"

"It's too small," Bianca said, showing her the purse.

The woman shoved the coins inside the handkerchief and then deftly knotted it.

"There we are. And be careful not to lose it! What's the matter?"

Bianca had started to cry.

"There, there now, what is it?" the woman repeated maternally, but Bianca kept on crying. Even she didn't know why. She had come there full of anxiety, and the simple cordiality the woman had shown her had suddenly snapped something inside her.

"I don't know! Forgive me! It's that . . . "

The woman embraced her.

"It's tough for everybody these days, little girl. You'll see, when your husband comes back, things will get better."

Bianca nodded, sobbing all the while.

"I'd offer you a glass of wine," Lady Regina said, but hurried to add, when she saw Bianca stiffen, "but it's forbidden, I know. You Christians can't eat or drink in our homes. The only thing missing is a law that prohibits you from crying, but probably sooner or later they'll make that one too," she added, bitterly.

Bianca wiped away her tears with her shirtsleeve and got up.

"I don't know how to thank you," she said, trying to smile.

"Not at all," the woman replied. "Ah, just a minute!" she added, calling her back. "I'm looking for a Christian servant girl. You wouldn't happen to know someone who'd like to come into service here with me?"

Bianca's eyes thrust open.

"But isn't it forbidden?" she stammered.

"No," Lady Regina said. "You think it's strange, eh? But the fact is we need Christian servants in order to be served on Saturdays. We're not allowed to do anything on Saturdays, not even light the fire or a candle, and we can't cook. That's the Lord's will. So, whoever can, hires Christians; it's not forbidden. But then they're not allowed to eat or drink in the master's house, or sleep there. They all have to leave the ghetto before the gates are closed. So if you know somebody's who's interested, send them to me, alright?"

Suddenly Bianca had a crazy idea. That woman appealed to her so much that all of her prejudices evaporated in a minute. The maternal tone that she used, not only with her, but also with her servant, had touched her deeply. When she had been in service with Faustina, she was certainly not treated like that by her mistress.

"Couldn't I be the one, signora?" she blurted out. Lady Regina smiled and shook her head.

"But you're too young, my child. They'd never let you come here."

"Why not?" Bianca asked, astonished. The woman laughed, but it was a bitter laugh.

"Can't you figure it out? They're afraid. Young people can be influenced. And young women are more at risk than the old ones."

"But I'm not in any danger! I beg you, signora, try me!"

"You don't understand," the woman said. "You have to file a request with the magistrate. They summon you and examine you, then if they approve they give you a permit to come and work in the ghetto. But they'll never give you a permit."

"Let me try!" Bianca exclaimed. Lady Regina tried to dissuade her, but on seeing how obstinate she was, she relented. She explained to her the name of the magistracy where she had to apply, and where the offices were. Then she bid her farewell. Bianca bowed and left. Lady Regina followed her with a tender look, shaking her head, until she was out of sight.

So it was that the next day Bianca presented herself to the Officials of the Cattaver, the magistrates charged with oversight of public works contracts, the collection of excise duties, and the activities of moneylenders, and who for a number of years now had also been meddling in the private lives of the inhabitants of the ghetto, on the pretext that most of the moneylenders in the city were Jews. After four hours in the waiting room, an usher led her to the office where three magistrates, all rather young, had just finished eating lunch. A servant was carrying off the remains of the meal and the wineglasses; one of the three was cleaning his teeth. All three of them were looking with interest at the young woman who was standing respectfully at the threshold.

"Come ahead," said the president, who was the youngest of the three. Bianca obeyed, told them who she was, and explained why she had come. The three knitted their brows.

"And why do you want to go to work for the Judeans?"

"I need to work," Bianca said. "Lady Regina told me that

she wants a Christian servant girl to light the fire on Saturdays," she added, all in the same breath.

"But how old are you?" asked the president.

"Seventeen," Bianca said. The three looked at each other and shook their heads.

"What is this, a joke? Don't you know that you have to be at least forty to go into service in the homes of the Jews?"

"But why is that?" Bianca asked, naively.

"What do you mean, why? Those people are dangerous; they can't wait to get their hands on some young person who doesn't know anything, so they can pull them over to their side!"

"But what do they do that's so bad? It seemed to me that Lady Regina was a perfectly good woman," Bianca objected bravely.

"There are no good Jews!" the president replied brusquely. "And by saying that, you are demonstrating just how dangerous it would be to let you go to her house!"

"Without even taking into account," said the one who was cleaning his teeth, "the other danger."

Bianca looked at him questioningly.

"Temptation! Can't you imagine what can happen to a young woman in the home of Judeans?"

Bianca wanted to respond that if that was the issue, it was well known what happened to servant girls in all houses, even those that belonged to Christians, but instead she objected:

"But that house belongs to a woman!"

"And aren't there any men?"

"There's the old master, but he's eighty years old."

"You don't know the Judeans, they go after it even when they're eighty," one of the three said vulgarly, and all three of them laughed.

"Enough wasting time," the president concluded. "The answer is no, and now be gone with you. If you want to work, look for a place in a Christian home, understand?"

Bianca bowed and left.

In the following months, not only Bianca but all the widow's tenants started looking for a house where they could go into service, because none of them were able to maintain themselves anymore with the jobs they had. The month of March was the coldest month in human memory, and they needed to buy more firewood. In the meantime the price of bread continued to rise while everybody waited anxiously to know how the new harvest had gone. But there were too many women looking for work, and none of them managed to find anything. So the little community began to shrink. The newborn orphan they were caring for on behalf of the Mount of Piety died after coughing desperately for three days straight, and that small source of income also vanished. Daniela decided from one day to the next to go back to her hometown, in the Po river delta, and nobody managed to dissuade her. Marta, who besides herself had a child to maintain, didn't know what to do. She looked for a shop where she could place her son as an apprentice, but he was still too little and nobody wanted him. While she was looking, however, she ran into a young man from her hometown, a ne'er-do-well, everyone said the first time he came to the house to ask her out, but she insisted that it wasn't true, it was all envy because she had found a man, and after a while she too rolled up her bundle, took her son by the hand, and disappeared. Her bed was occupied by another woman with two small children, who lived by begging. She didn't talk much, and she wasn't clean, but she paid the rent regularly, and the widow couldn't afford to be picky.

Bianca, who was still earning just enough at the washtubs to feed herself on brown bread, was very impressed by the new tenant, and during the gradually longer evenings she managed to get her to tell her story. Her name was Chiara, and she was the widow of a carpenter. As long as her husband was alive, her family was well off, because like all the carpenters in Venice, when he didn't have enough work at his shop, he had the right to go to the Arsenal and get paid for the day, whether there was something to do there or not. But when her husband took sick and died, it wasn't long till the larder was empty. Chiara went back to her parents, but after a while they died too. Her two brothers told her in no uncertain terms that there was hardly enough to eat for their two families, and since she hadn't learned a trade, she started begging.

"It's not really such a bad life," she asserted, with a wrinkly smile. "You get used to the heat and cold in no time. All you really have to do is defend your place, that's the name of the game. Every morning, I'm always the first one there on the steps of Santa Maria Formosa, and nobody dares try to move me from there. At the end of the day you've earned your pay. What do you say? You want to come along? The men are always anxious to give it to a beautiful girl; charity I mean."

"Really, you'd take me with you?" Bianca said, without thinking.

"Sure," the beggar replied. "But then we go fifty-fifty, clear?"

The next day was Sunday, and it wasn't a workday at the washtubs. Why not, Bianca thought. The money she'd got from the Jewish woman was dwindling fast, and when it was finished she wouldn't know even how to pay for her bed anymore. What was so bad about begging, after all? Just for tomorrow, and just to try it . . .

"Let's do it," she said, trying to smile. The widow and Camilla, who were sewing, gave her a long look, but said nothing.

The next day, before dawn, the beggar shook her awake. The children were already up, wearing their rags, and as usual they were moaning from hunger. Their mother only fed them at night, so they'd inspire pity during the day.

"You too, if you listen to me, you won't eat," she said to Bianca, who had pulled out her piece of bread. "If you look like you're hungry, they like you more. And leave your shoes at home."

They went out into the dark, barefoot, pulling the children behind them. Bianca hadn't slept much from the excitement, the fear, and the shame, but now what she was feeling was the cold and damp of the early morning air. They walked for a long time on the deserted streets all the way to Piazza Santa Maria Formosa.

"Here! This is a good place," Chiara said, hunkering down on the steps. Bianca imitated her, tried to warm the numbness out of her feet by rubbing them with her hands, and then wrapped her shawl tightly around her shoulders and waited, shivering.

She had expected to feel ashamed when the people passing by started casting their piteous glances, but she soon realized it wasn't like that. In the eyes of those who were going into the church to say a prayer or light a candle she was just a nameless beggar. The first time a woman put a coin in her hand, she murmured an ejaculation of thanks, as Chiara had taught her, and even that quickly became a habit. The cold was penetrating, but by huddling up close to Chiara and her urchins, she managed to resist. The worst was the hunger, but when she realized that the coins accumulating in her apron were enough for a ration of bread, and it was only midmorning, she mustered her strength, swallowing her saliva.

"Don't be thinking it's always like this," Chiara warned her. "Today is Sunday, and on Sunday you have to make enough for three days."

That evening, when they divided up the take, Bianca's share actually was enough for three days of bread.

"What did I tell you? In this business you've got to know how to keep your accounts, my dear," Chiara said. For her part, she'd earned enough to buy a little wine too, and she was preparing some bread soup in the fireplace for the children. When it was ready they sat down to eat, all four of them together, and Chiara poured a bowl of soup for Bianca too. Ever since Chiara had moved in, she and the children had eaten on their own. The others said they were dirty, and gave off a bad smell. Bianca, who had thought the same way, suddenly realized that now she didn't notice it anymore. I've already become like them, she thought.

14

The next day Bianca woke up with a sore throat, a cough, and a runny nose. She still got up at dawn to go to work at the washtubs, but while she was getting dressed she suddenly felt weak.

"Stay home, I'll give you some sewing to do," Margherita proposed.

"No, come with me," the beggar said, ready to leave the house.

"Are you trying to do her in?" Camilla intervened as she was combing her hair. The beggar looked at her with contempt.

"She can't work," she said. "You're the ones who want her to die of hunger. If she comes with me, all she has to do is sit there; and today it's not cold out."

The widow looked at Bianca, who was trembling with fever.

"Stay home," she insisted. But Bianca shook her head.

"No. What can I do? I have to make some money," she muttered.

"But you still have some money; the money you got from the Jewish lady isn't gone yet, is it? And look at how much you brought home yesterday!"

"No," Bianca said again, stubborn. "It's never enough. I don't want to die of hunger."

"Look, we're not going to let you die of hunger," Camilla said; but her mother shot her a glance, and she fell silent.

"Do what you want," concluded the widow, brusquely. "Surely it's better if you can manage to earn your bread."

The beggar smiled in triumph.

"Those two make me laugh," she said later to Bianca, as they were walking hand-in-hand with the children, fast, so as not to feel the bite in the morning air. "They ruin their eyes sewing, they kill themselves working, and we end up having more to eat than they do. There's no doubt you did the right thing by coming with me."

From then on, Bianca went regularly to beg with the woman and her children. The fever and coughing lasted a few days, but then she got better, and she realized that she had quickly gotten used to that life. She didn't feel the cold and damp nearly as much; her feet weren't as sensitive to the hard pavement of the churchyard. She even got used to not washing her face every morning, as she had done all her life, to not combing her hair whenever she had a free minute, to not worrying if her shirt or her skirt had a stain or a tear. She learned to hold out her hand with her eyes looking down, or to stick it out brazenly, depending on who was passing by, and the right tone for saying thank you, depending on whether the coin came from the hand of a man or a woman, a young person or an older one. At home, by now, she lived with Chiara and the two children, she ate and slept with them and didn't exchange more than a few words with Margherita, Camilla, and Lucrezia.

One day, as they were coming back from eating the soup distributed at the Celestine monastery, she came upon Senator Lippomano. She went over to him immediately, holding out her hand:

"Alms, your Excellency!"

Lippomano walked by without even looking at her. Bianca, even herself not knowing why, ran after him.

"Alms! My husband used to work for your lordship!"

This time the Senator looked at her. All he saw was a ragged, filthy beggar, half undressed, with an ambiguous, servile smile.

"Get out of my way, you slime!" he muttered, and went on his way. Chiara, stupefied, gestured for them to leave, but Bianca, foolishly, grabbed the patrician by the hem of his mantle.

"Alms!"

This time, Lippomano swung his cane over his head, and hit her.

"Go away, or I'll have you arrested! Shame on you!" he exclaimed. Bianca slipped and fell in the mud.

"Damn you! Those who serve your lordship die in the poor house!" she screamed, as the children started to cry and Chiara pulled her up and dragged her off.

"Have you gone crazy?" she scolded her.

"Yes!" Bianca exclaimed, and she too burst out crying. "Yes, I'm crazy, I can't take it anymore!" she repeated in between sobs, as she limped off toward home. "Let me go, so I can throw myself into the canal!" she shouted, as they were crossing a bridge. Chiara grabbed her even tighter by the arm.

"Hold still!"

"No. let me go, I want to end it all; I've had it with this life!"

This time Chiara glared at her in irritation.

"Listen, honey, go get yourself another life if you don't like this one. But don't throw yourself in the canal! You understand? Come on," she added, softening her tone, "I'll bet you're about to get your period; that's all it is. It'll pass, you'll see."

When they got home, Bianca was still weeping. Camilla, hearing them come in, came to greet them with a big smile on her face, but when she saw them she stopped short and changed her expression.

"What's the matter?"

"Nothing," Chiara said.

"What do you mean, nothing? Can't you see how bad she looks?"

Bianca, her face still lined with the tracks of her tears, tried to speak, but her sobs wouldn't let her. The widow ran over to embrace her.

"There, there, child, everything will be all right. What happened?" she asked the beggar woman.

"What do I know! To get her off him a man hit her with his cane, and she hasn't stopped crying since."

"But did he hurt you? Where did he hit you?" the widow asked, alarmed. Bianca shook her head.

"No," she sobbed. "It's that I can't take it anymore, I can't stand it, I feel so ashamed."

"I knew it," said Camilla; and both she and her mother looked disapprovingly at Chiara.

"Oh, take a look at yourselves, why don't you?" Chiara shouted, and grabbing her two brats she went off to sit in her corner of the room.

Margherita and Camilla did what they could to soothe Bianca.

"There, now! And to think that we were waiting for you so we could give you some wonderful news!"

"What news?" Bianca sobbed.

"I won't tell you unless you stop crying," the window decreed, astutely. Bianca dried her eyes and sniffled, and waited.

"Your mother-in-law sent someone to tell you to go see her right away, a letter has arrived from your husband."

"What?" Bianca said with a jolt, incredulous.

"Yes, and she's waiting for you to read it!"

Bianca's head was spinning. A letter from Michele! So it was really true that he wasn't dead; and not even gone away forever. He was still there, thinking of her, and maybe he was writing to say he was on his way home!

"I'm going right now," she exclaimed.

The widow examined her with a critical eye.

"Looking like that? Don't you realize what a state you're in? You'll kill her, the poor thing, if you let her see you this way!"

In her heart, Bianca knew that she had let herself go, and she felt a sort of perverse satisfaction in presenting herself in the worst way, ragged and dirty, in the face of the world that had treated her so badly. Toward strangers she was brazen and brash. With the other women in the house she felt a little ashamed, but all she had to do was stay in her corner with the beggar and her children, and not think about it. But with Zanetta she'd never have dared to let her see her like that, and in fact she hadn't gone to see her for months.

"What can I do?" she said.

"Come here, and let us clean you up a little. Do you still have a clean shirt?"

Bianca nodded.

"All right, then. Get the tub ready and put some water on the fire," the widow ordered her daughter. "You, in the meantime, come over here," she said to Bianca, as she sat down on the bed. Bianca went over to kneel down in front of her, and the widow patiently combed her hair, untangling the sticky strands of unwashed hair and squishing the lice with her fingernails. She continued until Camilla pulled the tin bathtub into the middle of the room, and filled it with a pot of hot water and a pot of cold.

"Now, get undressed," the widow ordered, and when Bianca, naked, got into the water she stated rubbing her down vigorously. Then she dried her off with a clean rag.

"Now you look like a princess. Get dressed, and get on your way."

A little while later Bianca arrived, panting, in the piazza of Saints John and Paul. To be able to run faster she'd taken off her shoes and now she leaned against the pedestal of the monument to slip them back on, before going to knock on the front door of the Derelicts. The servant who let her in told her that Zanetta was waiting for her in the ward. During the winter her health had not been good, and the old woman hardly got out of bed anymore. Bianca ran up the stairs and went into the room where all the beds of the residents were lined up in a row. Zanetta, all skin and bones, with tufts of white hair poking out from under her bonnet, was surrounded by five or six women, one of whom stood up on seeing Bianca and went over to greet and hug her. Bianca recognized her as one of her old neighbors, and hugged her back though she didn't know why. Then she went to give Zanetta a kiss. When the old woman recognized her, she laughed and pulled the letter out from under her pillow.

"It's Caterina you have to thank," she said, pointing at the neighbor. It turned out that Michele's letter had arrived quite some time ago, and the courier, on finding the house closed up, had knocked on the neighbors' doors; having come all that way, he didn't want to leave without getting paid. The first people he talked to shut the front door in his face; nobody had any desire to spend money to take delivery of a letter addressed to people who had left there long ago and wouldn't ever be coming back again. But Caterina had been close friends with Zanetta and she'd even gone to visit her in the hospital once. That morning she happened to have some change in her purse, and an impulse of generosity made her pay to take delivery of the letter. But before she was able to deliver it to Zanetta, she came down with a serious illness and was bedridden for several months, suspended between life and death.

"But I'm made out of some tough stuff!" she said proudly, showing off a toothless smile. "Now I'm back on my feet again, and here I am."

When she got to the hospital, Father Anzolo opened the letter and only then did they send a boy to go looking for Bianca. Her eyes shining bright, the young woman turned the page front and back in her hands. It was covered with all those marks that were so tiny they looked to her like so many spiderwebs and didn't mean a thing to her.

"But was it really written by Michele?" she finally asked.

"They wrote it for him," Zanetta explained.

"And what does it say?" Up to then she had been so pleased that she hadn't even thought to ask. The women got agitated and wanted to go call the priest, but Zanetta stopped them; she'd learned it by heart.

"My dearest wife," it began, "I am writing to tell you that I'm in the port of Corfu, on the galley *Loredana*."

So then it's true, Bianca thought, with a start. He's gone to sea. He's on a ship! The incantation was right!

"I knew it!" she exclaimed, unable to contain herself. Zanetta, surprised, interrupted her recitation, and Bianca frenetically told the story of the magic that the widow had taught her, and the vision that she'd had. All the old women listened to her enraptured, and then they made the sign of the cross.

"Don't tell Father Anzolo," Zanetta said. "You know how priests are, they don't like visions," and the others nodded pensively. But Bianca wasn't listening anymore.

"Corfu! And where is this Corfu?"

"Father Anzolo says it's an island on the route for the Levant," Zanetta informed her, satisfied to display her knowledge. "But listen to the rest of the letter!" And she went back to reciting the letter, which was actually quite brief. On hearing that Michele had written that she should answer him addressing the letter to Candia, Bianca became agitated again.

"But we need to write to him! Who knows how long he's been waiting! Let's ask Father Anzolo to write it; he wouldn't say no, would he?"

"Right now, Father Anzolo isn't here. But as soon as he comes back we'll ask him. But anyway, listen to the most important thing: Michele says he's coming back in November."

Bianca could feel herself going topsy-turvy and a marvelous feeling of warmth filled her entire body. Michele was coming back! Writing to him, which a minute ago seemed utterly urgent, suddenly seemed less important, since in just a few months she would be holding him in her arms in flesh and blood. But then something suddenly popped into her mind and she froze.

"But how can he come back? If they've banished him, he can't come back; they'll arrest him!"

Zanetta's eyes shot open, and the other women's with them. In their enthusiasm for the letter's arrival they hadn't thought of that.

"It's true," Zanetta acknowledged in a worried voice. "But why in the world didn't he think of it?"

"Is it possible that when he wrote he didn't know about it yet?"

"Maybe, and when exactly did he write?" asked Bianca, who until now had overlooked that detail. Zanetta scratched her head.

"I don't remember," she confessed. The page went from hand to hand, and they all squinted hard to try and decipher the date, but since none of them knew how to read, they couldn't make it out.

"It's no use, we have to wait for Father Anzolo," one of the old ladies declared.

"But isn't there a scrivener here," said Bianca, who was now in a hurry. The old women looked at each other.

"There's Signor Giacomo, in the storeroom. Go find him. You have to go across the courtyard, and go down the stairs on the other side."

Bianca grabbed the letter and stood up.

"I'll go right now. Excuse me!" and she ran out. A few minutes later, Signor Giacomo, an elderly scrivener with a big wart on his forehead and bad breath, was bent over the unfolded page showing Bianca with his finger the line where the date was written.

"You see here? 16 August, 1588. This letter is from last year."

"And now it's Easter time!" Bianca said with a fright. "So has he already come back? Virgin Mary, they'll have arrested him, and we didn't know anything about it!" The old man looked at her with a blank stare. Bianca was about to run out of there but then she thought that what she needed most right then was the advice of a man, a man who knew how to read. Between herself and all those other women, she thought, they wouldn't resolve a thing. So she told him the whole story. Signor Giacomo listened to her with his eyes half open.

"Well!" he said when she finished, "that's certainly not a pretty story! If he came back he's certainly in prison now, if they haven't already hanged him."

"Hanged him? Mother of God, help me!" Bianca exclaimed, her face turning white as a sheet. Satisfied, the old man held out his hand and caressed her cheek.

"But I don't think things have gone that way. You would have been summoned; you and your mother-in-law. You need to find out what happened. Maybe the galley didn't come back to Venice and went to lay up in some other port. Or else it came back and he wasn't on it when it did."

"And how can we find out?" Bianca asked anxiously.

"You have to go look at the logs," the scrivener explained. "Do you have any money?"

Bianca blushed and said no. The old man shook his head.

"Well then, my dear, there's nothing you can do. They don't show just anyone the logs. You have to go to a lawyer and present a writ for, I don't know, the recovery of your dowry, for example. Then you have the right to go see the logs to find out where your husband ended up."

Bianca was despondent.

"What am I supposed to do?"

The old man pondered.

"Or else," he finally said, "you can try asking around. At the Arsenal there's got to be someone around who sailed on the *Loredana*, if it's come back."

"I'll go ask," Bianca decided, perking up. She thanked the old man and went back up to the ward, where Zanetta and the other women were anxiously awaiting her.

"The letter is from last August!" she announced; and she told them everything that Signor Giacomo had told her. The women were astonished.

"If he'd come back," Zanetta thought out loud, "he would have come to the house, no?"

"But if they arrested him when he came into port?" Bianca despaired.

"In that case he would have written from prison. And if they put him on trial they surely would have sent someone to call us too. No, Signor Giacomo is right, either he never came back, or when he got back he discovered he'd been banished and he immediately went back to sea on another ship."

Bianca considered everything carefully.

"Yes, that must be the way it is," she admitted. "But why hasn't he written again?"

"And how do you know he hasn't written again?" Zanetta objected. "He could very well have written, but nobody paid to take delivery of the letter!"

"That's true," Bianca allowed. "If it hadn't been for Caterina, we wouldn't even have received this letter."

Everyone fell silent. As far as they could tell, they'd come to a dead end. Michele had gone to sea and he was still alive when he wrote the letter from Corfu, but almost a year had gone by since then, and what had happened to him in the meantime was anybody's guess. They didn't know where he was and he didn't know where they were.

When she left the hospital, Bianca took the letter with her. Zanetta wasn't happy to part with it but she had to admit that it was addressed to Bianca, and her daughter-in-law insisted on having it. She stuffed the folded page between her breasts, and went on her way toward Ca' Trevisan. The fatigue and excitement of that extraordinary day were battling inside her, and she went from feeling like her legs had turned to rubber to fostering a confused desire to do something, not to go to sleep without having accomplished something. Go to the Arsenal to ask for information? But she didn't even know where to begin, and vespers had already sounded. There wouldn't be anyone left at the Arsenal by now. Look for a scrivener to send a letter to Michele right away? But she didn't have a cent. All she could do was wait for Father Anzolo to come back. Yes; that was it; she didn't have any money. Tomorrow I have to go back to work, she told herself; and not to go begging, no, to go back to my work, so if Michele does come back he won't find me sitting with my hand out on the steps of Santa Maria Formosa!

So the next day Bianca informed Chiara that she didn't want to come with her anymore.

"I knew it!" the beggar said. "What do you think, that your husband can see what you're doing from where he is? Believe me, you'd do better to make sure that when he comes back you've got some money to show him, and he certainly won't ask you how you earned it! On the other hand, if he doesn't find any money, he'll take it out on you, you'll see!"

They argued for a long time, but Bianca wouldn't budge, and the other women agreed with her. So in the end Chiara shrugged her shoulders, took her two children, and left. Bianca grabbed her bag and went out and started making the rounds of the houses whose washing she'd done in the past. But she soon realized that it wasn't going to be easy getting back to work. Just about everywhere other washerwomen had taken her place. After the third or fourth house where the servant girl who opened the door responded to her question, whether she knew her or not, with a shake of the head, Bianca started to get discouraged. She hadn't slept well, dreaming and waking up constantly, while next to her Chiara snored. And she felt her bones aching. What am I going to do, she thought, sadly. I'll have to go back to Santa Maria Formosa.

"But aren't you Bianca?" said a voice from behind her. A passerby had stopped to look at her and now he was calling her. Bianca turned around and recognized him.

"Signor Nicolo'! Yes, it's me!"

It was the broker who just over a year ago had negotiated her marriage to Michele. Short in stature, even shorter than she was, with two sharp eyes and a gray goatee, he was looking at her with a mixture of good cheer and surprise. The young girl he remembered had changed a lot. Marriage wears them out in a hurry, he thought.

"You've become a full-fledged woman! I bet you've already served up a baby to your husband," he joked, trying to keep the conversation light. But Bianca stopped smiling, and the man noticed immediately.

"But what's wrong?"

Briefly, Bianca told him her story. It seemed like she hadn't been doing anything else since the day before, after all those months that she'd kept it inside like an unconfessable secret.

"Now I'm looking for work but I'm not finding any," she concluded, her eyes on the ground. The man smoothed his beard, observing her carefully. She was clean, and still gracious despite the fatigue and the malnutrition that had left their mark on her face. If he had run into her two days ago, dirty and ragged as she was, he wouldn't even have broken his stride. But instead he said, "Let it never be said that I refused to help a girl I married when she ran into trouble. Would you like to go into service?"

"If only I had the chance!" Bianca exclaimed.

"Well then come with me. I have to do an errand, and then I'll take you to a house where they're looking for a maidservant for the mistress."

Struggling to keep up with Signor Nicolo', all the way to the Rialto and then across the provisional bridge toward San Polo, Bianca tried to learn more. The broker told her the mistress was a young woman, the family a prestigious noble family, whose name, however, meant little or nothing to Bianca. The mistress too had gotten married just two years ago, and she had one daughter, but she had just gotten pregnant again. The lady's maid who took care of her in her private rooms was about to get married as well, and she would be leaving in just a few days.

"You'll see," the broker said, "Lady Clarice is a mistress like very few others. Her husband adores her, in the home she is in full command, even though she still looks like a young girl. Actually, she's probably no older than you."

"Are you the one who arranged the marriage?" Bianca asked. The broker started to laugh. "Are you serious? Me, arrange a patrician wedding? No, my dear, I arranged the maidservant's marriage! And with a fine young man, a caulker at the Arsenal."

"What wonderful work you do!" Bianca laughed.

"Ah, yes! Not to brag about it, but I'm the one that keeps Venice going!" the man joked. Meanwhile they had arrived in San Polo, and they started down an alleyway that ended abruptly at a canal. A small door was the only opening in the massive outside wall of the building at the end or the alley.

"Here we are," the broker said. "The main entrance is on the canal. You can only get to it by gondola. On foot you have to enter here."

He knocked several times on the little door before a man came to answer, introducing them into an unkempt garden, then into a second one, a vegetable garden, and finally into a third one, very small and full of flowers, arranged around a fountain.

"How wonderful!" Bianca said; and the place really did seem as though it belonged in a fairytale.

"The mistress says to wait here," said the doorman, who had gone in to announce their arrival. And the two of them remained standing in the garden, not daring to sit on the stone benches around the fountain, until a young woman appeared in the doorway, blond and bejeweled, a string of pearls around her neck, her face pale with circles under her eyes, her belly bulging slightly under her brocade dress. The man did a deep bow, quickly imitated by Bianca, and the woman responded with a nod of the head and a fleeting smile, then gestured for them to approach her.

Lady Clarice was the wife of Sir Lorenzo Bernardo, son of Senator Sir Alvise Bernardo.

15

C ome here," the killer repeated. Michele, hesitant, took a few steps toward the shadows.

"What do you want?" he insisted.

"You're in danger," Lupo said, in a whisper. He spoke softly on purpose, so the lad could hear but not hear well, and so he would instinctively come closer.

Michele trembled.

"What are you saying?"

By now he was fairly close. Lupo came out of the shadows and took him chummily by the arm.

"Let's get away from here, where they can see us," he said, with a worried air.

He led him away, and down a nearby alley. But there they both jolted to a stop because they nearly collided with a man who was walking at a fast pace straight at them. It was the officer with the red hair, the parone of the *Loredana*.

"Look who's here," he said.

The two oarsmen took off their caps and started to make their way around him; Michele frightened without understanding why, Lupo damning his bad luck.

"Hold on a minute," the parone said. The two came to a halt, waiting. "You, come here, I need to talk to you," the officer went on, referring to Michele. "You, take a walk," he told Lupo.

Disconcerted, Michele let himself be taken away by his savior, just as he had let himself be persuaded to accompany his killer, while the latter vanished amid the alleyways, cursing under his breath.

The parone's name was Cesare d'Anversa. He was the son of a Flemish merchant who had not had much luck in Venice and had died leaving him no inheritance except his name and his red hair. As for the parone himself, he was born on the lagoon and lived his whole life on the galleys of the Republic, so he felt as Venetian as anybody. That evening he too had gone ashore to have a good time, but after losing his share of the felucca's booty at the dice table, and then winning almost all of it back, he'd had the willpower to stop playing. While he was standing there watching the others play, he started to ponder a problem that had been bothering him ever since that morning. The sopracomito had shown him, as he had shown the comito, the list of the banished, and he who, like the comito, knew all the oarsmen on the *Loredana* one by one, had recognized Michele's name, without having to go check it in Don Muzio's register. He hadn't talked to anyone about it, because he wasn't sure what he wanted to do, and he wasn't a man used to acting on impulse.

Obviously, his duty would have been to denounce the banished criminal and have him arrested. But in that case he was sure that, as soon as he was hanging from the rope, the lad would tell everything he knew, from the theft of the zecchini to the capture of the felucca. Putting it all together, what it added up to was a story considerably different from the story the sopracomito had told on their arrival in Candia. As far as the authorities knew, the money had been recovered, but if an unexpected revelation were to put a flea in their ear it would take them no time to open an investigation. After the felucca affair, everyone on board, even those who counted for little or nothing, was all bound together with a double knot, and if the sopracomito got into trouble it was highly likely that they would all share his fate. The red-haired man watched the dice players spit on their hands, look up to the sky to ensure themselves a bit of attention from their protectors, and then throw the dice and exalt or despair, and all the while he was carefully calculating what he ought to do. He wouldn't denounce the lad, that much was certain. Nevertheless, it was likely that they would pick him up anyway, and when the time came he, Cesare, wanted to be as far away as possible. The next day he was going to start looking for another ship, and with a little luck he'd be able to find one; lots of ships passed through Candia. He was well respected on board, and the scrivener would pay him what he had coming without a lot of questions. As for the sopra-comito, he would be happy to have one less witness around.

But the lad would be in for a rough time. Confused as he was, maybe he didn't even realize the risk he was running by remaining in Venetian territory after the deadline fixed by the sentence. That's life, thought Cesare. There's nothing I can do about it. Or, on the other hand, maybe I can. He suddenly had an idea. At first glance, it wouldn't be easy to help Michele get away. He certainly couldn't sign up for another Venetian ship, nor could he hide out for very long on Crete, where sooner or later he'd be caught in some routine security check. He'd have to go a lot farther away, but Cesare knew the way to do it.

Yeah, he said to himself. All I need is for them to keep him hidden until the *Aquila* gets here. But why should I get involved, he objected; just because I like him? He who does good just for the love of God might be rewarded in the next world, but in this one here he's out of luck. Displeased, he looked around. The customers sitting at all the tables in the tavern were staring greedily at the players' table, where the coins were passing from hand to hand. Let's see, he said, give me a signal, if you're there. He spit on his hands, got up, went over to the players, and threw a zecchino onto the gaming table.

"Who's in? A round of zara, the first one to guess the total takes all."

The dice players looked at him, some with their eyes already glazed over from the wine, others with the astute eye of someone weighing the odds.

"So, you've decided to risk it again, eh?" one of them piped up. "Good, I'm in," he added, pushing a zecchino out into the middle of the table.

"That's too much for me," another turned him down; and then a last one shook his head and pushed back from the table the chair he'd been straddling. Cesare stared at his adversary.

"Your throw, Spada."

The man gathered up the three dice, and clenched them in his fist.

"Eleven," he shouted, and threw the dice. A murmur of disappointment welled up around him.

"Four, three, and three makes ten," Cesare announced coldly. "Now it's my turn."

As he shook the dice he made his calculation. All the regular players knew that the most frequent numbers were ten and eleven, and that the farther away from them you got the greater the odds that your guess would be wrong. But this was no ordinary match, a man's life was at stake, and the outcome didn't depend on arithmetic.

"Three," he shouted, and threw the dice. This time there was no murmur, but an exclamation of amazement. All three dice showed one dot. Cesare could feel his heart shaking. A clearer sign than that!

Spada had already jumped to his feet, gnashing his teeth; but Cesare spoke before he could.

"The dice are yours, Spada, don't say anything you'll live to regret."

The man stood there motionless for a moment, then plopped back down on his chair. Cesare picked up the two gold coins.

"Good night, everybody," he said. He paid for the wine

he'd drunk, went outside, and walked quickly into the night through the serpentine alleyways of Candia. When he got to his destination he knocked on the door and a servant girl, half asleep and half dressed, let him in.

"At this hour!" said the master of the house, who received him in bed, in a stifling hot room on the ground floor. He was wearing a nightshirt, the chamber pot was in plain sight under the bed, and next to him on the mattress and the pillow there had remained clearly impressed the shape of another body. "Weren't you supposed to come by tomorrow?"

"I've got some business to take care of before tomorrow," said the redhead. "Do you know yet when the *Aquila* is going to dock?"

"According to the agreement, next Saturday," said the man in the bed. "You're not thinking of going, are you?"

Cesare shook his head.

"No, you take this to him, as usual." He pulled out of his shirt pocket a piece of paper folded and sealed with sealing wax, but with no address. The other feebly stretched out his hand and took it between two fingers.

"Fine," he said. "Anything else?"

"And then there's one of our oarsmen who wants to look for another boat, and I'd be happy if you found him one. They're always looking for hands on the *Aquila* aren't they?"

"Could be," said the other, lazily. The *parone* laughed.

"I know darn well that they give you a zecchino commission for every rower you find them. You can bag it this time too. I don't want in on it. My zecchino I've already earned."

The master of the house made a vague sign of approval with his head.

"All you have to do is hide him until he goes on board," the redhead added. The other frowned.

"It's only for three days," Cesare insisted.

"Fine, fine," the other surrendered. "Who is he?"

The parone explained it to him without going into detail. Anyway, it seemed as though the two of them were used to understanding each other with no need for a lot of words.

"I'll send him to you tomorrow," the parone concluded. They embraced, then the man in the bed put out the candle and lay down again. The servant girl accompanied the redhead back to the door, yawning, then she went back to occupy her place in the bed as Cesare walked off at a fast pace along the sleeping street.

When he took Michele under his arm, the parone informed him that his name was on the list of the banished that had been delivered to the sopracomito, and that the next day he would help him disappear.

"Not tonight, understand?" he said, lowering his voice. "Now you go back to the galley, I'll come back later on my own, and tonight and tomorrow morning make sure your presence is noticed. Lupo saw us together and I don't want any trouble. It's risky but it's the only way to go. Tomorrow, you go ashore and disappear. After a while I'll go to the scrivener, pretend I want to check the logs and to notice for the first time your name on the list of the banished. I'll go immediately to denounce you, but you will have disappeared and nobody will ever find you again."

Michele listened, bewildered. The blow had left him breathless. Up to now he'd thought all he had to do was be careful and wait calmly for the *Loredana* to return to Venice. Now he realized that his situation was much more dangerous. An order of banishment was no joke, and if he got arrested there on Crete, or in any other part of the Overseas Dominion, there was a risk they'd hang him without even listening to his story.

"But where do I go?" he asked. The *parone* told him how to get to the house where he was to go into hiding.

"Are you sure you understand? The square with the new church, where there's a work site. The alley that comes up to the back of the bell tower. The house with the blue shutters. Knock, a woman will answer the door. You tell her that Signor Cesare sent you. She'll let you in and they'll hide you in the attic. You'll stay there till Saturday. On Saturday night, a galley of Genovese pirates will anchor in an inlet outside of town. They come here to take on wine and biscuit. There'll be a lot of movement that night, even though officially no one will notice a thing."

"And how do you know all this?" Michele asked. Then he bit his lip. Luckily, the *parone* didn't take it badly.

"That's my business, with the permission of his Excellency your lordship," he wagged. "Anyway, the point is," he went on, turning serious again, "that night they'll take you out to the galley and you'll sign on as an oarsman. It's the only way for you to get away from Crete. The boats that lay over in the harbor are almost all Venetian, and anyway there are too many checks. Once you're on board the *Aquila*, don't ever show your face again in the territory of St. Mark, and good luck."

Don't ever show my face again! Ah, no; Michele thought in his heart. I want to go back, and I will go back. It's just a question of making my fortune on this new galley, and buying myself clemency. On a pirate galley it must be easy to make a fortune, he reasoned, for despite all the time spent on the *Loredana* he still hadn't figured out that, as far as the oarsmen are concerned, fortune always passes close by without ever stopping. And if not, it will be the ten thousand zecchini that will make my return possible, with them I can even get the sentence of banishment annulled! For a minute he had the urge to tell the *parone* everything he knew, and ask his help in recovering the treasure; but then it seemed more prudent not to say anything.

The redhead hadn't noticed Michele's tumult of feelings, deeply involved as he was in imparting advice.

"Look," he said, "on the western galleys life is different than it is with us. There most of the rowers are slaves or convicts, and even the goodwillers have to get used to being treated the same way."

"The good what?"

"The goodwillers—the *buonavoglia*—that's what they call the salaried rowers. The only difference from the slaves is that at the end of the contract they pay you your salary, but for everything else the treatment is the same, understand? And you, don't be foolish. Keep your head down, take your clubbings if the galley-sergeant lets one fly every now and again, because it takes no time at all to get into trouble. Then, when you're nice and far away from here, maybe in Italy, if you get the chance to escape . . . well, I didn't say anything. Clear?"

"Clear," Michele confirmed.

"You remember the street you have to go down tomorrow and the signal for opening the door?"

Michele assented.

"Fine. Now go back to the galley. The two of us will not speak again. Good luck, lad."

When the next evening arrived, and with it permission for the crew to go ashore, Lupo pretended to be thinking of something else, but he never lost sight of Michele. He saw him undo his bundle, pull out a number of things, and fill up his pockets, but he didn't understand. When the lad put his cap on his head, headed for the stair, and climbed down onto the dock, he rushed to follow him. He didn't want anyone to see them together so he settled for following him at a distance, his hands in his pockets, waiting for his chance. The days had gotten much shorter, and the light was growing dim. Satisfied, the killer realized they were getting closer to the older, more deserted streets, and he felt the handle of his knife that he kept in his belt. Michele sped up and then slowed down, as though he were trying to find his way, and Lupo followed him in silence, keeping in the shadows. Then he saw him stop in front of a house with blue shutters and look around, uncertain. Now, Lupo thought, and drew his knife without making a sound. But in that very moment, Michele knocked on the door, and Lupo held his breath. An instant later the door opened and Michele disappeared inside. Nothing goes right for me, Lupo thought, miffed. Oh well, I'll stay here until he comes back out. I don't have anything to lose by waiting. So the killer squatted in the shadows and waited for his chance; but Michele never came out.

The master of the house was in bed with the windows covered and the end of a candle burning on the table.

"Come here, let's have a look at you," he ordered. He was holding a bowl of raisins in his lap, and chewing them slowly, one at a time.

"That's fine," he said. "Now we'll take you up to the attic, you'll have to stay up there until Saturday. Nobody will come looking for you here, but be careful not to make noise. Anastasia will bring you your meals."

The interview was over. With a yawn, the man sank back down into his pillows, then he nodded to the servant girl. The woman took the candle off the table and led Michele over to the stairs.

"You go on up," she told him. "There's a trapdoor."

Michele opened the trapdoor and when he got to the last few steps he found himself in a cramped attic. The woman, who had followed him up the stairs with the candle, showed him a pallet in a corner of the room, a water pitcher, and a basin. Evidently, he wasn't the first to use this uncomfortable lodging.

"When I go down, close the trapdoor. Then keep still and don't move around. When I come up to bring you dinner, I knock and then you open. Understand?"

Michele, puzzled, nodded his assent and the women went back down the stairs, taking the candle with her. Closing the trapdoor, Michele had the impression that he was in total darkness, but some light filtered in through the joints in the roof and slowly he realized that he could see well enough to locate the pallet. There was nothing else, except for a pile of old rags in a corner, where there was surely a rats' nest. Michele sighed and after looking around a little, resigned himself to lying down on the pallet and waiting.

In those three days he had time to get good and bored, but finally Saturday night came. The servant girl came to knock softly on the door. Michele was already dressed and went down. At the bottom he found a stranger there waiting for him. He too looked him up and down just as the master of the house had done, and he seemed satisfied.

"Let's go!"

It was a cloudy night, and it was hard to see. Tripping on the uneven pavement and stepping frequently on soft things whose precise identity he preferred to ignore, he made it to the city walls with his guide. Michele had wondered how they would be able to leave the city at that time of night without documents, but evidently the guide knew his business, because instead of heading toward the gate he went straight to the door that led to the bastions and whistled, staying hidden in the shadows. Almost immediately the door opened and a helmeted head appeared in the doorway. The guide went over and spoke briefly and then signaled to Michele to come too. Preceded by the soldier, they went through the narrow passageways of the fortress and finally came to another small door, closed by a heavy iron grate. It was one of the so-called sally ports, the openings that military engineers made on the sides of bastions, to allow the garrison to sally forth and attack the enemy forces in case the fortress was under siege. The soldier was busy for a long time with latches and locks. Then he raised the grate just enough so Michele and the guide could crawl under it to the outside. A minute later they were in the countryside and the guide pulled out a torch and lit it.

Come on, we've got a long way to go yet," he ordered, and they set off at a fast pace.

Three hours later they reached an inlet on the rocky coast, and as they headed down the path to the beach, Michele saw a galley anchored in the small mirror of water. Even though it was the middle of the night, a crowd of people was at work on the shoreline, loading firewood and barrels of water onto the tender that transported them out to the galley. The guide went right to an officer who was overseeing the work and spoke to him softly. He handed over the papers and then signaled to Michele to join hm. By now, Michele was used to being looked up and down, but he was still struck by the brusque tone with which the man said:

"Strip."

Michele complied, taking off his shirt, but that wasn't enough for the officer.

"Everything. Show me your legs."

Michele took his pants off too and stood there in his underpants. The man walked around him.

"That's fine!" he said finally. "So you've already rowed, eh?"

"Three months," Michele specified.

The officer briefly explained the conditions, the advance, the duration of the engagement; then he signaled to one of the rowers and told him to accompany Michele on board.

"Have him put the chain on, and then wait for me to assign him a place."

Michele was shocked to hear those words. He was about to ask what he meant when he noticed that the rower who was accompanying him had an iron ring around his left ankle. He looked around and saw that most of the men at work on the beach were shod in the same way.

"What's the story with the iron," he asked. He wanted his question to have an edge to it, even a tone of resentment, but his voice came out shaky. The other man looked at him like he was an idiot.

"Why? Don't you know that the oarsmen are all iron shod?"

"On the Venetian galleys they aren't," Michele shot back. Like all Venetians, he was used to thinking that the customs of Venetian seamanship were accepted by everybody as the best in the world, and was amazed when the other man began to laugh scornfully.

"Now, isn't that nice! But where have you been? We'll show you what a real galley is, come on!"

Humiliated and a little scared, Michele said nothing. Meanwhile they had arrived at the bow of the galley, which loomed over the water much higher than the bow of the Loredana. In general, Michele had the impression that compared to the Venetian galleys, with their decks just above the surface of the water, this one here was decidedly more powerful. But what struck him most was seeing that while some of the men were working on the beach, a lot of the oarsmen had remained on board, chained to their benches.

"And those guys?" he asked.

"Those are the convicts," the other replied. "We *buonavoglia* and the slaves are only chained at night, if we don't have to work on shore. But the convicts are always chained, they're too worried that they'll escape. Here we are; you wait here."

A few minutes later the man was back, accompanied by another oarsman and a sailor. The sailor knelt down in front of Michele and, with a few sure-handed moves, he fixed an iron ring around his left leg, closing it with a padlock. Then it was the turn of the other oarsman, who was the barber on the galley. He soaped down Michele's head and shaved all his hair off, or at least that's the way it seemed to Michele; but then feeling his head, he realized he still had a tuft in the middle.

"That's to distinguish you from the convicts. Their heads are completely shaved. But if you want my advice, grow a mustache. We buonavoglia are allowed to wear them but the slaves and the convicts aren't. When you've got your cap on, your mustache is the only thing that shows you're a free man."

To tell the truth, Michele was beginning to feel like he wasn't free at all, with that forced haircut and the iron on his ankle. To control his sense of panic, he reminded himself that signing on to the crew of that galley was his only way of escaping the sentence that was weighing on his head, and that he had to be as patient as he possibly could. After his head was shaved they took him to the scrivener, who carefully recorded in his register not only his name but his features, after examining him from head to foot for scars or other distinguishing marks.

"I'll credit you with forty lire," he said. Michele, who knew by now how things worked, assented wearily.

"It's the custom here," the scrivener continued, "that every new recruit leaves something for the Santa Barbara fund," and he pointed to a collection box, under the crucifix, attached to the wall of the stern cabin. "Then when the ship is unrigged, the drawer is emptied, and a donation is made to the church of Santa Barbara, who protected us during the voyage."

"That's fine with me," said Michele, puzzled.

"How much do you want to leave?"

"You tell me, sir," Michele was resigned.

"Generally, it's at least a *cavallotto*," the scrivener said. Michele, who was not used to coins other than the ones used in Venice, nodded his assent. He understood by now that you don't get rich on a galley.

In the meantime, the crew had finished loading the provisions, and the galley was preparing to get under way. The comito came to look after Michele and found him a place on a bench in the stern. There was a tall, well-built young lad, with a short blond beard, whose name was Pasquale da Spatorno. Alongside him was a bald sailor, with the eyes of a dead fish and bulging lips. He was the galley-sergeant, like the parone on Venetian galleys, the officer in charge of the custody of the oarsmen. He personally saw to it that Michele's ring was fixed to the chain attached to the bench, then he scrutinized his face with care.

"Listen to me," he said. "They call me the Calabrian, and I never forget a thing. If you give me trouble, you'll know it. If you play straight, we'll get along fine. Clear?"

Michele nodded, shrugging his shoulders, and the response he got was a slap in the face.

"You say, yessir!"

Someone nearby laughed scornfully.

"Yessir," Michele muttered, red with humiliation.

"Listen good to the rules: there's no cursing here, understood?" the galley-sergeant continued. "The first three times all you get is a clubbing, the fourth time we nail your tongue to the mainmast."

Pasquale confirmed, with a serious air.

"But if you hear someone curse and you turn him in, you'll get sailor's rations for a month," the Calabrian concluded. "Everything clear?"

"Yessir," Michele assented.

As soon as the two of them had gone, the oarsmen on the nearby benches turned to Michele with derisive curiosity.

"So where are you from, handsome?" When he explained that he was from Venice, he drew some more sneers.

"So when was the last time you got laid?" one of them asked, brutally.

"But can't you see he's just a wet chickling? That guy hasn't gotten laid in his life," another one laughed.

"Or actually, maybe he's married, and he left his lovely wife behind in Venice. Eh? Isn't that so, that you've got a little wifey waiting back there for you?"

Michele didn't say a thing, but the others got a kick out of the idea.

"Tell us now, handsome, how is your little wife anyway? Is she good in bed?" another one chimed in from behind, patting him on the back.

"What's it matter to you?" Michele shot back, turning abruptly and thrusting out his chin.

"Oh, to me, nothing at all," the other one responded, mockingly. "I'm just curious to know whether the guy she's fucking right now is having a good time or not."

Michele wanted to jump on him, despite the chain, but the Calabrian, who was out on the *corsia*, was coming their way, and everybody preferred to drop it right there. Michele wrapped his arms around his knees, put his head down on them, and closed his eyes, trying to calm the tumult of emotions that was stirring in his chest. How did I end up here? he asked himself. But his strongest thought was for Bianca, whom the rowers' vulgar comments had brought rushing back into his head. He'd already noticed long ago that the nights when he thought of her were harder to get through than the ones when he managed not to. And this time his desire for her and his anguish over losing her were so strong they were impossible to ignore. The only way he could calm himself down a little was by telling himself that he was going to make it back home. Yes, by God, he thought, I'll make it. I'll make it back to Bianca, I'll fall asleep again in her arms, in the smell of her skin.

16.

During the *Aquila*'s return voyage from Crete to Italy, Michele got to know the oarsmen who were chained to his bench. Both of them were slaves captured at sea, and spoke broken Italian, mixed with the lingua franca of the Mediterranean ports. The one on his left, on the sea side, was an older man, wrinkled and taciturn; it took Michele a while to figure out that he was blind in both eyes. On his right was the tall black African who had shut up the other oarsmen the night he came aboard. "My name is Ahmed, but some call me Big Prick," he said, laughing. He gave Michele the lowdown on his new placement and schooled him on the rules of survival. Wrapped up in his overcoat, with his red cap pulled down just above his eyes, he explained that the galley was Genoese, and belonged to a shipbuilder named Negroni.

"I and all the other slaves on board are his property. Master Ambrogio Negroni, my friend, is one of the richest men in Genoa. I know him. In the old days, he used to sail himself but not anymore. The captain is one of his men, and his name is Ettore."

Big Prick went on to tell him that the *Aquila* was a corsair commissioned by the Genoese government, and had gone to the Levant to try and capture a merchant ship in a convoy carrying gold tax revenues from Alexandria Egypt to the Sultan's treasury.

"But we failed. The convoy must have left ahead of schedule, but we really don't know. The fact is that all the officers are in a bad mood. We boarded a tartan and took on some slaves, but barely enough to replace the ones who died in an outbreak of typhus here on board. Don't worry, it's all over by now; there haven't been any more deaths in weeks. Now that we've taken on firewood and water, I hear we're headed for Messina. It's time, because the season is over. Winter's coming on; we have to go back into port."

Michele wanted to know his story. Big Prick told him he'd been captured six years ago by a Sicilian galliot, off the island of Pantelleria, and sold in Palermo to one of Negroni's agents, who had come to buy slaves for the principal's fleet.

"But I was already a slave," he added calmly. He explained that he had belonged to the rais of a fishing boat out of Tunis, and had been captured with him when the galliot boarded them.

"I'll tell you, I thought I was done for. These Christians have the idea that we black Africans can't row. They say we let ourselves die from melancholy, and there are galley owners who won't buy black slaves. When the pirate ship boarded us, I heard one of them say: what should we do with this one? I thought they were going to throw me overboard. Then, luckily, they decided to try and sell me anyway, and Negroni needed people, so his orders were to buy, without a lot of haggling. That's how I got here. See the blind guy over there? He was the rais, my master on the fishing boat, and now both of us are here, and if I wanted to steal his food and let him die of hunger nobody would notice. Ehi, Mahmud bey!" he said, shaking the sleeping blind man vigorously. He woke up with a jolt and muttered something in a language that was incomprehensible.

"See," said the black man. "He's not only lost his eyes, he's pretty much lost his mind too. He thinks he's still on the fishing boat, and that he's still the master. Go back to sleep, Mahmud bey," he added, with a rough caress. The other man muttered something else and then nodded off again.

"What can you do? It's God's will," the black man sighed; and Michele automatically made the sign of the cross. But then he thought of something else he wanted to know.

"Hey, why to they call you Big Prick?"

The black man laughed.

"Why do you think?"

He tinkered a bit with his pants and then gestured to Michele to take a look. Michele looked and his eyes popped open.

"Hey, what do you say? You want to touch it? Touch it, go on!"

Michele drew back, alarmed.

"I'd rather not," he stammered. The black man laughed good-naturedly.

"No, eh? Oh well, we'll see if you get the urge to touch it after a few months on the chain."

Michele soon realized that life on a Genoese galley was rather different compared to what he'd been used to up to then. Nobody, except for the officers, went ashore during lay-overs, and this meant the galley was ready to weigh anchor on a moment's notice, while it took a Venetian galley several hours to get all its oarsmen back on board. His new companions, knowing he was Venetian, took every opportunity to tease him about it, amusing themselves at his offended pride. On the bench in front of his there was an old convict who claimed to have fought eighteen years ago for the Holy League at Lepanto under the command of Don John of Austria.

"Sailing together with the Venetians was torture! When it was time to weigh anchor they were never ready. We'd be all set to go and we'd have to wait for them for hours. You know how many Venetian galleys got attacked by pirates before they could leave port because when the sails were sighted the crew were all ashore drunk?"

At first, Michele would counter by saying that on the Venetian galleys the oarsmen were free men, and that nobody got chained or whipped. But they shut him up right away.

"Nonsense. You've got plenty of convict galleys, it's just that you don't like to mix convicts and *buonavoglia*. That way the free men never see what happens to everybody else, because if they did, even you people wouldn't have anyone left who wanted to live on a galley."

Because, as Michele soon came to understand, the difference was exactly that. In Venice, rowing on the galleys was an honest job, albeit a job for poor people, while in the rest of Italy it was something to be ashamed of. Enlisting as an oarsman wasn't a choice for the unemployed, but for drifters who had no other alternative after gambling away the shirts off their backs; or for drunkards who let themselves be convinced to sign on after guzzling pitchers of wine. Even the language was different, because no one said "I enlisted," but rather "I sold myself onto a galley." And really, as long as their contract lasted, they were treated more like slaves than free men, as demonstrated by that iron ring around their ankles that was attached to the chain every night. Moreover, the night watches were taken extremely seriously. On the *Loredana*, the watch consisted of one of the officers walking up and down the *corsia* with a lantern, yawning from sleepiness, while here the galley-sergeant, accompanied by two mates, inspected every bench, checking all the chains one by one, to see if they had been chiseled. And the inspections were repeated four times a night, with the last one, the Diana, right before dawn, when the bell fixed to the foremast rang everybody awake.

Michele also had to admit that on the *Aquila* cleanliness was valued more and was enforced more strictly than on Venetian galleys. It had to be that way because a good half of the rowers were convicts who were never freed from their chains, neither during the day nor at night, unless there was a particularly taxing loading detail, for which they were called upon to help. The galley would have quickly become unlivable if those hundreds of men crammed on board, at least one hundred of whom lived chained to a bench, were not forced to wash themselves every day, and if the *corsia* and the benches were not inundated with water and swept every morning by teams of slaves and buonavoglia. Recalling the slovenliness of the oarsmen, sailors, and bachelors on the *Loredana*, the trash piled up in the corners that the officers only occasionally remembered to have thrown overboard, and the stench emanating from the hold after just a few days of sailing, Michele was forced to acknowledge, through clenched teeth, that the Genoese system was better.

But keeping all those people on board, without ever letting them go ashore except to take on firewood and water, under the control of soldiers with harquebuses in hand and their fuses lit, also had another consequence, and after his first nighttime conversation with Big Prick, Michele was only too aware of it. Living elbow to elbow for months, with their often naked or semi-naked bodies constantly rubbing up against each other, without ever having the chance to disembark to let off steam, many of those men felt desires that on land would have horrified them all, and would have easily attracted the attention of the Inquisitors. On ship, on the other hand, they seemed so natural that there wasn't even much effort to conceal them. At night, between one watch and the next, barely suffocated moans and suspect sounds could be heard coming from many of the benches, and everyone, by tacit agreement, pretended not to hear a thing. On his first night, Michele had rejected the alarming proposal from his bench mate. But after a few weeks of sailing, he noticed to his amazement that the black man's body, shiny with sweat, provoked in him an unexpected emotion, not all that different from the sensations he had felt in the past with Bianca, or with the few other women he had seen or touched. Satan is tempting me, he thought, trying to explain the phenomenon using the instruments that his upbringing had provided him; and he vowed to keep as great a distance as possible between himself and the man who was chained next to him.

After returning to Italy, the *Aquila* spent the winter months in the harbor at Messina, where a lot of corsairs licensed by the King of Spain took shelter. At first, Master Ettore, who was waiting for letters from Genoa and expecting to have to leave again from one minute to the next, had not wanted to unrig her. Tied up at the dock, covered by a large canopy of striped canvas raised once and for all on the day of arrival, it had become a sort of houseboat. Chained or not, the oarsmen never went ashore, except for those sent to take on food and water. Just about all of them spent most of their time snoozing, well wrapped up in their raw wool overcoats and blankets, trying to defend themselves from the cold and damp. A lot of them coughed all day long, and every once in a while someone took sick and died, but nothing could be done about it. The captain had a friar come on board, he performed a service, and then the body was taken ashore and buried in the pauper's field, while the scrivener drew a line across his register.

Toward the end of December the letters from Genoa arrived. The *Aquila* was ordered to winter in Messina, and, to cut costs, Master Ettore rushed to unrig her. The soldiers and most of the sailors were let go. Once the masts and tackle were dismantled, the galley was pulled out of the water and put in a shed at the Arsenal, and all the rowers were locked up in the slaves' bath. This was a dungeon adjacent to the Arsenal, with a courtyard enclosed by a high wall and surrounded with unfurnished rooms, where the shipowners of Messina kept their slaves during the off-season. There, even more so than on the galley, time slowed to a standstill, and Michele was able to reflect on his situation and make plans for the future. When he signed on to the *Aquila* he'd had to commit himself for a year; they didn't give him any choice, and he certainly was in no condition to refuse. If worse comes to worse, I'll run away, he would tell himself with youthful ignorance. And then, one way or another, he'd be able to make his way back to Venice. I know what really happened on the voyage of the *Loredana*, he would say, and in exchange for that secret they would certainly commute his sentence.

During the long months of reclusion in the bath, those who couldn't stand being idle worked on braiding ropes, or knitting socks. There were shopkeepers who brought them tools and raw materials and then came back to pick up the finished product and pay some miserable sum, half of which ended up in the pockets of the guards and their captain. Big Prick, Michele discovered to his amazement, took great pleasure in knitting, and he made so many socks that he managed to hang on to a decent sum of money. Being a slave, he didn't have an account with the scrivener, and his earnings were paid in cash. Michele learned how to knit from him and soon they were competing to see who was faster at knitting a pair of socks. But since Michele was a free man, the money was credited to his account. He still hadn't figured out if it was more dangerous to keep your money on your person, with the risk that someone would steal it, or have it recorded on the register, with the risk of being swindled by the scrivener. When he asked Big Prick for his advice, he burst out laughing.

"What are you worried about? If it's your destiny to be robbed, they'll rob you no matter what you do, my friend!"

Now that's comforting, Michele thought, and decided he had to respond:

"Why do you talk like that? If you take your life in your hands you can change your destiny!"

The black man looked at him, suddenly serious.

"No," he said, shaking his head. "Destiny doesn't change. Each of us has it written in the stars."

Michele shivered. What if it were true? And my destiny is to die on this galley, without ever seeing Venice again, without ever embracing my wife and my mother again?

"And according to you, what is my destiny?" he muttered. But Big Prick looked at him, astonished.

"How should I know? I'm not a soothsayer. Only God knows."

When spring came, the port of Messina slowly came back to life, and on board the *Aquila,* winter lethargy gave way to activity. The crew was let out of the bath and chained once again to their benches. Some military officers came on board to confer with the captain and negotiate the conditions for recruitment of a company of infantrymen to serve on board for the privateering season. But the most serious problem was the rowers. The commander was hoping to get some convicts from the governor but in the harbor along with the *Aquila* there was another Genoese galley, belonging to a rival shipbuilder, and three Sicilian galleys. And all of them were rigging up to leave in a hurry. When he came back from his meeting with the governor, Master Ettore was fuming mad.

"That damn scoundrel!" he said. "He couldn't manage to sentence to the galley any more than fifty men all winter long, and he wanted to give them all to the Sicilians! How do you like that?"

"That's what they always do," said Pasquale, the comito, philosophically.

"We had to cough up five ducats for every convict in order to get ten apiece for us Genoese, and he kept on saying he was losing out on the deal! Then it came out that when he said fifty he was just talking in round numbers, but actually there were only forty-eight, and one died in prison, so for us there were only seventeen in all, to be divided as we wished. And when I said that the *Aquila* belongs to Master Ambrogio Negroni, and that we had nine coming to us, the captain of the *Donzella* had the gall to say that his galley belongs to Master Nicolò Grimaldi and that the Grimaldis don't take a back seat to anyone! It was all I could do to keep from pulling out my sword, I swear to God."

"So in the end how many are we getting?"

"Eight for us and eight for him, and that's it. I wasn't going to lose face in front of that weasel."

For the next few days the rowers were put to work without respite, loading barrels of wine, oil and vinegar, casks of water, cases of sea biscuit, cheese, and salted fish, cannonballs and gunpowder, and all sorts of necessary equipment and hardware. Although the labor was hard, they were all glad to have the chance to stretch their legs and talk with someone other than their bench mates. The big topic of conversation, especially for the convicts, was why each of them had been sentenced to the galley. For his part, Michele got to know: a large landowner from the Salento area who had been sentenced to five years on a galley for having taken three wives, each unbeknownst to the other two; an olive oil retailer from Brindisi, sentenced to three years for committing sodomy with his shop boy; a notary from Mazara sentenced to life on a galley for heresy; a shepherd from Abruzzo also sentenced to life for raping a thirteen-year-old girl. Those men's stories, some told with indifference, some with an odd sense of pride, were met sometimes with compassion and sometimes with horror. But nobody kept their distance. They all listened avidly and had no problem sharing their bread and soup with men who had done even the most ghastly things. Somehow, the iron on their feet and the red caps on their heads made everybody equal.

While they were waiting on the dock for a load of cordage, Michele and some companions had the time to view a scene that seemed amazing to the Venetian, even though the others assured him that in the ports of the Kingdom of Naples and the Kingdom of Sicily it was played out quite often. On the contrary, a man from Lecce, reserved and brown as a Moor, assured Michele that he had been recruited in the exact same way. The captain had set up a counter at the head of the dock, and the scrivener from the *Aquila* was standing behind it, with a dice-tumbler and a pile of gold coins. Two soldiers with swords on their hips were stationed next to him to prevent any trouble, and very soon a sizable group of curiosity-seekers had gathered around them.

"Well now, step right up, gentlemen!" the scrivener shouted. "Who wants to try their luck? Five ducats! Five ducats against six months on the galley!"

It wasn't long before a man stepped forward; he was still quite young, but disfigured by a burn on his neck and cheek, and dressed in rags.

"Bravo!," the scrivener encouraged him. "Here are your five ducats. If you're lucky, you can take them home with you. Come, gentlemen, who else wants to try their luck."

The man, standing on one side of the table, coveted with his eyes the five gold coins that had been placed in front of him. The soldiers never took their eyes off him. When he put out his hand, the soldier nearest him put his hand on the hilt of his sword, but a glance form the scrivener made him take a step back. The man caressed the little pile of coins with is fingers, and a collective sigh went up from the crowd.

"I'll try it!" said a shoeless man with the air of a peasant and the contorted face of someone who had already been drinking at that early hour. The scrivener held out his hand to him with a big smile.

"Bravo! Come on up!"

The drunk walked up to the counter, reeling slightly, and the scrivener counted out five ducats for him.

"Now, gentlemen!" he announced in a stentorian voice as the crowd moved in tighter around the table. "Each of you has been granted a loan from the most excellent Master Ettore Spinola, captain of the galley *Aquila*, docked in this harbor of the royal city of Messina; the sum of five ducats in coin of the realm. Are you ready to put them in play?"

The two men nodded. The crowd was silent, expectant.

"For you!" said the scrivener, offering the tumbler to the disfigured man. The man grabbed the tumbler, put two dice inside, gave it a good shake, and tossed the dice on the table.

"Three plus two five!" the scrivener called out, as the man blanched and a groan of commiseration went up from the crowd. The drunk reached out and grabbed the tumbler, shook it, and tossed the dice.

"Three plus three six!" the scrivener proclaimed, as the onlookers gasped and the disfigured man put his hands over his face.

"Did I win?" the drunk asked, incredulous.

"Certainly," confirmed the scrivener, and he quickly pushed the other player's coins over to the drunk. The drunk stretched out his hands, with a greedy smirk.

"Just a minute!" said the scrivener. "We must do this right. You," he went on, addressing the winner, "have won five ducats fair and square, and they are yours. But the ones that you were lent by the most excellent Master Ettore must be returned."

He reached out, took five of the ten ducats and made them disappear into his purse.

"Now, take your money and go!" he continued. Then, turning to the other man:

"You received a loan of five ducats and you lost them. Since you are unable to pay them back, we will consider them as an advance, paid to you for your six months' service on the galley. Now you are legally bound to row six months on the *Aquila*, until the extinction of your debt. What is your name?" he continued, shifting to a pragmatic tone, taking out his book and a bottle of ink.

As the winner walked off with his money, followed by the excited crowd, and the loser recited in a broken voice his vital statistics, the man from Lecce said to Michele:

"That's what they always say, 'until the extinction of your debt.' But what extinction? You're flat broke and you have to row for six months on a galley! They debit your clothes. If you ask for a little wine, that's debited too. At the end of six months you owe them more money than before! I've been here for three years now, and I still haven't seen this extinction they keep talking about."

Just then a group of porters loaded with crates appeared on the dock, and the soldier who was accompanying the oarsmen ordered them to get to work. Michele and the others sighed and started loading the goods on board.

At the beginning of May, after loading all the supplies in the hold, embarking a hundred or so harquebusiers and enrolling all the rowers they could find, the *Aquila* left Messina and sailed east, following the mountainous coast of Calabria. A lot of the rowers grumbled, looking ahead to the five or six months of hard work that lay before them, but Michele was happy to have left behind the harbor, the gloomy, overcrowded dampness under the canopy, and the boredom of the weeks spent knitting or napping. The favorable winds enabled the galley to speed along so fast that in just two days they reached Otranto, without the rowers ever having to touch their oars. The Calabrian still made his rounds on the bridge with his whip tucked under his arm, but there was very little for him to do. Pasquale spent almost all of his time on the bow, searching the horizon. They were due to lay over in Otranto for just a day, just enough time to take on fresh water and get the latest information on the traffic, but in the early afternoon the sky began to grow dark. Heavy, threatening clouds appeared on the horizon, and by evening it was raining. The wind was so strong that, after consulting with his pilots, Master Ettore decided not to leave the harbor.

For four days the *Aquila* was stuck in the harbor at Otranto, the canopy was put back in place, and boredom set in again for everyone. On the evening of the fourth day the commander, impatient, decided the wind was dying down and that they could try to get under way, but Pasquale, behind his back, shook his head. Propelled by its oars, the galley got out of the harbor, and as soon as they cleared land the sailors started raising the sails. The foresail, which unfurled simply by pulling on the sheet, fell into place with ease; but the sail on the main mast, that had to be pulled up by force of arms, was a whole different story. The gusts of wind were so sudden and violent that the men in charge of the top edges kept staggering from side to side and losing their grip, and one of them fell overboard. When they fished him out he wouldn't stop protesting, while everyone around him chuckled. Intermittent showers soaked the sail before it could be raised, and the yard, straining under all that weight, rose so slowly that some of the sailors went to the captain to ask him to reconsider. Master Ettore insisted they keep trying, and Michele heard Pasquale grumbling to the pilot, who had come on board at Otranto:

"He's a good captain, but he doesn't understand the sails all that well."

Finally the mainsail was raised, and the commander, planted next to the helmsman, started giving the orders for the maneuver. The wind wasn't totally against them, but almost, and the sea was so rough you had to be constantly on the alert to keep out of trouble. It was pitch dark, and the lights along the coast indicated that the galley had hardly moved, when the wind, instead of dying down, began to get stronger. The ship was rocking frightfully on the waves, and nobody felt like laughing anymore. The pilot spoke heatedly with the commander, who listened to him with clenched fists. The soldiers, most of whom were on their first voyage, had already vomited their guts out, and were lying down, pale as corpses, moaning and praying. On the benches too, more than a few of the rowers had begun to pray.

The commander finally relented.

"What do you think, Pasquale, would it be better to take down the bastard and raise the marabout? It's smaller, maybe it will hold better."

Pasquale, ashen, shook his head. "It's too late to change sails, Excellency, we can't raise anything else! Instead, order them to lower the yard and may God help us!" Master Ettore, stiff-necked, refused to lower the sail, and ordered the helmsman to turn around toward the harbor. But with that sea and that wind, the galley had become almost impossible to steer, and worse, it was taking on water. All the oarsmen had their feet immersed in water up to their ankles, and the sailors who'd gone down into the hold to pull out the sacks of ballast and throw them in the water, came back up with the news that it was up to their knees. Michele, holding on for dear life to his oar handle, his stomach upside down, suddenly found himself thinking about what Big Prick had told him. What if his destiny and that of all the others was to drown in the sea that night? He looked at the black man, who was turning his head left and right with a terrified look on his face, and gave him an elbow.

"So, do you still believe our destinies are written in the stars?"

"Pray! You'll be better off," the black man replied. "Do what he's doing."

All curled up against the side of the ship, blind Mahmud bey was convulsively whispering a prayer in his incomprehensible language. Michele was about to say something, but then an even bigger wave slammed against the side of the galley with such violence that everyone on board thought it was going to turn over, and they all screamed bloody terror at the same time. The galley, completely out of control, turned on itself, and another wave hit Michele's side of the ship, sending it briefly underwater. Several oars broke in two with a deafening crack, and when the ship reemerged you could see that the foremast had snapped as well. Some of the oarsmen, crazy with fear, started screaming wildly to get their chains taken off.

"Silence," the commander shouted. "Caps in mouths!"

The oarsmen should have put their caps between their teeth, as they had been trained to do every time silence was ordered on board so as not to disturb the maneuver, but they were so terrorized that almost none of them obeyed. Pasquale, who was next to the helmsman, helping him to stay on course, called the Calabrian with a shout that could be heard above the roar of the waves, and he spoke with him briefly. The galley-sergeant spread his arms and went to talk to the commander. Meanwhile the oarsmen had stopped praying, cursing their destiny, and appealing to God, the Virgin, and the saints, and they cried out all together that they wanted to be freed. Master Ettore ran briskly down the *corsia* to check how many oars had been lost. When the Calabrian yelled something in his ear, he shook his head and pushed him away. Then, finally, he ordered the sailors to lower the sail, and the yard came down, a whole lot faster than it had gone up, swinging wildly back and forth and threatening, just before it slammed down on the bridge, to decapitate one of the sailors or knock him overboard.

"Now, listen to me!" The captain hollered, struggling to make himself heard over the roar of the billows. "A galley doesn't go down in the open sea! You understand that? As long as we stay away from the land we're not in any danger! All we have to do is make sure the wind doesn't drive us into the rocks! So, give it everything you've got! Row!" Pasquale immediately started blowing on his whistle. Some of the oarsmen refused to obey and kept yelling that they wanted to be unchained, but the Calabrian quickly beat them back into silence with a few blows of his whip. Despite all the effort, however, the *Aquila*, at the mercy of the waves, was unable to maneuver, and pushed by the wind, she kept moving closer to the lights on the shore. The few soldiers who had managed to stay on their feet were gathered together on the leeward side of the ship, staring anxiously at the lights. They hadn't understood anything the captain said, and it seemed to them that when they got close enough to the shore they would be safe. But the sailors knew it was exactly the opposite, and they were disconcerted to observe that the galley, now totally adrift, was getting closer and closer to the rocks. Despite the valiant efforts of the Calabrian, who berated them and beat them, the oarsmen stopped rowing and went back to praying. Master Ettore stood at the stern, pale as a dead man, flanked by the pilot and the captain of the harquebusiers. Up to a moment ago they had been arguing furiously, and such heated words had been flying back and forth that they nearly drew their swords, but now they all realized there was nothing more to be said.

"Let's wait," Master Ettore said. But suddenly the captain of the harquebusiers, who was in no better shape than his men and could hardly keep on his feet, slapped himself on the forehead.

"There's only one thing to do," he muttered; and he started rummaging through his pockets. Then he opened his hand and showed them all what was in it: a little gold *Agnus Dei*, the Lamb of God, attached to a gold chain.

"This will save us," he exclaimed. Then he knelt down, closed his eyes, and started kissing the *Agnus Dei* frenetically as he recited a prayer. The commander, the pilot, and

Pasquale, who had come to join them, made the sign of the cross, knelt down, and prayed along with him.

"Save us, Lord!" the captain shouted at the end, and with a grand theatrical gesture he threw the shining object into the sea.

The response came in the form of an enormous wave that pounded against the side of the galley and sent all four of them tumbling down on the deck. Utterly soaked, the officers struggled to their feet. The oarsmen went back to demanding to be unchained, beating their chains rhythmically against the benches. Michele and Big Prick were screaming at the top of their lungs too and even Mahmud bey, completely in the dark as to what was happening, repeated the same shout in his strident voice. But while they were all shouting, the wind suddenly died down, and the glow of moonlight came peeking through an opening in the clouds. The *Aquila* kept on rolling, but the waves, now, were less violent. The commander consulted feverishly with the pilot, who stubbornly indicated the right direction by sticking out his hand, even though it was so dark you couldn't see a thing. Then Master Ettore made his way, staggering, all the way to the mainmast, with Pasquale right behind him.

"Come on, the wind is dying!" he bellowed with all the strength he could muster. "To your oars! Row!"

All the rowers whose oars had survived the storm grabbed on to their handles and started rowing, while the comito blew on his whistle. The wind, all of a sudden, went completely calm, and a sickle-shaped slice of the moon stood out brightly against the darkness. An hour later the galley, the water in the hold now waist high, twelve of its fifty oars broken in two, and the foremast severed, reentered the harbor at Otranto, without having lost even one man. Everyone cheered the captain of the harquebusiers. He got a little color back in his face and explained with satisfaction that that *Agnus Dei* had cost him twelve ducats, and that he had had it blessed by the Capuchins before going aboard in Messina.

"We made it!" exclaimed Michele, who like a lot of the others on board, now that the fear had passed, was feeling brave. Big Prick nodded.

"It wasn't written that we were to die tonight," he declared solemnly.

"Couldn't you have told me that before?" laughed Michele, jokingly waving his fist in his face.

17.

It took several weeks before the *Aquila*, all its damage repaired, was ready to go back out to sea. The biggest problem was the oars. Each one of those huge monsters, made to be handled by at least three men, was carved out of a single trunk of beech, and there were no more than eight of them to be found, ready to go, in all the workshops of Otranto. The others had to be made to order, commissioning someone to cut down the trees in the forests of the Sila, in Calabria, and transport the trunks all the way to Otranto, at a price the made Master Ettore want to tear his hair out. Then, when everything was ready, the ship was coated with tallow to make the keel more viscous and faster in the water. A system of sheaves and pulleys allowed it to be raised and tilted next to the dock, half-suspended in air, so a boat could pass under the part of the keel that was out of the water, with a pot of melted tallow and two men to spread it, while on the dock more tallow was being melted in the boilers, and the crew all crowded together as far away as possible to get away from the smoke, the smell, and the heat. The whole operation was carried out very swiftly, in less than two days, because the pilots had advised that the wind was good and they didn't know how long it would last. So finally, one evening just before sunset the galley went out to sea.

When the Otrantine pilot who had steered them out of the harbor took his leave and got back on his boat to return to the harbor, the commander called Pasquale and the galley pilot into the cabin. He had opened out the nautical chart on the table, and since there was a strong wind, he put the sextant and the clock on it to hold it down.

"Listen up a minute, you two," he said. I've decided we should find ourselves a spot off of Valona and lie there in wait to make a strike. Do either of you know this island right here?"

Using his finger, he pointed out a little island that seemed to be blocking the entrance to the port of Valona. The pilot nodded.

"There's not much there. It's uninhabited. But there are a few coves, and you can find water there."

"Even on the side that's hidden from the port?"

"I think so."

"And does it have firewood?"

"From what I remember, it's all thickets and scrub."

Satisfied, Master Ettore nodded.

"Very good! Let's lay up there, we establish a guard post on the tip of the island, and the first boat that comes out of the harbor, we take them. From what they told me in Otranto, there's a fair amount of traffic in and out of Valona this time of year."

"There's traffic, especially grain, I hear," Pasquale commented, dryly. Generally speaking, grain was not such a precious cargo to be worth the expense of an expedition.

"You know what, Pasquale. The way things are right now, even grain would be just fine by me. The harvest is going to be poor again this year, you can see that. It'll end up being easier to sell grain than fabric, mark my words."

Pasquale didn't agree, but he couldn't say so, so he maintained a respectful silence. If I were the commander of this galley, he thought, we wouldn't go looking for grain! But this too was something that wasn't even worth thinking about. Where did it ever happen that a comito, a simple sailor come up through the ranks, could become the commander of a galley?

Someone had told him once that with the Turks that's exactly the way it was, and that quite often a comito who knew his job well got promoted to rais. But the Turks, everybody knew, were barbarians.

"There's something else," Master Ettore continued. "From the news they had received in Otranto, there's no plague right now in Constantinople, but there is in Syria and Egypt. So, when we capture a boat, before going on board, let's remember to find out where it's from, alright?"

The others agreed, exchanging meaningful glances. There was always plague somewhere, in one place or another of this wide world, and especially in the Turkish empire, as God's way of punishing the infidels. But it was one thing to know that in theory, and another to know that in practice there was always a chance of coming across a boat that was carrying the contagion on board.

"Let's hope for the best!" Pasquale concluded; and forced a smile onto his face.

The pilots were right. On their second day of sailing, when they could already make out the profile of the mountains on the Albanian coast, the sky clouded over. Master Ettore coughed all night long, and even now, as he scanned the horizon, he was still coughing.

"The lousy life of the galley!" he muttered, grumpily.

Pasquale, called in for a consultation, figured they wouldn't be able to reach the island before the storm. The captain of the harquebusiers, who was listening in, made the sign of the cross. After the tempest, a good half of his men had deserted, and the ones who stayed were not very cheerful.

"If we're hit by another squall, I'm not answering for anybody," he said brusquely. "Try to get us to shelter."

Master Ettore and Pasquale looked at him askance. Their faces clearly said: and what can we do? These landlubbers don't understand anything and they'll never understand. But in an effort to satisfy the captain, and to demonstrate that they had done everything possible, they put the crew under pressure anyway. Pasquale planted himself squarely in the middle of the *corsia* and blew his whistle. "Amain!" he bellowed. The amain command called for the rowers to strain their utmost on every rotation, tugging the oar with all of their strength rather than just letting themselves fall back down on the bench, dragging it with the weight of their body. The galley, which already had the wind at its back, increased its speed imperceptibly, but the sky was darkening fast. After a few minutes, whopping drops of rain started to fall, and some of the soldiers, white as rags, knelt to pray. Michele, straining under the exertion and shiny with sweat, still found the time to say to Big Prick:

"They seem to scare easily, these people!"

Since he had been on the galleys, not only had the muscles in his thighs and forearms developed enormously but he had also learned to manage his breathing so that even during the most strenuous activity he was able to exchange comments with his bench-mates. The black man agreed; he too, like everyone on board except the soldiers, knew how to read the signs in the sky, and distinguish a thunderstorm from a squall.

"We'll be dancing a little," he said, "and sure we'd be better off in the harbor. But when it comes down to it we'll get wet and that'll be it."

Not long afterwards the wind was so strong that the *Aquila* had to lower her sails in order to avoid getting thrown off kilter by the gusts, and it moved ahead solely on the force of the oars. Now it was raining heavily, and you couldn't see any further than a shot from a harquebusier; the island, which before had looked so close, had now vanished behind a curtain of water. After consulting with the pilot, Master Ettore decided that in those conditions it was better to stay in the open sea rather than risk getting too close to land. So he ordered the suspension of the rowing, and everybody, soaked and grumpy, waited for the storm to calm down, while the waves tossed the galley around as though it were a walnut shell.

Finally, just as suddenly as it had arrived, the storm ceased. A sliver of blue sky flashed through the clouds, and right after that the sun came out, setting now behind the distant, low-lying silhouette of the coast of Puglia. In front of them was the stark profile of the mountain looming over the harbor of Valona, and even closer, reachable in half an hour, the name-less island where Master Ettore had decided to establish their base. The sails were raised, to save the strength of the crew, given that they were still in hostile waters and there would be hell to pay if the galley let itself be surprised by a superior enemy with its rowers exhausted. And the wind, now a light breeze, lazily pushed the *Aquila* toward its destination. Everyone on board was trying to dry off under the last rays of sunlight, wringing out their dripping shirts and pants. The cap-tain of the harquebusiers checked his men's weapons, repri-manding those who hadn't managed to keep them dry during the storm.

"What would we do if the Turks came down on us now, eh? And you call yourselves soldiers!" he cussed, and then spat.

The pilot, looking out over the stern, six feet above the head of the helmsman, pointed out the direction to take in order to round a small cape that was blocking their way.

"Careful, not too far the other way! There's a sandbar. Stay as close to the edge as you can. That's it, just right, stay on this line and you'll be fine."

An instant later, the *Aquila* rounded the cape, discovering a wonderful blue cove, edged with white sand. And suddenly, several voices started shouting, not for the breathtaking beauty of the harbor, but because there was another boat anchored at the far end of it.

"A galley!" Master Ettore called out; then he instantly corrected himself. "No, A galliot! It's a corsair! Come on, let's take him! Row!"

On Pasquale's command, the oarsmen all started rowing in unison, while the few harquebusiers whose weapons were still in working order crowded onto the bow, and the gunners re-emerged from the hold where they had been playing cards for the last two days and went about opening a crate of cannon-balls. The galliot must have come into the cove seeking shelter from the storm, and to attain greater stability it had taken down its only mast; the last thing it expected was an attack without warning. A lot of its crew were ashore, undoubtedly on a firewood and water detail; you could see the Turks who were closest to it running along the beach to try and board the tender as it pulled away from shore, while the rest of them ran like crazy in all directions. It didn't seem that the corsair had the slightest chance of getting away, with no sails and so many of its oarsmen ashore. But the soldiers and sailors staring at the galliot from the bow of the *Aquila* yelled in anger on seeing the demasted ship beginning to move out to sea without waiting for the tender, from which men screamed and gesticulated in desperation. Evidently, the *rais* had decided to sacrifice the men on shore in order to save everything else. He put his faith in his rowers and he had calculated well: the galliot was already gaining ground. Pasquale, who had also run forward to the bow and had razor sharp eyes, made a quick count:

"Twenty-two benches," he judged. "We'll never catch her." The *Aquila*, with its twenty-five benches, had three benches more per side, but it was heavier than the galliot and was car-rying a lot more men. With a strong wind at its back, it could have overtaken her, but in that near dead calm, there was no hope. Master Ettore, who was so excited he had stopped coughing, grimaced in disappointment.

"Fire on the boat," he said to the gunner, pointing to the tender that by now had given up on reaching the galliot, and was trying to make it out to sea on its own, hoping to pass unobserved. The *Aquila*'s cannon splashed just short of the boat; a second round, long, plunked into the water just on the far side.

"Wait, let's see if they've heard the tune," the commander said, holding back the artilleryman who was preparing a third shot. Indeed, the boat, figuring it was going to be hit, had given up trying to get out to sea and had turned back toward the beach. One or two of the men on board had even jumped into the water and were now swimming toward shore.

"Let's come about," Master Ettore ordered. "Signor Annibale," he said to the captain of the harquebusiers, "get your men ready, we're going ashore to get those people."

The galliot, by now in open sea, was putting up its mast, and a few minutes later it was so far away you could barely make out the white triangle of its sail. The *Aquila* turned its bow toward land, and prudently headed toward the shore. The pilot and Pasquale measured the depth with a plumb line, while on the bow the gunners pointed their pieces toward the beach. Most of the Turks left on shore had gone into the scrub; only a few of them were still visible, uselessly firing their harquebuses against the approaching galley.

"Six fathoms. Stop!" the pilot said. The rowers stopped, the helmsman turned the wheel, and the galley, gliding on its momentum, spun around slowly on its axis. It took some doing, with the force of the oars, to point it toward the island, so the cannons could keep it in their sights.

"Lower the boat!"

The harquebusiers crammed on to the boat lowered into the water, and Master Ettore followed them, together with their captain.

"Pasquale! Fire on those people, clear the beach for me!" Master Ettore ordered, pushing his hat down on his head and feeling for the hilt of his sword. Then the boat, with six sailors manning the oars, headed for the shore. The Turks fired a few rounds with their harquebuses, but the balls fell into the water well short of the target. Then the main cannon of the *Aquila*, a culverin that shot balls weighing fifty pounds, thundered off a round of its own. The ball dug a hole in the beach very close to the Turks, throwing up a big spray of sand, followed an instant later by the balls from the smaller pieces. A second later the beach was deserted. The boat rowed in to within a few feet of the water's edge, then the soldiers jumped into the water and rapidly deployed in formation. Master Ettore and the har-quebusiers' captain were at the head with their swords drawn.

Their feet sinking into the sand, the soldiers advanced to the shrub-covered dunes that blocked the view from the sea; there they fanned out, leaving ten paces or so between one man and the next, and started moving into the scrub. The sailors on the galley followed the hunt attentively, commenting out loud and betting, while the boat turned back to embark more sol-diers. Every now and again, you could hear the echo of a shot coming out of the scrub, or a sudden shout revealed that the prey had been found. The boat had just landed another dozen soldiers when two harquebusiers were spotted coming back over the dunes, pushing three semi-naked men ahead of them. Shoved onto the boat, the three were taken aboard ship, while at the same time others could be seen on the beach. The whole operation took less than two hours, during which the entire island was combed, and fourteen Turks brought aboard the *Aquila*.

Master Ettore examined them one by one in the stern cabin, before they were chained at the ankle and assigned to an oar. The galley already had three oarsmen per bench, but there was room for four, and the oars were outfitted with four han-dles.

"What do you think, Pasquale?" the commander asked with a satisfied tone, when he came upon one who was particularly muscular. "In Messina, they'll pay us at least a hundred scudi for this one, am I right or not?" The prisoners were all sailors or janissaries, rugged and used to being at sea, the type of slave that brought a good price.

"Another two or three strikes like this one, and we'll have recovered our expenses," Master Ettore calculated; and Pasquale agreed. But in addition to pricing his goods, the commander wanted to know who he was dealing with. The brightest of the prisoners were interrogated, with no need of an interpreter, in the lingua franca based on the pidgin Italian that more or less everyone spoke in the Mediterranean. A janissary somewhat older than the others, with a long scar across his face form his mouth to his eyebrows, and a few white hairs in his long walrus mustache, confirmed that their ship was a pirate galliot, based in Duress.

"And who's the *rais*?"

The Turk said his name was Ali Ginoves. The two Genoese looked at each other.

"He's a renegade, isn't he?"

The Turk confirmed, and anyway most of the rais of the corsair galliots, in the Levant as well as on the Barbary Coast, were renegade Christians, that was no secret to anyone.

"Ali Ginoves," Master Ettore repeated, pensively. "I think I've heard that name before."

"Of course!" Pasquale exclaimed. "I've heard it too. Wait! Isn't he from Recco?"

"Bregante! Gregorio Bregante, who was captured by Ucciali in Tunis; I remember hearing somebody talking about it recently, that's him alright."

The janissary, who had been listening to their conversation without understanding a thing, nodded vigorously when he heard the name.

"Yes, yes," he confirmed cheerily, "Gregorio."

"Well, look at that," said Master Ettore. He was as pleased

as if he'd found an old friend. "I remember him perfectly, he was the crew chief on a frigate. Well, look at that!" he said again. "So, he's based in Duress?"

The prisoner confirmed that the galliot had its home in that port, and that it didn't let a Christian ship go by without attacking it.

"Last week we took two galleasses out of Venice, with over a hundred casks of olive oil, and some horses."

It turned out that all their loot was sold right there on the spot in Duress, and the rais always found buyers. Since the plundered vessels were Venetian ships, it was illegal, seeing as the Republic was at peace with the Sultan, but the qadi in Duress kept both eyes closed and he made a nice profit out of it too.

"The Venetians aren't going to be at all happy about this," Master Ettore observed, satisfied; and Pasquale laughed. Whatever might annoy the Venetians was always a source of pleasure; all the more so if it was the work of a Genoese, albeit a renegade!

"But how is it that the Venetian galleys haven't gone after him?"

The janissary chuckled.

"There's no way. Ali has friends everywhere. When the galleys come, they warn him with signals, day or night, anywhere within fifty miles of the harbor."

"Bravo, Gregorio!" Master Ettore approved. "I'm actually a little sorry I scared him so badly."

After interrogating the prisoners, the commander decided to feed the crew and let them rest a few hours, but to get back under way before dawn. The encounter with the galliot meant that place wasn't safe anymore, and even if it might be that Ali had gone back to Duress without worrying about warning Valone, it was better not to take risks. At two in the morning the bugler played reveille, and the *Aquila*, pushed by the full force of its rowers, went back out to sea heading south. Master Ettore called Pasquale and the pilot to communicate his orders.

"We'll go down as far as Pazù," he said, using the name the Italians used then for the Greek island of Paxos, south of Corfu. "We've got some friends there and we can lay there in wait for some cargo en route for Parga."

The weather had taken a turn for the better, the wind was light but constant, and the galley made its way south at a good clip, doing five or six knots. After the barber had shaved all their heads and mercilessly cut the janissaries' mustaches, the captured and chained Turks solicited some interest for a while, but it wasn't long before the novelty wore off. Big Prick always took an interest in each new rower assigned to the nearby benches, and since one of the new slaves captured on the island, a small Greek sailor, husky and very young, had ended up two benches in front of him, he had taken delight in contemplating his muscles, elbowing Michele with a smirk on his face and making all sorts of obscene comments. At first, Michele got annoyed with these games, but by now he had learned to put up with them. He'd figured out a while ago that his black bench mate was like that, he liked looking and talking about what he saw, but then he didn't bother anyone, and when he couldn't take it anymore he took his pleasure by himself, at night, when everyone was curled up to sleep.

Paxos was Venetian territory, and the galley took care to arrive at night, keeping well away from the fishing villages on the coast. It dropped anchor in an isolated inlet, and the commander sent two men ashore in a boat. The whole next day went by without anyone showing up, while the convicts gathered firewood and replenished the water supply. But the next night the two men came back, and not long after them a small convoy of mules came down through the mountains, loaded with barrels of olive oil and wine, crates of biscuit and cheese, and gunpowder. The supplies were loaded into the hold, filling the voids that had been opened in the first weeks of the voyage, a sum of money passed from hand to hand, and immediately afterward, in the deep of the night, the galley left as silently as it had arrived. At the first light of dawn, the stern third was rowing, and everyone else on board was snoozing to catch up on their sleep, when a sailor on watch shouted out:

"Ooay! Sail to starboard!"

18

On board the *Aquila*, as always, the sighting provoked immediate agitation. At every encounter on the high seas the crew didn't know whether to expect a prey to be hunted down, an enemy to fight, or, in cases where the unknown ship turned out to be from one of the realms of the Catholic king to whom the Genoese gave their highest allegiance, a friend with whom the engagement would be limited to an exchange of information. There was also a fourth possibility, never admitted but nevertheless rather frequent, and that was the case of a merchant ship belonging to a neutral power, such as the Republic of Venice or the Grand Duchy of Tuscany, for which there was no reason it should be treated with special attention. In that case, at a minimum the ship was boarded and if Turkish or Jewish merchants were found among the passengers their goods were seized. But if the ship's cargo was truly appetizing it could even happen that all of it was seized, just about any excuse would do, and if the poor victims wanted to protest, that was fine too.

"It's a cargo ship, your Excellency," someone came from the bow to inform Master Ettore. Having excluded the option of an enemy to be fought, the tension on board eased, although there was still a great degree of anxiety, especially among the officers, to discover if there was some loot to be had, and if so of what kind. Before long they could see it was a tartan, and from the way it sat in the water, those who knew about such things said that it must be carrying a cargo that was voluminous but not very heavy. The commander's eyes lit up and he rubbed his hands together.

"It's got to be spices, Pasquale," he exclaimed. The comito didn't respond. He'd been living on the sea less time than Master Ettore, but he had learned never to take anything for granted. The galley, under full power, with all the oarsmen rowing and the Calabrian cursing at them from the *corsia* and snapping his whip, gained ground rapidly, and after a while the head gunner decided they were within shooting distance. The tartan, having sighted the sails of the *Aquila* on the horizon, had tacked toward land, even though the harbor at Parga was still a way off, but it was clear that it wasn't going to make it.

"They're Turks," Pasquale said, on seeing them tack, and the sailors with the sharpest vision confirmed it: they could see their turbans.

"Let's fire a warning shot," Master Ettore decided. The roar of the culverin shattered the silence and a jet of water rose up very close to the tartan.

"Nice shot!" the commander said. "That's enough for now," he rushed to add, fearing that a too-well-adjusted ball might send to the bottom that fabulous cargo that he had already imagined was waiting for them: sacks and sacks of pepper, coriander, ginger, and cinnamon, each of which could be sold for hundreds of ducats.

The tartan must have had the same fear, because it lowered its sail. When the galley came up alongside it, a team of sailors got ready to board it, while the harquebusiers kept their weapons trained on the bridge of the cargo ship.

"Hey, wait a minute!" Pasquale remembered. "We have to ask them where they're coming from!"

"Dammit, that's right!" said the commander, who had totally forgotten. The two of them made their way up to the bow and climbed up on the boarding bridge; from there Pasquale yelled down in the lingua franca:

"Where are you coming from?"

"From Tripoli in Syria," came the reply of the frightened commander. Pasquale jumped backwards and swore.

"Damn! They've got the plague there!"

Master Ettore and the comito consulted rapidly and then Pasquale returned to question the Turk, asking him what cargo they were carrying. It turned out the tartan was loaded with citrons and raisins that they were counting on selling in Albania.

Master Ettore was disappointed, but not too badly. Even if it wasn't spices in the strict sense, the booty still had considerable value. One way or another, they'd have to transfer it onto the galley. Plus there was the crew of the tartan, eleven men in all, and that too was a bounty which was not easy to give up.

"What do you think?" he asked the comito. Pasquale squinted, thinking it over.

"First, let's ask them," he proposed. "How is everybody on board? You don't have the plague do you?" he shouted. You could see the commander of the tartan hesitate. If he answered yes, they might have let them go, but there was also the risk that for caution's sake they'd throw them all into the sea.

"No, what plague?" he then answered, reluctantly. Master Ettore and the comito looked at each other.

"Is he to be trusted?"

Pasquale thought about it again.

"I'd say we should start by washing them," he concluded, "Hey, you down there! Take off your clothes and throw all your stuff overboard!"

On the tartan, the Turks argued a bit with each other; but they had no choice, and at the same time that order seemed to indicate that the Christians didn't intend to throw them overboard too. Awkwardly, they took off their ragged clothes and turbans and threw everything overboard, remaining naked.

"Now, come underneath!" Pasquale ordered, and the sailors

on board the *Aquila* started to dose them with big bucketfuls of water. The washing went on for a good long while; then the Calabrian and two reluctant sailors went on board the tartan, trying not to touch anything, and chained the whole crew to the benches, because Master Ettore, as always following Pasquale's advice, had decided to take the tartan in tow.

"Shall we take it to Otranto?" the comito suggested, but the commander shook his head.

"The stuff they've got we can sell better in Palermo or Naples. Oh yeah, but come to think of it, if we come into port towing the tartan we'll have to declare where it came from, and they could well put us all in quarantine."

Pasquale sniggered. "But, if your lordship agrees, before going into port we can take the slaves on board, by then if they're all healthy it'll mean there's no plague, and we can transfer the cargo into our hold and scuttle the tartan."

Master Ettore was so accustomed to being gotten out of a bind by his comito that he didn't even notice anymore, as though he had come up with the idea himself.

"That's exactly what we'll do," he agreed, satisfied. "Is the towline ready? Well then, head west!"

Among the oarsmen the news that they had taken a ship coming from a plague-stricken country had spread like wildfire, starting with the benches called, for some unknown reason, the *consiglieri*, or "counselors", the last row on the bow end, and arriving almost instantly to the first row at the stern, called the *spallieri,* or the "backers."

"They want us all dead here," Michele protested. His memories of the plague were rather vague but immensely frightening. He was eight or nine when it devastated Venice, depriving him of two brothers, and the word alone evoked the anguish of being shut inside the house for what seemed like forever, the frightened and impotent adults who had no patience and who spanked him or took a belt to him for next to no reason, the smell of smoke from the pyres where they burned the infected furniture and household goods, and a vivid image of his mother to whom someone, from outside the house, was handing a loaf of bread through the window.

"Eh? Does that seem right? They're going to kill us all!" he insisted. For a while now he had been feeling like he wanted to be more aggressive. He was one of the few free oarsmen left on board, amidst a multitude of slaves and convicts, and he felt like it was right that he should remind them of that. But the Calabrian heard him and a second later his whip hissed and struck him on the back. Michele cursed, but he bowed his head.

"Silence on the benches!" the galley-sergeant yelled. "Today's not Sunday!"

"It's never Sunday around here," another rower grumbled, but under his breath.

"One day I'm going to kill that guy," Michele whispered.

"What are you talking about, kill him? He's just doing his job. Forget about it," said the oarsman behind him, and others voiced their agreement. Disconcerted, Michele, looked for a reaction from Big Prick.

"That's mankind, my dear," the black man laughed. "You hit them, and you tell them it's for their own good, and they're happy."

Then they stopped talking, because there wasn't even a breath of wind, and the commander ordered the sails lowered and the oars into action.

With the tartan in tow, the *Aquila* had become slower and less stable, and more difficult to steer. The oarsmen damned that booty of which they would never see a penny anyway, and which forced them to work even harder than before. As always happens in the Mediterranean, the winds that had favored the galley's voyage to the east were now hindering its return voyage west, so it took several days to make the crossing all the way to the coast of Puglia. After a layover to take on firewood and water, the two ships, joined by the towrope, slowly made their way south, and early one morning, amid filaments of mist veiling the horizon, they sighted Santa Maria di Leuca, on the tip of Italy's heel. Master Ettore had doubled the sailors on watch, because that place was famous for ugly encounters; and in fact, as soon as they had rounded the promontory and pointed the helm southwest they saw a sail shoot out of a hidden inlet and heard the rumble of a cannon.

"Galliot," Pasquale declared assuredly, and raced up to the bow to look and came rushing back to the commander to report, as the gunners scrambled down into the hold to get ammunition and the harquebusiers took out their weapons.

"What should we do?" asked Master Ettore, nervously.

"I'd say we wait," the comito advised. "If they're crazy enough to come right at us, we'll take them in any case."

"Uhm! And let's hope they're crazy," concluded the commander, as he rummaged through the cabin to search for the sword he'd forgotten to buckle around his waist that morning.

But the corsair, that for an instant must have been deceived by the sun and mistaken the galley and its trailer for a cargo ship, had already wised up, and the galliot was racing along with its helm to the wind, trying to leave the galley behind.

"With this wind we might just be able to take her, if we didn't have the tartan tied to us," Master Ettore pondered. Pasquale nodded, baring his teeth in a smile.

"Excellency," the whispered, "I say there is no plague."

"You're right," Master Ettore decided. "Give the orders!"

In short order the prisoners captured on the tartan were brought on board the *Aquila* and the sailors started transferring the cargo. There were so many crates being crammed into the hold that the galley's deck sank down almost to the surface of the water. Then, at a certain point it shifted dreadfully, and all of the oarsmen on the port side found themselves half underwater.

"Dammit," Pasquale swore and, stepping over the heads of the screaming oarsmen, he rushed toward the stern hatch where the new cargo was being loaded into the hold. When he got there he dressed down the parone who was overseeing the operation, had all the crates brought back out, and began stowing them again in a different order.

"If we don't manage to take the galliot, it'll be your fault!" he said into the face of the hapless parone. "How is it that you never learned how to stow a cargo?"

Under Pasquale's direction the crates were rearranged, as well as possible, so as not to compromise the ship's equilibrium, but precious time had been lost. When the towline was untied and the by-now empty tartan sent adrift, the galliot was already far away, out in the open sea.

"Let's try it anyway," Master Ettore ordered, after a glance at the sails bulging in the wind. "If it stays this strong we might just be able to catch her."

The chase was on. The comito's whistle sounded a hellish pace; the oarsmen, soaking wet with seawater and sweat, hardly had time to breathe. The Calabrian and the other sailors moved up and down the *corsia* with whips and clubs. But two hours later the galley had gained no more than a few lengths. The galley-sergeant came to speak into the comito's ear. Pasquale nodded, and went in to the commander.

"We can't keep up this pace any longer, Excellency," he advised. "The crew will be exhausted."

Master Ettore cursed.

"How can she go so fast?" he exclaimed, nodding toward the far off galliot.

"Shall we try changing sails?" the comito suggested. "We'll lose a little time, but in my opinion we'll get it back and then some."

"Do as you wish!"

At Pasquale's orders, the sailors got down to work, and in fifteen minutes the light sail the galley had been using all night was replaced by the bastard, the biggest sail of all. In the meantime, naturally, the galliot had gained ground; but as soon as the new sail was raised it was clear that the comito was right, and that now the galley was taking better advantage of that strong wind. Five hours later, the distance between the two ships was considerably reduced.

"We're within shooting range," Master Ettore declared, and ordered the gunners to open fire. The culverin flared, shaking the entire ship with the force of the detonation, but the ball ended up in the water in the galliot's wake, several lengths behind it.

"Let's wait a little," Master Ettore corrected himself, imperturbable. Another hour went by. By now the galliot was close enough that you could hear the sound of the drum beating out the rhythm for its rowers and make out the white caps of the janissaries stationed at the stern, their harquebusiers gleaming in the sunlight.

"Fire now, with all the guns," the commander ordered. Besides the culverin, the battery on the bow also included two aspics and two falconets, smaller pieces with a shorter range but still deadly; even more so since the corsair, its stern facing the galley, couldn't respond with its artillery. The first volley still fell short; then a ball from the culverin made a direct hit on the stern upper works right in the middle of the line of janissaries, raising a hurricane of splinters. Screams of pain and fear rose up from the galliot, answered by a chorus of triumph from the Christian ship.

"Come on! Let's go!" shouted Master Ettore, dancing with excitement, so carried away he tripped over his sword. But the rais of the galliot knew how to handle himself. Realizing that he was at risk of being blown to bits by the artillery, he maneuvered to come about, and did it in such a hurry that the galley wasn't able to follow him. Slowly but inexorably the galliot went into a large turn that took it out of range of the culverin, although not of the smaller pieces on the port side, which kept on peppering it with salvos. The galley, with its heavier sails, took so much time to execute the same maneuver that the two ships ended up parallel to one another and pointed in opposite directions. The harquebusiers started firing, and a cloud of smoke quickly became so thick that it was almost impossible to take aim. The chaser and the chased kept on maneuvering for quite a while, without either one succeeding in putting itself into a favorable position to shoot, and without the galley succeeding in getting close enough to the galliot to ram her and board her. Master Ettore and Pasquale, hoarse from shouting orders, were spouting imprecations, the sailors overwhelmed by fatigue, by the turmoil, and by the bullets from the harquebuses that every now and again whistled past their ears, were starting to lose concentration and mis-execute the maneuvers, and the rowers, despite the whip lashings that the Calabrian showered on them from the *corsia*, had totally lost their rhythm. Then, all of a sudden, the wind went calm, and the sails on both ships instantly went limp.

"Come on, let's get down to it!" Master Ettore shouted, and the comito's whistle blew the signal, known and feared by all the oarsmen, to row amain. But the crew was so exhausted that the galley hardly picked up any speed at all. In the *corsia*, the Calabrian looked crazed with anger, and he was dishing out lashes in all directions, but with no results. Master Ettore ran up to the bow and saw that the galliot too was rowing amain and that the crew of slaves, well-honed to toil, was holding up. There weren't enough of them to gain an advantage over the galley, but at this rate, the *Aquila* didn't have a chance of catching its prey before nightfall. The harquebusiers, short on bullets and powder, had stopped firing. Master Ettore raised his eyes as if to interrogate the heavens, and just then the sound rang out of a final harquebus volley from the galliot. First, they saw the puff of smoke; then they heard the detonation and the whistle of the bullet that hit the commander in the shoulder. Master Ettore cried out, more from the surprise than from pain, and staggered; one of the nobles from the stern cabin ran to hold him up.

Right then the curtain of the stern cabin on the galliot thrust open and a rugged man with a big white turban on his head came out and walked over to the taffrail, scattering the janissaries who had gathered there to look out.

"Hey, master! Master!" he shouted.

"What do you want?" replied Master Ettore, with a grimace of pain.

"Who are you?" asked the Turk who, oddly, didn't use the lingua franca but spoke in Genoese.

"The *Aquila,* of Master Ambrogio Negroni!" answered Master Ettore, proudly. The Turk made a half bow.

"Really? Pay him my respects!"

Pasquale, who had come over to them, spoke briefly to the commander, whose eyes opened wide before he nodded with decision.

"And who are you? Aren't you Gregorio Bregante?" he shouted back.

"That's me, always ready to serve the Republic!" the Turk replied. "Why did you attack us? Don't you know that I only take Venetian ships, and when I have news of interest to Genoa I send it on immediately to the consul in Ragusa?"

"And you, why didn't you tell me that right away? Look here, what you've done to me!" responded Master Ettore, showing his arm with the blood streaming down.

"Master," said Gregorio, "you have to be patient about what happened because that's the way it had to be. It is written in the stars that you had to have this. It happened: nothing can be done about it."

"Hey, Gregorio!" Pasquale interrupted. "Did we kill a lot of your people?"

"Six of my janissaries, you killed," the other replied.

"Oh well, captain," Pasquale shot back, "I tell you that it was written in the stars that those janissaries had to die in this battle. You can't go against the will of God."

The Turk spread his arms out wide; then he turned toward Master Ettore. "Master," he concluded, "it happened. The blame is yours and mine. We must have patience; and he who has been wronged, keeps his damage."

Master Ettore nodded wearily, then the men who were holding him up took him into the cabin and lay him down on the bed. In the absence of orders, the galley remained there, floating peacefully on the oil-smooth water, as the galliot, still driven by the strength of its slaves rowing amain, quickly disappeared into the open sea. The ship's barber, having rushed to the aid of the commander, helped him take off his jacket, then he cut open his shirtsleeve and saw that the wound was not very deep; in just a few minutes, skillfully maneuvering a pair of tweezers, he removed the bullet amid the moans of pain that Master Ettore tried heroically to stifle.

"Excellency, shall we go to Messina?" Pasquale asked respectfully. Master Ettore, pale from the shock and discomfort, quickly got back some of his color by recalling the cargo he had aboard.

"No. What are you, joking?" he said hurriedly. "I told you we can sell the raisins for a better price in Palermo. To Palermo, dear, to Palermo."

19.

By now Michele was hardened to the life of the Genoese galley, so different from the life he had known on the *Loredana*. It didn't seem strange to him anymore to have a chain around his ankle, to be shackled to his bench every night, and to be woken up several times during the night by the watchmen's inspections to verify that the chains were still fastened. He had also gotten used to almost never going ashore, except to help gather and load firewood and water, and always under the surveillance of the soldiers. Sometimes he was chosen to row the tender when the commander or some other officer had to be taken ashore. In those cases, the strongest and best looking oarsmen were chosen and in the year since his escape from Venice, Michele had become much huskier; his face, cooked by the sun, was more masculine; his arms and legs were as muscular as a wrestler's; and to his great joy, the first signs of a blond mustache had begun to sprout on his upper lip, so that now, donning the oarsman's red cap and red cassock, he cut a fine figure. But even if those outings were a pleasant distraction, he could just as easily do without them. He had learned from Big Prick to live each day as it comes, working when it was time to work, entertaining himself during the interminable hours of idleness by looking out at the sea or watching the seagulls fly, and enjoying intensely the sea biscuit that was distributed twice a day and the fava bean or chickpea soup on holidays.

Only his dreams came to disturb the almost animal-like passivity that had come over him. On occasion he would dream of his father and start writhing and shouting in his sleep as though he were fighting the police, so that on more than one occasion his annoyed neighbors had woken him up to the tune of punches and kicks. And it happened that he would dream of Bianca, and enjoy her in his sleep, and wake up soiled and sticky and inexplicably happy, before realizing with a pang of delusion that he was not on the mattress beside her but on the hard bench of the galley. And then, once, he dreamed distinctly of being discharged from the *Aquila*; the scrivener checked his accounts in the register, and began counting out in gold coins an enormous sum which had mysteriously accumulated in his account; after which, he disembarked, climbing down the ladder at the stern, with a sack of zecchini on his back, and everyone on board saluted him by doffing their caps, including the commander. When he woke up from that dream, it was tough for Michele to return to reality; all day long he kept thinking that the dream must surely have been prophetic, and that the ten thousand zecchini buried on the island were waiting for him to put an end to his odyssey. The hope of escaping from the galley before the term of his engagement expired seemed more and more remote, but at the same time the year was going by fast. As soon I'm free again, everything will work itself out quickly, he told himself.

After several days of smooth sailing, the galley entered the harbor at Palermo, passing under the towering castles that guarded its entrance. Master Ettore, with his arm in a sling and still very pale and sore, went ashore with the tender, and Michele was one of the six oarsmen chosen to row him in. After they tied up at the dock they stayed in the boat to wait for him. The wait lasted almost the whole day, which the oarsmen and the harquebusiers on the boat with them spent yawning and snoozing. At a certain point they were hungry, and decided all together to send someone to bring back something to eat from a tavern, given that all of them, more or less, had some money in their purses. What came back was a big cauldron of bread soaked in broth and flavored with roast spleen, and they all ate until they were full, happy for that unexpected variation from their usual, monotonous diet. Only one of the oarsmen declined, preferring to chew on a heel of bread that he had brought with him under his shirt.

"Hey, buddy, if you don't have any money, your friends will take care of it! Today's a holiday!" declared another oarsman, a Neapolitan who usually didn't talk very much, with thick eyebrows that made him look like he was half asleep, although darting in all directions underneath them were two alert, suspicious eyes. The other one raised his head and signaled a no.

"I can't eat this stuff."

"Ah no? Why not, aren't you Turks allowed to eat spleen?" the Neapolitan asked, as if to challenge him.

"I'm not Turkish, I'm Jewish," the other replied, with dignity. One of the soldiers started laughing, with his mouth full.

"And since when have you gone back to being a Jew? Didn't you say you wanted to become a Christian?"

The Jew shrugged his shoulders.

"Oh yeah? Well, I changed my mind."

"Again!" the Neapolitan mocked him. "You want to know this guy's story?" he went on, turning to the others. The rest of them pricked up their ears while the Jew made a face and went back to chewing on his bread. It turned out that he actually was a Turk, captured at Lepanto eighteen years ago. On the galley that captured him his benchmates and neighboring rowers were Jews and they convinced him to abandon his religion and take up theirs. But then he changed his mind, and started saying he wanted to become Christian. Maybe he thought he might be freed that way, or at least be treated better. When they told him that, in any case, baptized or no, he would remain a slave like before, he changed his mind again.

"Be careful the Inquisition doesn't find out!" somebody warned, mockingly. The Neapolitan stared at the Jew from under his thick eyebrows, then spit.

"All this stuff about I can't eat this and I can't eat that is beyond me!" he declared disdainfully. "So I guess that means you don't drink wine either?"

"No, why not? We Jews drink wine," the other one replied, offended.

"Oh bravo, our dear friend! Well then listen, old chum," the Neapolitan continued, turning to one of the harquebusiers, "what do you say we order up a little wine too, since we're a little thirsty?"

"But haven't we spent enough already?" objected Michele, who up to then hadn't said a thing.

"What are we, a bunch of ragpickers?" he said, threateningly.

Everyone fell silent for a minute; then another oarsman stood up. He was Neapolitan too, only recently come aboard. Michele had heard that they called him "'O Mussuto," but he didn't know that the nickname, given to him when he used to fry fish on the streets of Naples, meant "the Codfish."

"You heard what Don Tommasino said! Are we thirsty or not? Come on, cough up some dough!"

Everybody, including the harquebusiers, took out some money. 'O Mussuto counted it, and then bowed to his countryman.

"Don Tommasino, at your service"

"Ah bravo," said the other, clicking his tongue. "So you know me?"

"And who doesn't know your lordship?" 'O Mussuto replied, unctuously.

Michele followed this exchange without understanding a thing, and with a single, firm intention: if possible, to have nothing to do anymore with either of the Neapolitans. He didn't say a word, drank his wine when the soldier sent to get it came back and poured some for everyone, starting, naturally, with Don Tommasino, who, by the way, as Michele had noted, was the only one not to have paid a cent. Whether it was their full stomachs, the heat, the wine, or some other reason, silence came over the little group. They remained that way, digesting and dozing on the tender, rocked ever so slightly by the riptide until, just before sunset, Master Ettore and Pasquale appeared on the dock. You could see right away that they were not at all happy.

"It's not possible to be this unlucky! Tell me, Pasquale, is there someone on this galley who is a jinx? Think about it, because if there is, we'll leave him ashore; we can't go on like this!" the commander protested; and Pasquale shrugged his shoulders. The attempt to sell the cargo seized on the tartan had failed. Just two days ago, there had arrived in Palermo a ship from Ragusa loaded with raisins, and there was no more demand for them on the market. As the tender was carrying them back to the ship, the oarsmen were able to hear the commander, who was saying:

"You know what I say, Pasquale? They can go to the devil! Tomorrow we're leaving again and we're taking the cargo to Naples to sell it. I'll be damned if it doesn't go well for us there."

The comito agreed.

"That's a good idea, Excellency. If this southerly wind keeps up, we'll be there in three or four days."

On hearing they were going to Naples, Michele looked up to see the reactions of the two Neapolitans. 'O Mussuto seemed cheerful, he was chuckling. But Don Tommasino kept on rowing with his eyes fixed in front of him, as inexpressive as the eyes of a reptile under closed eyelids.

The voyage to Naples, as Pasquale had predicted, was fast and uneventful, except for one event that moved no one

254 · ALESSANDRO BARBERO

except Michele and Big Prick. One night, after trembling with fever for hours, old Mahmud bey passed away. They realized it at dawn, as the ship was about to weigh anchor; he was already stiff, so much so that the galley-sergeant who was called immediately had a hard time pulling him off the bench after removing his chains. They sewed him up in a canvas bag, and dropped him into the sea with no ceremony, as the scrivener drew a line through his name on the list of slaves. Michele made the sign of the cross, and Big Prick, as the cadaver was sliding overboard and sinking below the water, recited a formula in some unknown language, passing his hands over his face repeatedly. The old man was out of his head; he hadn't said anything comprehensible since Michele had arrived on the *Aquila*, and even now there was nothing more to say: yet both of them felt like their hearts were swollen and had no desire to talk.

They hadn't been sailing long when the Calabrian arrived, leading the oarsman destined to replace the old man. To his surprise, and also to his chagrin, Michele saw that the newcomer was 'O Mussuto. The other man recognized him too, and deigned to give him a nod of the head. He ignored Big Prick and installed himself comfortably in his place. He had two bundles, while all the other buonavoglia were allowed only one, and without hesitation he pushed Michele's out of the way to make room for his. The strangest thing of all was that he was assigned to the third seat, the *terzicchio,* where the rowing was least strenuous and where up to now old Mahmud bey had been more than adequate, while with the set of shoulders 'O Mussuto had he could easily have handled the post of *postizzo* or even *vogavanti*, as the *pianiero* was called on Genoese galleys. There are injustices here too, Michele said to himself, still naïve enough to be astonished.

On her arrival in Naples, the *Aquila* tied up in front of the towers of Castelnuovo and the commander went ashore with

Pasquale; 'O Mussuto and Don Tommasino were chosen again to row the tender, but not Michele, who took advantage of the opportunity to comment to his benchmate, now that the *terzicchio* was not there to hear them.

"Hey, what do you think of those guys, eh? They give me the creeps," he confessed.

Big Prick looked at him seriously and didn't say a word; he just silently raised a finger to his lips.

"But what is it?" said Michele, not understanding.

"Be quiet! It's better not to have anything to do with those people," Big Prick whispered.

The next day a merchant came aboard the galley to examine the crates taken from the tartan, and agreed on a price with Master Ettore, so that same evening the oarsmen were put to work unloading them. The work went on throughout the next day; the cargo had to be transported to a warehouse fairly far away, and Michele, like the others, had to go back and forth several times across the neighborhood near the harbor, pulsing with shops and porters, urchins, the unemployed, streetwalkers, people that ate, slept, and pissed in the open air. That night, when they got back to the galley, the weather turned: a storm was looming and they had to put up the canopy.

After finishing that job too the oarsmen were waiting for their evening ration when they heard the captain being called from down on the dock by a voice with a strong Spanish accent and a demanding tone. It was a police inspector, an elderly man with white hair and a white mustache, all dressed in black, accompanied by a team of halberdiers. Master Ettore looked out from the stern cabin and a strange dialogue began.

The police officer had been sent by the viceroy to inspect the galley. According to an anonymous complaint, there were two oarsmen aboard who had been tricked—hired to perform other services and then assigned to row against their will—and others whose contracts had expired but who had not been released. The commander replied heatedly that there was not a word of truth to the accusations, and that whoever had filed the complaint was lying. The inspector, turning red, replied that he would damn well see who was lying. The commander asked if by any chance he was referring to him. The officer responded that he would never have dared, but that he had been ordered to verify the allegations personally. Master Ettore replied that he should make himself at home. The officer asked that the canopy be lowered and the commander gestured to Pasquale to comply. The oarsmen, who had followed the exchange in a spellbound silence and with extremely close attention, stared avidly at the police officer. He made his way forward and loudly proclaimed:

"Anyone who is here against his will, say so."

At this point, the sardonic voice of the commander resounded from the stern cabin:

"Oh poor Master Ambrogio Negroni, today you'll be left without your galley. Lord, let me be left ashore, because I, who am the captain of this galley, have been here against my will for many years, and if I could stay on land I would. Just think what these people here will do, who have nothing but bread and water, garnished with the club."

Derisive laughter spread among the sailors and the oarsmen. The inspector shrugged, climbed on board, and started down the *corsia*, repeating the same question. Nobody responded; the large majority of the oarsmen were slaves and convicts, and none of the few buonavoglia trusted the viceroy of Naples. As the police officer approached Michele's bench, 'O Mussuto came to life, rummaged in his purse, and took out a coin.

"Hey, you want to earn a *reale*?" he asked Michele, showing him the silver coin.

"And how would I do that?" Michele replied, surprised.

"When the officer gets here, you wave him over and then

you whisper in his ear that Tommasino Buttafuoco is here on board."

"And then?" Michele queried, suspiciously.

"And then, nothing, you'll have earned a *reale*," the other replied.

Michele looked at Big Prick, who imperceptibly gestured no.

"So why don't you tell him then?" he responded. 'O Mussuto looked at him brazenly and spat.

"You'll get yours," he said, menacingly. The officer had already arrived at their row, and repeated once again his appeal: if there was someone there being held against his will, he should say so. Nobody opened his mouth and the officer, stiff and red in the face, went on. When he had completed his inspection, he returned to the ladder at the stern, climbed down to the dock, and turned to look at Master Ettore, who had watched the whole scene sniggering.

"Good night, sir," he said with a half bow, doffing his cap. The commander replied with an even deeper bow and the officer left, followed by the halberdiers.

The next day, word spread through the benches that the buonavoglia would be given special permission to go ashore. Master Ettore, happy about having the cargo from the tartan sold at a profit and even more so for the victory over the police inspector, wanted to compensate them for their loyalty, or at least that was the rumor that was going around, and Michele believed it.

"Enjoy yourself," Big Prick said sadly. "And if you get laid, remember all the details, so you can tell me about it."

Michele felt bad for the black man, but it never even crossed his mind that maybe the slaves too should be allowed to go ashore for once without carrying a load on their backs. After all, the fact that he was wearing a mustache while Big Prick's face was shaved must mean there was a difference between them! He pulled a clean shirt out of his sack and dipped his fingertips into the water cask to rinse his face. He was changing when he suddenly heard some arguing down on the dock and then a very clear cry:

"*Aquila! Aquila!* Help!"

All the sailors and the unchained *buonavoglia* still on board ran over to the side of the ship. The cry had come from Don Tommasino, who had been among the first to go ashore and was calmly walking along the dock, he too dressed in clean clothes and shoes on his feet, when the cops had stopped him. Don Tommasino had started crying for help; two men were holding him by the arms and another was busy trying to gag him. A roar of anger went up on the galley, and even without an order from the officers, the men crowded around the ladder and climbed down onto the dock. Almost no one knew the man who was being arrested but the fact that the police were messing with someone from the *Aquila* was enough to make everyone lose their heads. Several soldiers had their swords in hand, and all the sailors their knives. It was an instant: the group of policemen who were trying to drag off the prisoner was attacked by the crowd, and a second later one of them was lying stepped on and bloody on the dock, while the others ran to save their skins. Some of the men from the *Aquila* followed them to the head of the dock, then, prudently, preferred to turn back. Michele had just made it to the edge of the ladder to go down when he saw the first of them hurrying to come back aboard the galley.

"Well? What happened?" Big Prick asked.

"What do I know! The police had grabbed someone, but our boys showed them!" Michele replied, excited and happy. He sat down at his place, stretching his legs: the *terzicchio* wasn't there, so there was lots of room. Tumultuously, the oarsmen who had rushed to join the brawl came back to their places on the benches, while the officers, befuddled by the rapidity with which it had all happened, were yelling out useless orders. Word about what had happened must have spread quickly through the streets of Naples because over the next few hours the soldiers and sailors from the *Aquila* who had gone ashore earlier came hurrying back, in small groups and rather scared. Among the last, when night was already falling, was 'O Mussuto, who came back with a look of alarm on his face, and went straight to his post without saying a word.

"I've never been so happy to be chained to this bench," Big Prick laughed. "The rest of you are in for some big trouble," he prophesied.

20.

The black man was an easy prophet. No one slept that night on the galley. Master Ettore was furious and above all anxious, because he still had to collect his proceeds from the sale, and an imbroglio with the viceroy was the last thing he needed. Once he'd ascertained generally what had happened, he had the galley searched from top to bottom looking for Buttafuoco, but it was no use: after the melee the fiend had absconded. Equally useless was the attempt to discover who had wielded the knife or the sword that had created the cadaver. Several dozen men had gotten or were getting off the *Aquila* at that moment, but who, exactly, had gotten so far as to come to blows with the police could not be determined. And all those who were interrogated swore they had not been aware there was a victim until he was found lying on the pavement.

The commander, Pasquale, and the Calabrian were interrogating the last sailors, before going on to the soldiers and the buonavoglia, when a crowd of armed men was heard on the dock, with a great clanging of armor. Master Ettore looked down and saw the same police inspector from the other day, accompanied by quite a few soldiers, with their swords unsheathed and the fuses on their harquebuses lit. The dialogue between the two, as might be imagined, was even less cordial than the first time. The inspector, on behalf of the viceroy, demanded the immediate delivery of the banished individual, since it turned out that the aforementioned Tommaso Buttafuoco had already been condemned to perpetual exile from the kingdom of Naples for a congruent number of homicides, on pain of the gallows if he should allow himself to be captured. Master Ettore responded that he was greatly displeased not to be able to hand him over, for the simple reason that he was no longer on board. The inspector replied that he intended to ascertain that personally. Master Ettore responded that the ship was not one of the king's galleys and that he would not allow anyone to come on board. The inspector rebutted that that remained to be seen, and that in any case they had to turn over the policeman's assassin. Master Ettore replied that as commander of the galley it was up to him to conduct the investigation and to do justice. The inspector replied that that was not in fact the case, and pulled out some papers, which Master Ettore said he was unable to read because it was already nighttime and there was not enough light. The dialogue took place with some difficulty because as a cautionary measure the galley had pulled back some thirty feet or more from the dock and pulled up the ladder. On board everyone was holding their breath for fear of missing something. In the end, the inspector advised that he would return, and that then they would see who was right.

The officers on the *Aquila* continued their interrogations throughout the night, with no result. A dozen or so harquebusiers and sailors had to admit to having gone down on the dock in response to the appeal of the arrested man, and they were the same ones that Pasquale himself or some of the nobles from the stern cabin remembered to have recognized, but no one else opened their mouths, not even to denounce a colleague. Interrogated like all of the buonavoglia who had been unchained to go ashore, Michele told the truth, and that is that he had just arrived at the top of the ladder when the whole thing had ended. They didn't believe him, because practically everyone was saying the same thing, but they couldn't do anything about it, and they sent him back to his bench.

He was trying to get to sleep, despite all the movement on board and the light of dawn that was already visible behind the hills, when from the dock, where a guard of harquebusiers had remained on duty, a new appeal was heard. This time it was a Spanish army officer, with a large feathered cap and a red scarf knotted around his neck, who, after calling Master Ettore out of his cabin, repeated the order for the immediate delivery of the banished Buttafuoco and the police officer's assassin. In response to the commander's objections, the officer said that the viceroy, Don Juan de Zuniga, Count of Miranda, was giving him twenty-four hours to find them and hand them over, otherwise he would order an artillery attack on the galley, and with a gesture of defiance he pointed to the hulking mass of Castelnuovo that was reflected in the water. All those who heard him turned around to look, and saw that the artillery on the castle's turrets had already been pointed at the *Aquila*.

Dismayed, Master Ettore decided it was best to go and speak personally with His Excellency, and went ashore. He didn't return until that evening, a dour look on his face, and went straight to bed, without saying a word to anyone. After a while, everyone was asleep, aboard the galley as well as on the dock, where the soldiers on guard had wrapped themselves up as well as they could in their overcoats. Michele was asleep too, like all of his fellow oarsmen, when he was suddenly awakened by some movement nearby of a body much larger than a rat (the occupants of the galley had all gotten used to rats and no longer woke up when they felt them running over their feet). Michele opened his eyes and even before he got a glimpse of the dark shape of a man standing over him, he heard a desperate moan, immediately stifled, and was kicked by 'O Mussuto, who only a second before had been snoring on the bench and who was now wildly waving his arms and legs. But the whole thing lasted no more than a second, the noise ceased and the body of the *terzicchio* fell to the floor inert. All around them men woke up and grumbled, but nobody really knew what to do; it was a moonless night, and only a cat could have seen anything. But Michele noticed that the man stretched out on the bench was in an unnatural position, and after a bit he felt something warm and viscous dripping down on him. So he decided to call out. Amid the shouts of protest of the men he woke up, the Calabrian finally arrived, rubbing his sleep-filled eyes, with a lighted torch. With great exclamations of horror and surprise, everyone saw that 'O Mussuto had been stabbed to death, his throat slit like a sheep. The Calabrian bent down over the corpse and picked up a big piece of paper that had been pinned to his chest, half-soaked in blood.

"Who knows how to read?" asked the galley-sergeant. The response was a buzz of murmuring and laughter. Irritated, the Calabrian climbed back up onto the *corsia* and went to the stern cabin, where in the meantime the curtain had been pulled open and Master Ettore, in a nightshirt, had come to look out. The paper was brought to him and the commander read it in a low voice, but loud enough so the words could be heard and then instantly make their way throughout the galley. On the paper was written in large block letters: TOMMASINO BUTTAFUOCO, and underneath, smaller: "This same end will be met by anyone who tries to betray me."

"Well!" Master Ettore commented, with admiration. "Pasquale, come here a minute!" he ordered.

"Here I am, Excellency," said the comito, making his way through the oarsmen.

"Listen, Pasquale, do you think it's normal that this guy can come on and get off the galley whenever he pleases? Eh?"

Pasquale shrugged.

"Excellency," he began, but the commander cut him off.

"Forget the Excellency! Since when do you address the captain as Excellency? I'm sick and tired of having my chain pulled, you understand, Pasquale?"

Wisely, the comito didn't answer.

"Now, you tell me who was on duty this watch, and we dock him a week's pay, that way maybe they won't fall asleep next time!"

"Yessir!" Pasquale assented.

"And then you tell me once and for all what the story is here. Who is this Buttafuoco? And don't give me any bullshit; watch out because after you I'm going to call the Calabrian and have him tell me his version, and it sure as hell better coincide with yours."

Pasquale understood that it was best to come clean.

"So, Eminence," he began, "that guy came to sign on the last time we laid over in Naples last year; dressed like a bum, but with him were some knights, and they took me aside and explained that he had to leave Naples for a while, that there was trouble in the air, but that he was a friend of theirs, and that if I treated him well there'd be something in it for me."

"And how much did you get out of it?" Master Ettore asked him.

"Twenty pieces of eight," Pasquale replied without missing a beat.

"Liar! If you tell me twenty then it must have been at least fifty. Pasquale, you don't do things like that on my galley, you know that? I want to know about these things. And as punishment you'll put the twenty pieces of eight in the Santa Barbara collection box."

"Yessir," said the contrite Pasquale, whose take from Don Tommasino's friends had actually been a hundred pieces of eight.

"And the other guy?" Master Ettore continued. "The one who got stabbed?"

Pasquale shrugged.

"That one I didn't know. But the Neapolitans are a dangerous bunch. Who knows for what offense he was trying to get revenge."

"Anyway," the commander went on, calmer now, "there's always a silver lining. Now the viceroy will have to believe us that we're not keeping the guy stowed away in the hold. And besides, we've had one of ours killed now too, we're even."

"If I may say something, Eminence," the comito began.

"Tell me."

"I think Tommasino killed the policeman too."

Master Ettore pulled on the right side of his mustache, pensive.

"You know, I think you've hit the nail on the head, Pasquale," he said. "It couldn't have been anyone but him. Come to think of it, someone must have seen him do it too, don't you think?"

"I think so, Eminence," Pasquale nodded, serious.

"And you find me the ones who saw him, and then later today we'll go talk to the viceroy. Right now, I'm going back to sleep, it's the middle of the night."

Some sailors came to get the body of 'O Mussuto and carry him ashore, and in the confusion his bundles disappeared too. All that was left of him was a big bloodstain on the bench's leather padding and the wooden boards underneath it. Michele yelled that someone should bring a pail of water, but they told him to wait till tomorrow, and that he could take care of it himself instead of bothering people who were busy doing other things. In the morning, when they unchained him, Michele washed away the blood as best he could with a few buckets of seawater. Not so much as a trace was left of the man who in the last few days had been the *terzicchio* on bench number six, except in the scrivener's register; but even there his account was undoubtedly closed and cleanly balanced to everyone's satisfaction.

It took a few days of negotiation before the viceroy of Naples allowed the galley to leave port. When they were preparing to weigh anchor the man who was to replace the deceased rower was brought to the bench. After a year spent with that crew, Michele knew just about all the oarsmen on the *Aquila*, and he was waiting with curiosity to see who it would be. The man who sat down between him and the side of the ship and whose ankle was immediately chained to the bench turned out to be the Turk who had first become a Christian and then a Jew, whose story he had heard not so long ago. His name was Mami, and he had worked as a water seller in Constantinople before being forcibly conscripted into the Sultan's fleet.

"I had a wife and five children," he recounted bitterly. "They shouldn't have taken me. The Sultan's edict clearly stated that only bachelors could be forced to row on his galleys."

"So then why did they take you?" Michele asked. The Turk grimaced.

"Exactly because of that! All the bachelors went into hiding or left the city. The whole city went crazy, the shops closed, you couldn't find anything to eat. We were afraid the Christian fleet was coming to bombard Constantinople, but when it came to signing on to the galleys to defend the city, nobody wanted to be the one to volunteer; they all thought someone else should do it. You have to understand that never in human memory had it happened that the Sultan had forcibly drafted people in the capital; it was the peasants who were supposed to serve," and to better show his contempt for those poor wretches, the man cleared his throat and spat, "but us city dwellers, never! But instead they went and issued this edict and the people went crazy. In short, the janissaries blocked all the streets into and out of my neighborhood and went house to house, and since they couldn't find any bachelors they started getting mad, and in the end they took every man they happened to find."

"And so you ended up on a galley," Michele commented.

"Yeah! Oh, they paid me, fair and square. The Sultan had given the order to pay thirty scudi a head, and they paid up front, in cash."

"What, are you kidding? Thirty scudi, are you that rich down there?" asked Michele, amazed. Mami nodded proudly.

"Our Sultan is the richest man in the world," he declared, "and he didn't want any injustice to be done so he ordered them to pay thirty scudi which, even for us, is a tidy sum. But all the same nobody wanted to go to sea, because galley life is hard, and so many die of the plague, and then we were all terrified of the Christians, who, it was said, had built the largest fleet the world had ever seen. And, in fact, that's just how it was, and they took us apart in the big battle. As for me, I was captured by a Genoese galley, my first master was Prince Andrea Doria," he added proudly.

"And your thirty scudi?" Big Prick piped up, curious.

"By the grace of God I had left them with my wife! I wanted to take them with me on the galley but she caressed me so nicely that she convinced me to leave them at home. She swore that I would find them intact when I returned, and that she would compensate me for those months of separation as only she knew how . . . you see, she thought I'd be coming back at the end of the summer! How naïve; I haven't been home for eighteen years now, who knows if she's alive or dead, and all my daughters will be married!"

The man fell silent and turned to look out at the sea, drying his eyes. His story put Michele into a bad mood too; until then he had always been convinced that one way or another his return home would not be delayed and that he would be seeing his wife again soon. But despite all that he too had been away from home over a year now, and he had no idea what had happened to Bianca in the meantime.

"And how is it, then, that you became a Christian? Tell us

about it, you nasty miscreant!" Big Prick said, to break the silence. Mami flashed a toothless smile.

"What are you going to do? I've always liked thinking about these things. I lived in Pera, it's full of Christians there, there's even a Franciscan monastery, and I liked talking with them, even if I never set foot in the church, to stay out of trouble. Sometimes, in the summer, when it got really hot out, I'd go to the tavern to drink wine. We all went; Turks, Christians, Jews, although we Muslims had to be careful not to get caught by the vigilantes. There I learned that anyone can be saved as long as they believe in God and do no harm to others, and that praying at the mosque is a good thing just like praying in a church or a synagogue. God listens to us anywhere. Your Christian saints are a good thing too; they can help you a lot. And we Turks also have our saints, and they are good too."

"You keep saying, 'we Turks,' but didn't you first become a Christian and then a Jew?" Big Prick broke in, annoyed.

"Well, at some point, you have to make a choice!" Mami shot back. "I thought about it and I saw that the Christians fight to impose their religion, and the Turks fight too for the same reason; only the Jews refrain from fighting and they don't want to impose their religion on anybody. That's why I believe their faith is better than the others. Then, the ones who convinced me, on the galley where I was rowing then, the *Marchesa* of Prince Doria, insisted that you mustn't eat pork, and you must be circumcised, but you can drink wine, and you don't worship on Fridays but on Saturdays, and I pretended that I believed it, but that's not what interests me. If I have to, I eat pork, and so no one knows I'm a Jew, and I've never had any trouble."

"But aren't you the one from the other day that didn't want to eat the bread with pig spleen?" Michele objected.

"So what? I don't like spleen, that's all," Mami replied, spreading his arms. Big Prick started to laugh.

"Oh, bravo! But tell the whole story; didn't you get yourself baptized at one point?" he teased him.

"No way! I didn't make it in time. But that's a good thing too. The water washes away your sins, that much is certain. Only then you commit other ones right away. I'll tell you, when I was Turkish I remember that we washed often, and that water washed away your sins too, just like the baptismal water. The Jews, on the other hand, don't believe in that, but they're mistaken."

Michele wasn't used to this kind of talk, and he listened to it with great emotion, as though he were discovering a whole new world, whose existence he had never even suspected. Once or twice he tried to refute the Jew's arguments and defend the superiority of the Christian faith, claiming for example that the Virgin Mary was a powerful protectress, but his adversary disarmed him, smiling meekly and confirming that yes, Mary too was good and could very well be prayed to. Big Prick was more combative, but his argument consisted in stubbornly repeating that once you've made a commitment you can't go back on your word.

"The Christians, when one of them gets baptized and then changes his mind, they burn him at the stake. There's got to be a reason!"

"But why do you say that? Would you like to see me burn?" Big Prick was getting mad.

"What do you mean? Obviously not! But they'd have every right to."

Mami told them that one winter, in the public baths in Genoa, some Christian convicts had denounced some *morisco* slaves, new Christians captured in Spain at the time of the great rebellion, claiming that although they were baptized they continued secretly to practice the religion of the Moors. They had seen that on a holiday, when for the special occasion some cured meat had been given out, they had refused to eat it, even though it was December and no Christian would have dared do that. This last charge had seemed so significant that the Inquisition had arrested them immediately.

"And did they burn them?" Michele asked.

"In the end, no," the Jew acknowledged. "They gave them the rope, but they didn't confess, and that year the prince was very short on rowers, so they sent them back to their galleys."

"Anyway," Michele cut it short, "in my opinion it's not right to change. You're born into a religion and you're supposed to die in it."

Big Prick nodded, it seemed obvious to him too.

"But how do you know which one's the best if you haven't tried them all?" Mami objected.

"What do you mean, which one's best! The one they taught you is the best, right?" Big Prick declared, and Michele agreed too, totally convinced.

"Let's put it this way," Mami said. "We three, here, are a Jew, a Christian, and a Turk, right? When we die, we'll see where we're going to end up; if it's the Christian paradise, Michele will put in a word for us so they'll take us too, if it's the paradise of the prophet you, Moor, will be the one to do it, and if it's the paradise of the Jews, I'll get you in, alright?"

"But that means we all have to die together," Michele observed.

"Why, how do you think we're going to die? Just wait till the plague gets on board, or we get into a battle, and you'll see how we'll all die together!"

"When the galley lays up in October," Michele said condescendingly, "I'm getting out of here. I certainly don't want to spend my whole life rowing." At the end of the day, he thought with pride, he was a free man and a Christian, and his two companions, even if when they were rowing it seemed like they were all in the same boat, were slaves and infidels.

"Oh, yeah?" the Jew asked, and looked at him with commiseration. Michele, stung where it hurts, turned to Big Prick as if to ask him for confirmation of what he had just said; but he noticed that the black man too was shaking his head.

"Do you really think they'll let you go?"

"Why not?" Michele asked, baffled.

"You mean you still don't know yet how the game works? I've seen it so many times I can't believe that not everybody knows."

"Me too," Mami agreed.

"What game?" Michele asked.

"It's really simple!" Big Prick explained. "You have your account in the scrivener's book, right? They've credited your pay there, and every time they give you an advance they debit it to you."

"And so?"

"And so you don't notice it, because every time you think you're only taking out a little money, but over the long run it ends up that they've given you more than your pay, not least because they debit you with the clothes on your back; and at the end of your term you discover that you owe them money, and how can you pay it? You can't, so you keep on rowing! I've seen a lot of them who thought they were only going to do one season and they've stayed on the benches until their old age, my dear!"

"But I've always spent next to nothing!" Michele objected.

"In that case," Mami intervened, "they'll invent some debit that you can't remember. Then just try to prove it isn't true. Do you know how to read maybe?"

When he heard that, Michele went glum. He knew that going back to Venice, to barter the hiding place of the ten thousand zecchini against the sentence that was weighing on his head, meant facing a big risk, but he had been ready to do that for a while now and he had never thought that even getting all the way back there might prove to be impossible. The words of his two friends gave him his first glimpse of his situation as it might be seen from the outside, and what he saw he didn't like.

At their next layover, which was Messina, from where Master Ettore wanted to leave again for a last run through the Levant before the autumn weather forced him back into port, Michele took advantage of an idle moment to go look for the scrivener and ask him for an update on his account, because when the *Aquila* laid up for the winter it was his intention to take his leave. He returned to his bench with an expression so dark that the other two understood immediately what had happened.

"Didn't go so well, eh?" the Jew said.

"He says I've already used up all of my pay, and now I owe him a lira and five soldi," Michele reported. He sat down at his place and held his head in his hands. "Leave me alone," he yelled at Big Prick when he put his arm around his shoulders. The other obeyed, launching a meaningful glance at Mami, who gestured in resignation. Michele sat there like that for a while, not talking and not crying; but he had never been someone capable of holding it all inside.

"I am not staying here," he said at a certain point, looking first at Mami and then at Big Prick.

"Shut up!" Big Prick said to him abruptly. "Is that any way to talk?" But the Jew, even though he too had held a finger up to his lips as a cautionary sign, had tears in his eyes.

"It's not something you want to say right now, and especially not so loudly," he whispered. "But if you're serious, we'll talk about it another time, and you too, Moor, will see that it's a matter of interest to you too."

21

After leaving Messina again, the *Aquila* sailed for several weeks toward the Levant. Nobody on board, except Pasquale, knew the commander's intentions, and they were all surprised on seeing that the galley, after sailing along the coasts of the Peloponnesus peninsula and the island of Crete, laying over only as long as necessary in the customary places to take on firewood and water, kept the helm pointed east.

"We're going to Cyprus," the most expert oarsmen concluded after a while. And Master Ettore's plan was exactly that. Ever since Sultan Selim had taken it from the Venetians, about twenty years ago, the island had not been nearly as hospitable to Christian pirates, but if you were careful to keep away from Famagusta, where a guard of galleys was based, it was still possible to nest in some out of the way inlet, buy the silence of the local farmers, and lay in wait to make a good strike. By now it was too late in the season to attack the ships carrying pilgrims on their way back from the great hajj to Mecca, but on the routes to and from Alexandria and Tripoli in Syria traffic was steady throughout the winter; and with a little luck there was some hope of intercepting one of the cargo ships exporting Cypriot cotton.

But the *Aquila*'s luck for that year had run out. The galley cruised for several weeks along the island's southern coast, mostly spending the days demasted in a cove not far from Pafos, and the nights going up and down the coast as far as

Limassol Point, but they never even saw a sail, except for some chunky salt boats from the Salines, which weren't even worth the effort to board. With every passing day the officers grew more nervous because despite all their precautions, it was always possible that someone would advise the authorities of their presence and the galleys in Famagusta would come looking for them. The aga of the nearest rural village was a Greek nobleman who had become a Turk after the conquest and had been given back in fief from the Sultan the lands over which he had previously been lord, and the Christian pirates had always maintained good relations with him. His men supplied the galley with wine, olive oil, and rice, at a nice profit to boot, and there was no fear of betrayal. But the farmers from the other villages, who were much better off under Turkish rule than they had been under the Venetians, were not as reliable.

The day came when Master Ettore summoned Pasquale, the pilot, and the captain of the harquebusiers and informed them that he didn't want to run any more risks. The next morning, instead of taking shelter along the coast, the galley was going to set sail for home.

"In short, the entire voyage has been a total loss," observed the captain, whose contract provided that his and his men's compensation consisted largely of a percentage of the booty.

"That's the risk one takes in this business," Master Ettore pointed out.

"But we could go ashore and capture some slaves," said the captain, who evidently had been thinking of just such a move for a long time.

Master Ettore didn't understand.

"Going back up as far as the Turkish coast is too dangerous. There aren't any safe havens up there. All it would take is for a galley from Antalya to head out to sea and we'd be in big trouble."

"Why go all the way up there?" said the captain. "Let's take them here!" Master Ettore stared at him. The captain hailed from the Papal States and his name was Annibale da Fermo. He always wore garish clothes—red and silver—and his manners were not very polite; Master Ettore had noted that he didn't know how to use a fork properly. But like most soldiers he was from the mountains, and such people couldn't be expected to have refined ways.

"But the people here are Christians," Master Ettore objected.

"They might be Christians but they're not Catholics, and in any case they're still subjects of the Turk, and it doesn't seem to me that they deserve any special treatment," exclaimed the captain, pulling on his mustache.

Pasquale patiently started explaining to him that even if they should capture some Christian slaves, selling them would be anything but easy and, on the contrary, they'd risk getting into trouble. But Master Ettore interrupted him.

"You know, Pasquale, there just might be something to Signor Annibale's idea. All the villages by now have some Turks living in them. And they tell me that there are also a lot of Jews. We'll let the Christians be, as long as they hand over the Turks and the Jews; if they're rich we'll make them pay ransom . . ."

"The Jews are always rich," the other man broke in.

"And if not, we'll make them slaves. It's not a bad idea, my dear captain."

Pasquale was about to say something but he held back. The plan seemed risky to him, and he would have preferred if Master Ettore had nixed the idea, but he knew from experience that it wasn't wise to contradict him in public. We'll see, he thought, glumly; and he promised himself that, no matter what, he would stay on board and not take part in the raid.

That night after heading out to sea as on all the other nights and cruising for several hours toward the Salines, the *Aquila* turned around and went back up the coast to a cape, behind which was a hilltop village called Saint George. According to information available to Master Ettore, the aga of the village was a Turk, and its inhabitants included two Jewish shopkeepers. In the deep of the night the galley moved in as close as possible to the beach; then the tender started shuttling soldiers. Before dawn the whole company was ashore, and the captain led them, their harquebuses on their shoulders, up the slope of the promontory to the village. The soldiers were wearing shirts over their armor to make sure the moonlight didn't reflect off the steel and give them away, and they marched along quietly trying not to let themselves be heard in the nocturnal silence. Master Ettore was with them, along with the Calabrian and a dozen armed sailors. Every now and again, a dog barked in the village and the soldiers came to a halt a hundred paces or so from the first houses; they sat down on the ground and waited. When dawn lit up the eastern sky, the captain said softly:

"What do you say, Master Ettore, is it time?"

Master Ettore nodded, and they both unsheathed their swords.

"Forward! To Saint George!" the captain shouted. They all ran forward and, yelling like savages through vegetable gardens and chicken coops, invaded the village. The terrorized inhabitants came running out of their houses, half-naked, and the soldiers pushed and clubbed them until they were all rounded up in the square. Where the houses remained shut, the soldiers battered down the door and erupted inside, rounding up the people and pushing them outside. The desperate screams of the women mingled with the curses of the soldiers chasing after fugitives among the houses. Annibale stationed two harquebusiers in front of the church, ordering them not to let anyone in, to make sure nobody got the bright idea of desecrating it, then he began interrogating the people—barefoot, screaming, and crying—that the soldiers had rounded up. Nobody, however, could understand his Italian.

"These bastards! Up until twenty years ago they all spoke Italian, it didn't take them long to forget it!" he exclaimed angrily. One of the sailors who spoke Greek had to double as his interpreter.

"Where is the aga's house?" asked the captain. The farmers pointed to the only two-story house on the square, with a tile roof topped by a crenellated turret. The front door to the house and the door to the barn were wide open.

"Where is the aga? Where has he gone?" Are there any horses in the barn?" the captain shouted, more and more agitated. The women fell to their knees and tried to kiss his robe, but Annibale kicked them away. With some difficulty, since they were Turks and not Greeks, the interpreter managed to find out that when the soldiers arrived the ruler of the village had jumped on his horse and galloped off.

"Search the house, and bring out everything of value!" the captain ordered. "These people here, tie their hands behind their backs and get them out of the way," he added, indicating the women. Then he went back to plant himself with his legs spread wide in front of the terrorized prisoners.

"The Turks! All the Turks step forward!" he shouted. The interpreter translated. Some in the crowd were indicated, isolated, and pushed forward.

"Here behind us! Tie them up!" the captain ordered. The soldiers took hold of the hapless victims; they were mostly men but also women and some girls who were struck speechless with fear.

"The Jews? Are there any Jews here?"

This time the interpreter had to have a long discussion: then he turned to the captain.

"They say there's only one family. They own the warehouse

down there," and he pointed to a low building in the distance. "They live there, but there's nobody here."

"Who went down there? Somebody must have gone down there, dammit!" Annibale cursed. Then, since none of his soldiers responded, he sent some of them to search.

"Hurry up! Maybe they haven't gone yet! Search everywhere, up in the attic, down in the basement, in the well!"

Just then, from one of the houses in the village, came the shrill scream of a woman. The people in the square began to protest and the soldiers had to hold them back with the points of their swords. The woman screamed again, then she suddenly stopped, as though someone had shut her mouth.

"Captain, keep your men under control," intimated Master Ettore, ashen. The captain turned to him energetically.

"What can I do? They're soldiers. Don't be afraid, they won't kill anyone," he said mockingly. Master Ettore squeezed his hand around the hilt of his sword, but he saw that the harquebusiers, all around the square, had their eyes trained on him. He realized that there wasn't a whole lot he could do.

"Fine," he said, resigned. "But let's be quick about it."

The woman's screams could be heard again. Some of the soldiers began heading off in that direction without permission.

"Stay here!" Annibale bellowed, seeing that the situation was getting out of hand. The men, reluctantly, obeyed.

Just then a soldier came running from the Jews' house.

"Captain! There's nobody there but there's a warehouse full of bales of cotton!"

The captain and Master Ettore started moving at the same time, their eyes flashing with greed.

"Let's go take a look!"

The townspeople stayed huddled together in the square, surrounded by the harquebusiers. Many of them were down on their knees, praying. The woman who had been screaming had stopped.

The two commanders came back, gleefully.

"There's enough there to fill the hold!" Master Ettore announced.

"We need people to load it. Let's have them do it," said the captain, indicating the farmers. Master Ettore shook his head.

"I don't trust them. I'd prefer that these people stayed here. I'd rather have the oarsmen come ashore."

A mountain of furniture, carpets, and pottery had accumulated outside the front door of the aga's house. His women, huddled against the wall of the church, their wrists tied behind their backs, were weeping helplessly. By now, the sun was high in the sky, and it was hot. The soldiers allowed the people to sit on the ground. A woman whose face was streaked with blood because they had ripped off her earrings, begged for some water. Master Ettore sent some sailors to get a bucket from the well, and he had it passed around to the crowd. Meanwhile, the Calabrian had run down to the beach; he came back about an hour later, with about fifty oarsmen, among whom were Michele, Mami, and Big Prick.

"But what's going on here?" Michele exclaimed, horrified, on seeing the people huddled on the ground, the soldiers with their harquebuses trained on them, the houses with their doors broken in and their furniture thrown out the windows.

"What were you expecting?" Mami answered. "When pirates go ashore it's certainly no party."

"Let's get to work, people!" the Calabrian shouted, pushing the oarsmen toward the warehouse. "Down there. Load up the cotton and take it to the galley. Move!"

At that precise moment, an arrow whistled through the air, and bounced off the captain's breastplate.

"Dammit!" Annibale yelled, jumping back. More arrows whistled, sticking in the ground.

"It must be the farmers," Master Ettore said, trying to understand where the arrows were coming from. "But where are they?"

"I don't know where they are, but I'm going to take care of them right now!" the captain exclaimed. "To me! Drum, sound muster!"

The drummer, a crippled boy, started beating on his drum, and the soldiers who had dispersed to plunder the houses came running back into the square and lined up in ranks, some with their pockets bulging with booty, others buttoning up their pants.

"There's somebody down there!" said Annibale, who had run out to the houses on the edge of the village, where the dirt road met the open countryside, and now he was running back breathlessly, pulling his helmet down on his head. "That's where they're shooting from, now let's go get them."

"First, have them take the slaves down to the beach!" Master Ettore exclaimed. A corporal and a platoon of soldiers got the men and women up on their feet, with their hands tied behind their backs, and with the points of their swords and the butts of their harquebuses they pushed them onto the path that led down to the harbor. Meanwhile, the first oarsmen were coming out of the warehouse with the bales of cotton on their shoulders. But as soon as they realized there were arrows flying, they all threw themselves on the ground without waiting for orders.

"On your feet, you cowards!" the Calabrian yelled at them, purple with rage; but his voice got strangled in his throat, because an arrow had shot right through his neck, spurting blood. The Calabrian staggered for a minute, waving his arms in the air, then collapsed in the dirt.

The captain, cursing horrendously, led the soldiers out of the village. A group of men on horseback, who had pushed to the edge of the village and shot their arrows, rode off at a gallop, raising a cloud of dust. When they were out of range of the harquebuses, they stopped to yell something and wave their scimitars in defiance. A host of other cavalrymen appeared in the distance and were approaching at great speed, their tall pikes waving back and forth in the air.

"Damn, the Turks are coming!" Annibale shouted.

"The aga must have gone to inform them," Master Ettore remarked.

The two looked each other in the eye.

"I'd say we'd better get out of here," said the captain.

"And leave behind the cotton?" Master Ettore objected. "Can't you hold them off for a while?"

Annibale hesitated, unable to choose between greed and prudence.

"I don't have any pikemen. Harquebusiers can't hold off cavalry."

"How about if you take cover in the houses?"

"Let's try it!" the captain resigned himself. In the distance the ranks of the cavalry continued to grow. The soldiers were visibly agitated.

"Now then, soldiers! We are all experienced fighters and men of honor! Let's show these dogs what we're made of!" the captain yelled.

"You others, get going, take the cotton to the galley," Master Ettore ordered, walking over to the oarsmen and shaking his sword. The men pulled themselves up out of the dirt and shouldered their bales of cotton. The harquebusiers positioned behind the vegetable garden fence had started to fire, and the air was vibrating from the detonations.

There were only a few soldiers left in the square, keeping an eye on the people huddled on the ground, and they were looking around nervously.

"Listen!" Master Ettore had the interpreter say. "We are all Christians, we will do no harm to Christians! Stay there and don't get in our way, and very shortly we'll be gone."

Just then a barrage from the harquebuses sprayed chaotically through the air, followed by desperate cries, and some unarmed soldiers rushed into the square.

"They're here! Save yourself if you can!"

At the sound of those words the few remaining harquebusiers took off, and the people, no longer under surveillance, started screaming and running around in all directions. As soon as they saw what was happening, the oarsmen who were carrying the cotton bales, started running blindly too, throwing off their loads. Michele, Mami, and Big Prick went into a house whose door had been broken down. The inside had been devastated. The three of them scrambled up the stairs to the second floor. There, in an indescribable disorder, were the remains of a bed, the mattress and pillows cut open, and curled up in a corner of the room, with her eyes wide open in fright, was a naked girl, with blood dripping between her legs.

"Be quiet, for the love of God," they said to her breathlessly; but the girl seemed not even to have noticed them. She was trembling and mumbling something, staring into the void. The three of them squatted down in the opposite corner, trying not to look at her. They stayed there like that for a while, as the screaming and shouting gradually moved into the distance, until silence reigned in the square again, broken only by gunfire in the distance.

"It's over," Big Prick said, getting to his feet.

They covered the girl's shoulders with a sheet, and tried to talk to her, but she kept on murmuring to herself, without responding. While they were still hovering around her, from outside they started hearing the sound of hurrying footsteps again, mingled with neighing and confused yelling, which got louder and louder.

"Let's look out the window!" Michele suggested.

They looked out. A covey of Turks, on horseback, was moving through the square, dragging behind them a half dozen soldiers tied by their wrists to their saddles. Among them they recognized Captain Annibale, without his helmet, his face covered with blood and consternation. On the edge of the square was a gathering of farmers yelling scornfully in the direction of the soldiers; some of them picked up stones from the ground and threw them. The Turks didn't interfere. When they got to the front of the church, one of them who seemed to be in command, and who had two severed heads hanging from his saddlebow, dismounted and dried the sweat that was streaming down from his turban. The farmers pushed and shoved another dozen men in front of him, shoeless and bleeding, and the three in the window recognized some captured sailors and oarsmen. They were interrogated in Turkish; the ones who were Muslim slaves responded with joy in the same language, and the Turks let them up immediately, gave them something to drink, and began clumsily cleaning them off, while the others remained kneeling in the dirt.

Mami and Big Prick looked at each other in celebration.

"Friend, would you ever have believed it?" Mami said.

"Never in my life, I thought I was going to die chained to an oar!" the black man replied, weeping. "I guess it wasn't written after all." Then he remembered Michele, who was hiding in the corner at the other end of the room, pale as a cadaver.

"And him?" he said.

"Hopeless! They'll put him back on the oars."

"It's not fair! We have to hide him," Big Prick said. The Jew hesitated. "Come on! He's a good kid. Let's give him a chance," the black man said.

"All right," the other agreed, nervously. "But not here," he added, pointing to the girl. "If they find him with her, they'll skin him alive."

Cautiously, they went down to the ground floor. Luckily, nobody had come back in yet. The house had two rooms, one facing the square, and the other with a little door to the back-yard, still closed and latched. They opened it and saw that it led to a kind of outbuilding that in the past may have served as a stable. Now, however, it was empty, full of thorns and nettles, and the roof was half caved in.

"In here!" Mami decided. They shoved Michele inside, told him not to go anywhere, and locked the door.

"Now let's go and let them see us," the black man said. "May Allah protect us!"

22.

Michele stayed hidden in the stable for three days, buried under brambles and spiders, and sweltering in the suffocating heat. The villagers were in the throes of desperation; even though the Christians had carried off only the Turkish residents, all their houses had been devastated and looted, and several women had been raped. The spahi from the surrounding area, who had rushed to their aid to fight the pirates, had divided up the prisoners and returned happily to their estates; the Jewish merchants, back from the woods where they had managed to escape the attack, had the cotton brought back into the warehouse, but the aga, who had lost all of his women, had gone mad with grief, and the rest of the inhabitants were shut inside their houses, frightened and bewildered. Before leaving, the Turks ordered the Orthodox priest, who had locked himself in the basement during the melee, to put up and take care of the Muslim oarsmen who had been freed. Mami and Big Prick were also welcomed warmly when they went into the square and recounted their story in Turkish, and although the former was a Jew and the latter a black man, they were treated the same as all the others. On the second day, a blacksmith arrived from a nearby village and sawed off the rings they wore on their ankles, and the ex-slaves exchanged their red caps and cassocks with used clothing provided by the farmers.

In the house of the girl who'd been raped, there was a constant coming and going of women, and their plaintive cries could be heard day and night. Luckily nobody went to look around in the stable, but Mami and Big Prick didn't know what to do to get food or at least drink to Michele.

"He'll die in this heat," predicted the black man, anxiously.

In the end they decided to take the risk of telling the priest the whole story. The good man was frightened out of his wits, and declared that he didn't want to have anything to do with it, but the two of them insisted until he gave them a loaf of bread and a jug of milk, and on the second night, on the pretext of going outside to get some fresh air, they went all the way to the hideout. Michele was half dead from thirst, and when they passed him the milk through the collapsed roof, he chugged it down avidly.

"Try to get me out of here," he said afterwards, in a hoarse voice. "I don't know how much longer I can hold out."

That night, in a corner of the church that had been filled with straw for the oarsmen to sleep on, the two friends talked about what they should do.

"Let's reason it through," Mami said. "He's a Venetian, there's no reason for them to do anything to him."

"You're wrong," Big Prick disagreed. "First and foremost he's a Christian galleyman, with an iron on his foot. If they capture him they'll realize immediately that he was on the *Aquila*, and they'll sell him as a slave."

"Well then, the first thing to do is get rid of the iron. And then get him out of here, to the city, where nobody will care about him."

The next day the priest went to tell the aga that by now all those men had been captured and that for the love of God he should order them to get out of his house because they were ruining him. The aga spat in contempt, but came over to the church anyway to see for himself. He was an elderly man, fat, with thin white hair and a pained expression on his face that hadn't changed since the day of the tragedy.

"All right now, Muslims!" he said to the galleymen who had stood up in respect when he entered. "Now you are free men, what do you want to do?"

The men, feeling embarrassed, didn't know what to say. Most of them had been slaves to Christians for so long they didn't have place to go anymore. The aga explained that on Cyprus, after the huge number of casualties suffered during the war, there was work for everybody, and that the Sultan granted favors to those Muslims who wished to settle on the island. If instead some of them preferred to leave, they were free to look for passage and go with God's blessing. In any case, his advice was to go to the city, Nicosia, to register with the authorities, and see what opportunities fate might have in store for them.

After a brief discussion, the men decided that's what they would do. The aga promised he would accompany them part of the way and that he would make them a donation of ten aspers apiece, to pay their expenses during the journey; upon which everyone fell to their knees, kissing his hands and the hem of his garment.

"You will leave tomorrow; or rather, no, the day after. Tomorrow you'll stay here at the expense of this Christian!" the aga ordered, and everyone laughed, except for the priest, who was listening from the sacristy and holding his head in his hands.

"What do we do now?" Big Prick asked Mami.

"We've got to find a way to leave here on our own. If we go with them we sure can't set Michele free. I know! Why didn't I think of this before? You can tell I haven't been a Jew long enough. What does a Jew do in a situation like this?"

The black man looked at him quizzically.

"He asks for help from the local Jews! It doesn't matter how stingy they might be, Jews always help each other."

That very day Mami went to the Jewish merchants, the owners of the warehouse, to tell them his story. The merchants, two brothers, listened to him impassively. They'd seen all kinds of people in their lives, but they'd never met a Jew like him. Luckily, they weren't theologians either, so they didn't think of examining him too much about his faith; but it was clear they didn't want any trouble.

"What do you want from us?"

"A letter of recommendation, dear sirs, to enable us to get to Nicosia and from there find passage to the mainland."

"We don't know you," said the older of the brothers. "If that's really what you want, we'll prepare the letter for you, but we'll say that we can't vouch for you."

"All I need is to be able to tell the aga that I'm leaving for Nicosia with a letter from you, and so I will be leaving tonight, myself and my two companions, rather than wait for the others."

Just then a woman came carrying three glasses of raki on a tray. The glasses were tiny. The two brothers each took one, and pointed to the third for Mami.

"That it not be the last," the guest said, and they all drank.

"And why is it that you want to leave without waiting for the others? And who are these companions? Are they Jews too?"

On learning that they were a black Muslim and an Italian Christian, their faces clouded over even more.

"No, brother, something's not right here. You tell us the truth now, otherwise things are not going to go well," the older one said, crisply.

Realizing he was trapped, Mami told them everything. The two merchants blanched, and broke out in a sweat.

"Oh, this is perfect! A fugitive infidel hidden here in the village! Don't you know you could end up on the pole?"

"That's the way things are by now, there's nothing to be done about it. But if you help me, tomorrow we'll be long gone."

"And why should we help you?" the younger brother interjected aggressively.

"For charity," Mami said.

Now the two merchants really lost their tempers.

"No, brother, now you get out of here, in a hurry, and don't
ever show your face around here again. We know nothing and
we have heard nothing."

With the force of desperation, Mami shot back:

"If I leave here and I try to get the Christian out of the village without your help, it is very likely that we'll be discovered.
And if they catch us, they'll see that I am a Jew, and they'll never
believe that you didn't help me. I'll tell them. The two brothers? I'll say; the merchants? Certainly they helped me, they
knew everything, who else could I turn to? That's what I'll say."

The two looked at each other.

"But if we help you, you'll leave tonight?"

"Yes, your eminence," Mami confirmed.

"So what do you need?"

"Sir, tonight we can get our friend out of his hiding place;
that won't be hard, the wall is made of mud and the roof is half
caved in. The problem is the iron ring; we can't let ourselves
be seen on the road to Nicosia as long as he has that ring
around his ankle. You should call for the blacksmith to come,
make him swear to secrecy, and saw off the ring."

"And then?"

"And then, write a letter to your partners in Nicosia, saying
that the Jew Mami and his two companions have been freed
from slavery and that you are recommending them so they can
find passage on a ship"

The merchant looked at him, tightening his lips.

"Go outside. My brother and I have to talk."

Mami left the room and the woman who had served the raki
had him sit on a bench. But he didn't have to wait long; the
merchants called him back in after just a few minutes.

"Fine," they told him. "We'll do everything you've asked of us, for the love of God. But then make sure we never see you again."

Mami fell to his knees and kissed both their hands.

"We'll come as soon as it's dark," he promised.

That night Michele, more dead than alive, was pulled out of the stable and carried to the warehouse. The merchants had arranged for some wine to be there along with some lentil soup and some halva; when they found out he hadn't eaten for three days, they were afraid he wouldn't be strong enough to leave right away, and they were in a hurry to be rid of him. The blacksmith came, after having sworn to secrecy, and sawed off the ring, after which the three friends set off. Michele, dressed in a used shirt and a wool fisherman's cap, walked with a limp and had so much trouble staying on his feet that they had to give him a cane. After leaving the village they walked for a little over an hour, then they had to stop to sleep on the side of the road because Michele couldn't go on. Besides the letter, the merchants had given them a knapsack with something to eat a wineskin, and a handful of aspers to make sure they made it to Nicosia, where nobody would notice if there was one man too many among the slaves freed from the Christian galley.

For the next few days the three friends walked at a good pace, stopping only to sleep in the hottest hours of the afternoon, buying food in the roadside villages, and journeying on during the night; the famous letter of recommendation was a good enough document to keep them out of trouble if they ran into a guard post but Mami and Big Prick were mostly afraid that the other galleymen, leaving the village fresh and rested, could catch up with them, in which case Michele risked being recognized and reported.

For six days they marched along in the middle of dry, rugged mountains; in many places the sparse vegetation was reduced to burnt tree stubs and the barren land was covered with white ashes from the fires ignited by the summer heat. Then, finally, they started down into the plain of Nicosia and, as they neared the city, the landscape became more civilized, with cotton fields and orange groves. On the evening of the seventh day, they entered the city; the letter that told of their liberation from slavery and directed them to the leader of the Jewish community was delivered to the soldiers at the guard station, together with the last remaining aspers in the knapsack, and thanks to this precaution it was judged sufficient to let them enter the city.

It was the hour of the evening prayer, and the muezzins were calling the faithful from all the minarets. Michele had never heard such a thing, and he was struck by it, even more so on seeing the Turks on the street interrupt whatever they were doing, roll out a prayer rug, if they had one, and get down on their hands and knees, while the Greeks and Jews, respectfully making their way around them, went on about their business. Big Prick found himself a corner that wasn't too filthy and he too got down on his knees, while Mami and Michele waited nearby.

"I never did it at home!" the black man laughingly confessed when the prayer was finished. "But right now thanking God seems like the thing to do!"

"And is this what you do every evening?" Michele asked.

"Every evening? Five times a day, you mean!" Big Prick responded proudly.

Michele whistled.

"You have to have a lot of time on your hands!"

Luckily the black man did not get offended.

"To each his own," he said philosophically.

While they were looking for the home of Rabbi Abram Abravanel, leader of the Jewish community, they saw that Nicosia, though it was full of people, shops, and warehouses, churches and mosques, still showed a lot of signs from the war of twenty years ago, of the shelling and the terrible plundering, in which the entire Christian population had been killed or reduced to slavery. In the square in front of the Catholic cathedral, which the Ottoman authorities had transformed into a mosque, the noble palaces built in the Venetian style were still dilapidated ruins and uninhabited, their courtyards full of rubble and weeds, the walls charred from the fire. The three stopped to stare, their mouths agape.

"War!" Mami commented.

Just then a man popped out of an alleyway and stopped to look with them. He was dressed like a farmer, and he was a little tipsy. He made a gesture with his arm and said something in Greek. When he saw that they hadn't understood he repeated it in Turkish.

"He asks if we saw what happened," Mami translated for Michele. When he heard Italian spoken the man jumped.

"Are you Italian?" he said to Michele, with a hostile tone.

Michele nodded, on the defensive.

"Venetian," he said. The man spat in contempt.

"Can't you see what happened to the Venetians?" he exclaimed, in broken Italian, indicating with a wide sweep of his arm the ruined facades of the buildings. "They treated the farmers like slaves. Truly, like slaves," he repeated. "They weren't masters, they were devils. They made them work like animals. And look what happened to them; the Turks came, and they killed them all," he concluded, satisfied.

"Come on, let's go," Mami said; and he dragged the others away with him.

"All of them! Not a single one got away!" the drunk shouted behind them.

"You can see that it's not a good idea for you to stay here. Cyprus is no place for a Venetian."

"You're right," Michele acknowledged dryly.

During the journey the three of them had talked a lot about their future. Mami wanted to go back to Constantinople, and with the help of his coreligionists he would succeed in doing that, without a doubt, but deep in his heart he was afraid of what he would find; he'd been away for eighteen years and who knew what had happened, in the meantime, to his wife and daughters. But above all, if he found them again, he'd never be able to confess to his having become a Jew; the Muslims, like the Christians, punished apostasy with death.

"So I'll go back to being a Turk. I've been thinking about it for a while. I miss going to the mosque," the bizarre man said.

Big Prick didn't have anywhere to go back to; in Tunisia he'd been a slave, now he was a free man.

"I'll stay here. If it's true that there's work for everyone, I'll find something and settle down," he declared with a smile.

As for Michele, after their unexpected liberation from the galley, he'd excogitated a new plan. He knew that there was a permanent bailo in Constantinople, sent by Venice to represent the government of the Serene Republic and protect the interests of the Venetian merchants. If he went to see the bailo he could tell him the story of the *Loredana* and the ten thousand zecchini without running the risk of entering Venetian territory, where he could be arrested at any moment. If that money might really be the price of his freedom, it would be better to discover it there, where the Venetian authorities couldn't do anything to him. He couldn't tell the truth to his two friends, but he pretended to be seduced by the arguments made by Mami, who wanted to convince him to come with him to Constantinople, instead of staying in Cyprus with Big Prick.

"Here, I might find work, but the city has the whole world in it," he said with dreamy eyes. "There, you never know what kind of opportunities will come your way."

They were still talking when they came to Rabbi Abram's

house. It was an elegant building, which testified to the importance of its owner.

"The Jews are well off here," Michele couldn't help but observe, with a touch of acrimony. Mami looked at him, surprised.

"It's thanks to these Jews that you'll be able to find work or passage on a ship. I'd say it's lucky for you too that they're well off here." Michele realized that he'd said something wrong, but he'd been raised his whole life to feel hatred and contempt for the Jews, and it wasn't easy for him to get over it. Sure, Mami was a Jew too, at least for the moment, but he was different. The whole thing was too complicated. Michele shrugged his shoulders, embarrassed.

Rabbi Abram made the three wait for a long time; he was tied up in a meeting with the secretary of the beylerbey, the Turkish governor of Cyprus, and meetings of that kind, from which the secretary usually left with his purse heavier than before, were an essential part of the rabbi's political work. When he finally received them, he seemed tired but satisfied, and they could tell he was anxious to get rid of their annoying presence quickly; nonetheless he listened without showing signs of impatience. Mami, who knew how the world works, cut their story as short as possible and showed him the letter. The rabbi read through it quickly.

"Very well!" he said cheerily. "What can I do for you?"

"Eminence," Mami said, "the Christian and I would like to get on a ship for Constantinople. Help us and God will reward you. The Moor, on the other hand, would like to find work here."

The rabbi looked at him attentively.

"A Jew, a Muslim, and a Christian," he said pensively. "It really does seem like someone wants to put me to the test! There's a great little novella—" but he stopped himself short. "What could the three of you know about that? But tell me something more about yourself, Jew. Where are you from?"

Mami was in a fix. He had wondered for a long time if it was better, when dealing with other Jews, to tell the true story of his conversion or pretend to be a Jew from birth, and he had deduced that this second strategy was the better one. He had also made up a fictitious story in which his parents, Jews from Constantinople, had died when he was a baby, and he had been raised by their neighbors so he didn't remember anything about his family or where they had come from. The rabbi listened to the end and then, without warning, spoke to him not in Turkish, but in a language that Mami didn't know. Mami, utterly lost, sat there with a stupid smile on his face.

"If you're a Jew from Constantinople, why don't you speak Ladino?" the rabbi asked severely, returning to Turkish. Michele, who hadn't understood a word of the whole conversation, looked first at Mami, then at the rabbi, then at Big Prick, who did speak Turkish and who had started to sweat.

Mami tried to justify himself.

"Eminence, I know that my family did not come from Spain, they came from the East, I don't know where, maybe even from Baghdad, we never spoke your Ladino!"

The rabbi kept quiet for a while, observing them. He'd had the impression right from the start that he was dealing with three con men, and now he was sure of it. I should have them thrown out on the street and order them to never come back, he thought. But he realized that he didn't feel like doing that. Wasn't it less trouble, after all, to help them out? They were asking for so little, and even that would be a good deed pleasing to God. And maybe, who knows, God had sent them on purpose, those three, to test his goodwill. It really did remind him of the story by Boccaccio that the rabbi had read many years ago, in a Castilian translation, and had never forgotten. A rabbi, and the three religions of the Book . . .

"Say no more," he decided abruptly. "I don't want to know anything else. I will help you, for the love of God. You, Moor," he said, "you want to work? My warehouses always need people who know how to work hard. I'll give you a note for my administrator. And you two want to go to Constantinople? Fine, I'll give you a hand. A galleon is supposed to arrive next month from down there, to take on a load of cotton. If I ask him, the owner will take you on board, but you'll have to work, maybe even row, if necessary, understand?"

The three fell to their knees and kissed his hands.

"Fine, that's enough," the rabbi sighed. "Now go downstairs, they'll give you something to eat and a place to sleep."

Later, as they were eating a soup of rice and fava beans, the three had tears in their eyes.

"Our paths are separating," Mami said.

"You know?" Big Prick said, "the Koran says that Christians and Jews who do good deeds will be saved. Up to now, I never understood what that meant, it didn't seem possible. But now I understand," he concluded, his eyes shining.

"I never heard anyone say that," Michele admitted. "But now I believe it too," he added; and he blew his nose on his shirtsleeve, to hide his emotion.

23

Bianca had never set foot in a palace as big as the Bernardos', and in the first few weeks she often got lost in it. On the first floor lived Sir Alvise with his wife and their servants, and it seldom happened that she was sent there; Sir Lorenzo and Lady Clarice occupied the whole second floor, but in addition to the main stairway they had a smaller independent one that went down to the garden, and another, on the opposite side of the house, to reach the atrium and the peristyle that opened on to the embarcadero on the Grand Canal. Then there were the narrow stairs that went up to the granary and down to the kitchen, to the storage areas in the back and the damp basement beneath the level of the canal, where a not very bright scullery maid assured Bianca that in days gone by the masters punished the servants by shutting them inside—but it wasn't true and Lady Clarice laughed when Bianca told her about it.

At first, Bianca was surprised by just how many stairs there were to be climbed up and down continuously. For a while her ankles would get sore, and one day she vowed to count all the stairs she had to do; but when she got to three hundred fifty-six she lost count and gave up. In the brief interview she'd had with the mistress when she was hired, while the broker negotiated on her behalf the contract terms and her salary, Bianca had been struck by Lady Clarice's sharp eye, by the precision and economy with which she chose her words, and also by the good cheer that shone in her eyes betimes, despite the fatigue of the pregnancy that was all too easy to see in her wearyness-laden features. I'm going to like it here, she told herself with confidence; and she wasn't mistaken.

Naturally, the work was hard. Bianca slept in a corner of the spouses' bedroom, within earshot of the large brocade-curtained bed that dominated at the center of the room; the master's manservant slept instead on a mattress in the antechamber, just outside the door. Bianca got up before dawn and if it was cold she went to light the fire in the fireplace; usually there were embers still burning from the night before, because Sir Lorenzo liked to stay up late reading in front of the fire, but sometimes the embers had gone out and she had to busy herself in the dark with tinder and flint for what seemed like forever, her hands numb with cold. But Bianca soon learned to go down to the kitchen with the copper hand warmer and ask for some live embers from the cook, who at that hour was already working at full rhythm, and then hurry back up the stairs before they went out.

As soon as there was a little light she and the other servant girls swept and cleaned the rooms, keeping an ear turned toward the bedroom so they could hear if the mistress was awake; Sir Lorenzo usually got up very early too, and vanished into his rooms, where he had breakfast before getting down to work with his secretary. But now that she was pregnant, the doctor had ordered Lady Clarice to stay in bed as much as possible. When her mistress called her, tired of being alone in the dark, Bianca went in, opened the bed curtains and the drapes, and the window just a crack, even though the doctors had advised Lady Clarice not to get too much fresh air; she helped the mistress get into her slippers and dressing gown, then she went down to the kitchen and came back up with breakfast: a glass of Cypriot wine and some biscuits or sweetmeats. While Lady Clarice ate she sometimes kept Bianca with her to chat, then she went back to bed and left her free in turn to go down to the kitchen and eat a bowl of soup.

On Sundays, when she had to go to Mass, or on days when visitors were expected, Lady Clarice combed her hair, put on her jewelry, and got dressed. Bianca was always there to learn, but at first two more experienced servant girls did almost all the work, which on the most solemn occasions took a few hours. The fashion of the moment called for the most complicated hairdos, with strings of pearls running through her hair, and everyone complained about it, including Lady Clarice, but there was nothing anyone could do. Otherwise the mistress stayed in her dressing gown all day, in bed, or in an armchair in front of the fire; called for, in turn, the cook, the governess, and the wet nurse; talked about shopping and expenses, sugar, barley, and wine, about household items and linens; then she had her baby girl come in, Francesca, who was just barely starting to walk, and amused herself playing with her.

Bianca and the other servant girls, five in all, finished the cleaning and did the washing, which soon came to be entrusted almost entirely to Bianca's direction, given her experience. It was the first time she found herself giving orders to someone, and at first it didn't feel natural; but she got used to it, and none of the other servant girls protested because Lady Clarice didn't tolerate fighting or spats between her people, and anyone who might be inclined to instigate arguments or divisiveness knew they risked being fired. The master and mistress had lunch together, but Sir Lorenzo's manservants waited at table, while the women ate in the kitchen; it was their turn then to clear the table and wash the dishes, although most of that work was shouldered by the scullery maid.

In the afternoons, if no visitors were expected, Lady Clarice played a bit of music on the harpsichord, which Sir Lorenzo listened to with pleasure; then they walked together in the garden, read, or played chess. This last was an obsession of Lady Clarice's, and Sir Lorenzo was always reluctant to take part in it because he always won, and the consequences on his wife's mood were unpredictable; but Lady Clarice stubbornly insisted on playing, announcing at the beginning of every game that maybe this was her moment and she was finally going to win. Sir Lorenzo often told himself that he should try to lose, at least once; but it was too much for him, he just couldn't do it.

If instead, as happened quite often, her husband was away on business, Lady Clarice liked to call all the women together and, while they sewed and mended, have them tell her the gossip they heard in the stores, the news from the market, the thousand little household events. She laughed heartily with them on hearing their accounts of a sleazy storekeeper who came on to them every time, or of a porter who made some salacious remark, and none of the servant girls could recall a time when something that came out during those conversations was used against them; but all in all it didn't take Bianca long to realize that, in the end, even though she lived her life shut inside her rooms Lady Clarice always found out everything, and when she gave an order it was always the right order.

It didn't take her long to know everything about Bianca as well. When she hired her, it had been enough for her to know that she was looking for work because her husband had signed on as a galleyman; the reassurances of Signor Nicolo', who knew her family and had arranged her marriage, were all she needed. Later on, without letting on and never pushing her, Lady Clarice had sometimes dropped a hint about that faraway husband, about his misfortune of having to earn a living by doing such a hard job, and also about the fact that in any event, when winter comes the galleys lay up and usually the oarsmen come back home. She'd noticed right way that Bianca was embarrassed, and didn't willingly respond, even less so when there were other women present; and by talking to the other servant girls in the house she had verified that the new girl had not confided in anyone. Her curiosity piqued, the young mistress waited until she was alone one evening with Bianca, who was undressing her to put her to bed; Sir Lorenzo was away, in Padua, on certain family business.

"So then, Bianca!" she said to her, while the younger woman was removing her makeup with a cotton flock. "Tell me a little about yourself, when did you get married?"

"It was just a year ago, at Easter," Bianca replied, after thinking a minute.

"And how long have you been alone now?"

"Poor me! We were together for less than three months."

"But tell me, when you were married was your husband already a galleyman?"

"Oh, no!" Bianca said, impulsively. "No, he worked with his father. They were masons."

"And so why did he go to sea?" Clarice asked immediately. Bianca, who was taking the barrettes out of her hair, and had two of them in her mouth, took advantage of her situation to delay her answer; she made a hemming sound to indicate that she couldn't open her mouth. But when she put the barrettes away and began combing the mistress's long blonde hair, Clarice repeated the question, politely, but firmly. When Bianca didn't answer, the mistress turned around and saw that her mouth was pressed shut and her face contracted in fear.

"Look, you can talk about it with me," she said tenderly. "Relax, Bianca, whatever it is you don't have to worry. And I want to know everything about my women."

Bianca hesitated.

"Come on now, sit down here and tell me everything," Lady Clarice insisted, making her curl up at her feet and stroking her hair. Bianca, embarrassed and reassured at the same time, started into her account. She expected the mistress to get cross on hearing about the misdeeds of old Matteo and about Michele's becoming a fugitive from justice; but then she realized that, from a moral point of view, the whole incident didn't faze her at all.

"And you say they've sentenced him to banishment! We'll have to see if it's possible to have the sentence commuted," Clarice pondered. It had never crossed Bianca's mind that such a thing could be done. The mistress saw her astonishment and burst out laughing.

"You don't think that can be done? It happens every day, believe me!"

Seeing her laugh, Bianca smiled.

"But I don't even know where to begin," she confessed. Clarice ruffled her hair with her fingers.

"What do you have to do with it? If it's to be done, it will be up to your mistress to take care of it. But help me understand; you said he ran away and you haven't seen him since then, how do you know he went to sea? Or was that a lie?"

"Oh, no!" Bianca said, blushing; and she told her about the letter.

"And where is this letter?" Lady Clarice asked, curious.

Bianca explained that it was in the trunk where she kept her things.

"Go get it, I want to read it," the mistress ordered. Bianca obeyed, and came back an instant later, having found the paper among her blouses and shoes. Clarice took it, unfolded it, and read it quickly under her breath.

"But here," she noted immediately, looking up, "it says he plans to come home in November, when the galley comes back to lay up, and he's talking about last November. It's been almost a year."

Mortified, Bianca shrugged.

"I don't know anything, Signora. I've never heard from him again. Maybe . . ." she interrupted herself. Clarice urged her to continue.

"Maybe? What were you going to say?"

Embarrassed, Bianca was wringing her apron with her hands. "They told me that you can find out if the galley has returned, and who disembarked, but I didn't know how to go about it. Maybe her ladyship could help me?"

Clarice thought for a minute.

"Why not? Let's start from there."

Some time passed without the mistress raising the subject again; then one morning, she called for Bianca while she was meeting with her administrator. Clarice owned a number of houses that she rented out, and she lent money at interest. During the negotiation of her marriage contract, she had asked that half of the assets in her dowry should remain in her hands, rather than entrusting the management of all of it to her husband, as was usually done, and her indulgent father had agreed to insist on that condition. Sir Alvise and Sir Lorenzo had argued against it at length but they finally gave in, provided that Clarice accepted the assistance of an administrator chosen by her father-in-law. Sir Agostino the notary was a tall and imposing man, with a red face and elegantly dressed; it was evident that his engagements earned him a handsome compensation.

"Here is Bianca," Clarice said cheerily. The notary looked with pleasure at the gracious young woman, "Now tell this gentleman your story and let him see the letter."

Sir Agostino already knew everything, but Clarice was amused by the simplicity with which Bianca told her story, and, she wanted to see if in telling it to a stranger she might change something. The notary listened attentively.

"So, the *Loredana*, rigged in July of last year, bound for Candia, and due to return in November," he summarized. "Very well, Signora, we'll check into it and I'll let you know right away. And don't you worry," he said to Bianca with a big smile, "if Lady Clarice takes someone to heart, everything always works out well."

A few days later the notary returned and related to Clarice what he had discovered. The *Loredana* had indeed returned to unrig toward the end of December; for some reason it had gotten a late start on the return voyage from Crete, and unfavorable winds had kept it laid over in Zante and Cephalonia before it could manage to get back into the Adriatic. The oarsmen had all been dismissed, but Michele, son of the mason Matteo, was no longer aboard; in the log it was written that he had been paid all of his credits in Candia and that he had not been seen again; in sum, he had deserted.

"But that wouldn't amount to anything, on the contrary, it's better that way, otherwise sooner or later they would have arrested him," the notary continued. "I, however, Signora, took it upon myself to check the registry of sentences." Clarice approved; this man, she knew well, kept for his own pockets a percentage of her profits that was a bit too high, but he served her well. Sir Agostino told her that Matteo had been sentenced by the Ten to having his tongue cut out for sedition and treason, and had died resisting arrest; and that Michele had tried to help him escape, and had been later sentenced to banishment *in abstentia*, he too on the charges of sedition and treason.

Lady Clarice was indignant.

"That's it, the extent of his sedition and treason is that he tried to keep the police from arresting his father?"

The notary shrugged.

"We all know how these things go."

"It seems to me these lordships of ours are afraid of their own shadows!" Clarice raised the ante, ready for battle.

"That I am not permitted to say," Sir Agostino replied prudently. "But please know that those present at the Council meeting that issued the sentence included your dear father-in-law."

"I'd very much like to speak to him about it" Clarice concluded. "Thank you, Sir Agostino, you can always be counted on."

That afternoon Lady Clarice was walking in the garden

with her husband. It was autumn by now, and although it was sunny that day, in her condition it would soon be too cold to go out. Sir Lorenzo had just returned from Padua, where he had tried without success to convince the bishop's vicar to support his request of a canonry for a priest cousin of his. But he always hid his bad moods from his wife, and Clarice didn't realize that it wasn't the right moment to talk to him.

"I wanted to ask you if your dear father is still one of the Ten," she began, taking the long way around, as she was cutting the last roses of the summer to take them into the house.

"No," her husband replied. "His health is too far gone, he preferred not to be reelected. But why are you interested?" he added, struck by such an unusual question.

"Oh, nothing. An order of banishment issued by the Ten can only be annulled by them, not by the Senate, am I right?" Clarice replied. "One of my women was telling me that her husband has been banished, she hasn't seen him for over a year, actually she doesn't even know where he is."

Sir Lorenzo explained to her that yes, those banished pursuant to a sentence issued by the Ten were always excluded from amnesties.

"So to obtain a pardon, a request must be made directly to the Ten?" Clarice insisted.

"That's right," Lorenzo confirmed. "But as for me," he went on, his temper rising, "I don't at all agree with pardons being dispensed so easily as they seem to have gotten into the habit of doing. A sentence is a sentence!" he exclaimed. "It's shameful to see those who have been banished be pardoned for their crimes just because they promise to recruit soldiers and oarsmen, or because they have ingratiated themselves to the papal nunzio. But they're all in on it anyway, and protesting is just a way to make your blood rise for nothing," he concluded bitterly, "this is the world we live in and we have to take it as it is." After his final word, however, he stood there with his mouth open, because Clarice had suddenly gone white, and was leaning on him for support.

"What is it? Don't you feel well?"

"A little nausea," Clarice said, trying bravely to smile. "And it's started moving again. Yes, feel it! Oh, how it kicks!"

She took her husband's hand and put it resolutely on her belly.

"Can you feel it? Yes, right there. There it is again!"

Sir Lorenzo was moved and also a little embarrassed, and he had already forgotten the reason his wife had undertaken that conversation.

"Let's go back in," he said. "The air isn't good for you today."

Sure, let's go back in, thought Clarice, passing her arm under her husband's. But you'll see, you're going to help me get a pardon for that lad, whether you want to or not.

24

The pregnancy went ahead, and the time came when Lady Clarice was about to give birth. Her belly was so enormous she struggled to carry it around, and she spent most of her time in bed. The baby kicked very frequently now, causing moans of pain, and on seeing the marked and pointed curve of her belly the women all predicted that this time it would be a boy. For two weeks already Sir Lorenzo had given up sleeping in their bedroom, moving into another room in the palace, and every night two midwives slept next to Clarice's bed; by day, two seamstresses hired for the occasion worked on preparing linens in the next room, helped by any of the servant girls who had a free moment. Another room hosted an accumulation of wall hangings, ribbons, and garlands to be used after the birth to decorate the nuptial bedroom for visitors to be received in a dignified manner; when she got out of bed, Clarice went to check on them, approving and discarding, adding new orders, calling in new artisans, so there was a continuous coming and going of people in and out of Palazzo Bernardo. Little Francesca, who was walking flawlessly by now and had begun to mumble a few words, came in every day to see her mother, but Clarice tired quickly and sent her back to the nanny, after making her a present of some ribbons.

"Children are wonderful, but tiring," she confided. Actually, to Bianca it seemed that the young mother spent precious little time with her daughter; as she remembered her own childhood, she had never for a moment detached herself from her mother's skirt. But the nobility, naturally, see everything as they please.

"And you, why didn't you have any?" Clarice continued, cooling her face with a fan. "Open the window a little, it's suffocating in here!" she commanded, even though it was cold outside.

"What can I say! At first, our Lord didn't send us any. We thought we had a lot of time!" Bianca replied after cautiously opening the window, whose small round panes were so fragile. She preferred to keep it to herself that in those early months of their marriage, when they thought they had a long time ahead of them, she and Michele had done everything possible not to have one.

"But luckily he sent them to us right away," Clarice continued. "You know what Sir Lorenzo says?" she laughed. "That all he has to do is look at me and I get pregnant!"

Bianca blushed, and went to put a log on the fire.

"If it's really a boy, you know who'll be happier than anyone? My father-in-law," Clarice continued. "He's always saying he doesn't have much longer to live, and if he lives to see the birth of an heir he'll die content."

"You're born and you die, that's life," Bianca commented, repeating something she'd often heard from her mother and Zanetta.

"Yes," Clarice agreed. Then she groaned, "Oh! He's moving again." She was pale, and Bianca went over next to the bed.

"Does it hurt?"

"I don't know . . ." Clarice whispered in pain. "The midwives are here, aren't they?"

"They're in the kitchen eating," Bianca said, with a touch of contempt. The midwives were two mature women, nice and plump, and since they'd been in the house they'd done nothing but eat.

"Go call them," said Clarice. "No, wait! It's passing. Close the window, all that's coming in is the humidity. Why can't I find a position that's comfortable!" she protested, twisting awkwardly among the pillows. "What torture! And to think you have to spend half your life like this!"

"When the baby comes, you should be the one who nurses him," Bianca dared suggest, hesitantly. "As long as you're nursing you can't have another one. My mother said that where she came from they nursed babies until they were three, that way they were sure not to have too many!"

Clarice looked at her with a condescending smile.

"For us noblewomen it's different. It's our job to have babies for our husbands, and I want my husband to be proud of me. And then, nursing makes you ugly, it makes you skinny and your hair falls out! You certainly don't want to see me get skinny do you?"

Right after that Bianca saw her go white again.

"Another pain? I'm going to call the midwives," she said.

"Wait another minute," Clarice called her back. "The other time I went on like this for weeks before the time came. I don't want them hovering around me right now, I'm tired."

"Do you want to sleep?"

Clarice shook her head.

"No, I'm tired of sleeping too. There, now I feel hot again. This is truly impossible! The last month is the worst. My mother used to say that the first months were the worst. She vomited all the time. But I hardly even noticed, not the last time and not this one either. But instead at the end you can't take it anymore. With this belly that feels like a trunk . . ."

They both laughed.

"My lady certainly has gotten a whole lot bigger," Bianca said, entering into her confidence.

"What can you do? With the hunger that comes over you! I haven't done anything but eat!"

More than one woman Bianca had known came to mind,

who even when she was pregnant ate only bread and water, and not always till she was full. Those women there, she remembered, didn't get this fat.

"That reminds me," Clarice said, "I'm hungry now too. Go get me some sugar and a little candied fruit. And a cup of Cypriot wine."

Bianca went down to the kitchen. While she was waiting for the tray to be prepared, one of the scullery maids went to talk to a woman who was sitting near the fire together with the two midwives, and she pointed at Bianca. The woman looked at her, got up and came over to her smiling. She was tall and she moved gracefully, as if she were young, and not until she was very close did Bianca see that she had a wrinkly face and lots of white hair.

"Are you Bianca?"

"Yes, signora," Bianca replied, used to treating elderly women with respect. The woman laughed.

"You don't know me, but I know you very well. I knew your poor father-in-law too. My name is Foscarina," she added. "Listen to me, I need to talk to you, that's why I came here this morning."

"Tell me."

"First of all I want to tell you how sorry I am about your misfortune," the woman began. She knew what had happened to Matteo, she knew that Michele had disappeared, that after the famous letter he hadn't sent any more news of himself.

"I know what it means to be left alone, without a man in the bed. Ever since my poor husband died I've never had a good night's sleep."

Bianca listened, astonished.

"You're young, for you it must be worse," the woman continued. "Now, listen to me closely. There is a young man who has seen you in church; he's been watching you now for several Sundays. Maybe you've even noticed him," she insinuated.

Bianca shook her head.

"Oh! You'll notice next Sunday all right. Look at the men's pews, he always sits right across from you, he has a peacock-colored doublet, and a bit of red beard, but short. Handsome, you know? If I were young I'd want him for me."

Bianca turned to the fire.

"I'm a married woman," she said, her eyes shining. "How dare you come here and make these proposals to me?"

Foscarina didn't bat an eyelash.

"Are you really sure you're still a married woman? With a man who's gone who knows where and you haven't heard from anymore?"

"He's coming back," Bianca said, obstinately.

"You want to believe no matter what? If that makes you happy!" Foscarina laughed. "But anyway, listen to me, next Sunday at Mass look for that young man! I'm not trying to rush you into anything, that's all I'm asking. Take a good look at him, and then I'll come back, and you'll let me know. His name is Sir Giacomo, he has a spice shop right near here, in Piazza Sant'Aponal, he's very well off, you know! And if you want, he'll make you well off too. Good-bye, beautiful, see you soon." The woman blew her a kiss and left, while Bianca, shaking herself out of it, ran into the cellarman, who gave her a disapproving look.

That night Bianca had a hard time getting to sleep. Despite herself she kept thinking about that woman and her proposal. Up to now she had been hanging on with all her strength to Michele's expected return, and she hadn't wanted to admit even to herself that she was finding it hard to believe anymore. Too much time had gone by since the arrival of that one letter, which no others had followed. The discovery that the galley Michele had left on had already come back a while ago to unrig, and that he wasn't part of the crew anymore, had cut the last thread that could still let her try to imagine where he was and what he was doing. By now it was almost a year and a half since she'd seen him, and her memories of the few months they had been together were beginning to fade. The mistress had promised that she would help her to find him, even to have his sentence annulled, but a long time had also passed since those promises had been made and Clarice, totally absorbed by her pregnancy, hadn't spoken about it again. Servants can't trust their masters, Bianca thought, her eyes wide open in the darkness, unable to get to sleep . . .

That Sunday Clarice wanted to go to Mass, even though she hadn't gotten out of bed for two days. Her husband and her father-in-law tried to convince her that it was better not to risk it, but without success.

"In my day, a gentleman could have a priest come to say Mass in his home," Sir Alvise muttered in irritation.

"In your day they did a lot of things that weren't right!" Lorenzo rebutted. "Today it's prohibited and that's as it should be. That's not the point! The fact is," he continued, turning to Clarice, who was looking at him from her bed with a defiant air, "that I have looked into it. I asked my confessor and he assured me that in your state there is no obligation to go to Mass."

"I don't doubt it," the woman responded, ashen but obstinate. "But it's me who's got this putto in my body and it's me that will have to pull him out, and that could happen any day now, and if before it starts I still want to go hear Mass there's nobody who can stop me!"

In the end, the two men, exasperated, got her to agree to ask for an opinion from the midwives, and they left, as the two women went over to Clarice and began tapping her gently. When Clarice was covered again Sir Alvise and Sir Lorenzo were allowed back in the room, and the midwives declared their agreement that milady could still go to church, provided she was taken there in a sedan chair and came directly back home.

Bianca had been waiting for that Sunday in a tumult of mixed emotions. The irritation provoked by the matchmaker's brazenness had still not dissipated; I'll go to church and I'll stare directly in front of me, she told herself with pride. But at the same time knowing that for who knows how long a man, during Mass, had been looking on her with desire, aroused her curiosity. Sure, she was married to Michele, and had no right to let herself be looked at by another man. But who knows where he is, she thought sadly, and who knows with whom. If he loved me, he would have found a way to get in touch with me. As Sunday drew nearer, the idea that there was nothing wrong about a man looking at her, and the curiosity to see his face, gathered strength. That morning she was so distracted as she combed and dressed her mistress that she earned herself a harsh reprimand.

The church of San Polo was teeming with people, and Bianca, who despite all her good intentions, kept glancing around out of the corner of her eye, was afraid she wouldn't recognize the man. Clarice leaned on her as they made their way up the central nave and entered the Bernardos' pew, and nodded to her to sit next to her, so that Bianca found herself in the best possible position, closest to the men's pews. She didn't want to look their way too obviously, for fear that her mistress would notice, but as soon as she managed to cast a glance that way she flinched, because there really was a man there with a short red beard, wearing a peacock-colored doublet, who was staring at her. Bianca felt an inexplicable sense of triumph, and fought with herself for the whole time of the Mass to keep from turning to look again; she could feel the man's eyes on her as though he were touching her. On the other hand she didn't hear a word of the Mass, and she hardly noticed, on seeing everyone stand up, that it was over and it was time to go back home. Clarice wanted to wait until most of the faithful had left, and when they started down the aisle on their way out there were no more than a few isolated individuals. The man with the red beard was near the door; when the two women passed by he moved next to Bianca as though he wanted to go out with them, bowed his head quickly to her ear and whispered:

"You're beautiful, you know that?"

Then he disappeared, as Bianca tripped, nearly making her mistress fall.

Three days later, Foscarina came to Palazzo Bernardo, and stopped Bianca on the stairs as she was going up to her mistress with the water for her to wash herself.

"He sent me to tell you he's in love with you," she told her, with her eyes laughing. "Now that you've spoken to each other he has no more doubts."

"But we didn't speak to each other!" Bianca said immediately. "I didn't speak to him at all," she added. But the woman had no trouble seeing that the phrase had been spoken without any energy.

"You'll speak to him the next time," she said maliciously. "Wait!" she exclaimed, on seeing that Bianca was impatient to go up the stairs before the water got cold; and she grabbed her by the arm. "Sir Giacomo sends you this," she said, taking a roll out of her bosom. "He wanted to give you a ring, but I told him it was better not to. Your mistress, my dear, is one who sees everything, I know her. If she sees you with a new ring on your finger she'll notice right away. I told him it was much better this way. Come on, open your hand!"

Bianca wanted to refuse but this time too her curiosity got the better of her, and she obeyed. The woman unfolded the roll, which turned out to be a handkerchief of embroidered silk, and let fall into her hand a gold chain. Bianca's eyes thrust open.

"You see how serious he is? With that one you've found your fortune, my dear!" Foscarina continued cheerily, while she adroitly wrapped up the chain again in the handkerchief and stuck it in Bianca's bosom. "Just be sure to wear it under your blouse, so your mistress doesn't see it."

"I have to go now," Bianca said, confused. Luckily she knew that her mistress was patiently waiting for her hot water.

"Go, honey, go," the woman reassured her. "And expect to see me soon, and we'll have more time to talk, all right?"

Bianca tore herself away and ran up the stairs. Milady Clarice was waiting for her sitting on the edge of the bed, half naked, contemplating her great belly. Bianca was red in the face as she poured the water into the basin, but for once her mistress didn't notice her turmoil.

"He's kicking," she whispered. "He wants out. It won't be long before he starts pushing."

She seemed so tender, scared, and defenseless that Bianca was shocked. As she handed her a towel she murmured:

"Don't worry, the Virgin Mary will help you, it will all go fine."

Clarice made the sign of the cross, and Bianca immediately followed suit.

"I've been praying a lot that this time it won't hurt so much," she said, trying to smile. Bianca didn't know how she should act; she had already seen other times that Clarice was not at all embarrassed to let her into her confidence and she would have liked to reach out to her, but they had taught her that servants had nothing to gain by fraternizing with their masters, and she couldn't manage to be spontaneous.

"Does it hurt a lot?" she asked, without looking at her. "My mother used to say it wasn't true, that there was nothing to be afraid of, it hurt a little but nothing a woman can't handle, and when it's all over you can't remember the pain."

"My mother used to tell me that too," Clarice nodded. "I

think mothers always tell their daughters that. And you know something? I'm going to say that to Francesca too. It's not good for a bride to know how it really is."

"Is it really so terrible?" Bianca asked, fearfully.

"I thought I was dying. It lasted a day and a night, and the whole time I thought I was dying. I screamed, asking the Virgin and our good Lord to take me right away and end it." Clarice saw that Bianca had gone white and she took her hands.

"But don't you get scared, eh? I'm going to need you too, and you've got to keep your feet on the ground, when the time comes. What can we do? We're women and that's what we have to do. If our husbands could see us at those times I think they'd faint; they who always know everything and have an answer for everything. But we've got to go all the way without fainting, you understand that, Bianca?"

"Yes, signora," the young woman said, swallowing.

"Oh, damn!"

The imprecation came out of Clarice's mouth so loud that Bianca turned to look at her in astonishment.

"It's broken," Clarice said, irritated; and showed her an earring.

"Oh, what a shame!" Bianca exclaimed, sympathetically. They were her most beautiful earrings, the ones Sir Lorenzo had given her when their baby girl was born, and that Clarice would be wearing to receive visitors after the upcoming delivery.

"We'll have to get them repaired right away," the mistress decided.

"Shall I call someone?" Bianca asked. Clarice bit her lip.

"It annoys me to let everybody know. They're capable of thinking it's some kind of bad omen. Listen, do you know where my jeweler's shop is? The street that goes to San Stae, right at the bridge. Ask for Sir Vincenzo, tell him I sent you, and that he has to fix them right away, and wait there and bring them right back."

"Yes Signora," Bianca said; and she took out the handkerchief that had enclosed the gold chain to wrap the earrings in it.

"What a lovely handkerchief!" Clarice was surprised.

"Really? It was a gift," Bianca stammered, quickly concealing it in her bosom. She had already noticed that the handkerchief, with its fine needlework, must have been very dear, and she felt stupid for taking it out.

"I'm off, Signora," she said, trying to regain her composure.

"Bianca, please be careful with those earrings, all right?" Clarice cautioned, and let her go.

So it was that Bianca, who never left the house except to accompany her mistress or, increasingly rarely, to go and visit Zanetta, suddenly found herself out and about on her own. She still hadn't closed the front door when Foscarina's words came back to her: he has a spice shop in Sant'Aponal. To be honest about it, to get to San Stae there was no need to go that way, but it really wasn't out of the way. Her curiosity was so strong that her feet took her in that direction all by themselves, with no decision on her part. When she got to Canal Sant'Aponal she started looking around, and since she didn't know the area, she asked an old man if he knew the shop of Giacomo the spice dealer.

"Take this portico here, when you come out the other end, go left, you'll see a bakery, the spice shop is right in front of it," the old man said.

Bianca walked quickly through the dark, muddy portico. When she came out on the street she smelled the aroma of bread. She walked over next to the shop and pecked inside. He was there, dressed in black this time, with a cape around her shoulders against the cold, and he was arranging some jars on a shelf, together with an apprentice. The store had no windows and what little light came through the door was enhanced by an oil lamp hanging from a beam under the ceiling. The two men were working and you could see their breath as it condensed in the cold air. Then Sir Giacomo turned toward the door and Bianca took a quick step backward; she didn't want him to know that her curiosity had dragged her all that way. Then she heard him giving orders to the apprentice, in a calm voice, and she leaned forward again to see better.

"My goodness, it's cold today," Sir Giacomo said. "Go close the door, if somebody comes they'll knock!"

Bianca jumped backwards, turned around and started off stepping quickly in the direction of San Stae, with her heart beating fast.

Foscarina kept her word. Less than three days later, Bianca spotted her in front of the kitchen, where she had come down to eat, after having served dinner to milady Clarice, who never left her bed now. The woman was on friendly terms with the scullery maids, who were used to seeing her around the house, and also to receiving gifts from time to time; they knew exactly why she was there, and had been gossiping behind Bianca's back, curious to see how it would end up.

"Come! Sit over here," said the woman, sitting on the step in front of the fireplace, with a bowl of soup on her knees. Conflicted, Bianca looked around; apparently no one was paying any attention to her. She went over to the woman, remained standing, and began sipping her soup noisily, waiting to see what happened.

"Here, look," said Foscarina when she'd finished eating; and she pulled out another handkerchief. In it were five little silk handkerchiefs.

"These are the mates to the one you already have. Sir Giacomo sends them to you as a token of his affection. But now," she continued, lowering her voice and putting a hand on her shoulder, "you have to send him a token too."

"And why is that?" Bianca stiffened.

Foscarina looked at her severely.

"But the gold chain, you took," she whispered.

Eh, Bianca thought, but you put it in my hand! But the idea of a man who desired her enough to send her gifts did not displease her at all. Even that little bit of gold, for someone like her, was already a small fortune. And if there was more where that came from? And behind the gold—a man, a man to hang on to in times of need. Sometime I have to start thinking about taking care of myself, she rationalized.

"I'm not asking you for anything big," Foscarina was going on. "A token, that's all."

"And what can I send him?" Bianca whispered. Foscarina smiled.

"One of your garters would be just fine. Now you go and get one from your trunk and bring it down to me, while I warm myself up a bit more here in front of the fire. It's raining out, you know? I've already been rained on quite a bit for you, it's a good thing it's worth it!"

As she climbed the stairs Bianca's heart was in her throat. She knew for certain that this was a move that she'd never be able to take back, and part of her wanted to turn around, tell the woman to her face that she wasn't doing anything, and give her back the chain and the handkerchiefs. But another part was dominated by the wish to give something back to this man who was willing to do so much for her; this living man, in flesh and blood, who was there, in Venice, so close to her, and who thought of her constantly . . .

In her trunk she looked for a garter of black ribbon, rolled it up in her fist, went back down and put it into the woman's hand. Foscarina accepted it with a big grin.

"Good girl, my little Bianca. Now listen, I'm going now to

take it to him. You don't know how happy he'll be. He truly loves you. And it's no use my coming back here again to waste time. Let's come to an agreement right now. You know where he lives? Right behind here, on the big canal that goes to Sant'Aponal, the one where the bakery is."

Bianca was careful not to tell her that of course she knew where.

"Next to it is his shop, and he lives above it," the woman continued. "Tonight you ask your mistress to let you off for two hours tomorrow to go and visit your mother-in-law at the hospital. It's been a while since you've been there, isn't that right?"

Bianca felt bad. It was true. Clarice needed her constantly and didn't willingly give her permission to go out, and Zanetta was more feeble all the time; the last time she had been to Saints John and Paul she had hardly recognized her. Bianca felt a little ashamed of herself, but she didn't have much desire to visit her. She didn't say anything and bowed her head.

"So then, you'll tell your mistress that before the baby is born you want to visit her one more time, that afterwards you know there will be too much to do, and she'll let you go tomorrow and the day after; and when you go out you tell everyone you're going to visit your mother-in-law, and instead you go to Sir Giacomo's shop, and everything will go fine, you'll see."

Bianca kept quiet for a minute, then she decided to jump.

"All right," she whispered.

"Good girl! And I pray you, be nice to him. He's a wonderful man. He'll make you happy. But between us women, you don't need me to teach you certain things, right?"

The next day, without daring to look her mistress in the eye, Bianca asked her permission to go visit her mother-in-law. Clarice noticed her embarrassment right away, but although she was used to seeing into the souls of her women, this time she misunderstood; she thought that Bianca was afraid she'd be reprimanded because she wanted to leave the house when the delivery was imminent.

"Go right ahead, that's a good thing to do," she decided. "But go right away, tomorrow morning."

So the next day Bianca got up earlier than usual, took care of as much of her work as she could, and then at shop-opening time she put on a clean blouse and her good dress, made the sign of the cross, and left.

25

It was stinging cold and drizzling. The streets were nearly deserted. The brick walls were oozing with dampness, the rooftop chimneys spitting gray smoke. Bianca walked along, hugging the walls of the houses, trying not to ruin her heeled slippers in the mud. In a few minutes she came to the spice shop, where a workman was still taking down the wooden boards they used to shut the shop at night. There was nobody else around.

"I'm here to see Sir Giacomo," Bianca said hurriedly. The workman hardly looked at her.

"The owner is upstairs," he said, pointing with his chin to the balcony overlooking the street, with the shutters still closed.

"I have to see him," Bianca insisted, obstinate. "He told me to come," she added.

"Well then, come ahead." The man carefully put down the board he was holding, and then signaled to her to follow him. In the back of the shop a door opened on to a dark staircase.

"This way," he said. "At the top, knock."

Bianca breathed deep and started up. She was hoping that the man would come to the door, but instead it was opened by an old servant woman, who gave her a hostile look.

"I'm here to see Sir Giacomo," Bianca said again, her look just as hostile.

"Wait here a minute," the woman said rudely, and went shuffling off into the dark interior of the house. Bianca stood there tormenting the hem of her apron with her fingernails, until the woman reappeared.

"Come with me," she said, and led the way. They went through an icy room, with a floor of black and white tiles and a spent fireplace; then the woman showed her into a room and closed the door at her back. It was a bedroom, a little less cold, with a brazier in the center, and a big bed against the back wall, its curtains drawn. At a table in front of the window sat the spice dealer, intent on staring at a fuming cup, a puzzled look on his face.

"You came!" he exclaimed; and rose to greet her, opening his arms out wide. Bianca could see that he was younger than he had seemed, his face slightly pockmarked, and his hair even redder than his beard.

"I came," she said, lowering her eyes.

"Do you feel cold?" Giacomo said, embracing her. "Come here, next to the brazier."

He grabbed a chair from against the wall and placed it between the brazier and the table. Bianca sat down and he smiled at her in contemplation.

"How good of you to come," he said. He was decidedly less than a great conversationalist, but Bianca didn't notice. She smiled too, and waited.

An embarrassed silence followed.

"Oh!" he exclaimed after a while, as though he had just remembered something. "You came at just the right time. Let me have you taste something you've never tasted before."

He took the cup in hand and held it up to her. It contained a dark, dense liquid, with a sharp odor. Bianca must have made a strange face because the man started to laugh.

"Don't be afraid, I won't poison you!"

He drank a sip and paused to savor it.

"I'm not saying it's good. It's still missing something. I've been trying all the spices. This has cinnamon and ginger. Come on, try it."

Bianca awkwardly took the hot cup in both hands, and

drank a sip. The flavor was different than anything she'd ever tasted.

"But what is it?" she asked.

The spice dealer started to explain.

"It's called *chocolate*. It's made from a berry that the Spanish have brought from America. They drink it, and they like it very much. They've just sent me a sack of it. But I'm not sure I've prepared it the right way."

"No, it's good," Bianca said, pensively. "Only, you're right, there's something missing. Have you tried adding some sugar?"

"Sugar? No. There's an idea, I'll have them bring some right up."

The apprentice arrived with a lump of sugar, and Sir Giacomo crumbled some into the cup.

"You taste it," he said.

Bianca's face lit up.

"It's wonderful!"

The spice dealer tasted it too, and smiled.

"It really is wonderful! And you, my Bianca, are so smart. You've helped me make a great business deal as soon as you walked in the door."

He came next to her and embraced her. Bianca let herself go in his arms, and when his mouth went looking for hers she did not pull back. They both tasted like sweet chocolate.

"Come here," Giacomo muttered, leading her toward the bed. Bianca let herself be led, but when she got there she sat on the side.

"Wait, I'll ruin my clothes," she protested.

"Then take them off," the man said. He was behind her, sitting in the middle of the bed, and he started kissing the back of her neck. Bianca smelled the odor of an aroused man who wanted her, and she got busy with the latches of her dress, while he kept on kissing and biting her neck from behind. She got down to her blouse and stockings, turned and rolled under the covers, sinking down into a soft mattress. The man closed the bed curtains, and leaned over her in the half light.

"I've wanted you for a long time," he whispered.

"Me too," Bianca replied, without even knowing what she was saying.

"Can you feel how much I want you?" he continued, taking her hand and putting it between his legs.

"Oh, yes," Bianca laughed, embarrassed.

He pulled out one of her breasts from her décolleté, and caressed it. The nipple perked up and stiffened. He put his mouth over it and licked it.

"You're tickling me," Bianca laughed, wriggling to free herself. Then she pulled him to her to kiss him. She squeezed his back with her hands, then slid further down. She began to get aroused too.

"I like you," she whispered, between one kiss and another. Then she opened her eyes wide because he was already pushing to get inside her.

"Be gentle, you'll hurt me," she murmured.

"No, I won't hurt you, relax," he said, determined; and he pushed again. Bianca moaned.

"There, there, don't fight it, relax," Giacomo said again. He pushed again, and he was all the way in. Bianca, breathless, grabbed on to his shoulders and dug in with her nails. He laughed, wriggled free, and blocked her arms.

"No scratching!" he exclaimed, still laughing; he covered her mouth with his, still moving on top of her.

"Don't come inside me," Bianca warned anxiously, as soon as she managed to free her mouth.

"Relax, relax, little one. God, do I want you," the man repeated. And he kept his word: right after that, with a painful wrench, he pulled out of her, just in time; then, with a satisfied groan, he rolled over and lay on his back.

"Amazing," he said, with a dreamy voice. "I've waited for you so long."

Bianca smiled, a bit shamefully, as she dried herself with the sheet. She wasn't sure if she'd liked it, and now she felt a furious burning between her legs. But it was the first time she'd had a man since Michele had disappeared, and her whole body had come alive with sensations that had been dulled for too long.

"I love you," she said, without even knowing herself if she was lying or not.

When she got back home, Lady Clarice was feeling bored and wanted to chat. She asked about the visit to her mother-in-law, and Bianca immediately started digging herself into a hole.

"She's totally confused," she declared. "She didn't even recognize me."

That had seemed to her the best way to keep out of trouble; she wouldn't have to make anything up. But then it crossed her mind that in the future the pretext of going to see Zanetta might still be a good ploy.

"But she was still really happy to see me," she corrected herself. Clarice raised an eyebrow.

"But did she recognize you or not?"

Damning her own stupidity, Bianca tried to cover her tracks.

"Yes, in the end, yes," she fibbed, without looking at her mistress, only to realize to her dismay that she was blushing. Luckily Lady Clarice showed no further interest in her servant girl's mother-in-law, and the conversation stopped there.

When she went downstairs to eat, Bianca was expecting to find Foscarina; indeed the woman was there, and came up to her in a festive mood. She embraced her and, after casting a furtive glance around the room and ascertaining that nobody was observing them, she dropped a pair of earrings in her hands. They looked like the ones Bianca had pawned and not yet managed to redeem, so much so that when she took them in hand she twitched as a torrent of memories flooded her brain.

"He sent them! You made him happy, he can't wait to see you again," Foscarina went on breezily, not knowing what was going on in Bianca's soul.

"All right," Bianca sighed, forcing a smile. "But I'm not sure when I'll be able to, with the mistress in the state she's in."

"No matter! We'll find a way," the woman said. "Naturally," she added, adopting a pensive manner, "things can't go on forever like this. You'll have to quit your job and go live with him."

Bianca started.

"But how can I quit here? Don't even mention it!" Foscarina shot her a cold glare.

"As far as you've come, my dear, there's no point in turning back. Look, he's downright crazy about you; he'll shower you with gifts."

"I don't know," Bianca said, avoiding the woman's eyes.

"Apart from everything else, suppose your mistress comes to find out what happened. She'd throw you out on the street in no time, you know? And then, who knows if he won't have changed his mind? Mark my words, it's best that you decide, and soon." Foscarina's tone was tinged with a hint of a threat that didn't escape Bianca.

"I'll think about it," she whispered; then, luckily, they called her, and she ran off.

On Saturday, Lady Clarice declared that she would not be going to Mass the next day, and ordered Bianca to go to the early morning one, together with the other servant girls, and then not to go out again the rest of the day.

"I can feel that we're almost there," she said, forcing a smile.

Both of them slept very badly that night; Clarice kept waking up, asked for something to drink, sent Bianca to open and then to re-close the window, feeling like she was going to suffocate. In the morning she was ashen, and when Sir Lorenzo came in to wish her good morning, her appearance scared him.

"I can't force you, but if you love me send for the doctor," he said.

Clarice's glaring response took him aback.

"Let's not get into this again! This is a women's affair, and we're not going to have some doctor poking around; you already let me do it that way the last time, remember?"

Sir Lorenzo mumbled something. Clarice smiled at him, as though to beg his pardon.

"There now, have some breakfast with me. And a game, wouldn't you like that?"

The chess board was set up on a little table next to the bed. Bianca, just back from Mass, brought in a tray of biscuits and a small carafe of wine, then she went to sit in the corner and sew while the two of them played. But very shortly a cry of pain coming from the bed made her jump to her feet. Clarice, white as a sheet, her eyes thrust open, was holding on to her belly. Bianca ran over to her.

"This is it," the mistress said, her voice taut. "Run and call the women. You, please go away," she said to her husband. "This is not a place for men right now."

Sir Lorenzo, pale himself, stood up, kissed her forehead, and left. The midwives, having rushed upstairs from the kitchen, pulled the sheets and covers off the bed and without a lot of formalities, examined Clarice between her legs.

"I don't know," the first one said, after a minute. "It's too early, you can't see anything." Just then Clarice felt another stab in her belly, and howling with pain, put her hands over her pubis, and then fell backwards onto the pillows. The midwives looked at each other.

"This is it all right."

Bianca was sent to fetch a cloth to moisten the laboring mother's forehead, and servant girls and seamstresses came running from every corner of the house, ready to make themselves useful. In no time at all there were a dozen women standing around the mistress's bed, commenting, smoothing her covers, caressing her, assuring her that everything would be fine. Every time Clarice moaned, they all encouraged her in chorus, trying to keep her calm. Nearly all of them had been in the house at the time of her first delivery, and they began to make comparisons out loud.

"Remember how hot it was the last time?"

"It was summer. The end of August."

"It was the day after the Assumption," said one, who valued precision.

"And it started in the morning then too."

"And Francesca was born that night."

"Actually, it was more like the next morning."

"But this time it will be faster," the governess prophesied, leaning down lovingly over Clarice, who was breathing heavily between one pain and the next. "The first time is always the hardest. I should know, I've done it nine times; from the second one on it's all very fast, the chute has already been oiled."

"Let's hope so," Clarice mumbled, a lost look in her eye. Then she screamed, "Ohi!" her whole body contracting. "This one was stronger," she commented, her forehead beading with sweat. Bianca refreshed her with the cloth. Two women kneeling beside the bed held the mistress's hands, caressing them softly. Every so often one of the midwives came over to the bed, pulled down the covers, bent over to look, and then straightened up again, shaking her head.

"It hasn't really started yet," she proclaimed. Clarice puffed with irritation. At times ten minutes went by, even fifteen, while nothing happened, and some of the women began looking to the others as if to ask if they'd been mistaken after all; then, Clarice howled again, and they all leaned over her. Finally, after an especially strong pain, the midwife who examined her exclaimed:

"Bring me a cloth!"

She wiped Clarice clean between her legs and then showed everyone the cloth, soiled with mucus and also a little blood.

"Now it's started," she said with satisfaction.

Five hours later, enervated and drenched in sweat, Clarice began, not to howl, but to scream at every contraction. Some of the younger women were shocked. Bianca, standing in back of her, kept wetting her forehead, as she had been told to do. She'd never seen a delivery, and she wasn't feeling too well; only the serenity of the midwives, who were joking with the governess and crudely encouraging the laboring mother, helped keep her spirits up, because she figured that if there was some real danger they wouldn't behave that way.

"What do you think, this is a good time to go have something to eat, no?" one of the two said. Clarice shot her a ferocious glance, but actually you could tell that their serenity was good for her too.

"Signora," the other said, "tell the cook to prepare something for us two women; we'll serve you better on a full stomach than on an empty one."

Clarice barely had time to nod; then her eyes shot open and as much as she tired to avoid it, she screamed again, as though she were in agony.

"Virgin Mary, I'm dying, I'm dying, please help me" she murmured, when the pang had passed. The midwives looked at each other again.

"Take a look," the older one said. The other one got down on her knees, made the women who were blocking the light move out of her way, and pulled back the covers. Without a lot of preliminaries, she pressed her hands on Clarice's thighs and examined her fissure.

"Maybe yes," she said. "Let's wait for the next one."

They remained in silence for two or three minutes, waiting. Then, suddenly, Clarice screamed and arched her back, putting her hands on her kidneys, and thrashing the midwife with her legs.

"No, that's not good!" the midwife said, annoyed, while Clarice kept on screaming. "The next time, hold on to her arms and legs." When the pain stopped, Clarice closed her eyes and nestled into the pillows. Seeing she didn't object, the women held her wrists and ankles.

"Spread your legs," the midwife ordered, "and hold on tight."

After another three-minute wait, which seemed it would never end, Clarice started screaming and writhing again, and the midwife bent over to look between her legs. When she straightened back up she had a big smile on her face.

"Let her go! All right, milady Clarice, we're almost there, it's opening. You, girl," she said, addressing Bianca, who was pale as a corpse, "get that look off your face! Go downstairs, go see if there's something ready to eat, because before too long we're really going to have to roll up our sleeves."

Bianca bolted out of there, more than happy to get away; she was still on the stairs when she was reached by another of Clarice's screams, first muted as if the woman were trying to contain herself, and then wild like a wounded animal. She was about to open the door to the kitchen, when the door opened from the other side and Giacomo appeared in front of her.

"Here she is!" the man smiled happily, and threw open his arms. Bianca, caught by surprise, took a step back.

"There now, come here. I want to give you a big hug! Why haven't you been to see me anymore, eh?"

"But I can't right now!" Bianca said hurriedly. "I have to go back upstairs, the mistress is about to give birth!"

"I know, they told me," the man said, more serious now.

"But I couldn't resist any longer, I wanted too much to see you. Come on, give me a kiss at least."

Bianca gave in and let herself be hugged; then she wriggled free.

"Let me go, now."

She raced into the kitchen with her heart pounding. At another time, maybe she wouldn't have minded being kissed by Sir Giacomo, feeling his soft red beard tickle her throat, but now she was too focused on the drama unfolding up there in her mistress's bedroom. When she went back to the stairway to go back up, Sir Giacomo was still there.

"Toll," he said, blocking her way. Bianca had no desire to fight, and gave him a kiss in the mouth; then she ran off.

"I'll wait for you down here, come back soon!" the man beseeched her. She was too much in a rush to even notice. She climbed the stairs and, short of breath, advised everyone that food had been prepared and the women who wished to eat could take turns going downstairs. Clarice kept screaming with every pain, then she fell back down exhausted, soaked with sweat; the women all around her touched her and spoke to her; the covers had been stripped altogether and piled on top of the trousseau chest, so now the mistress was lying with her naked legs for everyone to see. The older midwife went downstairs with a few others to eat, and came back a half hour later, wiping the grease from her lips with the back of her hand. Clarice was in the middle of a pain and she was screaming desperately, arching her back. The midwife bent down to look.

"That's fine!" she decreed with satisfaction. "It's coming down in a hurry," the other one said, "in a minute or two, we'll be on our way."

The ones who hadn't eaten yet gathered at the top of the stairs. Clarice had closed her eyes now and between one pain and the next she lay curled up with her arms crossed over her breasts; behind her, Bianca kept wetting her forehead, and couldn't help glancing out of the corner of her eye at those legs, which every few minutes or so kicked with agony, and at that round belly, which would soon deflate like a burst blister, letting that little putto come sliding out. Another half hour went by, during which Clarice screamed and writhed ten times, then the door opened and the women came back in. Clarice welcomed them with a look of gratitude, then she turned around to look at Bianca.

"But you haven't eaten."

"It doesn't matter, signora," Bianca replied. But Clarice wrinkled her brow.

"It certainly does matter! I need you to be strong. Go downstairs and eat!"

Bianca obeyed and rushed off. As she was going down the stairs she remembered Giacomo, and she almost expected to find him in front of her again on the stairs, but she didn't see him anywhere. She quickly ate a bowl of soup, standing by the fire, and went back up. She got there just in time, because all of the women were lined up even closer around the bed, making anxious and cheerful sounds.

"Yes, they've broken, they've broken!" they were saying. Bianca moved in closer and saw that one of the midwives was wiping Clarice's thighs with a cloth; the laboring mother, despite being disfigured by the pain, had a new light in her eyes.

"Ohi!" she cried soon after that, and put her hands on her groin.

"Now's the time to start pushing, lovely lady," the midwife told her. "The rest of you make room; you're suffocating her!"

Clarice, sweating copiously, did her best to obey; but she was soon writhing again, kicking her legs into the air and screaming in pain.

"No, that's not good!" the midwife said severely. "Look, if you don't stop that I'll have them hold your legs down. Come on, be a good girl, this isn't the first time, no? And this time will be easier. Come on, push!"

Clarice, with her eyes wide open and struggling not to scream, gave it all she had. Bianca, fascinated, never took her eyes off her mistress's groin.

"Are you watching, Bianca!" Clarice said to her, trying to smile. "Remember this when your turn comes. It's not hard. It's like shitting."

One of the woman couldn't contain an embarrassed titter, but the older midwife nodded with satisfaction.

"That's exactly right, the signora said it well. Come on now, push!"

But the baby's head was nowhere to be seen. After a while, Clarice couldn't control herself anymore, or hold back her screams. The two midwives both got down on their knees to look, then, after consulting, they began to push cautiously on her belly, first on one side and then the other. Clarice cried out in desperation and called on the Virgin to release her. All of the women had moved back in silence, waiting. The wait lasted a long time, and now the midwives weren't smiling anymore.

"I don't understand," muttered one of the two, feeling the belly. As far as I can tell it's in the right position, this putto."

"As long as the chord isn't wrapped around its neck," the other one whispered.

"Shut up!," the first one lit into her. "Don't say such things even as a joke!" and she made a quick sign of the cross. Then she looked at Clarice to see if she had heard.

"I just know this putto is going to kill me!" the mistress shouted suddenly.

"The Virgin will help you. Come now, women, what are you doing there? On your knees, and say a Hail Mary!"

The room filled with the monotonous murmur of the prayer, interrupted by Clarice's ever sharper cries. Bianca had made to kneel down too, but the mistress had stopped her, grabbing on to her arm.

"Stay here," she murmured, and Bianca stayed there, caressing her sweat-soaked hair.

"It's not coming," one of the midwives whispered, despondent. She spoke softly, but Clarice heard her.

"And what am I supposed to do?" she shouted desperately.

Out of the blue, Bianca had a vision of a childhood experience, buried for years in the deepest recesses of her memory. The barn, the warmth coming off the cows, outside the winter darkness, a woman lying on the straw, her mother's sister, surrounded by women just like Clarice was now, and also like her sweaty, screaming, and terrorized; and then one of the women, an old woman, forced her to change her position, to get up on her hands and knees.

Cows give birth that way and humans can give birth that way too, the old woman had said.

"In my town they say that when the putto won't come out, you have to get up on your hands and knees," Bianca blurted out all at once. For a second it seemed as though Clarice hadn't heard, but then everyone saw her pushing herself up on her elbows, trying to turn over.

"Girl, what foolishness comes out of your mouth!" the younger midwife shouted at Bianca.

"It's true," one of the women interjected. "That's what they do in my town too."

"That's the way they deliver cows . . . and peasants!" the midwife retorted.

Clarice shook her head.

"Me too. I can't take any more of this," she grumbled; and gathering all her strength, she pulled herself up and got on her hands and knees. The younger midwife looked at the older one. The older one shrugged her shoulders.

"It doesn't make any difference. Let's not fight about it," she whispered.

Clarice had started screaming again. The women who were kneeling started praying again. The midwives changed their position too, and Bianca, now that Clarice couldn't lean on her shoulder anymore, got down on her knees too, beside her mistress.

Then, one of the midwives yelled:

"There it is, it's coming! God be praised!"

All the women stood up and ran over to the bed.

"Stay back! Back!" the midwives admonished them. Each of them took hold of one of Clarice's thighs, opening them as wide as possible.

"Come on, it's coming! Come on, it's coming!"

"Virgin Mary!"

Clarice screamed again, like a stuck pig, the women who had been peasants all thought at once. Now, on the sheet underneath her a pool of blood formed; but something was moving in her opening. The older midwife stuck her hands right in there, Clarice screamed again, and a second later the midwife was up on her feet, energetically shaking a little bundle that was dripping blood and mucous. A few seconds went by, and then he bundle let out a desperate cry.

"It's born! And it's a boy, signora!" the midwife announced, triumphantly. Clarice, exhausted, let herself fall on her side, and tried to smile.

"Hot water, fast! And towels!" the midwife commanded. "And you, girl," she ordered Bianca, "go downstairs and get some firewood, the fire is just about to die! Up to now the signora has been sweating, but now she has to be kept from catching cold!"

Confused, Bianca rushed to the stairs, went down to the kitchen and from there out into the first courtyard, where the woodshed was. But as soon as she was outside in the cold air of the winter afternoon, she pulled up short: there, wrapped in a mantle, was Giacomo.

"Finally! You've kept me waiting, you know?"

"The mistress has given birth! It's a boy!" Bianca announced, out of breath.

The man doffed his cap.

"Congratulations!" he exclaimed, with a smile. "And where are you off to?"

"They sent me to get some firewood," Bianca said, indicating the door to the woodshed; a small structure made of bricks and plaster, as tall as a man, with a roof of displaced tiles.

"That sounds like an excellent idea, we won't be disturbed in there," Giacomo said. Bianca paled.

"But I don't have time! I have to go back upstairs with the firewood!"

"I don't have time either, but I've waited all day for you. Come on, be a good girl, go inside and stop fussing about it," said the man, not smiling anymore.

26

Bianca opened the door to the woodshed and the man accompanied her inside, putting his arm around her shoulders; then he closed the door. There was barely enough room to move between the wall and the woodpile; the ceiling was so low that Giacomo had to stay bent over, and there was no light except what came in through the cracks in the door. It was bitter cold. The man kissed her and, confused, Bianca let him have his way. His hands squeezed her around the waist and then went down lower. Bianca tried to squirm free.

"I can't! Today I can't. Please!" she whimpered.

"Just for a minute. I can't take any more of this waiting. Be good," the man said again, in a hush. "Here, lean against this," he added, taking her by the shoulders and pushing her against the woodpile. Bianca bit her lip. A residue of the desire that had driven her to go to his shop the other morning was still welling up inside her, but it wasn't as strong as the fear that someone would discover them, her eagerness to get back to her mistress right away, the discomfort of the cold, the darkness, the rough surface of the wood against her skin. Nevertheless, she leaned forward, and waited. Giacomo pulled her clothes up to her waist and then went about unlatching his pants. A minute later she felt him up against her and then inside.

"Be quick" she mumbled, gritting her teeth in pain.

"Yes, my beauty, relax, I'll let you go right away, don't worry, but move, little one, move. There, like this . . ."

Giacomo whispered, in a dream-like voice, as he squeezed her hips. Bianca realized that his pleasure no longer stirred up any excitement or desire in her, only the wish that it would all be over fast.

"Don't come inside me," she warned him, when she noticed that his voice was becoming more excited and his breathing more labored. The man didn't respond. Bianca, in a panic, squirmed and wiggled and got him to slide out of her just an instant before it was too late. Giacomo moaned with pleasure and disappointment at the same time.

"I have to go now," said Bianca, determined, after wiping herself off as best she could with the edge of her apron. Giacomo opened the door, went out into the open air and stretched in satisfaction.

"I love you," he said, watching her come out with her arms full of firewood. "Next time I'll bring you a nice present," he added.

"Yes, but now good-bye," Bianca said in a rush; and she ran off.

That same day Clarice's bed was disassembled and taken down to the receiving room on the ground floor of the palace. While the midwives were looking after the exhausted mother, soothing her lacerations with perfumed ointments and making her drink warm wine and chicken broth, the man servants climbed up and down ladders and ramps, hanging the walls with new tapestries, specially commissioned for the occasion by old Sir Alvise. The tapestries portrayed the birth of Hercules and his exploits in the crib, like his strangling of the serpent who wanted to devour him, and the women of the house stood there admiring them with their mouths agape, hindering the passage of the workmen. Even before the decoration was finished, relatives began to arrive: two of Sir Lorenzo's sisters, one of Lady Clarice's, six Bernardo cousins, and four Pesaro cousins on Clarice's side. In the end, the salon was full of women, all of them dressed in voluminous formal gowns, and although out of respect for the new mother they forced themselves to talk softly, the chatter was so thick it was deafening; not nearly so bad, however, as what was heard in the anteroom, where the visitors accompanying maids were stationed. They all arrived loaded with gifts, and a little table set up specially next to the bed was piled with costly confections, rolls of silk and velvet, and silver jewel-cases.

In the next room, the wet nurse, already arrived a month ago from the Bernardo's country estate near Treviso, suckled the baby, who was to be called Alvise, after his paternal grandfather. His father and grandfather were admitted to admire him only that evening, after the room had been completely decorated; Clarice, pale and wan, had been made up with vivacious colors, her hair combed and done up with dozens of false curls laced with lines of pearls, and over her nightgown she wore a brocade robe. The two men stood solemnly in front of the bed looking at her, their eyes shiny with emotion and pride.

"I always knew this marriage would mean the prosperity of our family!" Sir Alvise declared.

"It's the most wonderful day of my life, after the day I married you," Sir Lorenzo said; then he picked up a jewel case that a servant, behind him, was carrying on a plate. He put it down on the bed in front of Clarice and opened it to take out a gold chain with emerald pendants and he placed it, clumsily, around his wife's neck, not without getting her curls entangled in the clasp.

"Thank you, kind sir. It's marvelous," said Clarice, rubbing her fingers over it, and feeling its heft.

"It will always be too little for what you've done for me."

Sir Alvise in turn gave a slight nod of his head and another manservant came in with a tray, presenting it to Clarice. On the tray was a miniature chess board; its squares made of porphyry and diaspore, and the pieces marvelously crafted in gold and silver.

"With this you'll beat your husband," the old man joshed.

Clarice lit up with a joyful smile and examined the pieces, holding them in her fingers; but it was clear she was exhausted. The elder midwife stepped forward and respectfully but firmly asked the two gentlemen to withdraw; it was time for the mother to be quiet and get some rest. Which, however, did not mean being left alone; throughout the night her most intimate female relatives, the two midwives, and Bianca stayed with her. At first, the bustling and excitement, and the shrill cries of the baby in the next room, kept them all from going to sleep; then little by little sleep came over them. Clarice, exhausted and uncomfortable, was the first to fall asleep, then all the others dozed off, the gentlewomen in their armchairs around the bed, the midwives and Bianca on mattresses specially arranged in the room next door; by three o'clock, after the baby had taken his second suck, they were all asleep.

As soon as the light of day began filtering through the shutters, Palazzo Bernardo came to life and prepared for a new day of celebration. All the relatives who had not stayed there to sleep the night before came back early in the morning to keep the new mother company, and the flow of visits and presents started back up almost immediately. Bianca was amused to see that the men entered the room cautiously if not awkwardly, not knowing how to behave, and after paying their respects to Clarice they stood around like wallflowers, not talking much and admiring the tapestries for lack of something better to do, while the women acted like they owned the place, totally at ease, giving orders to the servant girls, as though they were in their own homes, every time they perceived, or imagined, some desire of Clarice's, or espied some sign of fatigue in her drawn and made-up features. All day long there was a constant parade of the Bernardos' relatives, friends, clients, business associates, and tenants, with clothes and gifts appropriate to their social rank, and Clarice received them all royally, despite her exhaustion and discomfort, always surrounded by women who talked to her, complimented her, mopped her brow, and offered her things to eat and drink; all day long she drank Cypriot wine, munched candies, and kept an ear stretched to hear the baby's cries, commenting favorably on his energy, and sending her servants to ask for news of his appetite. Bianca didn't have a moment's peace, and that evening she was so tired Clarice noticed it and sent her upstairs for the night so she could get a few hours sleep.

The next day presented itself exactly as the preceding one had: it seemed as though there were still a lot of people connected to the Bernardos who had not yet managed to be received in the throng of the day before, a lot of women who had already come to bring a gift came back to inquire into the health of the new mother and the baby, and the relatives gave no sign of going. Clarice was feeling decidedly better; the roll of the queen surrounded by her obsequious subjects suited her perfectly, and that day there was no need for makeup to give color to her cheeks and make her eyes twinkle. Bianca too, despite the fatigue, was enjoying herself; for the first time she appreciated in all its significance her role as the personal chambermaid of the mistress, and it made her laugh to see some of the visitors of more modest rank treat even her with deference. But the first time she was sent to the kitchen on some errand she was brusquely brought back down to reality, because waiting for her again in the anteroom she found Sir Giacomo.

"Great festivities, eh?" he said to her by way of saying hello.

"Oh yes," Bianca replied, embarrassed.

"Is your mistress feeling well?"

"Thanks to God and the Virgin, they are both doing fine!" Bianca exclaimed.

"Good," said the man, and rummaged in his pocket. "I've got something here for you," and he showed her a silk purse, embroidered with pearls. Despite herself, Bianca couldn't help but admire it, and she reached out her hand. Giacomo, making fun, pulled the purse back, then, on seeing the disappointment in Bianca's face, he put it in her hand.

"But it costs a kiss," he joked; and went right ahead and kissed her.

"Listen, Bianca," he began again after their lips had separated, "when will these festivities be over?"

"I don't know!" she marveled, "Why?"

"Because," the man replied, fixing his eyes on her, "when they're over it's time you came to live with me."

Bianca felt the world come crashing down on her.

"But, but I'm not sure!" she stammered. The man bristled.

"What do you mean you're not sure? You're not joking, are you! After all, you came to bed with me! And you've accepted my gifts."

Fiery red, Bianca mumbled something incoherent.

"Let's not play around," the man started back in, his tone peremptory. "You went along willingly and you can't pull out now. I'm inviting you to come live with me, what more do you want? What kind of an ingrate are you?"

"But I don't know if the mistress will let me," Bianca muttered, unable to find another excuse.

"Then you'd better persuade her!" Giacomo exclaimed. "If not, somebody could spread some things around, and you'll be better off if things don't ever get that far!" he added, with a hint of a threat.

"All right," said Bianca, who was ready to say anything if it would let her get out of there.

The man breathed easy.

"Good girl! Come on, smile. At my place you'll have everything you need, wait and see."

"All right, Bianca said again, nodding hurriedly. "Now I have to go."

"I'll see you when the festivities are over!" the man shouted after her.

That evening Sir Lorenzo came to see his wife. Clarice had sent for the baby and the wet nurse and was observing the feeding, weary but her eyes shining with satisfaction. Sir Lorenzo sat down beside her and the two of them gazed intently at their newborn baby as he sucked with animal-like relish on the woman's swollen tit. When the baby dropped off to sleep, having had his fill of milk, the wet nurse carried him away with her and Clarice and her husband were left alone for the first time in many days. Lorenzo, visibly moved, took his wife's hands in his.

"Their hot," he exclaimed, worried. "You don't have a fever, do you?"

Clarice shook her head.

"I'm fine," she assured him, smiling; and she pulled her husband toward her. After kissing her, Lorenzo calmed down.

"Yes, you're lips are cool. But I beg you, you mustn't get sick."

"I won't get sick," Clarice declared, sure of herself.

Lorenzo sat silently for a moment, then he cleared his throat.

"I want to tell you again," he began, "how proud of you we all are."

Clarice smiled and caressed him. That familiar gesture made Lorenzo forget what he wanted to say, so he kissed her and fell silent again a little longer.

"And I want to tell you," he started back in, "that I know I am still in your debt."

Clarice laughed.

"I've only done my duty."

"Oh no," Lorenzo insisted, sincerely. "Ask me whatever you like. I've spoken with my father, and he agrees with me."

Clarice stretched herself voluptuously on the pillows. Her face and her body, still deformed by the pregnancy and the delivery, emanated a luminousness that affected Lorenzo deeply.

"Really?" said the young mother. "Well then, do you remember my maid, Bianca? Do you recall that her husband has been banished, and that some time ago I asked you to obtain a pardon for him?"

Lorenzo opened his arms.

"I remember. But I also remember explaining to you that it was impossible."

"No," Clarice corrected him, "you explained to me that you didn't think it was right."

"And even if that were so?" Lorenzo rebutted, on the defensive.

"Well, you've just finished saying that I can ask you whatever I like. I have your word."

Lorenzo remained silent.

"So, get me that pardon. A lot of time has passed and all he did was what any boy would have done. You and my dear father-in-law still count for something in Venice. I can't believe you won't succeed."

Lorenzo wrinkled his brow, then he sighed deeply.

"I'd prefer you asked me for something else," he finally said.

Clarice sighed.

"There's something you don't know," she said. "You owe it to Bianca that your son was born." And she told him that Bianca had been the one to explain to her what position to put herself in so the baby could manage to come out.

"The midwives didn't think of it. If it had been up to those two, I don't know if we'd be here talking like this," she concluded. Sir Lorenzo, embarrassed, had been listening without looking her in the eye; now he sat in silence for a while.

"Well?" Clarice insisted.

Sir Lorenzo shook himself energetically back into the moment.

"Let's play!" he said cheerily, pointing at the chess board. "If you win, I'll make you a gift of a pardon for that man."

Clarice looked at him, her eyes shiny with tears.

"Sir!" she exclaimed. "I'll not stake a man's life on a game of chess, and neither will you. I understand, from what you tell me, that obtaining a pardon for that poor man is not something impossible. Well, did you or did you not give me your word that I can ask you for whatever I want?"

Lorenzo tightened his fists. In that precise instant, from the room next door, came the cry of their baby boy, who had just woken up. The eyes of husband and wife met. Lorenzo held up for a minute; then he lowered his eyes in defeat.

"All right, signora, you will have your gift," he declared, standing up and preparing to go. Clarice wriggled under the covers, kicked with one of her naked feet and grazed her husband's leg. Surprised, he stopped in his tracks.

"And I'll have it from my husband, as a sign of his love and of the trust that he has in me," the woman said softly; and she stretched out her hands toward him. Sir Lorenzo hesitated for a moment, opened his mouth as if to reply, then closed it again, shook his head laughing, and let himself be pulled into her embrace.

"That's right," he said tenderly, before kissing her. "I couldn't have said it better myself."

That night Clarice couldn't get to sleep. The lacerations provoked by the birth were still a long way from being re-absorbed, notwithstanding the midwives" ointments, and they tormented her; even though the fire had nearly gone out, it felt to her as though the room was engulfed by a suffocating heat. When the familiar voice of the San Polo bell tower rang out three o'clock, she couldn't take it anymore and woke up Bianca to have her get her something to drink.

"Listen," she said after taking a sip, putting the crystal goblet down on the bedside table and gesturing to Bianca to come sit at the foot of the bed. "Have you had any news of your husband?"

"No, signora," Bianca replied, surprised.

A mischievous smile crossed Clarice's face.

"Well, I can give you some."

"You, signora?"

"Yes! I wanted to wait until everything had been taken care of, but I'm too eager to tell you about it now. Master Lorenzo my husband will obtain a pardon for him."

Bianca's jaw dropped in amazement.

"Oh, signora!" she said, choking on her voice; then she took her hands and kissed them.

"There, there," said Clarice, who was not at all displeased by such manifestations of gratitude. "Then we'll have to find him," she added, "but we can do it, you'll see." But then, right after that, she noticed that Bianca was sobbing.

"But you're crying!" she exclaimed. "What is there to cry about?"

Confused, Bianca tried to use the sleeves of her blouse to dry the hands of her mistress, which she had gotten wet with tears and snot.

"Stop that!" Clarice said, impatient, and she wiped herself with a handkerchief. Then, more gently, "Come on, talk," taking the young woman's chin in her hands, and seeing that the tears were still lining her cheeks. Frightened and unhappy, Bianca told her, with a lot of hesitation, many omissions, and a few embellishments, what had happened to her with Sir Giacomo.

"And so you've promised to go live with him?" concluded Clarice, who knew enough to understand fully how things had gone, despite Bianca's reticence. The girl nodded in affirmation, and started crying again.

"Stop it!" Clarice ordered her abruptly. "He certainly can't force you to do it."

"But what else can I do?" Bianca sobbed, crying even more profusely.

"But why? Are you expecting a baby perhaps?" Clarice pressed her, still looking for an explanation. Bianca shook her head vigorously; then, between sobs, she said that the mistress would certainly not keep her in the house anymore, now that she knew what happened; and Giacomo, if he spread it around, could make sure she was fired from any job she might find. She didn't have any choice but to give in.

Clarice was liking the situation more and more. She was there, at night, in the sleeping palace, with her favorite maid crying desperately at her feet, and only she could put a stop to all that pain. How marvelous to be a mistress, she thought, with a tremor of delight.

"It's true," she said, measuring her words. "I should throw you out on the street." Then, because Bianca's weeping was turning into a moan and they might hear her in the other rooms, she rushed to add:

"But I'm not going to. And if you stop crying right now, I'll tell you what we're going to do."

Bianca looked up at her with two red, questioning eyes.

"First, I am the mistress of this house, and I decide whether or not to get rid of one of my servants, and it happens to be the case that I don't want to get rid of you, is that clear?"

Bianca opened her mouth, but the words wouldn't come, and she nodded; then she went back to convulsively kissing her mistress's hands.

"Second, I decide if what you've done is serious or not, if it deserves punishment and if so which, and if someone else needs to know about it or not. For example, I say that when your husband comes back, there is no need for him to know about it, what do you say, Bianca? He has been who knows where for years, has done who knows what in the meantime, and you are a wise wife and you won't ask him about it, right? He, on the other hand, because men are not wise, will want to know everything from you, and you, about this story that you've been telling me about tonight, will not tell him a thing, understand? That's an order from your mistress; I take responsibility for the consequences. All you have to know is this: that I have given you an order and it is your duty to obey."

Bianca had stopped crying; she was holding on for life to Clarice's hands, and she kissed them every minute. But then she pulled back and turned to her mistress with a lost look in her eye.

"Bur Sir Giacomo, he'll tell everybody!" she exclaimed, her face ashen.

Clarice looked at her, wrinkling her brow.

"You think so? We'll see!" she exclaimed.

27

Two days later a man form Palazzo Bernardo went to Sir Giacomo's shop and told him that his mistress needed to talk to him right away. The spice dealer, alarmed, threw his mantle over his shoulders and followed him. When they came to the rear entrance to the palace, he was invited to enter and pass through the garden and the vegetable garden to the door that led to the stairway and on up to the first floor. Clarice was waiting for him in bed in the receiving room, still sporting all of its festive decorations, and Sir Giacomo, hat in hand, made his way rather awkwardly across the carpets covering the floor.

"Are you Giacomo the spice dealer?" Clarice addressed him.

"At your service," said the man, bowing.

Clarice examined him at length and without regard. A handsome man, she thought, with approval.

"So you've fallen in love with Bianca?" she then asked him, point-blank. The redhead flinched.

"Well, I . . ." he stammered; but Clarice cut him off.

"Be still! I already know everything. You saw her in church. And you took the liberty of sending a procuress here in my home to court her," she said severely.

The man was sweating and tormenting his hat with his hands.

"Signora, I . . ." he began.

"Be still, I said! You sent her a procuress and you showered her with gifts. You may as well have sent her money! Some lover you are!"

The man opened his mouth to speak, but immediately thought better of it.

"Well done, Sir Giacomo! You fall in love with married women and court them in other people's homes!" Clarice continued. "Yes, my dear man, Bianca is married, and don't tell me you didn't know that!"

"But by this time her husband is certainly dead!" the poor man cried.

"Silence!" That's what you think! You're in for some more surprises, dear man! Fortunately, when Bianca's husband returns, he'll have no reason to come looking for you with a knife, given that his wife had the good sense to tell me everything, and despite all your gifts nothing has happened between you."

"But that's not true!" exclaimed the man, his blood rising. "Signora, if that liar told you that . . ."

Clarice transfixed him with a glare so cold the man was stunned, and fell silent yet again.

"Sir Giacomo, let's try to understand one another. I've already told you that I know everything, everything, is that clear?" Clarice said, pressing hard with her voice on that *everything*. "Therefore, I know that you have courted Bianca, that you have sent her gifts, that she has been careful not to give in, and that she has immediately told me everything, and that is all to the good, extremely good, that things have gone that way, because if you had dishonored my maid, in my home or elsewhere, you wouldn't easily come out of it unscathed. Do you understand?"

Sir Giacomo was no fool. Despite being thrown into confusion by the unexpected turn their conversation had taken, he understood very well what the noble woman was telling him.

"Signora, yes, I understand," he swallowed.

"Are you sure? Be careful," Clarice pressed him. "Because if I should ever discover that you haven't understood, and that you have imagined some things, and that perhaps, heaven help us, you've told someone about it," and here she interrupted herself, and then resumed, lowering her voice and giving the words a sinister twist, "then, Sir Giacomo, watch your neck."

The spice dealer was staring at his shoes and tormenting his hat.

"I understand, signora," he said again in a whisper.

"Just one more thing," Clarice added.

"Tell me."

"You know those gifts that you sent too my maid?"

Sir Giacomo didn't know how to answer, and he shrugged his shoulders.

"Well, if you've already forgotten them, that's fine, we needn't say anymore about them. You can go," Clarice declared royally. "Oh, just a minute," she corrected herself. They tell me you're a spice dealer."

"That's right, signora."

"And you keep the shop on the street that goes from San Polo to Sant'Aponal, am I right? And they tell me you live above the shop?"

"Yes, signora, Sir Giacomo confirmed; and for the first time since he entered the room, a slight smile came over his face.

"Why are you laughing?" Clarice reproved him; but she was laughing too. "Now, listen carefully, Sir Giacomo, maybe someone from my house will come to buy a little pepper, and perhaps some sugar, and candles. I'm disappointed with the spice dealer I have been using till now."

"The signora shows me too much honor," Sir Giacomo said, bowing.

"Indeed," Clarice agreed. "But you seem to be a man who understands things, and if you serve me well we will be friends. Now, go."

"I don't know how to thank you, Signora," the man declared; he bowed again and headed for the door.

"Sir Giacomo! Remember, it doesn't take much to twist a man's neck!" Clarice shouted behind him, already worried that she'd put him too much at ease.

As soon as the door was closed again, and the man's footsteps had faded away on the stairs, Clarice turned to the other door, ajar, that led to the next room.

"Bianca! Come out," she called.

Bianca came in the room, her eyes low and her cheeks on fire.

"Quite a beast you chose for yourself!" Clarice exclaimed, in a tone of disapproval. "If your mistress wasn't here to get you out of trouble," she added.

Bianca, embarrassed, said nothing.

"Well?" Clarice queried.

"Signora, I . . ." Bianca mumbled.

Clarice couldn't wait to have a laugh.

"Get that look off your face!" she exclaimed. "Yes, quite a beast he is, like all men! Tell me," she continued in a jocular tone, "does his beard scratch?"

Bianca timidly looked up and saw that her mistress's eyes were bright with good cheer. The sight perked her up.

"A little!" she confessed, starting to laugh now too.

Clarice was about to ask her something else, but she realized she was getting too confidential. That had happened with another maid, and she had learned that it wasn't wise.

"That's enough now," she concluded. "Now, come over here and comb my hair."

At this point, our story becomes intertwined with that of a dossier, which for some time now had been slowly fattening up on the desk of Master Zuanne Morosini, one of the Lord Heads of the Council of Ten. The dossier had been opened three months ago, after a lengthy private discussion between

Master Zuanne and Master Simone Guoro, the *Sopramasser all'Abbondanza*, or the man charged with feeding Venice by making sure the bakeries always had bread. All you had to do was look at Master Simone's face and his red eyes to understand that his office caused him a lot of sleepless nights. That winter, after the second straight bad harvest, people had started dying of hunger throughout the Po river valley, and everywhere the crowds of beggars were thick and threatening. Luckily, the Republic had money, and ships, and ports in the Levant, but even so the task of making sure enough grain arrived in the city everyday to avoid riots and tumult was certainly not an enviable one. But what Master Simone had to tell Master Zuanne was so important that the two of them discussed it in low voices behind closed doors; and when the *Sopramasser* left Palazzo Morosini, the master of the house walked out onto the open gallery on the Grand Canal, exactly opposite what the local population continued to call the Ca' d'oro, even though the gilt on its façade had long since disappeared; and he tarried there quite a while to think. Then he walked back inside, sat down at his desk, took out a piece of paper, and began to write. "Pro memoriam of how today, 28 November 1589, his Magnificence Master Simon Guoro, Soprammasser all'Abbondanza, came to me, Master Zuanne Morosini, and reported . .". He wrote for a long time, filling the entire sheet; then he folded it in four, and sealed it with wax and the ring he wore on his finger. After thinking some more, he took out a larger sheet of thick, stiff paper, folded it in two making it into a file folder, stuck the sealed paper inside, and wrote on the cover three apparently innocent words: "Grain from Constantinople."

From then on, the dossier remained buried under other dossiers on the desk of the illustrious Morosini, opening its maw from to time to swallow new sheets of paper. It gathered extracts from anonymous announcements published in

Constantinople, Alessandria, and Tripoli in Syria, sent by the consuls, merchants, and spies operating in those Turkish cities. A place was found in it for the transcripts of depositions taken from certain Venetian, Turkish, and Jewish merchants, secretly summoned to the seat of the Ten; the summary of a second meeting with Master Simon Guoro; the sworn statement of a certain Sir Zaccaria da Candia, owner of a Cretan xebec; and the transcription, which Master Zuanne set down personally in his own hand rather than entrust it to his secretary, of some passages taken from official dispatches sent by the Venetian ambassador, the bailo, to the Sublime Porte—the man responsible for the Serene Republic's relationships with the most powerful, unpredictable, and dangerous of its neighbors, and whose office was considered the most prestigious to which a Venetian diplomat could aspire. Then, one fine day, the dossier was taken in hand by Morosini, slipped into a case that he wished to carry in his own hands to the Ducal Palace, and became the topic of a very long conversation between Master Zuanne and the Doge, Pasquale Cicogna, which lasted from after lunch into the middle of the night.

A few more days went by and the dossier reappeared, even fatter, on the table of the Lord Heads at a meeting of the Council of Ten. More than one of the documents contained therein were extracted, unsealed if necessary, and read in a low voice by Master Zuanne, amid exclamations of incredulity. Then, when there was nothing left to be read and each of those present recognized that there were no possible doubts, there supervened a worried silence.

"We have to recall him," said one, in a tone of resignation.

"We have to try him," said another, with the tone of someone who realizes the enormity of what they are saying.

"And the scandal?" a third interjected.

They all fell silent. Then the doge said what his role compelled him to say.

"There is no scandal that counts more than the honor of the Republic."

"Nevertheless," someone objected, "if it were possible to avoid it."

This time the silence was more prolonged.

"We'll see," Master Zuanne concluded. "Meanwhile I would like to ask for a vote on the proposal to send someone down there to get him."

"Isn't it better just to recall him?"

Master Zuanne shook his head; the naiveté of his colleagues never ceased to amaze him, and to think that this was the Council of Ten! No wonder then that the Senate, with a hundred of so votes, always cost so much effort to arrive at a reasonable decision. It would be so much better if we weren't a republic, he thought to himself, as he had so often.

"Recall him before his term expires? And on what pretext? And if we were to find a pretext do you think he'd fall for it? You don't know the kind of man he is."

They all acknowledged he was right.

"There's nothing else to do," said Master Zuanne. "Someone has to go get him."

"You mean to arrest him?" someone asked. Master Zuanne nodded.

"Of course. We'll have to write to the Porte, explain everything, ask for their authorization; otherwise it can't be done."

Reluctantly, the others nodded their agreement. Nobody liked having to tell the Turk about the weaknesses of the Republic, and having to ask his permission to make the arrest, but this time they all saw there was no alternative.

"And who can we send?" the doge asked. They all avoided looking at their colleagues. The assignment they had before them was so delicate and important as to project whoever took it on into the highest echelons of power in the Republic, but also so problematic and dangerous as to send chills down your spine.

"It must go to someone who has been there before," another suggested.

"It must go to someone who is still young and knows how to use a sword, because he could be forced to manhandle him," the doge decreed; and no one dared add anything else.

"And so you promised her?" asked old Sir Alvise. His son shrugged his shoulders.

"I know I shouldn't have," he admitted, disappointed in himself.

"Your wife is a great woman," Sir Alvise said suddenly; and Sir Lorenzo, surprised, realized that his father was not as irritated as he had feared. Clarice had bewitched him too, he thought, torn between admiration and alarm.

"The fact is," he replied, "that I am forced to use my influence to obtain a pardon for someone I've never seen; or even worse, who until yesterday I didn't know existed."

Because the point was exactly that: if it had been a relative, or even just a domestic servant, the Bernardos would have thought it obvious to use their influence to resolve it. The family could only gain from it being known in Venice that whoever was under their protection could even beat up a policeman with impunity.

"But this woman, how long has she been in service to your wife?" asked Sir Alvise, who evidently was thinking along the same lines. Sir Lorenzo shook his head.

"Not long. When the incident happened she lived in another parish."

He got up from his chair, went over to the window, and pulled the curtain. It was still raining outside. A bad sign, he thought, mechanically. A rainy winter means a bad harvest, and that winter it had done nothing but rain, even on the mainland. It had been that way last year too, when Sir Lorenzo was serving as podesta in Udine, and he remembered the squalor of the fields ravaged by the winter rain, without a blanket of snow to protect them, and how sparse and stunted had been the wheat that came up in the spring, and the glum faces of the farmers at threshing time. If it doesn't snow, he thought, it will be the third bad year in a row, and in that case God help us.

Sir Alvise was in bed, immobilized by a new attack of gout. The pain in his leg had kept him up all night, but on the other hand, at his age, he didn't need much sleep.

"Listen a minute," he said, caressing his white beard, which he had recently been letting grow longer. "By now you can't avoid it, so let's see if we can't get some advantage out of it."

"Oh, there's one advantage for sure; if I ever have to outfit a galley I'll have secured myself an oarsman," his son replied sarcastically.

Alvise chuckled.

"You want to know something I've learned in all these years?" People think that by asking favors you make yourself weaker because then you're in debt to those who did it for you."

"And so?" asked Lorenzo, surprised.

"And so," the old man said, pleased with himself, "that's not the way it is at all. Asking for a favor is like asking for a loan to invest the money in an important business deal. Then you're in debt, certainly, and then you have to pay it back. But in the meantime the guy who lent it to you has become, let's put it this way, your partner. He has an interest in having the thing go well, not having it go badly. He's done you a favor and he wants you to be in a position to pay it back. He wants it to be known that people who ask him for favors are crowned with success.

"He wants it to be known that you've gone to him with your hat in hand," Sir Lorenzo disagreed. Sir Alvise gestured his annoyance.

"That could be! It's not always a dishonor to take your hat

off. It all depends on whether you do it before the right person. Someone who can ask the doge for a favor certainly doesn't feel humiliated by doing it. On the contrary, everybody else looks on him with respect and envy, because he can ask a favor of the doge and they can't."

"And therefore," probed Lorenzo, who was beginning to understand.

"And therefore, I say: whom should we ask for this favor? The boy has been banished by the Ten, without an opinion from the Ten he'll never be pardoned. This year I," he said as though excusing himself, and nodding at the bandage around his leg, which was oozing yellow puss, "I'm on the sidelines, but in any case if I were still on the Council it's not at all certain that would be enough. On the contrary, I say it's good luck that things have fallen out the way they have."

He stopped because he was short of breath.

"Don't wear yourself out," said Sir Lorenzo, anxiously. Sir Alvise signaled a no and remained silent for a minute, until his breathing went back to normal.

"To obtain this pardon you need an opinion from the Ten. Now, I'm certain that nobody remembers anything about this poor fellow, and the case is so insignificant that nobody would dream of opposing it, if the proposal is put on the agenda by the Lord Heads. Therefore, you'll go to Morosini, who is a friend of ours, and you'll ask him for this favor. Don't tell him about Clarice, though," he grinned.

Lorenzo laughed.

"Perhaps not."

"Tell him he's one of our men, the husband of a woman in our house, and that's it. He won't ask you anything else, it couldn't matter less to him by now."

"And then?"

"And then, that's it! At this point Morosini will remember you. He'll remember that you owe him a favor. He'll remember that you went to ask him. A little experience under your belt you've already got, it's time to become a candidate for more important magistracy, especially now that I'm laid up with this leg. And Master Zuanne can do a lot."

Master Zuanne had had it up to here with posing. The sumptuous purple robe trimmed with ermine, symbol of his august office, was weighing on him, he wanted to scratch his head and blow his nose, and generally, to devote himself to something else; but the painter had begged him to be patient for another half hour, the sketch of his head was nearly finished, and he had resigned himself. But when they came to tell him that the magnificent Master Lorenzo Bernardo had asked to be received, he decided that was an excellent excuse to interrupt the sitting.

"I'm sorry, Sir Jacopo, come back tomorrow, if you can. Anyway, it looks to me like we haven't got much light left."

Tintoretto bowed obediently and started gathering up his things. Master Zuanne got down off the high-backed chair where he'd been sitting, walked by the canvas mounted on the easel and took a look. The figure was barely sketched, but the head and the face were easily recognizable. The similarity is surprising, he admitted. Even too much; there wasn't a wrinkle around his eyes, a groove in his forehead, flab on his cheeks that hadn't been reproduced. The barely open eyelids, the cold, severe gaze, the mouth hidden under the thick well-groomed beard were more to his liking. I did well to call him, he decided. It's a shame about those bags under the eyes, so puffy and cracked, as only someone who has slept too little and drank too much can have. Those who consume their lives worrying about the health of the Republic end up having the same faces as the drunks who waste all their time in taverns, he thought, vexed.

In the anteroom he went over to greet Sir Lorenzo, excusing himself for receiving him in such solemn garb, and explaining why. He was curious about this visit; he was well acquainted with old Sir Alvise, who on more than one occasion had given him fits in the Council, but he knew little of this son who had only begun his career a few years ago, holding minor magistracies on the mainland. But he knew that an heir had just been born to him, and he offered his congratulations.

"I" said Sir Lorenzo when they had exhausted the formalities, " have come to disturb you to ask you a favor"; and without wasting time he explained Michele's case to him and told him he wished to obtain a pardon.

Master Zuanne had no recollection of the incident, and was not reminded of it even when Sir Lorenzo recounted the details for him; but precisely for that reason he realized almost immediately that it wouldn't be difficult to grant the request. If he didn't remember it was highly unlikely that anyone else would; and who would want to go against him and raise an objection, if on the basis of some excuse he proposed to pardon the poor lad?

Morosini thought it through quickly because his guest was waiting. Was it useful to him or not, to take this on? If old Alvise's son had come to ask him a favor it was clear that the significance of that gesture went well beyond this specific case. Lorenzo, now that he too was the head of a family and had a male heir, was preparing to take his father's place in the political life of Venice, and he wanted to do so with his friendship. All right, thought Master Zuanne. That's just fine. All he had to do was avoid giving the impression that the thing was as easy as it actually was.

"We'll have to see," he grumbled, pulling at his beard. "But why is it, excuse me, that the Bernardo family has decided to take up this case at this time?"

Sir Lorenzo shrugged his shoulders.

"At the time, the man was not a member of our household. It was only after the fact that his wife joined our staff."

"And is she a domestic servant of Lady Clarice's?" asked Morosini, spritely.

"Her personal chamber maid," Sir Lorenzo specified.

The two men looked each other in the eye; then, realizing that they had reached an instant understanding, they burst out laughing.

"Sir Lorenzo," the master of the house said then, "I understand completely, one cannot say no to one's wife at times like this, am I right?

"That's so, unfortunately," he acknowledged. His father would have pulled out his hair to see him acting so undiplomatically, but his frankness went down well with Morosini. And then, all of a sudden, taking a better look at the man sitting before him, strong, still young but already mature, with his short blonde hair already thinning on his forehead, a strange idea came into his head.

"I'll be very happy to do a favor for Signora Lady Clarice, and in return I'll ask her if she will allow me to kiss her hand, when I have the sentence," he began. "But since we're here, let's talk a little more. You, I gather, have not yet had an office this year, is that right?"

Lorenzo confirmed; the management of the family estates on the mainland and his wife's pregnancy had left him too little time. "But now I think I'll launch my candidacy for a post," he added instantly. Morosini stared at him attentively.

"And if it involved a long journey?"

Weeks passed and it continued to rain. The stinging cold of the winter became a bit less brisk, but people kept on shivering and coughing, passersby hurried along the streets full of water and mud, chimneys kept spitting into the sky billowing clouds of smoke, until the price of firewood rose so much that the poor had to stop warming themselves. As in previous years, March was cold and it rained unceasingly; Venice was covered by a permanent blanket of gray clouds, and the sun never showed its face.

"Ever since they changed the calendar, the seasons have gone mad!" the women complained. Sir Lorenzo tried patiently to explain to Clarice the astronomical reasons for which Pope Gregory XIII, eight years ago, had introduced the new calendar, eliminating ten days and passing directly from the 4th to the 15th of October 1582; but Clarice stubbornly refused to acknowledge them.

"The fact remains that now they say we're in March, but instead we're still in February, no wonder it's so cold! Think for a minute if it was right to go playing around with the seasons as they were created by God just to make the astronomers feel good!" she exclaimed.

Sir Alvise was puzzled as well.

What I still don't understand," he said, "is how they turned Monday into Friday. Because that famous 15th of October was supposed to have been a Monday, if you count the days the way you should. So then Sundays are no longer Sundays! But is a day Sunday because man decided to call it that or because it's the seventh day made by Our Lord?"

"But it's not like that!" rebutted Sir Lorenzo, who was about to lose his patience. "Look at it from this other point of view: the 4th of October, a Thursday, it was decided that the next day, Friday, instead of being called the 5th of October would be called the 15th. But it was still a Friday! And Sundays are still Sundays! Only the number has changed!"

"I suppose," Sir Alvise replied, unconvinced.

At the beginning of April, God willing, the weather stabilized a bit, and the sun peeked out of the clouds more often. In the garden the trees sprouted their first leaves, and the mud slowly dried up, until one day after lunch Clarice proposed to her husband to go take some air. Sir Lorenzo had been wanting to talk to her for a few days now but had not yet had the opportunity, so he was more than happy to accompany her out to the garden.

"You haven't said anything more about the pardon for that poor boy," his wife broached the subject, as soon as they were alone between the hedges of laurel.

"Ah, yes! I've been wanting to tell you," said Lorenzo, gravely. Clarice couldn't help but notice the seriousness of his expression, and she tightened he grip around his arm.

"So tell me then," she urged him, with a hint of apprehension.

"It's done," said Lorenzo. "the Council of Ten will not oppose it. The day after tomorrow it should go to the Senate, together with five or six other pardons, all with favorable opinions."

"So it is sure to pass?" asked Clarice.

"I'd say yes," Lorenzo agreed.

The woman dropped her hand from his arm, to better look him in the eye.

"Thank you! I never doubted it. But permit me then to ask why you have such an air of gravity?"

"But that's not why!" Lorenzo marveled. "It's that I have to give you some other news."

"Good or bad?" probed the woman, her heart throbbing.

"Good, if you don't worry about me."

They both remained silent for a minute, then Clarice broke a twig.

"You have to go away," she guessed.

Lorenzo thrust his eyes wide.

"How do you know that?"

Men are all alike, Clarice thought, and signed.

"It doesn't matter. Tell me all about it."

"I'm going to Constantinople."

"To Constantinople? To do what?"

Sir Lorenzo held back, undecided.

"I shouldn't tell anyone," he declared. Clarice stared straight into his eyes, until her husband lowered them.

"You can't not tell me," she declared simply.

Lorenzo pulled her to his chest, smelling the perfume in her hair.

"You won't tell anyone, ever, until I've returned." It wasn't a request, but an order, and Clarice understood.

"I swear," she said.

"Well then, our bailo in Constantinople is robbing the Republic. He buys wheat in the Levant, cheats on the price, and pockets the difference."

Clarice was the daughter of Venetian patricians, and she knew the rules.

"But that's extremely serious!" she exclaimed.

"It will cost him his head," Lorenzo agreed, serious. "But I have to manage to arrest him and bring him back to Venice before he knows he's been discovered. That's why nobody must know, really nobody, I mean it Clarice, not even my father."

"And they've chosen you to go and arrest him?"

"Yes, and you know, Clarice, the credit is all yours. Lorenzo said.

"Mine?" the woman was dumbfounded.

"It was Morosini that proposed me. If I hadn't gone to ask him for the pardon, it never would have crossed his mind."

Clarice didn't know whether to laugh or cry.

"It's a very important assignment, isn't it?"

"I'll say," Lorenzo said. "My future could depend on it. If I don't fail," he added gravely.

"You won't fail," Clarice affirmed, determined. Then she blanched.

"But will it be very dangerous?" she asked. Sir Lorenzo raised his shoulders.

"A trifle. Imagine, all I have to do is cross half of the Turkish empire, get to Constantinople, convince them to let me arrest the bailo, then go and get him in his own home without him ever suspecting a thing, and then go back across the Turkish empire to bring him here."

"And they've chosen you!" Clarice exclaimed, her eyes shining with pride. "Oh, you'll see!" she added, without specifying exactly what. Then another question came to mind.

"And who is this bailo?"

"I don't know if you know him. He's been there for over a year. Girolamo Lippomano.

Clarice thought.

Then she said, "Lippomano? I don't think I know him."

28

The Saturday after Easter, the Senate, to which the true purpose of the expedition had not been revealed, approved the appointment of Sir Lorenzo Bernardo as special envoy to Constantinople, and ordered him to depart as soon as possible on a galley made available to him expressly for the mission. Following his appointment, the Council of Ten and the Inquisitors for the Protection of State Secrets added that Lorenzo, after arresting Lippomano, was to send him back under escort and remain temporarily to serve as bailo until a successor was named. Sir Lorenzo took another three days to prepare his baggage, decide which servants to take with him and hire other hands for heavy work, and then went by boat to the Lido to speak with the commander of the galley. After a brief interlude of nice weather the sky had filled with clouds again, and a cold wind was blowing in from the north. The sopracomito's name was Giambattista Calbo, and he welcomed him with open arms.

"With this weather, you can see for yourself, we can't leave the harbor!"

Sir Lorenzo puffed with impatience.

"But we have to move fast, Master Giambattista, very fast."

"I know!" said the sopracomito. A secretary from the College had just come to bring him his orders: the galley *Calba* was to take on Signor Bernardo and all of his entourage, and take them where the same illustrious gentleman wished, without asking anything else and without first knowing the destination, which was to remain secret so as not to threaten the success of the mission. Having received such an order, the sopracomito was bursting with curiosity.

It took another three days until a man finally came from the Lido to Palazzo Bernardo to advise him that the weather was promising, and that they could depart that afternoon. The baggage had already been stowed on the galley for days, and the servants had also gone aboard the day before. At the Lido Sir Lorenzo met his secretary Francesco Vianello, his dragoman, or official interpreter, Marchetto Spinelli, and the captain of the police of the Council of Ten Filippo Casalini, who were to accompany him on his journey. The secretary was a young man with a long nose who often couldn't resist the impulse to laugh; the captain too, despite his occupation, was a jovial and jocular type; the dragoman, on the other hand, was a man well along in years, portly, and afflicted by a wheezing cough, who would have gladly done without the assignment. But there was no one else in Venice who knew Turkish that could be trusted with such a scabrous affair, and so Spinelli had received a peremptory order from the Signory to prepare to depart.

"Let's hope for the best!" he said, struggling up the ladder to the galley, and he made the sign of the cross.

The wind had died down, and the waters of the lagoon were sparkling calm. The sopracomito recited a prayer out loud, standing before the oarsmen and the rest of the crew on their knees; then the bugle sounded the departure, the oarsmen bent to their oars, and the galley pulled away from the dock. Sir Lorenzo was expecting the sopracomito to come and ask him for their course, but nothing happened. As the galley broke into the open sea, Master Giambattista was leaning on the railing of the stern boarding plank, eating an apple. It was evident that having to answer to someone else on board his own ship irritated him, and he had no intention of cooperating. Sir Lorenzo thought that it would be much better to try to tame him.

"Signor sopracomito," leaning next to him on the rail, "when can we look at the charts together, to decide our course."

"You are in command," Calbo grumbled, throwing the apple core into the sea.

"No," Lorenzo declared, "you are in command of the galley, and both of us are accountable to the Most Serene Lords. Come, if you will, I need to discuss our course with you."

A corpulent man, dressed in black, was strolling up the right nave of St. Mark's basilica, stopping every now and again to sign himself in front of the images. When he came to the end another man stepped out of the shadows of the columns and walked up to him. The corpulent man looked up high, as though his gaze were lost in the gold of the mosaics.

"So tell me," he whispered. The other man, looking around with feigned self-assurance, launched into a long story. The corpulent man listened intently, and at a certain point he flinched.

"Are you sure?" he hissed.

"Unfortunately, yes, your eminence," the other excused himself. "I saw the orders myself before sealing them."

The corpulent man lowered his eyes, and sighed.

"You have always been devoted to us. You will be compensated," he said; and he held out his chubby hand, glittering with rings. The other man kissed it, bowed deeply, and walked off. The basilica was deserted at that hour. The corpulent man stayed a little longer, kneeling to pray in several of the chapels; then he decided he had waited long enough. He made his way out at a surprisingly rapid pace, given his age and build; once outside, a servant who had been waiting for him, jumped to his feet and fell in behind him deferentially.

Half an hour later the corpulent man was sitting in his office in the same Palazzo of the Carmines where Senator

Lippomano had lived before his departure for Constantinople. The man was his brother, known as Prior Lippomano, because he lived on the income from a rich benefice in Brescia, even though he had not yet bothered to receive holy orders, so for all intents and purposes he was still a layman. As the evening darkness fell on Venice and the screeching calls of the seagulls resounded through the canals, the prior sat there in reflection, until the room was dark. Then he had the candles lighted and ordered his man servant:

"Go call the Mule."

A few minutes later the Mule was standing before him. He was the bastard brother of the two Lippomanos, thus coming by his nickname, and raised from birth as the most trusted of their servants.

"Listen, Mule," the prior said. "We have a serious problem and you're going to have to deal with it."

In a few words, he explained that he had come to know, from a reliable source, that the special envoy to Venice had orders from the Council of Ten to arrest the Senator and send him under escort to Venice. The Mule listened, impassively.

"Bernardo left yesterday, on the galley commanded by Giambattista Calbo. Nobody knows what route he wants to take. Listen to me, Mule, you need to leave right away. My brother knows nothing, warning him before Bernardo arrives down there is a matter of life or death. You'll take him this letter," he added, taking pen and inkwell in hand and starting to write rapidly. Curious, the Mule sharpened his gaze and saw that the letter was written in cipher; from the speed with which his master was writing, you could tell he was accustomed to using it. When he had finished, he folded the paper in four, took some sealing wax, tilted the candle and sealed the letter with one of the rings on his fingers.

"Is that all," the Mule asked laconically. The prior looked him up and down.

"No," he said. "I told you that nobody knows what route Bernardo will take. But you could find out. Rent a frigate, stop to ask in every port, find some trace. You don't need me to tell you what to do."

"No, eminence," the other man grinned.

"When you find him, see if the opportunity presents itself. Take your time, following him for a few days; anyway you'll have plenty of time to get ahead of him. All you need to do is get to Constantinople before he does."

"But if the opportunity were to present itself?" the Mule asked.

Prior Lippomano looked away.

"If Bernardo shouldn't arrive in Constantinople at all, that would be even better for my brother, you understand?"

"I understand," the other said.

"Bravo! Go, and don't worry about expenses," the prior ordered, taking out of his drawer a purse that was already filled to bulging.

"I'm off," the man said. Bowing, he doffed his cap, uncovering, under his hair that fashion dictated must be worn short, one whole ear and one ear cut in half by a shot from an harquebus, many years ago at Lepanto.

"Go with my blessing," said the prior; and dismissed him with a slow movement of his hand.

The *Calba*'s voyage started out smoothly; but on the third day the wind changed. The galley, which had stopped the night before in the little harbor of Veruda near Pola, wasn't able to leave again for three days. Sir Lorenzo, who hadn't had much experience at sea, was champing at the bit, but everybody on board was taking it so calmly that he became convinced there was nothing to be done; so he killed time by taking long walks on the beach, in the shade of the maritime pines, marveling at the whiteness of the fine sand and the iridescent reflections on the water.

The morning of the first of May it looked like the weather was changing for the better and the sopracomito declared that before nightfall, if it kept up like that, they could weigh anchor; right after that, however, a sailor came to say that an approaching sail had been sighted.

"A frigate," Master Giambattista judged, after observing it a little.

"As soon as it come into port, have its master come to me," said Lorenzo, who had orders to interrogate all the commanders of boats coming from the Levant to see if they had letters from Constantinople.

It was a frigate from Cattaro, and when he was interrogated the master immediately said, yes, he was going to Venice and he had been given a packet of letters. Sir Lorenzo ordered him to being them aboard the galley. The man was puzzled but in the end he obeyed. The packet was opened, and out of it came a dozen letters, several of which were sealed with the crest of the bailo of Constantinople.

"As you know, I have the authority to open them," declared Sir Lorenzo . The sopracomito, the secretary, and the dragoman, who were with him in the stern cabin, assented.

"Sir Francesco, let's keep a record," Sir Lorenzo ordered Vianello. "You, gentlemen, please do me the courtesy of going outside."

When they were alone the secretary broke the seals.

"They are in cipher!" he exclaimed, on seeing the letters. Ser Lorenzo nodded. "That was expected. They also provided me with the cipher used in Constantinople," and he put a bound notebook known as a quinternion on the table. "Get to work, Sir Francesco."

The secretary began toiling away at deciphering the letters, transcribing them into the record. It took a few hours; at the beginning, Sir Lorenzo was impatient and looked over his shoulder to read the lines already transcribed. Then he got tired and stood there waiting. The wind had died down, the galley had stopped rolling, it would have been a good time to leave port, but it was too important to verify what Lippomano had written. When the transcription was finished, Sir Lorenzo read through it quickly. The letters had been written between 15 March and 4 April, and they were similar to all those received by the Signory, every two or three weeks, from each of its ambassadors. The bailo had been invited to lunch by the aga of the janissaries, in his villa on the shores of the Golden Horn, and conversing in the garden, that dignitary had assured him that the sultan loved peace and appreciated its benefits; a Neapolitan slave who was working on painting a wall in the antechamber of the Gran Vizier had overheard a conversation concerning certain spies who were leaving for Venice, and had come to report it to the bailo, certain he would be compensated; in the Arsenal no preparations for war had been observed and no extraordinary personnel had been hired, a sure sign that the Turkish fleet would not be going to sea that summer; in the Jewish neighborhood some suspect cases of plague had been discovered, but there was no cause for worry because the same thing happened every year; the bailo had sustained an unforeseen expense for reparations to the roof of the palace; the price of grain in Constantinople was going up, as was inevitable at that time of year, and the merchants reported that it was going up even more in Salonika, because it was expected that the harvest would not be good. On reading these last lines, knowing what he knew about Lippomano's trafficking, Sir Lorenzo winced, then he turned to Vianello.

"All right. Now let's put the letters back in the packet, but we'll seal them together with a letter of ours addressed to His Serenity, where we explain where and when we broke the seals. And now that I think of it, Sir Francesco, wouldn't it be better to write as well to the Inquisitors for the Protection of State Secrets, advising them that we have read these letters?"

"It's always better to be safe, and put everything in the record," confirmed the secretary, who, though he was young, had learned how to stay afloat in a bureaucracy.

"Let's do it, then. Still more work for you," Sir Lorenzo smiled; then he went out to advise the sopracomito that they would be ready soon to weigh anchor.

Having left port that evening, the galley crossed the Gulf of Quarnero; then, since there was haze on the horizon and the pilot advised against going out on the open sea, it continued along through the narrow channels between the islands. At times the mountainous coast was so close it seemed they were sailing on a river, instead of the sea. A light northerly wind permitted them to use the sails, using the rowers only when they had to overcome a current or hug the shore for the night.

"This is almost a pleasure cruise," Vianello commented to Spinelli. The dragoman responded with a grunt, and the secretary, offended, decided it was better to drop it.

On the evening of 5 May they entered the port of Curzola, and Sir Lorenzo took Calbo aside. Up to that moment, obeying his instructions, he had discussed their course with him every evening, sketching out the next day's sail; but by now they were close to the last stop on their sea voyage.

The sopracomito spread out his nautical chart on the table in the cabin. It was drawn by hand, on parchment; and where the sheep's skin came to a point, in correspondence to the animal's neck, there was a brightly colored painting of our Lady of Perpetual Help. The Venetian bases in the Adriatic and the Ionian seas were marked with a red lion of St. Mark, and another much bigger lion marked Venice; it was so big that the city covered half of northern Italy. Genoa in comparison, Sir Lorenzo noted with satisfaction, was an insignificant dot.

"Can we get to Ragusa tomorrow evening?" he asked. Every time he asked him such a direct question Master Giambattista shrugged his shoulders, spread his arms, and talked about the wind and providence, avoiding an answer; but by now Sir Lorenzo was used to it.

"I ask you," he specified, "because Spinelli has to disembark there."

The sopracomito looked at him, surprised. He could tell me a little more, he thought. Sir Lorenzo read it in his eyes.

"Be patient, Master Giambattista, I'm obeying orders. So, can we get there tomorrow?"

The sopracomito pretended to examine the chart with care, and to reflect.

"If the wind doesn't change, yes," he finally admitted.

But the next day in the afternoon the wind did change. Maneuvering the sails it was possible to go on, but their speed was greatly reduced. Impatient, Sir Lorenzo looked at the sun going down fast behind the green mountains of the island.

"Let's put down the oars," he ordered.

The plunging of the oars immediately began to form a long frothy wake behind the stern of the galley. Even so, however, Master Giambattista and the pilot declared that they would not get to Ragusa before nightfall.

"If it were one of our ports they'd let us in even in the dark, but the Ragusans will never do that," the sopracomito predicted; and he spat. His contempt for Ragusans was shared by all of Venice: there's a city that pretends to be Christian , but it pays tribute to the Great Lord, and it informs him about everything that happens in Christendom, and if that weren't enough, it enjoys commercial privileges in the Turkish empire that would make things so much nicer for us Venetians, and instead we are denied them! There was enough to hope that one day or another God would grow tired of the Ragusan's hypocrisy and send them to ruin, them and their damned city. In the meantime, however, they had to make the best of a bad situation, and to tell the truth it wasn't without a certain utility even for Christians to be able to avail themselves of a place of encounter and exchange on the border between the two worlds: a no man's land to conduct a lot of business that otherwise they would not have known how to conclude.

"We can take to land a little sooner, if there's a suitable place,' Sir Lorenzo suggested. "We'll put the dragoman ashore there and tomorrow morning he can go on to Ragusa."

"And us? Aren't we going there too?" the sopracomito asked.

"No, Master Giambattista, we're going to Cattaro. And there I will probably leave you on your own."

I get it, the sopracomito thought, you're going to Constantinople. Until that night he had believed that their destination could be Ragusa, but if Bernardo was having himself taken all the way to Cattaro, the last Venetian base in the Adriatic, and with all that secrecy, and then he was going to disembark to continue the journey by land, they couldn't but be directed to the Sultan's capital. But why the devil did the dragoman have to stop at Ragusa? Oh well, let them do what they like, seeing as it's such a secret mission, he thought, with a touch or resentment.

A little before sunset the galley drew near to the shore a few miles before Ragusa. They found a local fisherman who spoke Italian and he was sent to find a horse or a mule to take the dragoman into the city. While they waited for him to come back, Sir Lorenzo gave Spinelli his final instructions. According to his calculations made before they left Venice, in order to carry all the people in the entourage and their baggage they would need to rent thirty-six horses.

"Try to get a good price, but don't bargain too much, we're in a hurry," Sir Lorenzo urged him.

"They'll want a deposit," the dragoman pointed out. Sir Lorenzo assented.

"You're too fair." He had someone bring him the bag where he kept the funds for the mission, took out a certain number of gold coins, counted them carefully, and had Spinelli sign a receipt.

"And as for the escort, what do you say?"

The dragoman shrugged his shoulders. Everybody knew that to travel in the Ottoman Empire without risking aggravation from the local authorities, to easily find hospitality in the caravanserai, or in the homes of local leaders without always having to take out your purse, you needed to have official escorts, able to attest that the travelers were under the protection of the Great Lord and to threaten punishment for those who might obstruct them.

The ideal would be a *chaush*," Sir Lorenzo observed. With that title, the Turks indicated the sultan's personal envoys, feared and obeyed wherever they presented themselves, with their enormous white turbans and the club that was the symbol of their rank. On receiving the news that a chaush was arriving in his territory there was not a provincial governor who did not tremble, asking himself if he was simply bringing him an order to carry out, or the notification of his destitution, and perhaps also a strip of silk with which to obediently strangle himself.

"It all comes down to whether there happens to be one in Ragusa who has to return to Constantinople; there may just be, there are always a lot of them on the roads," said Spinelli. "But he'll cost us very dear," he advised.

"And if not, two or three spahi or janissaries," Sir Lorenzo ordered, knowing that the Turkish military rarely refused an offer to earn a few zecchini by escorting Christian travelers, as well as drink wine at their expense as long as the journey lasted. "But let me remind you, you must negotiate without saying on behalf of whom, nor where you have to go. I don't want the Ragusans to inform the Porte that a Venetian envoy is on his way. You'll merely take them with you to Cattaro and there they will find out everything they need to know."

A few hours before dawn the dragoman set off for Ragusa with a mule and a servant, and the galley went out to sea and sailed south. At noon it entered the shallow waters of the Bay of Cattaro, filing past the Turkish fortress at Castelnuovo. Everybody looked with respect and a little apprehension at the powerful bastions, whose artillery had fired so often during the wars of the past against Venetian ships trying to get through the narrows to bring help to the city under siege; but now the Serene Republic and the Great Lord were at peace, and the castle, recognizing the flag of St. Mark waving on the stern, fired only one salvo as a salute.

That evening, after a slow and tortuous slalom through the shallows, the galley came into the harbor at Cattaro. From there on, along the coast, there was no longer a single port that had not fallen into Turkish hands. Sir Lorenzo went ashore to confabulate with the governor, to decide together the itinerary to follow on the land journey. They always had fresh news there from the bordering Turkish provinces, known as sanjaks, and they always knew more about their current situation than was known in Venice. The governor, or sanjak-bey, who had just finished dinner, insisted on preparing a new dinner and hurriedly summoned three or four of the city's best-heeled merchants, to get their opinions. They sat around the table talking late into the night, drinking the governor's malmsey.

The merchants weren't sure which route was the best. Although they forced themselves to speak Italian, every once in while they consulted among themselves in their Slavish tongue, and it was evident that sharp words were flying back and forth. In the end, the governor summed up the majority opinion: it was best to stay on the galley to the port of Alessio, and begin the land journey from there, going through the Turkish sanjak of Scutari, rather than take the road directly from Cattaro, through the sanjak of Ducagni.

"Oh, well," Sir Lorenzo sighed, "I was hoping not to have to get back on the galley. But if, as you say, the road isn't safe, we'll take the road from Scutari."

"You're better off that way. The Scutari sanjak-bey is a friend, and he's a good neighbor," the governor vouched for him; and the merchants, relieved, nodded their assent.

It's all very clear, Sir Lorenzo thought: the Ducagni sanjak-bey must have raised the percentage of his take for closing an eye to smuggling, and these good people, who are in it up to their ears, haven't yet worked out a deal with him.

"You, however," he ordered the governor, "will send someone immediately to the Scutari sanjak-bey, since he's such a good friend, so he'll do us the courtesy of writing us some letters of recommendation to use on the journey."

On the way back to the galley, Sir Lorenzo couldn't help but share his impressions with his secretary.

What a bunch of fine gentlemen!" he exclaimed. "Between them and the Turks, I don't know who steals more."

"That's true," Sir Francesco commented with a chuckle. "But at the same time you've got to sympathize with them. They live here, we might say, in the mouth of the Turks. How could they survive if they didn't adapt?"

The next day Spinelli arrived from Ragusa. He hadn't found any janissaries but he had worked out a deal with a transporter, a *caravanbashi'*, as the Turks called him, to rent thirty-six horses as far as Constantinople. The man had come with him to close the deal; he was dressed as a Turk but swore that he was Christian, and said his name was Xarco. He was a man with bristly black hair, turbid eyes, and an enormous mustache on the face of a heavy drinker. At the start he was cheerful, but when he learned that the deal was off his mood darkened.

"I'd offered a good price! Who else would give you all those horses for 950 aspers a head?" the Turk said heatedly.

"How much is that in ducats?" Sir Lorenzo asked Spinelli, after he had translated.

"Fifteen zecchini, at the local exchange rate," the dragoman responded promptly.

"That really isn't much," Sir Lorenzo exclaimed, pleasantly surprised.

"It's that the asper has depreciated. They've run out of silver and they coin them lighter. For us who come from Christendom, where we have gold it's a big advantage. Even now, you'll see, when they figure out we're Christians they'll want to be paid in zecchini rather than aspers.

"The fact remains that we're no longer leaving from here, but from Alessio. Ask him if he can let us have the horses down there."

The interpreter translated. There followed a long discussion in Turkish, of which Sir Lorenzo understood nothing, except that the other party was increasingly irritated.

"He says it can't be done," Spinelli translated in synthesis.

"Well then, tell him to go to the devil," Sir Lorenzo concluded abruptly; and started to get up. But the other man, his face red with anger, pounded his fist on the table.

"You don't tell me to go to the devil, you Venetian dog," he proffered in broken but perfectly comprehensible Italian. Sir Lorenzo turned red, and put his hand on the hilt of his sword.

"For goodness sake," the dragoman cried; and literally resorting to physical violence, he forced him to sit down, thanks also to the help of the secretary, who had made the same gesture on the other side.

"We can't mistreat this man! He's the son of a brother of the Aga of Castelnuovo," he explained excitedly.

"But didn't he say he was Christian?" Sir Lorenzo asked, dumbfounded.

"And so? Here anything is possible and you mustn't let it take you by surprise."

Xarco, speaking half Turk and half Italian, made it understood that he felt deeply offended.

"So what does he want?" Sir Lorenzo asked when he had finished, exasperated but nevertheless determined to bring the incident to a close. The dragoman reflected a moment.

"I gave him four zecchini as a deposit. I'd say that if we let him keep them that should be enough.

The man shook his head and added something.

"He wants one more," the interpreter translated.

"Let's give it to him then," concluded Sir Lorenzo, relieved, and sent him to the devil in his heart, given that he couldn't do it out loud.

With Xarco sent back to Ragusa, eight porters were hired to carry the litter that Sir Lorenzo had brought with him, in anticipation of a long and onerous journey. The merchants, called again into council, advised taking with them a dragoman for the Slavish language, since it was spoken by most of the peoples subject to the Turk; Sir Lorenzo approved, and they found a certain Master Vincenzo Pitcovich, who for an adequate compensation agreed to accompany the expedition to Constantinople.

In the days that followed, the wind from the Levant remained strong and steady, pushing the galley into open sea, and forcing the sopracomito and pilot to order frequent layovers. In those rare moments when the wind died down, the galley could proceed by rowing, and at a certain point a bit of northerly wind enabled it to get up some speed for a few hours; but overall Sir Lorenzo had the impression they were getting nowhere.

"I can't take anymore of this sailing!" he commented, when the crew of the ship were out of earshot. "Luckily, we're getting off now and we can continue on foot."

In a fishing village near Dolcigno, where they had stopped to take on firewood and water, Sir Lorenzo was eating lunch as the invited guest of the local priest, when a man came to knock on the door of the parish house to ask if the illustrious Signor Bernardo was there.

"I am he," said Lorenzo, surprised. The man was looking for him, and was going to Dolcigno, where he was expecting to find him; but noting from the road the galley anchored near the beach he got the idea to come and see. He was carrying two letters from the man that the governor of Cattaro had sent to the sanjak-bey of Scutari; Sir Lorenzo read the first and swore.

The secretary and the two interpreters, who were with him at the lunch, looked at him with surprise.

"Oh, it's really nothing! You remember the sanjak-bey of Scutari, the one that is such a great friend of ours, and whom the governor felt was such a good neighbor? Well, it seems they were a little too friendly, because he's been recalled, has already left, and nobody knows who's going to take his place."

"Oh, that's just great!" exclaimed the secretary.

"Gentlemen, that's the way it always is when you travel in the land of the Turk, you have to be ready for everything, be patient, and trust in God" said Spinelli. "But there's another letter, it looks like."

Sir Lorenzo broke the seal and read.

"Much better! Our man, seeing as he couldn't conclude anything in Scutari, decided to go to Alessio, and has contacted the transporters, he says there are horses. He also found a guide and two janissaries, but he didn't come to terms because they want too much."

The group calmed down.

"As for the janissaries, your lordship could also request them from the Aga of Dolcigno," Pitcovich suggested.

Sir Lorenzo nodded. The priest had prepared the lunch to be eaten under an arbor outside the parish house, sheltered from the sun, which at that hour was murderously hot; a light breeze brought them some cool air and below them the calm sea was shimmering. All around them, in the pine trees, the cicadas were buzzing like mad.

"Oh, what a lovely spot! If only we could stay here for a while, without a mission to carry out," Sir Lorenzo smiled. The others all laughingly agreed. The priest's wine was good and above all fresh from the wine cellar, so they had already drunk quite a bit.

"And if we didn't have to embark again on that damned galley," added Spinelli, whose cough had certainly not been cured by the humidity during the nights at sea.

"We'll do this," Sir Lorenzo decided. "You, Master Petrovich, will go tomorrow to Alessio to reserve the horses, and to find out the best route. You, instead," he continued, addressing Spinelli, "will go to Dolcigno to speak with the aga, and somehow see to it that he finds us two janissaries. I will stay here to wait for you. When everything has been arranged, we'll have a boat take us to Alessio with all our people and gear.

"And that's enough of the galley?" asked Spinelli, satisfied.

"Enough of the galley," Sir Lorenzo agreed; and he gave a sideways glance at secretary Vianello, who on hearing the news had comically raised his arms to thank the heavens.

29

The next day in the late afternoon Pitcovich returned, accompanied by a crowd of people: in addition to two Turkish merchants, he had brought with him several local notables, Albanians and Montenegrins, to discuss the rental of the horses. They had to give all those people something to eat and drink, sitting on cushions in the priest's house, because the weather had broken and it was raining. Sir Lorenzo asked the price of the horses; the elder of the two Turks, with the green turban of a hajji who has been to Mecca, answered gravely that he had to consult with his friends, that the price depended on the distance, and that it was by no means certain that the could find all the horses he was asking for, and let him take them so far away. The notables, sinking their fingers greedily into the rice and with their mustaches smeared with grease, had a long discussion in various languages. The whole business was taking forever, Sir Lorenzo was getting antsy, the priest's raki was streaming down all those throats like it was water. In the end a consensus was reached: the horses would be found but it wasn't possible to let them take them all the way to Constantinople, at any price. The notables, eating halva and finishing off the raki, suggested that he could take them as far as Salonika, and change them there; but the hajji shook his head vigorously. He wasn't willing to let them take his horses that far. If the most excellent gentlemen wished to take the road through Elbasan, he would let him have his horses as far as Elbasan, for ninety aspers a head.

"So little?" Sir Lorenzo marveled. Instead of translating, Master Pitcovich explained that Elbasan was only three days ride. Sir Lorenzo signed.

"If we have to renegotiate from scratch every three days, we'll never get there. Are we sure, at least, that we'll find horses down there?"

The two Turks gave him a big smile; there was no doubt, they guaranteed it.

It was already night when Spinelli arrived with two janissaries he'd found in Dolcigno, who had agreed to accompany the expedition to Constantinople; and after a few hours sleep, the baggage was loaded onto a boat, the servants boarded another, Bernardo said farewell to the sopracomito of the galley and climbed aboard the caïque, and the convoy sailed into the mouth of the Drina.

It took them two hours to reach Alessio, owing to the slow hull speed of the boats and the struggle against the current. The broad stream was placid and swampy, edged with bamboo and willow trees, and infested with mosquitoes.

"Will there be a Catholic church in Alessio?" Sir Lorenzo asked the janissaries. "Today is Sunday!" he added, addressing captain Casalini, who nodded: the last thing they needed while undertaking such a dangerous journey was to miss hearing Mass. The janissaries started laughing. "They say not to worry," Spinelli translated. "There is a church and we can hear all the masses we want." From the way they were laughing uncontrollably, it was evident that the janissaries had added something less respectful, but the dragoman avoided translating it.

In the stable on the ground floor of a palace in Ragusa, a mare was giving birth. The other horses, nervous, were kicking up their heels and neighing. A bull's-eye lantern, sitting on the trough, illuminated the stable boys who were standing around the animal, caressing her and talking to her in low voices. The owner, off to the side, was looking on with his hands on his hips, chewing on a piece of straw. When a servant came to call him, he gestured his annoyance, then he turned forcefully and followed him to the door of the stable. Standing out against the moonlight was the long shadow of a man wearing a mantle.

"Are you Xarco?" the man asked.

The other man answered yes.

"I've been told," the man went on, "that you rent horses."

Xarco nodded and invited him to come in the house. The man accepted with a brief bow. They sat down at a table and a servant lighted a candle.

"Where do you have to go?" Xarco asked, in bad Italian.

"To Constantinople," he said.

The other man raised an eyebrow.

"That's a long journey. And what road do you want to take?"

The man gave a hint of a smile.

"That depends on the information that you're able to give me. I pay well," he hurried to add, putting his bag on the table and loosening the purse-strings to show off the glitter of the gold. "You haven't already rented the horses to a Venetian gentleman and his entourage, have you?"

Xarco thought for a minute. In the stable the horses were neighing. The zecchini were shining in the candlelight.

"I didn't give them to him," he said in the end, with regret. "We couldn't agree on terms. But they came through here, if that's what you want to know."

The man nodded.

"And what road did they take?"

"They went to Alessio, from there on I don't know."

"Is there more than one road from there?"

"You can take the road to Skopje, or the road to Elbasan. But the Skopje road is safer," said Xarco. "So do you want the horse? You'll give me a thousand aspers, all the way to Constantinople."

"It's a deal," said the Mule.

There was indeed a Catholic church in Alessio, below the castle, served by a trio of shabbily-dressed Franciscans. Sir Lorenzo insisted that his whole entourage hear Mass, and he left a big donation, so God would be with them on that part of their journey. Then the company entered the city, and went to spend the night in the caravanserai, which turned out to be filthy and half-abandoned, Two Venetian merchants were camped there, on their way back from Salonika, and Sir Lorenzo talked with them about the price of grain. There was nobody else in the whole caravanserai but them and their servants.

"Why is there so little traffic?" Sir Lorenzo asked. The two shrugged their shoulders.

"Because of the Albanian brigands," they replied. Nobody feels safe passing through here."

Sir Lorenzo would have liked to ask why the two of them, on the other hand, felt it was safe, but he realized it was better to let it drop.

The next day, he had everybody awakened two hours before dawn, but it took so much time to load their baggage that by the time they left the sun was already high in the sky. In Sir Lorenzo's judgment, the porters hired in Cattaro didn't have much desire to work. As long as there was no need for it, his litter had been loaded onto two horses, rented especially for that purpose, and those people had practically nothing to do; but they were always at the end of the caravan. Sir Lorenzo, who went ahead on horseback together with the secretary, the captain, the two interpreters, the janissaries, and the servants he had brought from home, never stopped complaining about how slowly the caravan moved. The sun was sizzling;

after leaving Alessio they crossed a swampy area, with the road flooded and water up to the horse's knees, and they were eaten alive by mosquitoes. God willing, they made their way out of the swamps and came into a forest of poplar, and two hours later they came out into a plain cultivated with oats and wheat. To their left, a crest of barren, rocky mountains obstructed the horizon, while to the right, at certain sudden turns in the road, the sea stretched all the way to Dolcigno. The fields were deserted under the sun, and there were no houses to be seen anywhere.

"One thing's for sure, in a place like this a man could die of starvation!" Casalini commented, looking around him with surprise.

In the early afternoon they came within sight of a village.

"We'll have to stop here for the night," Pitcovich advised. "The aga is a relative of the bey of Dolcigno; he's already been advised that he's to offer us hospitality."

"But it's early yet. We've only been riding for five or six hours! We won't have done eighteen miles," Sir Lorenzo objected, perturbed.

"In the Turkish countryside you don't keep track of hours, or miles, but only days," the interpreter declared. "From Alessio to here is a day's journey, because farther ahead there is nowhere to sleep, and we'd risk spending the night out in the open at the mercy of brigands."

Sir Lorenzo resigned himself, but the next day he made everyone get up even earlier. The little caravan started out on the road before dawn, across an arid plain surrounded by mountains.

"This," said Pitcovich proudly, "is the great and famous country of Scanderberg, known as Tirana."

Sir Lorenzo knew the name of the hero, who had made famous throughout Italy the resistance of the Albanian Christians to the Turkish invasion, but he looked around in vain for some monument to his greatness; all he saw was a dust-blown village, with a battered minaret.

"The brigands live up there," the interpreter continued, pointing out some barely visible clusters of buildings way up in the mountains. "From up there they can see everything, and when some isolated traveler passes by, they come down to attack him. They can see us now too, but they won't attack because there are too many of us."

"Let's hope not," said Sir Lorenzo, steadfast; but deep inside he felt a chill.

But the merchants who had worked out some sort of arrangement with the brigands must have been fairly numerous, because crossing the plain of Tirana they encountered several caravans of horses loaded with wheat, headed to Alessio.

"The harvest has already begun in the land of the Turk," Spinelli remarked.

"And apparently it's going to be a good one," the secretary added. "To think that in Italy we're starving!"

Sir Lorenzo turned to Pitcovich.

"Master Vincenzo, when you come back through here, you should buy some of this grain and send it to Venice. It would be a great public service in this penurious year."

"That would take some capital," Master Vincenzo replied, prudently.

"There would be a large profit to be made," Sir Lorenzo hurried to add. "Think about it! I'm certain that if you proposed the deal to some of those merchants in Alessio, you'd find someone who'd be interested."

"I'll think about it," Pitcovich agreed.

The next day, after an exhausting trek of sixteen hours on horseback, on a rocky road that climbed up through the mountains, they finally came to Elbasan. Sir Lorenzo, who had had it with being jerked and jolted by this horse, decided it was time to make use of the litter. Where the road was smooth and flat the cumbersome piece of equipment remained attached to two horses, but in certain points the road was so steep that the animals couldn't make a go of it, and the porters had to called in. The jolts, on the shoulders of those eight men, were no less annoying than those Sir Lorenzo would have had to endure if he's stayed in the saddle, but in the litter, at least, he could stretch out, and even doze off a little. The only advantage was that as they went up the mountain the heat became less suffocating; but in the afternoon, after going through a pass, the road started to go down, and by evening they were back on the plain. There, enclosed within a circuit of ancient walls, rose up the city of Elbasan, bristling with minarets.

"It's a good size city, there are two caravanserais and a lot of trade," Pitcovich remarked with pleasure. At the gate, the janissaries explained to the guards that they were accompanying a Venetian envoy who was going to the Great Lord, and the travelers had no trouble.

"We'll have to go render homage to the sanjak-bey," Pitcovich observed.

"What's he like?"

"His name is Mehemet bey. He's the brother of a Persian lord, who during the last war swore allegiance to the Turkish Sultan. He likes gifts," the interpreter replied.

"Wouldn't you know it!" Vianello commented.

There were a lot of people staying at the caravanserai, Turkish and Italian merchants, and also a group that attracted Sir Lorenzo's attention: some rather unwholesome looking oversized men with a slave in handcuffs. On hearing Italian spoken, this latter, who appeared to be immersed in the most profound apathy, was startled into wakefulness; he exchanged a few words with his keepers, then he stood up and, still in handcuffs, went to present himself to Signor Bernardo.

"Excuse me, Signore, are you Italian?" he asked, in a Neapolitan accent.

Sir Lorenzo nodded courteously, and feeling a bit ridiculous, asked how he could be of service.

"You can take note of my name, and when you go back to Italy you can spread the news about me," the man said, dramatically displaying his wrists. His name was Master Polidoro Apricola, and he was a nobleman from Positano. He told of how the Barbary pirates had captured him several weeks ago, in a raid along the Neapolitan coast; and since he was a man in good condition, the rais had decided to send him as a gift to the Sultan.

"So they are taking me to Constantinople, and I don't know what's going to happen to me there," Master Polidoro concluded, in a tragic tone. Sir Lorenzo assured him that he would do everything he could for him, but for prudence sake he did not tell him that they too were headed to Constantinople

"Would you like me to pay those men something to take off your handcuffs?" he asked instead. The Neapolitan grimaced eloquently.

"I thank you! But they would put them back on as soon as you left."

At that point, his masters called him, and the man went back to sit with them; despite the handcuffs, Sir Lorenzo noted, he managed to eat the rice and mutton the pirates had had themselves served. Later that evening, his conscience started bothering him a little, but he told himself he'd done the only thing he could have done in the circumstances. He was a servant of the Republic, charged with a most serious mission, and he mustn't jeopardize its success in any way. Christian slaves captured by pirates were in great supply, and there were special institutions at work for their liberation, it wasn't his responsibility. Sir Lorenzo promised he would make a special donation to the brothers of Mercy, on his return to Italy.

The next day, having sent the horses back to the merchants

in Alessio, the search for new horses began. As Sir Lorenzo had foreseen, the task was anything but easy; luckily the san-jak-bey, pleased with his gifts, sent a safe conduct pass and four of his spahi to escort the caravan. Secretary Vianello, who kept the accounts, was tearing his hair out at the thought of having to pay all those people, but the assurance they offered was decisive for the horse dealers, and after two days of exhausting negotiations, they were able to get back on the road, with horses as far as Monastir.

It was pouring rain, and along the way the travelers were surprised by a furious hailstorm; the road climbed steeply up some rocky slopes, amid gloomy pine forests, so the litter had to almost always be carried by hand. They spent the night in the farmhouse of some dirt-poor farmers, so filthy it grabbed you by the throat. There was no bread, and the travelers had to eat the biscuit they'd brought with them; the worst was that there was no wine, and the wine they'd brought from Venice was finished.

"No wine!" Vianello and Casalini kept repeating, looking at each other in consternation. "What a country!"

Spinelli and Pitcovich, who knew the territory, maintained an air of superiority.

"My dear sirs," they said, "from now on you'll have to get used to it; the more the land is inhabited by Turks, the less wine we're going to find."

Vianello made everybody laugh by pointing out that the janissaries and the spahi, intent on consuming their frugal meal in a corner of the only room, had followed with great attention the conversation about the wine between the interpreter and the farmers, and not even they seemed very satisfied at the out-come. On the preceding days the janissaries had never shown themselves to be bashful when it came to swilling their share of the wine.

"What can you do?" Spinelli said. "The janissaries were all

born Christians, the Great Lord takes them when they're children, clips them, and turns them into Mohammedans"—with that *clips them*, the dragoman was referring to circumcision—"but they've had the wine habit since they were children; it's hard to give up! Those born Turks, on the other hand, easily do without it."

Pitcovich rebutted that it wasn't true, and that he had known a lot of born Mohammedans who drank like Germans; this gave rise to a discussion that brought some cheer to an otherwise gloomy evening. Then they all went to sleep on piles of straw, some in the house and some in the barn, while the pouring rain kept up a drum beat on the roof.

The next day the company came to an enormous lake, and they rode along the shore for nearly the entire day.

"Lake Ocrida," Pitcovich said, rubbing his hands together. "Here we're going to eat well."

They stopped for the night in a big village on the shore of the lake.

Sir Lorenzo was moved to see that the straw roofs of all the houses were home to stork's nests. For some reason he was particularly fond of birds. As a boy back in Venice he could spend hours watching the seagulls from the balcony of Palazzo Bernardo.

"How wonderful," he exclaimed, pointing at the great birds solemnly crossing the horizon. "And doesn't anyone mistreat them?" he added. Pitcovich shook his head.

"On the contrary, everybody respects them, because they believe that these birds bring god luck where they build their nests."

"What do you think, Master Pitcovich, how much longer do we hve before we get to Salonika?" Sir Lorenzo asked that night. The interpreter counted on his fingers.

"If everything goes well, we can be there in a week."

"And from there to Constantinople?"

"With a little luck, another two weeks."

Sir Lorenzo pondered. It was 21 May; by mid-June they could be in Constantinople.

The rain was pouring down. The caravan was crossing fertile plains, planted with grain; and Sir Lorenzo could not help but contemplate that sea of ears of wheat, all ready for the harvest, and think about the famine that for three years had afflicted Italy. Before Lippomano had left for Constantinople he hardly knew him, and he had formed no opinion about him, except perhaps that he was a little too haughty with his peers. When Morosini had explained the mission to him, more than anything else he had been amazed at the audacity of the scam, and persuaded that a man capable of orchestrating it was a danger to the Republic. Now, however, he realized the revolting immorality of this particular scam, raising the price of grain distributed to the people by the government in those years of famine, and the difference, pulled out of the empty bellies of the poor, ended up in the pocket of Senator Lippomano. It would be good to hear what Clarice thought of it, Sir Lorenzo reflected; and he felt more acutely than ever the distance from his wife. But they had taught him that a Venetian patrician must be ready to sacrifice his feelings and his domestic happiness for the good of St. Mark.

The fatigue of that exhausting and monotonous journey was beginning to make itself felt; they had all become more taciturn. Sir Lorenzo almost always traveled in his litter, and although his porters didn't dare protest, you could see they were unhappy. Every day it took them longer to get ready to leave, and it took solicitations and threats to get them up and back on the road after meals. For a while they went along the shore of another big lake, then they stopped at a farmhouse for lunch; from the rooftops the storks looked down, vaguely alarmed, at all those men and horses. The farmer, who had brought them some brown bread, fresh cheese, and wine, warned them that from that point on the road was dangerous.

"Dangerous, why?" Sir Lorenzo wanted to know.

"Murderers," Pitcovich replied, after questioning at length the farmer, whom he had a lot of trouble understanding. "The wood is a good place for ambushes."

The man explained, half in words and half in gestures, and with repeated signs of the cross, that right there, just the day before, a traveler had been murdered; and he offered to take them to see the place.

"That's just great!" Vianello said, trying to joke about it; but nobody was in the mood. The farmer led them down the road to the point where it went into the wood.

"Here it is."

On the side of the path there was a big patch of congealed blood surrounded by confusing footprints and horses' hooves.

"And who was he?" Sir Lorenzo waned to know.

The farmer explained that the victim was a Turk, sent by his master to Salonika to buy supplies for a wedding feast.

"Poor guy," Vianello commented.

Sir Lorenzo ordered that all those on horseback keep their weapons at the ready and that the pack horses and people on foot should proceed in the middle of the armed riders. He himself rode in the avant-garde, together with Casalini and the two Janissaries with their harquebuses loaded and the fuses lighted. The wood, in and of itself, was a common beech-wood, full of birds that noisily took flight when the travelers went by; but everybody thought it looked haunted, all the more so since they proceeded in silence, their ears perked up to hear any revealing noise. They were expecting to see at any moment the flash of a weapon amid the smooth, shiny trunks of the beeches.

"Wait!" Sir Lorenzo said. "What's that?"

Behind them they could hear the trot of a horse. The four

of them, suspecting, turned around. But it was only Vianello, who had spurred his horse to join them.

"Eminence," he said, "there is a man who has followed us and asks if he can make the crossing with us, for fear of brigands."

"And who is he?" asked Sir Lorenzo.

"A Venetian. An agent of the Dolfin house, on his way to Salonika."

Sir Lorenzo tightened his shoulders.

"That's fine with me," he said, with a hint of arrogance. The Bernardos had never had much to do with the Dolfin bankers, though they certainly were not enemies. Vianello spurred his horse, and shortly afterwards the new arrival joined them. With one glance he recognized, from his clothing and his attitude, which of the four was Sir Lorenzo.

"Signor master," he said, "your slave. Permit me to thank you. Without your company I wouldn't have dared take this road."

The man doffed his cap, displaying a handsome virile face, short-clipped iron-gray hair, and a mutilated ear. Sir Lorenzo made a gesture of consideration.

"You work for the Dolfin house?"

"Yes, your eminence," the Mule confirmed, with enthusiasm.

"Fine, you can come with us," said Sir Lorenzo. "Do you have weapons?"

"Eminence," the other laughed, pointing to a small harquebus, hanging from his saddle-bow, "and who would undertake this journey without a weapon?"

"Excellent, then you too keep your eyes open!" Sir Lorenzo concluded.

In the end, they didn't see any brigands; and when they came out of the wood, after several hours, they all breathed a sigh of relief. After crossing over a torrent on a wooden bridge, the caravan climbed a hill to a shabby little village, dominated by the ruins of a castle. The caravanserai was half-abandoned, on the edge of a swampy depression, and the Turk that ran it had a face that did not inspire trust.

"If you ask me he's the one who murdered that poor guy back there," Vianello joked.

Rather than that portico full of spider webs and rubbish, they preferred to stay out in the open; but the humidity soon forced them to come back in.

"This place is called Vodena," Pitcovich told them, "You see all this water? Well, in Slav water is called *voda*. So the place probably takes its name from the water."

"Even worse, I'm afraid we won't get any wine," Sir Lorenzo predicted. But the Turk surprised them.

"No, why do you say that?" said Spinelli, who had questioned the Turk in his language. "Certainly, there's wine"; and he produced a cask, together with some large loaves of brown bread.

"Well, these are conditions we can adapt to," Sir Lorenzo concluded philosophically.

Since the Turk assured them that from there they could reach Salonika in two days ride, Sir Lorenzo decided to send ahead at a gallop two men from the entourage together with a Turk recruited on the spot, to start looking for horses. In Monastir, the Jewish consul had given him some letters for his brother, Rabbi Abraham, insisting that he look him up in Salonika.

"Go to the Jew and see what he can do for you. Maybe that way we won't have to lose another three days!" Sir Lorenzo ordered his men.

The man from the Dolfin bank also came to bid them farewell. Now that the road was safe, he said, he would go on alone, since riding alone he could go much faster than the caravan, slowed down as it was by the litter, all that baggage, and the men on foot. Sir Lorenzo said good-bye to him with indifference, climbed into the litter, and didn't think about him again.

Fortunately, the road turned flat again, among fertile fields of grain and villages with their houses covered with tile roofs, instead of straw like the ones they'd seen up to then. The weather was dry and the fine, white dust of the road made them thirsty. At a certain point a great cloud of dust rose up on the horizon and threw them all into alarm; they prepared their weapons and waited to see who they would encounter, but almost immediately the two janissaries, who had gone ahead, came back laughing.

"It's just some peaceful merchants," they explained.

"If you say so, but they look pretty strange to me," said Vianello, sharpening his gaze. And indeed, the figures that began to come into view out of the distance were disturbing, and the Venetians looked at each other with anxiety, until Spinelli started to laugh as well.

"They're camels!"

Sir Lorenzo rejoiced; like all the others, with the exception of the dragoman, he had never seen those fabulous beasts.

"We will be able to say that we've also seen this!" Casalini repeated in amazement.

"The Orient starts much nearer than I imagined," Sir Lorenzo commented, pensively.

The caravan reached them and passed them by. The Venetians stood there with their eyes thrust open watching those strangely swaying beasts go by, and they kept on talking about them for the longest time. Later on, however, at a bend in the road some more camels appeared: an entire small herd this time, that a merchant was taking to Monastir to sell. Sir Lorenzo wanted to examine them again up close, but the other Venetians, and especially the servants, had lost a lot of their enthusiasm.

"We've already seem them, they're all the same," they grumbled.

30

The company was proceeding laboriously, scaling the side of a mountain, when all of a sudden the sea opened up on the horizon.

"That's the Gulf of Salonika," Spinelli announced.

"*Thalassa! Thalassa!*" Sir Lorenzo said; but nobody understood.

"Smell the air!" the secretary exclaimed, opening his arms out wide. And it was true; the sea air made it all the way up there from the gulf. Sir Lorenzo decided to go a ways on foot and got down off his litter. The porters made some comment in their language, and Sir Lorenzo was glad not to have understood.

They stopped for the night in a walled city, which as far as they could tell was called Genizzè. A Greek took them to the caravanserai; it was positioned in an out of the way location, far away from the harbor, but instead of having to stay in the barn with the horses, or under a portico around a courtyard, as in all the other caravanserais they'd encountered, this one had bedrooms on the first floor.

"Stay here tonight, and shut yourselves inside," said the Greek, in labored Italian.

"What's that?" asked Sir Lorenzo, who hadn't understood.

"I say don't go outside in the dark, and you'll be fine," the man insisted.

The travelers wanted to know why. The Greek explained that the city was inhabited by both Greeks and Turks.

"Our people are peaceful, but the Turks who live here are

violent. They kill each other. It's better to stay in the house at night," he said again.

The Venetians looked at one another. Spinelli shrugged his shoulders.

"Could be," he said. "But don't worry, usually the Turks are the most peaceful people in the world."

Vianello laughed.

"I guess that's why they've conquered just about everything!"

"Go tell that to Bragadin," Sir Lorenzo said, glumly, remembering the defender of Famagusta, skinned alive after surrendering.

"But that was an accident," Spinelli was fervid. "Brigadin was a hothead, everyone knew that. They called him the fair. And pasha Mustafà was someone who easily got a fly up his nose. Brigadin provoked him, he went to tell him to his face that before surrendering he had killed all the prisoners and that he wasn't the least bit sorry about it, and it went the way it went. Everyone in Constantinople was upset by all that butchery, I can guarantee you that. And later on even Mustafà regretted it. I know that, I was the dragoman for Master Andrea Bodoer, when he went to negotiate the peace with the Porte; we also went to the home of Mustafà, who gave us a warm welcome; he said he was sorry to have exaggerated."

"So let's call it an exaggeration!" Sir Lorenzo remarked. "Anyway, even if the Turks are peaceful people, these ones here look like they've had a change of character, so order everyone to stay inside tonight; I don't want any trouble."

Despite everything, the night passed without incident, and at dawn the caravan was back on the road, across a wide stretch of grassy hills.

"So much land!" commented Sir Lorenzo, thinking of his country estates outside of Padua and Treviso, where there wasn't a patch of land that wasn't occupied by wheat, vineyards, or the newly arrived American corn, which the farmers called *meliga*, even though, who knows why, some had started calling it *granturco* or Turkish grain. It wasn't until after midday that they came upon a farmhouse and stopped to have lunch near the well, in the shade of the age-old plane trees. As the first horses approached the spot, a deafening caw rose up out of the trees as a huge flock of crows took flight. Vianello made the sign of the cross, and Sir Lorenzo, observing his people, noticed that many of them had taken it as a bad omen.

"Be brave!" he exclaimed. "We've come this far, what do you think can happen to us now?"

Reluctantly, the men unloaded the horses. Just then, some barefoot girls emerged from the farmhouse, carrying baskets atop their blonde heads; they put them down on the grass, and pulled out some appetizing buns cooked under the ashes.

"So much for your bad omen!" Sir Lorenzo laughed, as the secretary took out his purse and the men, feeling cocky again, crowded around the girls, playing around and trying to strike up a conversation. The buns were good and everybody ate their fill. Every now and again a scream was heard, when one of the men let his hands go a bit too far, but it was clear that the girls were used to dealing with travelers passing through, and they knew how to handle themselves. Suddenly, however, one of them, sitting on the grass talking animatedly with one of the janissaries, gave herself a slap in the forehead as though she had forgotten something, blurted out an exclamation in her language, got up and raced toward the farmhouse. Sir Lorenzo looked with delight and also, without letting on, with a hint of arousal at the barefoot figure as she ran, her blonde hair blowing in the wind. A second later the girl came back, carrying another bun, and came to offer it to him with a bow.

"For the lord and master," Pitcovich translated.

Sir Lorenzo took the bun in hand, it was browned and filled with raisins.

"What a shame," he said, "I'm not hungry. Tell her she should eat it!" he concluded, giving it back to her with a smile. The girl bowed again, ran to sit down in the grass and bit into the bun. The janissary wanted a piece of it, but the girl, laughing, held him off and kept on eating, kicking at him to keep him away.

"It's time to leave," said Sir Lorenzo. "Tell the men to get up."

"That's won't be easy," Vianello observed. "It's so nice here."

"It's nice, but we have to leave," said Sir Lorenzo, severely.

Just then, a scream made them all turn around. The girl, suddenly ashen, was holding her hands over her belly. Then she screamed again, and tried to get to her feet, but she couldn't do it. Her face had turned a greenish color, her eyes were popping out of their sockets, and she was writhing on the ground, screaming. The janissary had jumped up on his feet, and was looking around, lost. The other young girls came running over and knelt down next to her, chattering away at her. The girl struggled to respond, then she cried out again and contracted in pain. The men were all there, forming a circle around her, as they girls screamed and tore at their hair. An old man and an old woman came out of the farmhouse. But when they arrived at the spot, the girl made one last cry and died.

"Poison!" said Casalini, with an air of professional competence, after leaning over her for an instant.

"The bun," Sir Lorenzo noted, his face pallid.

Pitcovich questioned the girls and the old couple. It came out that the night before a man, a foreigner, had stopped to sleep at the farmhouse.

"He slept with this poor thing," the interpreter translated. The old woman added something in a harsh tone.

"She says she was one who went along."

"A foreigner," Sir Lorenzo repeated. "And then?"

"And then he advised them that today a caravan would be arriving, and that they should prepare some food, because the travelers would pay well. And he had them make a sweet bun for the lord and master, saying they had to offer it directly to the master and to no one else, and that way he would pay even better."

"He had them prepare it?"

"He insisted on seeing how we prepared it," the girls replied, in tears. Sir Lorenzo and the others looked each other in the eye, mute.

"He wanted you," Spinelli finally remarked.

"We'll have to be on the alert," Sir Lorenzo said, matter-of-factly. "Give these poor people some money so they can give her a Christian burial," he added. He gave the girl one last look but glanced away immediately from that swollen, clay-green face.

"A foreigner," he repeated under his breath, pensively.

From then on the journey continued in a sinister atmosphere. Knowing he was an assassin's target, having to beware of ambushes even in areas that were free of brigands, having to scrutinize what he ate at every meal, robbed Sir Lorenzo of the pleasure, which up to then he had enjoyed, of discovering a new world. With their harquebuses at the ready, they went over the wooden bridges that crossed the muddy waters of the Vardar, swollen from the recent rains. Soon afterwards they came upon a large number of men and horses. Most of the men had dismounted, but some were still in the saddle; on their shoulders they were carrying long lances made of bamboo, and two of them were carrying pennants made from horse tails. On seeing the caravan approach, a small group of those horsemen moved toward them; Sir Lorenzo sent the dragoman and the janissaries to meet them. After a brief discussion, the horsemen rode away and Spinelli reported that it was the bey of Salonika, who was on his way to conduct investigation, accompanied by two companies of cavalry.

"Could it have something to do with what happened to us?" Vianello wondered.

"How would they have found out about it?" Casalini judiciously objected.

"True enough," the secretary acknowledged. "Well then, could it be about that other murder?" he hazarded.

"That's not possible," Spinelli patiently explained. "The river we crossed is the border between Bulgaria and Tessaglia. The bey would never go to investigate outside of his sanjak."

"And not only, imagine the bey bothering to look into something so small," Sir Lorenzo added; but Spinelli shook his head.

"I wouldn't rule it out. Anything can happen here. They steal, and everything is for sale, but it also happens that an incident of that nature, which in Venice would be immediately forgotten, they go out of their way to find the culprits and punish them. With the Turks you never know; and that's how they get all the other peoples to obey them."

Sir Lorenzo didn't respond. That journey through the land of the Turk gave rise to reflections that surprised even him, as though now that Venice was so far away everything they had taught him and that he had always taken for granted had suddenly become less certain. Spinelli, on the other hand, as he gradually penetrated deeper into Turkish territory, became transformed. The heat had cured all of his ailments, and the food and air, evidently suited him better than what he was used to at home.

A few days later, when they had also left Salonika behind them, the travelers saw some additional signs of reinforced surveillance as they moved closer to Constantinople. They were sleeping, as usual, under the portico of a caravanserai, when they heard the sound of a large number of approaching horses, and the travelers, brusquely awakened, saw a group of lancers come into the courtyard. You could tell they were only an advance guard, because outside the gate the clopping hooves, the neighing, and the shouting in Turkish were in crescendo.

"We're going to end up being thrown out of here," said Spinelli, who had gone to hear what was going on. "Some big shot is arriving."

The owners of the caravanserai had a long discussion with the leader of the horsemen; then the leader made a sign and left.

"It went well!" the dragoman reported. "Outside there's an envoy from the Sultan on his way to do an investigation, with one hundred and thirty horses, and they wanted to sleep here! They ordered the owners to throw everybody out but luckily they decided to leave things alone; they've got their own pavilions and they'll put them up in the countryside."

"Another investigation! All they do in this country is conduct investigations!" Sir Lorenzo marveled.

"That's how the Great Lord governs," Spinelli declared respectfully.

The secretary started laughing.

"And this one is also about that poor guy who was killed up there!"

The joke was gruesome but they all couldn't help laughing anyway.

"It won't be long till the Turk and all his Janissaries come to investigate in person," Vianello upped the ante.

Now they were all laughing so loudly that someone came to look out the upstairs window.

"Enough now! Signor Francesco, let us go to sleep!" Sir Lorenzo intimated, struggling to hold back the laughter.

But it was their fate not to sleep that night. They had all been asleep for a while when they were wakened again by the sound of a shot nearby, followed by a chaotic shootout, shout-

ing, and neighing. A minute later they were all on their feet
with their weapons in hand. From outside they were knocking
on the locked door of the caravanserai and calling repeatedly.
Finally someone opened the door and a group of horsemen
erupted into the courtyard. Shouting, they made it understood
that they wanted to speak with the leader of the Venetians. Sir
Lorenzo, together with Spinelli, took a step forward; and the
servants were all around them with swords and harquebuses.

"Are you the Venetians who arrived last night?" shouted
the commander of the cavalry.

Spinelli answered yes.

"And how many are you?"

Sir Lorenzo and his interpreter did a quick tally. Between
porters and stablemen hired on the way, guides and escorts
who had joined up with the company, it wasn't easy to be certain. Finally they decided on a figure.

"And this one here is one of yours?" the Turk shouted.
Through the front door came a group of foot soldiers, dragging a body behind them. They pulled him through the dirt
to the portico, and abandoned him at Sir Lorenzo's feet. In
the moonlight you could see right away that he was dead,
with his jacket pierced by two harquebus balls and soaked
with blood. Sir Lorenzo bent down to look at his face and
snapped back up.

"It's the man from the Dolfin bank," he said softly. He had
recognized him more by the mutilated ear than by his features,
contracted by death spasms.

"He's not one of ours," Spinelli responded. The Turk
pulled on his mustache.

"But is he a Venetian or not?" he replied.

"He's a Venetian, but we don't know him, he's not one of
ours," the dragoman said again, after consulting briefly with
Sir Lorenzo. The Turk sneered and then he jumped down off
his horse and walked over to them, dragging his scimitar in the

dirt. When he got near the body, he kicked it in contempt and started talking in an irascible tone.

"They say this man was surprised outside here, he was roaming around outside the caravanserai and he was armed. The patrol decided to stop him. He shot at them and ran away. They shot him and killed him."

While Spinelli was translating what he had said the Turk observed the faces of the two Venetians intently.

"Tell him that none of our group is missing, he can verify that for himself, and that he can do whatever he wants with this body," Sir Lorenzo said, his voice flat. The Turk listened to his response. Then with the point of his sheath he began turning the dead man's clothes inside out. From one of his jacket pockets a packet of letters slid out into the dust. Instinctively, Sir Lorenzo bent to pick them up, but the Turk stopped him, pointing his sheath at him. Then he courteously moved him out of the way, gathered up the letters, glanced at them and stuck them in his turban, saying something in a slightly derisive tone.

"He says if we don't know him, we can't be interested in his papers," Spinelli translated.

The Turks left, taking the body with them. It was the middle of the night, and they all went back to throw themselves on the straw, but nobody wanted to go to sleep.

"You know what I think?" Casalini said.

"I know, Signor Filippo" Sir Lorenzo intimated. "That that man was here for us, and that perhaps he was the mysterious foreigner who poisoned the bun."

"That's it, exactly," said the captain, disappointed.

"If we could get those letters!" Vianello observed.

"We can always try to buy them," Sir Lorenzo reasoned. "You," he said to Spinelli," tomorrow morning you'll go to the captain to see whether for the right amount of money he's willing to let us have them. You'll tell him that since the man dressed like a Venetian, we're afraid he might have been a traitor and we want to be able to report him to the Signory."

But the next morning, when the doors of the caravanserai opened, the Turks had already dismantled their camp and vanished.

The next day the heat granted them a truce. Having got under way at the first light of dawn, they circled yet another lake and then entered a gorge between the mountains.

"What refreshing coolness, how wonderful, what a beautiful country!" Spinelli delighted. At mid-morning they stopped below a rise, dominated by the ruins of a castle.

"Who knows whose this was! Maybe it was built by Constantine, and we know nothing about it, eh, Signor Filippo?" Sir Lorenzo said. The captain spread his arms.

"As far as I'm concerned, they could be ancient ruins or just as easily the house of the current sultan's father, they're still rocks."

Spinelli shook his head; such irreverence annoyed him. But they were all happy to eat and with good appetites. The death of the man from the Dolfin bank, as they continued to call him among themselves, although it confirmed that someone was really aiming for Sir Lorenzo, made them think that for the moment at least the threat had been neutralized.

In the afternoon the Gulf of Kavala opened up on their right, and they went along the shore for hours, in the shade of the maritime pine trees, enchanted by the rhythmic rasping of the cicadas. The heat was rising again, despite the sea air, and on the following days the situation got worse. Under a searing sun they crossed a dazzling stretch of salt flats; then the road began to climb again through a barren, rocky valley. The wagons had such a hard time making headway that they fell behind, and at a certain point Sir Lorenzo, the secretary and the dragoman found themselves alone with the litter carriers.

If someone got the idea to assassinate us here, it wouldn't take them long," Spinelli observed.

"But we're all armed, and they're not," Sir Lorenzo pointed out.

"I still say we'd be better off waiting for the others," the dragoman stuck to his guns.

It wasn't until the second day that they came within sight of Kavala. The city rose up on a spur that stretched out over the azure waters of the gulf, surrounded by turreted walls, and dominated by a castle of white limestone. Spinelli came over to Sir Lorenzo and pointed out a mountain that you could barely make out in the distance, almost suspended between sea and sky.

"That," he said, "is Mount Athos. It is said that there are more than twenty monasteries there of Greek monks, and it's the most sacred place in their entire country."

But Sir Lorenzo wasn't interested.

"Signor Marchetto," he said, "we'll go there in pilgrimage another time, now let's think about our journey, which it seems to me is not moving ahead."

"It's the heat," the secretary observed. "The men and the animals can't take it." And truly, despite the vicinity of the sea, the heat was dreadful; when they came to a stream the horses couldn't be pulled away from drinking.

"If we decided to travel by night?" Sir Lorenzo proposed.

They consulted with the janissaries and with the local people, and it turned out that the area was so safe by now that they could allow themselves to travel by night.

"That's what we'll do then," Sir Lorenzo decided, pretending not to notice Spinelli's sighs.

That afternoon, after they had something to eat, they all went to sleep. There wasn't a living soul in the whole city; even the stray dogs were sleeping, all curled up wherever there was a bit of shade. But Sir Lorenzo couldn't get to sleep. He'd had more to drink than usual, and a lot of confused images were whirling around in his head: his first-born son, whom he had been able to enjoy for such a short time before he'd had to leave; the endless fields of grain in the land of the Turk, and Lippomano negotiating with merchants from his palace in Pera and cheating on the price; the man with the mutilated ear, who had tried to kill him; Clarice with whom he had been sleeping again for just a few days, three months after she gave birth, her tiny breasts, not deformed by nursing, since she hadn't nursed the baby even for a day, her slender legs, the sparkle in he eye. Certainly, by this time, there were letters from her trying to catch up with him, and maybe they would reach him in Constantinople; maybe they would even announce to him that she was expecting again! Then he realized that it wasn't possible, the times didn't correspond. The first letters that would reach him would have been written just a few days after he left. Like the ones, he thought, that the assassin had in his pocket . . . He went to splash some water on his face, then he decided to go down to the marina for some fresh air; here it was suffocating. He woke up two servants and headed out; one of the two preceded him, the other followed holding an open parasol over his head.

Going down to the beach, he looked inside an improvised shed and saw the skeleton of a boat under construction. Curious, he went over to get a better look. The lumber and tools were carelessly scattered all around, and a dozen or so workers were sleeping in the shade of the shed. As the three men arrived one of the workers awoke and pulled himself up, and Sir Lorenzo saw from his dark clothes and beard that he was a Greek priest.

"Good day," said Sir Lorenzo, in Italian. The other responded in the same language, albeit with a comical accent and jumbling the words. On seeing that he could communicate, Sir Lorenzo asked him what he was building. The other explained that it was a twenty-three bench galliot, being built for the bey of Kavala.

"But the bey is not here now," said the priest; and he laughed, indicating the sleeping workers.

Sir Lorenzo was amazed to see a priest working in a shipyard, and on top of that working for Turks. The priest spread out his arms.

"What can I do? I've got to make a living somehow. I'm certainly not the only one," he added, with a gesture; and Sir Lorenzo noticed that several other sleeping workers had the tunic and the beard of the *papas*. "How do you put it? We have families to feed!"

It's true, Sir Lorenzo thought, Greek priests can marry, and here they are even working in a shipyard. The world upside down!

"Is the pay good?" he queried. The other thrust open his eyes.

"Good! Good! The bey pays seven aspers a day."

Sir Lorenzo made a quick calculation. Seven aspers are ten and a half *marchetti*; more or less what a manual laborer gets in Venice. Strange! The laws are different, the religions too, but money has the same value everywhere.

"And is today's work paid too?" he asked, nodding with a smile at the snoring workers.

"Sure it is!" the priest nodded, with a serious look. "And where are you from?" he then asked. From Venice, Sir Lorenzo answered with pride. The other bared his toothless gums in a big smile.

"Venetians and Greeks, friends! One face, one race!" he declared.

Sir Lorenzo was afraid that in a minute he'd be asking him for a donation; so he hinted at a bow, given that the other man was still a priest, albeit a Greek one, and he left. The priest stood there for a few minutes watching him, then he went back behind he shed to throw himself down on the sand.

Just before sunset they had dinner, and at the *Ave Maria* they headed out again, as planned, to travel by night. It was almost dawn and they were just ferrying across a stream, when a band of horsemen came upon them, with lances and harquebuses.

"And who are they?"

Spinelli sharpened his gaze.

"A chaush!" he exclaimed, indicating the unmistakable white turban of the squad's commander. When their boat reached the opposite shore, the horseman spurred forward and came to meet them. He was still young, muscular, and tanned, with a long mustache and a metallic flash in his eyes. Without getting down from his saddle he exchanged a few words in Turkish with Spinelli, then he jumped down to the ground, bowed in the direction of Sir Lorenzo and made him a long speech in the same language, after which, he fell silent, looking him calmly in the eye. Spinelli seemed embarrassed.

"Well," Sir Lorenzo urged him.

The dragoman cleared his throat.

"The magnificent Kubat chaush," he said, "asks if your lordship is the magnificent Master Lorenzo Bernardo. I told him yes."

"And then?" Lorenzo insisted.

"He said," the interpreter continued, "that he had been sent by the Porte to meet you, and he has orders from the Gran Vizier to suggest to the illustrious gentlemen that he speed up the journey, because he is awaiting you with great desire, having already been advised of your arrival."

Sir Lorenzo was speechless.

"Advised! And who was it that so advised him?"

"Who knows? The Turk always knows all," Spinelli affirmed.

"Try asking him!" Sir Lorenzo ordered.

"Are you serious!" the dragoman protested.

"Ask him, I tell you!"

"That's not courteous," the interpreter stubbornly insisted. In the end, however, he asked; but the answer, as was predictable, was that the chaush didn't know a thing. After Spinelli had translated, the Turk added something, and the dragoman made a strange face.

"Well?" asked Sir Lorenzo.

"I don't understand," said the interpreter. "He says your lordship needn't worry, that Signor Lippomano has been told nothing. I don't know what he means."

But I understand, Sir Lorenzo thought, dismayed. He alone, of all the entourage that was accompanying him, knew why they were going to Constantinople, but from all appearances the Gran Vizier knew perfectly well the purpose of his mission. What a country! he thought.

When his man servant entered and pulled open the curtains, Girolamo Lippomano was already awake. Actually, he hadn't slept at all; and for days and days now he had been sleeping little and badly, with confused, threatening dreams, waking up more tired than when he'd gone to bed. For the last ten or twelve days there was talk in Constantinople of a Venetian ambassador who was about to arrive; the Gran Vizier, who undoubtedly was the first to be informed, had been careful not to let him know, but Sir Girolamo, like all Venetian bailos, had his informants. He had a whole network of confidants on his payroll, from the Jewish doctor who treated the young men of the seraglio to the Venetian slave who had opened a shop in the bazaar, and there was hardly a rumor that circulated in the city without someone sooner or later passing it on to the bailo, in his palace among the vineyards in the suburb of Pera, looking out on the Golden Horn.

When he first learned that a Venetian envoy was about to arrive, Sir Girolamo was puzzled and worried. In such circumstances, official procedure always provided that the Signory notify the resident ambassador in advance, and this time, instead, nobody had told him anything. That menacing silence didn't promise anything good. In wartime it could happen that a courier would be captured and a packet of letters intercepted, even though everybody recalled that during the Fourth Ottoman-Venetian War the bailo, Marc'Antonio Barbaro, confined to the palace and with all the windows and balconies boarded up, still managed to maintain a copious correspondence with Venice for three years. But now it was peace time and what's worse Lippomano had received letters during those very days from the Senate and the Ten, which didn't contain the least mention of the arrival.

For a week or so he had acted as if nothing were afoot, trying to dispel his suspicions; then, five days ago, a courier had brought a new packet. He had left Venice in early May, made the whole voyage by sea with favorable winds, and he was carrying top secret letters, with the order, he said, to deliver them personally to the most excellent bailo. Sir Girolamo had the letters brought to him and dismissed the letter carrier; at first glance he saw that they were from the Lord Inquisitors for the Protection of State Secrets, and he broke out in a cold sweat. He was about to open them, when he noticed they were not addressed to him. The address, scribbled and half-hidden by the wax of the seal said: "To the Magnificent Master Lorenzo Bernardo, our bailo in Constantinople."

Sir Girolamo buckled under the blow and had to sit down, his heart beating wildly. If the Signory had appointed a new bailo, and had sent him there without notifying him, that could mean only one thing. Trying to reason coldly, despite the panic that was washing over him, he assessed what he could do. To escape without a trace into the immense empire was not even thinkable; besides everything else he didn't have any cash, nor the time to raise it, and anyway the Porte always found a man if it wanted to. His only chance was to deny everything, try to understand what evidence they had, and defend himself all the way to the end; he was sure that his business deals had always left very few traces, and if his brother the prior, who no one could suspect of complicity, made the right moves, even those few traces could be eliminated.

Trying to stop the trembling in his hands, Lippomano went over to his desk, and began going through his papers. To one side he put all the letters of the merchants with whom he had corresponded, and he read them again attentively. There was nothing that would allow anyone to see behind the scenes, he had always been very careful. In another pile he put all the letters from his brother the prior, and when he read them he knitted his eyebrows; to those without suspicions they could appear to be innocent, but not to anyone who already nourished some doubts. It was summer, the heat was unbearable, and the braziers had been put into storage; they wouldn't be needed again until October. He called for a lighted candle and a pewter plate, shut himself in his study under lock and key, and burned all the letters in the plate. Then he realized that it would seem strange if he had saved all the letters from his other brother, the bishop of Verona, and not those of the prior, so he burned them too, even though they were completely innocent because the bishop didn't know anything about the whole business. When this work was done, he shut all the remaining papers in a desk drawer, and got up to go open the door; but all his strength had been sapped and he had to go back and sit down. He looked at his hands: they were trembling madly. Lorenzo Bernardo! he thought. Damned . . .

That same day Lippomano took to his bed, and he never got up again. Every morning his man servant, on entering and throwing open the windows to change the stale air, found him more livid, with the bags under his eyes injected with blood. And finally the morning came that Sir Girolamo had feared:

the man servant, on entering, said there was a secretary downstairs just arrived from Venice, who was waiting o be received by him to inform him of things of the utmost importance.

"You'll tell him that I am unable to leave my bed," said Lippomano, ashen.

"I've already told him so, eminence. He says your lordship absolutely must receive him."

Sir Girolamo dragged himself over to the window, stuck his hands into the basin that the servant had filled with water, and washed his face.

"The barber!" he commanded.

An hour later, secretary Vianello was admitted to his bedchamber. Lippomano had not managed to get himself up, and was lying in bed in his nightshirt, but he had shaved. The secretary, who had seen him many times before then, found him dreadfully aged.

"Eminence," he said, after having bowed, "I have come to inform you that my master, the magnificent Signor Lorenzo Bernardo, has entered Constantinople this morning an hour after dawn; he has been sent by the Council of Ten and by the Lord Inquisitors for the Protection of State Secrets to confer with your lordship, and he will be here presently."

31

After the encounter with the chaush, Sir Lorenzo's caravan had traveled for fourteen more days before arriving
in the capital of the empire. The harsh terrain, the suffocating heat, the fear of new attempts on their lives which
forced them to remain constantly on the alert, had tested the
travelers' endurance, and the porters were on the verge of
rebellion. But the ill humor and weariness from the over-exer-
tion of the journey dissolved when the company finally came
within sight of Constantinople. They all crowded together with
exclamations of surprise, contemplating the vast city of
wooden houses amassed around the colossal bulging bodies
and tapered minarets of the great mosques, and the waters of
the Golden Horn flickering in the distance. The dragoman,
who had already been there, smiled as though the travelers'
admiration of the city was somehow also a compliment for
him.

"And that down there?" asked Sir Lorenzo, pointing to a
spire silhouetted against the red disc of the sun, beyond the
strait.

"The tower of Galata," Spinelli explained. "The bailo's palace
is just below it."

On hearing those words Sir Lorenzo sharpened his gaze as
though he might be able to see Lippomano standing in the window.

"But with this heat," the dragoman continued, "we'll
undoubtedly find him in his summer villa, in the vineyards of

Pera. It's a beautiful spot; the garden is composed of rows and rows of grapevines."

Sir Lorenzo cleared his throat, and gave the order to get moving. When they came to the walls they expected a long search of their baggage, but the janissary in command at the gate bowed obsequiously as soon as he learned that the group was accompanying a Venetian ambassador.

"He says he's sure," Spinelli translated, "that there are no goods that have to pay duty, and even if there were he would like to do a kindness to your lordship, and he will send one of his men to pay homage to you at your palace. You'll have to send him back with a gift," he added needlessly.

Once inside the city, they went down to an embarcadero to arrange for boats to take them over to Pera. Having reached an agreement with the boatmen, Sir Lorenzo, Vianello, Spinelli, and Casalini boarded the ferry without waiting for the servants and baggage. It was morning, the air was still brisk, but all the signs pointed to another dog day of summer. Amazed, Sir Lorenzo noticed that the boatmen called him "Signor Padron".

"Here everybody speaks the lingua franca with foreigners," Spinelli said. "They see so many of them! For us Italians it's a real convenience."

The boat left them at the dock of the Tophane, the plant where the Sultan's cannons were cast and where his artillery and gunpowder were stored. The place was teeming with people, and Sir Marchetto saw someone in the crowd whom he knew.

"Look there," he said, "that's Master Pasqual, the dragoman of the lord bailo. Hey, Master Pasqual, what are you doing here at this hour of the morning?"

The man so apostrophized was tiny in stature, dressed in the Venetian style, with a round, smiling face that was now wearing a stupefied expression.

"Signor Marchetto! Well then it's true!"

Introduced to Sir Lorenzo, before whom he bowed down to the ground, the dragoman told them that their arrival in Constantinople had been expected for quite some time.

"And does Sir Girolamo know about it?" Sir Lorenzo inquired, disgruntled.

"Certainly!" the other man nodded. "But he doesn't know the reason for the visit of your illustrious lordship, just as no one does."

"And how is it that the news arrived?"

The dragoman laughed.

"Oh, it arrived from all sorts of places! By way of the Ragusans," he enumerated; "and of a caravan who advised us from Cattaro; and of the sanjak-bey of Elbasan, who immediately advised the Grand Vizier; and then there were some pirates, who said they had met your lordship on the road, and then they boarded a ship in Salonika and evidently made it here ahead of you."

And we hoped we could arrive incognito! Sir Lorenzo thought; but he didn't say anything. "Sir Francesco," he said instead to the secretary, "you will go immediately to the palace to announce my arrival to the illustrious lord bailo; we will refresh ourselves a bit and then we will follow."

When Sir Lorenzo arrived, Lippomano was still in bed, and in his nightshirt; and looked even more distressed and afflicted than when he woke up. Sir Lorenzo went into the bedroom by himself, but prudently left waiting in the anteroom Captain Casalini, Vianello, and two servants, who had joined them in the meantime.

"Hand on your sword, Signor Filippo," he whispered as he went in; the captain assented with an imperceptible nod.

To be received in that way, by a man who was feigning illness, didn't please him in the least; nevertheless, he bowed his head and introduced himself.

"I knew it was you who was supposed to arrive," said Lippomano, with an air of reproach. Sir Lorenzo was baffled, but managed not to show it, at least he hoped so.

"And how is that?" he asked, impassively.

Lippomano, with a weak smile, pointed to a packet on the window sill. It held the letters from the Inquisitors, addressed to Sir Lorenzo, and still sealed.

"They arrived four days ago. Evidently, you weren't able to travel very fast," he observed, venomously.

Sir Lorenzo was very annoyed by the direction the conversation was taking, but he didn't let it show. The instructions he'd received on behalf of the doge before his departure were unequivocal: he was to notify Lippomano that His Serenity no longer wanted him as bailo, that he was removing him effective immediately, replacing him temporarily with Sir Lorenzo, and recalling him urgently to Venice; but all of this, the Council of Ten had ordered, was to be handled with dexterity and prudence, without giving him the impression that he had already been convicted, precluding him from thinking, even for a moment, of offering resistance and refusing to obey.

"I am stunned," said Sir Girolamo in a gravely voice, barricaded behind pillows and sheets.

"I was stunned myself," Sir Lorenzo confessed. That much was the pure truth; he had been ordered to conceal the truth, and he would do that, but it bothered him to lie, and as long as he managed to avoid it he felt more at ease.

"My conscience is clear," Lippomano resumed. "I can't imagine why this misadventure has been visited upon me. My health is already bad as it is, and now this! My conscience is clear," he said again.

"I don't doubt it," Sir Lorenzo courteously concurred. "But I beg you not to lose heart. I am sure that in Venice you will find a way to dissipate all of those tiny suspicions that may have arisen with respect to I don't know what." Here Sir

Lorenzo fell into an embarrassed silence, and the other man resumed:

"So, I must depart for Venice?"

"Immediately," said Sir Lorenzo, in a tone that was calm but admitted no rebuttal.

"And how?"

"It will be taken care of. You will be accompanied by Signor Filippo Casalini, captain of their excellencies the Lord Heads of the Ten."

Hearing that, Lippomano turned even whiter.

"My conscience is clear," be muttered once again.

Sir Lorenzo steeled himself.

"But signor Girolamo," he said, trying to display good cheer, "come now, be assured that once there, and this is the point, you will be able to demonstrate it, and everything will be fine. A man such as yourself, a pillar of the Republic, certainly cannot be guilty of anything. It must be a misunderstanding," he added; and he fell silent again.

Lippomano, wary as an animal forced to come out of his lair, was trying to figure it out. This young man they had sent appeared to be naïve; is it possible that he really knows nothing? But as much as he tried to sound him out, Sir Lorenzo didn't give anything away. As far as he knew, there must have been some accusation or other directed at the bailo, "perhaps even a maneuver of these Turks, in an attempt to ruin your reputation," he suggested. "You'll have no trouble exculpating yourself," he concluded, matter-of-factly.

Lippomano invited him to take possession of the palace and to excuse him if he didn't get up. The blow, he said, had overwhelmed him.

"Shall I see you this evening at table?" asked Sir Lorenzo.

"If God gives me the strength," replied Lippomano, letting himself fall back against the pillows.

Sir Lorenzo bowed and left.

What a scoundrel! he thought; and ordered Casalini to put some of his men on the doors, and to remain himself in the anteroom, to ensure that Lippomano could not communicate with anyone unbeknownst to him.

The rest of the day was taken up with searching all the palace furniture, confiscating all the papers and examining them attentively. Lippomano, upon express request, had surrendered the keys to his desk, and all the documents were found there regarding the grain purchases he had carried out on behalf of the Signory, the records of his ordinary and extraordinary expenses, and his correspondence; but Vianello, who carefully read all of the papers one by one, didn't find anything compromising.

"The only thing strange is this: there are no private letters here."

"Not even from his brothers?"

Vianello spread his arms.

"We'll see!" said Sir Lorenzo, impassive.

That evening Sir Girolamo came to the dinner table, a bit bent over and limping, but back on his feet, and dressed in black.

"Master Lorenzo," he said, forcing himself to look cheerful, "I can do nothing but accommodate myself to the will of God. I know I am innocent, and even more than that I am anxious to leave immediately for Venice, to get there as soon as possible in order to justify myself."

"I'm delighted," said Sir Lorenzo; and once again summoning his theatrical energies, allowed that it wasn't right that the illustrious lord bailo was dressed in black.

"But since I'm a prisoner!" Sir Girolamo rebutted, bitterly.

"Oh! A prisoner in your own home! You've been recalled to Venice, but I certainly have not been ordered to treat you as a prisoner," said Sir Lorenzo. As much as his conscience pricked him, he noticed that he also felt a certain degree of satisfaction at how well he was playing his part.

"I beg you," he insisted, "go dress yourself in purple."

After an exchange of compliments, Sir Girolamo agreed, and went back up to his room, returning shortly thereafter wearing the ample purple robes of a magistrate.

"That's much better!" said Sir Lorenzo, with a smiling face.

The dinner, however, was not amusing. Lippomano tried repeatedly to discover whether Sir Lorenzo had any idea of the charges that had been made against him, and the other, not to betray himself, preferred not to talk much. Then, because Lippomano kept at it, he decided to strike back.

"My lord bailo," he said, "we have examined your papers, and I thank you for giving us the keys; naturally, we have found nothing that was anything less than legitimate."

Sir Girolamo nodded proudly.

"However," Sir Lorenzo continued, "I expected to find some letters from your brothers, or from other relations, and instead there are none."

Lippomano remained impassive.

"I don't keep track of them," he replied, curtly. "I'm in the habit of tearing them up, if they don't contain something of importance for my affairs."

"That's only natural," said Sir Lorenzo courteously; after which everyone went back to dealing with what they had on their plates.

"Ah, that's how it is!" said the Grand Vizier. He repeated several times, caressing his long beard; then he called a secretary and told him something. Since he hadn't taken the precaution to ask his two Christian guests to leave the room, Spinelli decided it was not impolite to translate his words for Sir Lorenzo.

"His Magnificence has ordered him to go immediately to

the Great Lord, advise him that the Venetian ambassador has arrived, and that the matter is nothing important."

Sir Lorenzo, despite himself, felt a little bit offended; but on seeing the cheerful gaze in the eyes of the Grand Vizier, he told himself it was better this way. The day before Master Pasqual, the bailo's dragoman, had told them that there had been great expectations in Constantinople regarding his arrival, in the belief that he was coming to discuss the European situation, and to present some grand proposal; now the Grand Vizier's reaction was visibly one of relief, and this was the best thing that could have happened, because without his consent Sir Lorenzo would never have been able to complete his mission.

After dismissing the secretary, the Grand Vizier wiggled a bit on the cushions he was sitting on, making his turban tilt to one side, and he had to straighten it. Sinan Pasha was an old Albanian, slender and gritty, with an unpleasantly penetrating gaze that was often illuminated by a flash of irony.

"The illustrious bailo," he said, after adjusting his turban, "is viewed quite favorably by this Sublime Porte. He has always behaved well and has served the interests of His Serenity. It upsets us to hear that our Christian friends—may God enlighten them!—the lords of Venice are dissatisfied with him."

Here we go, thought Sir Lorenzo. He cleared his throat and replied, assuring His Magnificence that the bailo would certainly be able to clear himself of the accusations that had been made against him, and that it was specifically in order to allow him to clarify matters completely that he had been urgently recalled to Venice. After all, Sir Lorenzo told himself in his own heart, lying to a miscreant, and for the sake of a mission so necessary to the Republic, was not really a sin.

After listening to the translation, the pasha spoke again, briefly and in a tone that was courteous but firm.

"His Majesty—that God should render him ever victori-

ous—desires that at his Porte everyone should feel safe; therefore, he will not allow the illustrious bailo to be sent back to
Venice by force," Spinelli translated him.

"He is not being sent back by force, but he himself wishes
to leave, in order to dissipate all suspicions and reassume his
place among the lords of Venice," Sir Lorenzo assured him.
The Grand Vizier listened to him with a flash of amusement in
his eyes.

"If that's the way it is," he said, "we will let him leave."

Sir Lorenzo bowed deeply.

Sinan Pasha looked at his fingernails, then resumed the conversation. This time he spoke a little longer, smiling throughout.

"He says that Venice must not fear the Great Lord, even
though the other Christians must fear him and how," the
dragoman translated. "He says that very soon there will be
great things, naval enterprises; that His Majesty has remained
at peace with the Christians too long, and now he wants to fleet
to go out to sea and undertake some enterprises. He says that
he personally is a great enemy of the Christians, and although
he is old as we can see, he wishes to be part of the enterprise
too, and he will embark on a galley."

The Grand Vizier kept on smiling, and nodding affirma-
tively, so much that his turban moved again and he had to
straighten it again with a gesture of annoyance.

"But he's laughing," Lorenzo objected, puzzled.

"I believe," said Spinelli, the expert, "that he has to tell us
these things because the arrogance of their nation requires it,
but he wants us to understand that behind the words there is
no ill will."

Sir Lorenzo bowed once again and thanked the Grand
Vizier for the audience, assuring him of the unshakeable
friendship that the Most Serene Republic nurtured for the
Porte; after which the two Venetians took their leave.

"What a chore dealing with these people," Sir Lorenzo

remarked as soon as they were back out on the street. "And what a language! They talk and it always sounds like they're shouting."

"The language reflects the character of the people, who are arrogant and insolent, Spinelli confirmed.

In the meantime, Sinan Pasha had called his secretary back in, and a slave to redo his turban. Tapping cautiously with his fingers his bald and speckled cranium, he grumbled with contempt, "What a chore dealing with these people! To see them, all dressed in purple, you'd say they were a bunch of emperors; yet among the Christians their leader, the doge, ranks even lower than a king."

"They are insolent by nature," the secretary confirmed. Yet among the infidels they have been given the nickname of 'fishermen'.

The two Turks burst out laughing.

"Are you really going to let their bailo leave?" the secretary asked. The Grand Vizier gave him an ironic look.

"If he really wants to so much, we will let him," he replied.

As their boat was passing in front of the gardens of the seraglio, Spinelli caught Sir Lorenzo's attention.

"Look at the kiosk right across from us, the one covered with an arbor of red vines. But don't let them see you."

"Well?"

"Well, the man sitting inside there—you see the window with the marble grate?—the man that's looking toward us, that's the Great Turk in person."

Sir Lorenzo could barely make out a man in sumptuous dress, with an enormous white turban, seated on a mountain of pillows, and surrounded by a large number of servants, immobile as statues.

"Those," Spinelli explained, "are his mutes. The Great Lord is always surrounded solely by mutes and he speaks and signs with them, because he likes to live in silence, his tranquility undisturbed. Now he must have gone down to the kiosk to see your lordship go by, since they will have told him that you were bringing with you who knows what grand proposals!"

Knowing he was, in that very minute, under the impenetrable gaze of the Great Turk, Sir Lorenzo felt a small chill go down his spine; and he was glad when the boat, rowing toward the Tophane, left behind the kiosk, the sultan, and his mutes.

In the days that followed, they had to go visit the others pashas, taking all of them, as was the custom, sumptuous gifts of garments and fabrics. Last on the list, in accordance with the immutable order of precedence established by protocol, was the visit that Sir Lorenzo awaited with the greatest curiosity, the visit to *kapudan pasha*, as the Turks called the commandant of their fleet. Hassan Pasha was a Venetian, captured during the Cypress War on a transport ship where he was he scrivener; and as little sympathy as he had for renegades, Sir Lorenzo couldn't help but be curious to see him. The pasha, whose own men called Hassan Venetian, was on holiday in his yali on the Bosphorus; a one-storey wooden villa, with a dock for boats and a vast garden scattered with kiosks looking out over the water. In the shade, drinking rose syrup, Hassan talked at length and in proud tones, delighted to entertain a Venetian patrician decked out in purple who was forced to listen to him respectfully. At the start he spoke in Turkish, and Spinelli translated, whispering directly into Sir Lorenzo's ear, so that between one sentence and the next he could introduce, without the other man noticing, some comments of his own.

"They told me he didn't speak Turkish very well, and it's true, the words don't come to him!" he whispered.

"And why is he speaking to me in Turkish?" asked Sir Lorenzo, also whispering.

"Good heavens, to make an impression!" replied Spinelli,

with a grin. After a while, however, the kapudan pasha had had enough, and dropped the Turkish; but he didn't switch to Venetian, but to the lingua franca. In the mouth of Hassan Pasha, however, the lingua franca was more Venetian than usual, and even though he mixed in a large dose of Spanish, Sir Lorenzo managed to understand him without an interpreter.

"I've always heard that the Republic is governed with the utmost prudence," said the pasha, staring at his listener with his deep black, penetrating eyes, "but it was a big risk, Signor Bernardo, sending you hear to arrest Signor Lippomano, carrying him off as a prisoner from the court of the most important prince in the world, without saying a thing either to His Majesty nor to those entrusted with the government of this empire. If it were up to me, I would find this way if proceeding highly insulting to the authority and dignity of our emperor."

Sir Lorenzo was in a cold sweat. Spinelli was right, he thought, when he suggested that I double the usual gift for kapudan pasha, explaining to me that he is very greedy and that he is the most dangerous man in this government for us, precisely because he is Venetian and knows us well; and thank goodness I took his advice!

"Why arrest?" he said, when the other man fell silent and gestured that he had the floor. "I didn't come to arrest the bailo, but only to notify him that certain accusations have been raised against him, and to allow him to return as soon as possible to clear his name!"

The Kapudan Pasha laughed.

"Signor Bernardo," he retorted, "you have enchanted everyone in this court with your prudent and skillful way of negotiating; our pashas have all shown themselves to be without eyes, ears, and hands, and you have hoodwinked them all. But I'm Venetian, I know what it means that you brought that captain from the Council of Ten with you."

Sir Lorenzo wanted to protest, but the pasha stopped him with an imperious gesture.

"Don't be afraid that I want to interfere in your affairs! Others have already decided on behalf of the Great Lord, and it's not my place to criticize them. The operation, it seems to me, is underhanded, and this Porte will have occasion to regret it; but good for you. I'm telling you these things so that you'll know that this Lord too has people around him who understand the ways of the world. In the past there have been things even more difficult to negotiate, and never has the Signory resolved to send a representative here in secret as it has done with you. You have handled yourself well, and you have my compliments!"

And the Venetian scrivener turned, first, a slave on Turkish galleys, and then commandant of the Sultan's fleet, raised his goblet of rose syrup, and drank to Sir Lorenzo's health.

That evening, as Sir Lorenzo was re-entering the palace, the secretary told him there was a man waiting to see him. He had arrived right after lunch, and had been sitting in the waiting room ever since.

"A man? Who is he?"

"A Venetian. A common lad, quite young. Not well dressed. But he says he has to inform your lordship about things of the utmost importance and that he cannot speak with anyone except yourself."

Sir Lorenzo was accustomed to the ways of the Council of Ten and he knew that anyone, even a poor fisherman, a street vendor, an unemployed soldier, might be the carrier of a secret message; so he ordered that the man be brought in to see him.

The visitor came in and remained respectfully on his feet, his cap in his hands. He was dressed in rags, his shoes broken, and his cap was the simple wool cap of a fisherman; but the man was solid, muscular, and tan.

"Tell me," Bernardo prodded him, after assessing him with a quick glance.

"Are you the illustrious lord bailo?" the lad asked.

"I am. Do you have letters for me?"

The visitor shook his head.

"No, your lordship, but I have a story to tell."

Sir Lorenzo was surprised, but nodded that he should proceed. The lad tormented his cap with his hands, and couldn't bring himself to begin.

"Well?" Sir Lorenzo prodded him, beginning to lose patience. The lad hesitated for another minute and then took the leap.

"So, your eminence, I have been banished from Venice, but I didn't do anything wrong, and plenty of witnesses will tell you that, but when I signed on to the galley *Loredana*, which was bound for Candia with a sack of gold zecchini, I saw how the comito of the galley stole them, I mean," the lad got confused, "two others stole them, but he killed them and buried the sack and I know where it is. And then the signor sopracomito captured a felucca and they took other coins from there and made the delivery with them and nobody found out about it, but the zecchini are still buried on the island," the lad concluded, more confused than ever.

Sir Lorenzo looked at him carefully. He'd never heard anything about this story, and in general he had no sympathy for exiles who tried to get themselves pardoned by making up who knows what revelations; but the lad had an air of sincerity, nothing brazen about him, and the way he got embroiled in the details made it seem that he was telling the truth, and not a made-up story learned by heart.

"Wait!" he said, raising a hand. "Let's proceed with some kind of order. When did this supposedly happen?"

The lad reflected.

"Two years ago."

"And why did you come to tell about it now?"

"Eminence, I was on the *Loredana*, and I stayed on it until Candia. Then, while we were there I found out I'd been banished, because before that I didn't know, I had run away from the police, but I didn't know I'd been banished, and so I was afraid to stay there, and to get away from Candia I signed on to a corsair galley, and I was with them until last year, and then on Cyprus I ran off and from there I managed to get here to Constantinople, because they told me there was a Venetian bailo here and that I could tell you everything and you could help me get a pardon."

"And would you know how to find the island again, and the place where the zecchini were hidden?"

The lad nodded his assent.

"The night before we were in Zara. The island is a day's voyage toward Cattaro, when I see it I'll know it."

"Listen to me," Sir Lorenzo said slowly. "If this story is true, only an investigation will be able to establish that. If you want to return to Venice, I can give you a safe conduct pass, that will guarantee that you won't be arrested on arrival; then it's up to you to demonstrate that you're telling the truth. First, however, tell me why you were banished."

The lad shifted back and forth on his feet, with his eyes looking down. Then, after a minute's hesitation, he raised them again and looked frankly into Signor Bernardo's eyes.

"The police wanted to arrest my father, at the Rialto. I don't know what he had done. They hit him with a halberd and he ended up in the Grand Canal and drowned. I ran away, and they ran after me. I got down to the Slavonian waterfront, there was a galley there that was weighing anchor, I had spoken the day before with one of the oarsmen, and he had told me they needed men. I jumped on board."

Sir Lorenzo realized, with astonishment, that he had already heard this story.

"And then you say you were banished, how do you know that?"

"Eminence, on Candia the parone told me he had seen the list of the banished, and my name was on it."

It can't be him, thought Sir Lorenzo, amused. If Clarice could see them now! He had to reflect a minute to recall the name of the man for whom he had obtained a pardon from the Council of Ten, the husband of his wife's favorite little chambermaid. Matteo? No, Michele.

"Tell me now, what's your name?"

"Michele son of the mason Matteo, parish of Sant'Agnese," said Michele, all in one breath.

Sir Lorenzo laughed.

"Listen to me, Sir Michele, I've got good news for you."

32

For Michele those days were like living in a dream. He couldn't bring himself to believe that it was all true: the pardon already obtained even before requesting it, the safe conduct pass signed by Bernardo, and what's more, news of Bianca; that she was alive, doing well, and had a good job. He had just started to believe it when another surprise happened: Sir Lorenzo's servants told him what they knew about their master's mission, and about the bailo who had to be taken back to Venice in the custody of a captain of the Council of Ten. As soon as he saw him, Michele recognized that Lippomano whom he had seen for the last time the day of the accident at the work site and the death of Zorze. He remembered him only too well; his father never stopped cursing him, saying that he was to blame for all his misfortune. When Michele happened upon him in one of the rooms of the palace, he instinctively stepped aside, torn between fear and loathing; but Sir Girolamo never looked the servants in the face, and he didn't even notice him.

By order of Sir Lorenzo, Michele spent hours with the secretary Vianello, recounting all the details of his story; the secretary transcribed them, read them back to him, and had him put an X at the bottom of the page. Then he sealed it together with other letters addressed to the Council of Ten.

"Mind you, back in Venice, make sure you repeat it in the same way!" he urged him. "The lord master," he added, lowering his voice, "has written to the Lord Heads that you are the same man to whom they granted a pardon, upon his petition, before he left Venice. He says that in his view your story deserves to be verified, but from now on it all depends on you."

The day of the departure Michele went to say good-bye to Mami, with whom he had arrived in Constantinople not long before. It was not a very festive arrival. Mami, who had not been back for nineteen years, was sure that he wouldn't find either his wife or his daughters, and in fact that's exactly what happened. The neighborhood where they had lived was still there, with its torturous streets piled with garbage, the stray dogs and children playing in the dirt, the houses of rotten wood, tilting a little more each year until they were almost touching, but the person living in his house was a stranger. On seeing Mami's yellow turban, which marked him as a Jew, the man sent him away rather brusquely, and he and Michele rushed out of there before a hostile crowd could form.

"What will you do now?" asked Michele, after they'd reached the seashore, and were sitting down to rest in the shadow of a wall.

"I don't know," Mami admitted, disheartened. "I'll have to go to the Jews to look for work," he added. But Michele, who knew him well by now, realized that he wasn't convinced. Mami looked around with an anxious air, as though he were meditating and couldn't make up his mind.

"It's the city that has this effect on me," he said. "I didn't think I'd ever see it again."

Just then a man came out of a courtyard. He was dressed very poorly, barefoot, and with big earrings hanging from his ear lobes. He was followed by a tumultuous pack of stray dogs, and other dogs, attracted by their barking, came galloping from the surrounding streets. The man was carrying a bucket, and he emptied it in the middle of the street; it was full of tripe and roast liver, and the dogs tore into it avidly. The man stood there contemplating them for a minute, then he went back inside, and came right out again with a full bucket, and repeated the same routine.

Michele, amazed, turned to Mami.

"But what's that guy doing, is he crazy?"

Mami looked at him not understanding.

"Why? He's giving alms to the dogs. They too are God's creatures."

"Is that the custom among the Turks?" Michele laughed.

"Not everyone does it, but there are some good men who believe that this too is a form of charity," said Mami, very seriously; and when the man came out for the third time, he got up and went over to him. They spoke for a long time in Turkish, and Michele, who didn't understand a word, saw that they were both smiling; then Mami bent over to caress one of the dogs, which had rubbed up against his leg, and he came walking back with his eyes shiny with tears.

"Holy men!" he said. "I think I'm going to stay here with them for a while."

When he came to say good-bye to him, Michele found Mami in the back of the courtyard, where, in the open air and without any defense against bad weather, there lived a small community of dervishes. To look at him, he had already become one of them, and nobody would have ever suspected that until a very short time ago he was a Jew. He walked around barefoot as though it was the most natural thing in the world, and he had two heavy earrings hanging from his lobes.

"God is great!" he said to Michele, embracing him. "If it is his will, you will arrive home safe and sound, and you'll see your wife again."

Michele embraced him fighting back the tears, telling himself one more time that the world was more complicated than he had been taught to believe.

The first Venetian ship out of Constantinople was supposed

to leave in ten days, which Sir Girolamo used to prepare his bags, make his round of farewell visits, and go over the accounts with secretary Vianello. He sold nearly all of his robes, garments, furs, silver, horses, wines, wood; Sir Lorenzo, who was to stay on in his place until the Senate appointed a new bailo, purchased most of the household furnishings, and the rest was bought by Jewish merchants and taken to the bazaar. The last Sunday before his departure, Lippomano went to hear Mass at the Franciscan monastery, went to confession, and ostentatiously received communion; that same evening Sir Lorenzo summoned the monk who had heard his confession and entertained him for several hours, without succeeding in getting him to reveal anything of what he had heard. Sir Girolamo dressed in purple, went around with his head held high, proclaimed his innocence, and made large donations with the money left in his purse after settling his accounts. Finally, one evening the ship *Manolessa*, master Sir Demetrio della Canea, finished stowing its cargo of leather, salted fish, porcelain and alum, and Lippomano went on board with his servants. Sir Lorenzo accompanied him onto the ship, then he shut himself in the cabin with the master and captain Casalini.

"Master Filippo," he began, "you understand your orders. You are to take Signor Lippomano back to Venice; with this ship you'll go as far as Chania, and you'll wait there until they send a galley from Venice. You must never leave him alone for an instant, never leave his presence, you will not allow him to go ashore nor to board another ship, is that clear? And you," he continued, addressing the master, "will do the same, at the cost of your head. You will go straight to Chania, laying over as little as possible, and not in inhabited places."

The master, a short, bearded Greek, nodded in resignation. You could see that he would gladly have done without all that bother.

"Once arrived in Venice," Sir Lorenzo continued, this time

to Casalini, "you will take him to the prison of the Lord Heads, and once there your mission will have been completed. Here," he added, handing him a bundle of papers, "these are sealed letters for the authorities in Candia and for the Council of Ten, which you will deliver to the intended recipients. Is everything clear?"

The captain nervously assented.

"Ah, Master Filippo! I almost forgot," added Sir Lorenzo, who had already stood up to head back to the dock. "I'm also putting in your charge that young lad whom I pointed out to you. He will be given the same ration as my servants. Do not lose sight of him, but remember that he is not under arrest. I've given him a safe conduct pass and in Venice you will take him to the Lord Heads. And then, if I may ask you for a personal courtesy, you will go to pay respects to my wife Lady Clarice, and you will give her these letters," he concluded, handing him the packet. The captain stretched out his hand and bowed.

"And now, gentlemen, be on your way, and may God be with you and grant you a prosperous voyage."

The ship got under way in the early hours of dawn, and made its way into the Sea of Marmara. Michele stood at the stern to look at the minarets of Constantinople until they disappeared in the morning haze. In the afternoon they stopped at Silviria, where the Venetian consul came aboard, carefully examined all the passengers, then signed a certificate attesting that they all looked healthy; in the land of the Turk there was always a suspicion of plague, and no ship could dock in a Venetian port without a certificate like that one. They next day the ship pulled in to the shore under the turrets of the Castle of Anadolu Hissari, which guarded the narrowest passage of the Dardanelles, and the Turkish customs agents came on board to inspect its cargo and bill of lading. The visit was very brief because Master Demetrio had prepared a little bag of aspers, which he passed around in plain sight; the customs agents pocketed them, went down into the hold and came back up a few minutes later, saying everything was in order. The ship raised its sails and an hour later it was on its way to the open sea. Michele, who was on the bridge, saw Lippomano coming up from the cabin, dressed in black, and beside him Captain Casalini. The two of them went over to the edge of the ship and stood there for a while in silence.

"Do you see those remains of walls over there?" Lippomano said after a bit. Casalini sharpened his gaze.

"When I arrived here, last year, they told me that this was the point where the ancient city of Troy rose up, and that those ruins are its walls. But who knows if it's true!"

The captain said nothing.

"Since this ill luck has befallen me," resumed Lippomano, who seemed particularly pale in his black outfit, "it seems to me that it's no longer possible to know what's false and what's true."

Sure it's possible, thought Casalini.

"For me," he rebutted, "the only thing that's true are the orders of the Lord Heads, and that is the revealed truth."

Lippomano sighed and bit his lip. Not that he had hoped all that much, because the Council of Ten knew how to choose its servants, but he now had confirmation that it was not by arousing the captain's sympathy that he would be able to squeeze out some useful information.

The voyage as far as Chania lasted two weeks, with a favorable wind, and without any unsavory encounters. As they were arriving in Crete, Michele was moved to see again the scraggy silhouette of the mountains dominating the big island. When they came into the harbor, the ship disembarked its human cargo, to the great satisfaction of Master Demetrio, who could now go back to devoting himself to his affairs without being involved in the dangerous conspiracies of state; Casalini,

Lippomano and the entire entourage, including Michele, were housed in the palace of the regent of Chania, while they waited until there was a galley ready to take them to Venice. The lay-over lasted more than ten days, during which Michele tried to stay as far away as possible from Lippomano; he was in the throes of an irrational fear that the man might recognize him and somehow do something bad to him. Just once he happened to be close enough to overhear a conversation between the prisoner and the master of the house, and he couldn't help but perk up his ears.

"How can it be that my brother knew nothing about this, that he didn't write to me? I can understand that his letters may not have made it all the way to Constantinople before my departure, but I was sure I would find some here," Lippomano was saying.

"And yet there aren't any, and none have arrived here," the other man replied coldly. To his great surprise, Michele noticed that Lippomano, usually so haughty, now seemed almost to be begging.

"Tell me the truth," he implored.

"But that is the truth!" the regent said impatiently. "No letters and no news of your brother the prior have arrived here, for several months."

Lippomano shrugged his shoulders. "I can't believe it," he concluded.

The prisoner was free to move around the regent's palace, but not to leave it, and Captain Casalini slept in the same room with him. He was never left alone; but his long years of diplomatic dissimulation had accustomed him to isolating himself and reflecting on his own even in the midst of strangers. He calmly went about making his calculations, assessing his chances of getting off. He had hoped that in Crete he would find letters in cipher from his brother, that would inform him about his situation, helping him to understand if besides the suspicions there was also some concrete evidence against him, since everything, or almost everything, depended on that. When he found no messages from he prior he lost heart; but almost immediately he told himself that probably that was not at all a bad sign. On the contrary, if his brother hadn't written to him, it must be because nobody in Venice knew anything; no scandal had blown up, and he, the prior, had not been disturbed. Aside from the two of them, nobody knew the truth about his trafficking; and only a very few of their employees could even so much as suspect there was something amiss. I'll have to fight the Ten, Lippomano thought, but I'll make it, I'm more clever than any of them. And then, one way or another, I'll figure out who talked, and I'll avenge myself; and I'll also avenge myself of that Bernardo. Oh, yes, how I will avenge myself of him! When he was thinking these thoughts, Lippomano sometimes forgot that he was not alone, and a ferocious grin bared his canines; one time when Captain Casalini was observing him on the sly, he was surprised to see that grin come over his face, and his blood went cold.

Finally the day came when they all boarded the galley of sopracomito Benetto Gritti, which was supposed to take them to Venice. Going on board, Michele noticed uneasily that it was not a common galley, but one of those that the Venetians called a convict galley, with its crew of oarsmen composed exclusively of chained convicts. His most unpleasant memories of his days on the *Aquila* came to mind, and along with them a certain fear, at the thought that he was voluntarily returning to Venice, to put himself into the hands of the Council of Ten, protected only by the word of Sir Lorenzo Bernardo. Let's hope for the best, he told himself, while, together with the servants and laborers of Bernardo and Lippomano he put down his sack and looked for a place to sleep.

The weather continued to favor the voyage; the galley sped

passed Citera, pushed by the wind, sailed up the Morea, keeping itself constantly in sight of the coast, passed Zante and Cephalonia, laying over every two or three days to take on water and firewood, and after a few weeks it came within sight of Corfu. There the weather changed and for five days it was impossible to leave port. The regent of Corfu came on board to confer with the sopracomito and Captain Casalini, and when he came out of the cabin headed for the ladder he ran into Lippomano, who greeted him, bowing low. The regent responded courteously to the greeting, but it was clear he was embarrassed.

"Signore," said Sir Girolamo, "grant me this favor."

"What is it?" the regent grumbled, furrowing his brow.

"It's not possible that here there is no news from my brother, the lord prior. I haven't heard anything from him and I am terribly anguished."

The regent opened his mouth to say something, and then held back and remained silent.

"Well?" said Lippomano, leaning his head forward avidly.

The regent looked away.

"Tell me, it's obvious that you know!" Sir Girolamo demanded.

"Signor Lippomano, since you want to know at all costs, your brother has been accused of complicity in your crimes, and has been banished from Venice and from all territories belonging to St. Mark, under pain of death if he should return," the regent declared.

"Banished!" Lippomano bellowed, reeling from the blow. "Complicity in my crimes! So then I too have already been convicted and sentenced!"

"I didn't say that," said the regent, embarrassed, noticing the look of disapproval in the eyes of Captain Casalini, who had also come out of the cabin.

"Go back inside, Signor Lippomano," said the captain; and

taking him courteously, but firmly, by the arm, he led him away.

From that day on, everyone noticed that the prisoner was in the throes of a deadly agitation. He ate little or nothing, despite always being invited, together with Captain Casalini, to the table of sopracomito Gritti, where delicacies were served at every meal; macaroni at lunch and dinner, caviar and roe, while the officers, sailors, and servants had to settle for a soup of rice and salted meat, and the convicts at the oars dined on sea biscuit soaked in water. Lippomano's servants competed for the chance to serve him at table, because his plate always remained full, and whoever cleared the table had the right to empty it. Master Filippo and Gritti, a thin, bony man, with a short gray beard and steel blue eyes, never took their eyes off him, and noted with growing unease that he wasn't eating, was losing weight, and had a feverish look in his eye.

"I'll be glad when I've delivered him to the Lord Heads," Casalini said to Gritti one evening, as they were drinking a goblet of wine; it was hazy and dead calm, the wind had died, and the convicts chained to the benches were sweating to push the galley over the oil-smooth sea, under the surveillance of the galley-sergeant armed with a club.

"I'll be glad too," the sopracomito agreed. "I don't want to make any more stops, even if it means arriving in Venice with the crew completely spent. I don't like that man," he added.

Finally, the time came when the galley came within sight of the Lido. Almost all the passengers crowded onto the bow to be the first to make out, in the morning mist, the bell towers of Saint George's and Saint Mark's. The sailors prepared to take down the sails, because the difficult maneuver to enter the Lagoon, passing between the two castles of the Lido, could only be done under oars. Casalini and the sopracomito came out from behind the curtain of the poop cabin, stretching themselves; for some days now the heat had become so unbearable that instead of going below deck to sleep in the commander's quarters, they and Lippomano had been sleeping there.

"I have never been so happy to see Venice again!" Casalini said, laughing.

Lippomano came out behind them, in shirt sleeves, with the red eyes of someone who hasn't slept and a shadow of white beard. Squinting, he recognized the bastions of the castles, rife with cannons, and breathed a deep sigh. Then with a brusque gesture, he headed for the door leading to the ladder.

"Where are you going?" Casalini asked severely.

"To piss," Sir Girolamo responded, in a hostile tone. When he got to the door, he opened it and stepped down onto the top step of the ladder; then, in a flash, he threw himself into the sea.

33

S top! Stop!" Casalini cried out, his eyes popping out of
their orbits.

"Strike the sails!" shouted the sopracomito. "Let's turn
her around. You on the benches, glide and row!" The officers
rushed onto the *corsia* repeating the order for the convicts on
the starboard side to stop rowing and those on the port side to
row backwards to turn the galley, which, driven by the wind,
was visibly moving away from man overboard. As the sailors
were running around to take down the sails, all of those gathered on the bow with nothing to do rushed back to the stern
to see what was happening.

"He fell in! Man overboard!" Casalini screamed.

The sopracomito gave the order to throw empty water casks
and other wooden objects into the water so that Sir Girolamo
could grab onto something and keep himself afloat until he
could be rescued. But instead of swimming toward them,
Lippomano was swimming toward the open sea.

"But are you sure he fell?" Gritti said softly. Casalini, frightened out of his wits, spread his arms, and kept quiet.

"It doesn't look to me like he wants to save himself," the
sopracomito remarked.

It took the galley a long time to stop and turn on itself; by
now Lippomano was no more than a dot on the horizon.

"He's an excellent swimmer," Gritti noted, provoking a gesture of impatience from Casalini. Finally, the galley picked up
speed, and started closing in on the fugitive. "Everyone who

knows how to swim, in the water, and a zecchino for the one who grabs him!" the sopracomito cried. Several sailors quickly stripped off their clothes and jumped into the water. In the meantime the sea had gotten much rougher, and the galley was rolling dangerously.

"What a mess!" Casalini muttered to himself. Dozens of men, now crowded together again on the bow, were anxiously following the chase. Propelling themselves forward with powerful arm strokes, first one sailor and then another moved in close to Lippomano; but when they were just about to reach him, he ducked under the water. On board the galley a collective cry went up, followed immediately by another when the fugitive resurfaced behind the two pursuers, and began swimming vigorously in another direction. But other swimmers were coming toward him. Lippomano escaped yet again, took another few strokes, and then he was seen thrashing his arms wildly before disappearing under water. Another collective cry went up from the crowd. Two of the pursuers went under water too, and resurfaced soon after, struggling to hold up an inert body.

The fugitive was brought back on board unconscious. He was purple, with his eyes bulging out of their sockets, and swollen from the water he'd swallowed.

"Is he alive?" Casalini anxiously asked the galley's surgeon, who was the first to examine the body. The man looked up and shook his head.

"More dead than alive."

"But is he breathing?" the captain insisted. The surgeon put his ear next to the drowned man's mouth, while others felt his pulse and listened for a heartbeat.

"He's breathing a little bit" was the response.

"Try to bring him to!" Casalini shouted. "Master Benetto, let's take him ashore here at the Lido, and get it over and done with.

In coma, Lippomano was transported to the monastery of San Nicolo of the Lido, where physicians and surgeons were rushed in; blood was drawn, massages were done with vinegar and other urticant substances, but none of the remedies succeeded in keeping him alive. At midnight, Sir Girolamo Lippomano ceased breathing, without opening his eyes again or speaking.

"And so there's no doubt that it was not an accident?"

"No, there's no doubt. He did everything he could not to be saved."

Master Zuanne Morosini fell silent, and tapped on the table top with his fingers. The benches in front of him were full, not one member of the Council of Ten was absent, the doge Pasquale Cicogna, sitting in the president's chair, was running his bejeweled fingers through his long, thick beard, and Captain Casalini, standing with his hat in hand, was waiting in a sweat to see if he would be reprimanded or not for what had happened.

"So he confessed his guilt by himself," the doge remarked, in the end. Casalini breathed deep; despite the silence with which they had listened to his report, and the impenetrable expressions that all of those old foxes painted on their faces when there was a stranger in the secret room, it didn't seem that the Ten were all that unhappy with how it had ended up.

"Very well, you can go, but remain outside to wait," Mososini ordered, after exchanging a few words under his breath with the doge. With the captain dismissed, the discussion became much more heated.

"He's dead, fine; but that doesn't mean he shouldn't be given the punishment he deserved," said Sir Giambattista Soranzo. He was a little bald man, with a thin black beard, who was easily excited.

"And how so?" someone asked.

"He's no longer here, but his body is," Sir Giambattista

declared. "I propose that it be dragged through the dirt, decapitated, and held up to public scorn."

"In sum, his dead body should be given the treatment he deserved in he same manner as if he were still alive," the doge reassumed.

Master Zuanne Morosini cleared his throat.

"I believe," he began prudently, "that inflicting punishment on a cadaver is not something becoming to the decorum and the clemency of the Republic."

"The world has seen many examples of traitors drawn and quartered or hanged after death, and those princes that treated their enemies in such a way were certainly not the less feared for it," Soranzo interrupted him.

"That's true, but in those cases the betrayal was publicized and known to all," Morosini rebutted. "The point is if it behooves us or not to let it be known that the bailo who His Serenity" and he nodded toward the doge, silent and absorbed, "sent to Constantinople, and who prior to that had represented the Republic in many important posts, a man from one of our most noble families, deceived us so unworthily, and for filthy lucre!"

"There are rumors afoot," someone objected.

"But as long as they are not confirmed and the secret remains here among us, rumors do no damage. On the contrary, the fact that rumors are spread without being confirmed increases the fear and respect of the rabble.

"I continue to believe that that man deserved to be tortured and put on the rack, and if we can't do it to him alive, we have to do it to him dead," Soranzo said again ferociously.

The doge sighed and took the floor.

"Even wild beasts do not vent themselves on cadavers," he began.

"Except for jackals," a voice said.

"Exactly!" the doge retorted. "I believe it behooves us to

show clemency, and to permit his family to bury him. Where are the tombs of the Lippomanos?"

"In the church of the Frati dei Servi" interjected the secretary who was keeping the minutes.

"There! Well then, I ask for a vote on this motion: that the dead body be turned over to the family, with no further demonstrations, and that they be given permission to bury it in the family tombs at the Servi."

The secretary prepared the ballot box and distributed the little balls of fabric. The Ten voted in silence. When the box was opened, it was evident that the majority had voted in favor of the motion. The secretary made a note for the record, specifying the number of votes in favor and against.

"I want to hope that we will at least approve the seizure of his assets, and the demolition of the house where he lived," Soranzo spoke again, still cross. The others looked at each other, puzzled. It was, in fact, habitual to take such measures against traitors. But this time?

"You don't understand," Morosini said, his patience growing thin. "This whole matter must be kept quiet, and that's it. What do you think people will say when they see his property confiscated and his house torn down?"

"So, about justice we don't give a damn. Fine, as long as we know that," said Sir Giambattista, miffed.

"Justice is one of this Republic's greatest preoccupations, but we must be coherent with our objectives," the doge intervened. "We have voted not to proceed against the cadaver, and neither will we proceed against the house."

Sir Lunardo Michiel, who until now had remained silent, suddenly got to his feet.

"Let it be said," he began suavely, "that this man has rendered us a great service by killing himself. Because if it had been necessary to try him, I don't know what could have come of it. Worse still: imagine if down there in Constantinople he had got the bright idea to resist being recalled. He could have put himself under the protection of the Turk, and refused to leave; and we would have been greatly embarrassed, and we would have presented a not at all flattering image of ourselves to the rest of the world."

"All of that," Morosini interjected, "goes to the credit of Bernardo, who managed the whole affair so ably."

"That's true," more than one agreed.

"I can tell you," Master Zuanne continued, "that Lippomano was all set to resist the recall and refuse to leave. But Bernardo used his diplomatic skills to persuade him that was not a good idea."

"So you see!" Soranzo spoke up, agitated. "And you come and tell me we have to be grateful to him for so docilely letting himself be brought back! Yet you will all recall what Bernardo writes in his report, that one day, in conversation, he said to Lippomano, to keep him calm, that he was very happy with his obedience, and that in that way he had given a great sign of his innocence; and Lippomano responded: my dear sir, what else could I do? Here with enough gold one can obtain anything he wants, and you can spend so much more than me!"

Many of them laughed.

"The fact remains," Sir Lunardo resumed, "that Lippomano has freed us from serious embarrassments, first because he has seen to it to punish himself, and then because in Constantinople he so readily obeyed our orders. And I believe that despite his enormous demerits, this bit of merit we can recognize; and therefore, I would like to move that no further punitive measures be taken in his regard."

The vote approved Lunardo's motion with just one dissent, evidently coming from Soranzo, who went back to his bench to sit down, shaking his head.

"Therefore, this matter is closed," Morosini declared. "Now, gentlemen, there is another matter that our brave Captain Casalini has brought back from Constantinople."

"Our brave Captain Casalini deserves to be put in jail for letting his prisoner escape that way! If this goes on much longer we'll end up giving him a commendation!" Sir Giambattista sounded off.

"Don't doubt that we will let him know what we think of his handling of this affair, and it will not be a commendation," Master Zuanne said sinisterly. "But there is another man we must discuss, the exile whom Bernardo has sent back to us under safe conduct, and who, it seems, has a very strange story to tell. It's still early and we have time. I would propose to send for him and hear what he has to say."

Fifteen minutes later Michele was brought in by two policemen. He was still dressed in the clothes he was wearing when he left Constantinople, almost two months before, and he had a disheartened look about him. He was expecting to be let go upon arriving in Venice, but Captain Casalini had orders to take him directly to the jail of the Ten, pending questioning. Those twenty-four hours in solitary confinement, without being able to notify Bianca that he had returned, and in the uncertainty of not knowing what was going to happen next, had demoralized him more than the entire exhausting voyage.

Master Zuanne Morosini looked at him with curiosity. So this was the man for whom Sir Lorenzo Bernardo had come to ask him a favor. In effect, it was thanks to him that he had gotten the idea to send Bernardo to Constantinople, and that had been a very good idea. How strange, though, that the lad had turned up out of nowhere right in Constantinople of all places, and with such an outlandish story to tell! Morosini made it a habit not to trust anyone, and not to believe in coincidence. So he was suspicious and prudent when he began questioning Michele.

"The magnificent Sir Lorenzo Bernardo," he said, sizing up

the young man who was standing before him, hat in hand, "writes that you have recounted a long story. Tell it to these gentlemen as well."

Stammering from the emotion, Michele began telling the story of what had happened to him. He told about how he had signed on to the *Loredana*, all of a sudden, because he was running from the police.

"Only later did I learn I'd been banished. But the lord bailo told me that the ban had been lifted, and that the pardon has been signed, isn't that right?" he asked, looking around the room warily.

"That's right," Morosini confirmed, "and you needn't be worried about that. But we're interested in what happened on the galley. Do you confirm that you are referring to the galley of the sopracomito Master Andrea Loredan, which left the port of Venice on 27 July 1588?" he asked, after glancing at the dossier which he had spread open on the table in front of him.

"I don't know the day," Michele swallowed, "but that's the right galley."

"Go ahead."

"So," said Michele, "among us oarsmen the rumor started to spread right away that the sopracomito was transporting a sack of zecchini."

The doge looked at Morosini, who confirmed with an eloquent nod.

"A sack of zecchini to be taken to Candia," Michele continued. "And one day, while we were laying over on an island in Dalmatia, two men stole the sack."

"Two men?" Soranzo interjected.

"Two oarsmen! Two who sat on the same bench as me, two lads from Chioggia."

"And then?"

"And then the soldiers went ashore to search for them, and I was already ashore with the detail sent to gather firewood and water, and I saw them run off into the woods, and the soldiers caught up to them and killed them. And I was hiding nearby and I heard everything: the comito said why don't we keep the zecchini for ourselves? And he said, all we have to do is say we didn't find them, we bury them here and nobody will know about it."

"And do you know the comito's name?" someone asked.

"No, eminence, I don't, I was just an oarsman," Michele said.

Master Zuanne cleared his throat.

"That's not really a problem, we know what his name was, I've already had the ship's log recovered. Go ahead."

"Well, the soldiers said that was fine by them, and so they buried the two lads, and the gold too, and then they went back on board to say they hadn't found anything. And I saw where they dug the grave, and I took note of the place, and I'm sure I could find it again."

"And what was the name of the island?"

"I don't know, but I could find it again, sailing from Zara. I got a good look at the profile of the mountains, I impressed it on my brain. It's a day's sail from Zara," Michele repeated.

Giambattista Soranzo shifted on his bench.

"And why didn't you report what you saw immediately?"

"I know I was wrong not to," said Michele, solemnly. "I was afraid, eminence. How can a galleyman denounce a comito?"

"You should have denounced him, and the sopracomito would have done justice," Soranzo rebutted, icily.

"Sir Giambattista, excuse me, but the story isn't over yet," Morosini intervened. "Was there no more talk on board about the sack of zecchini?"

"Sure there was!" Michele resumed, taking heart. "Everybody said they hadn't been able to find it, we were sent to search the whole island looking for the thieves."

"And only you knew it was useless, and you didn't say anything," Sir Lunardo Michiel noted.

"Yessir," admitted Michele, downcast. "I was afraid. I didn't talk right away, and later on I couldn't anymore."

"And since the thieves were never found, what happened after that?"

"Well," said Michele, "before we arrived in Crete we boarded a Turkish felucca. There were some Jews on board with some merchandise and some gold. His lordship the sopra-comito had everything seized, and then they told us that those Jews were the thieves, and that they had recovered the stolen gold. But I know that's not true."

"And how is it that nobody ever heard anything about this felucca?" Michiel piped up again.

"I didn't see because I was on my bench. But they say they killed everyone who was on board, so nobody would know."

Michele fell silent, sweating and scared, trying to figure out what those gentlemen dressed in purple thought of his story.

"Very well," the doge thundered, after a moment of silence. "Take him away."

The guards came in to get Michele and they took him out-side. As soon as he was out of the room, the Ten all started talk-ing at the same time, and the Lord Heads had a difficult time maintaining order.

"I've never seen such a bold-faced liar!" Sir Lunardo Michiel protested. "The sopracomito Loredan arrived in Candia and delivered the gold according to protocol, it's all in the log, the rest is all nonsense!"

"Master Lunardo," said Sir Zuanne, staring him right in the eye, "am I mistaken or is that sopracomito the husband of one of your nieces?"

Michiel admitted that was the case but he didn't back down.

"And so?" He rebutted with a combative air. "Here a Venetian patrician is accused of letting himself be robbed of money entrusted to him by the Republic, to have assaulted a Turkish vessel, killed the crew, and in turn to have stolen money and delivered it in place of the other without reporting even one word of what happened, and this whole story, which has no place in heaven or on earth, is told to us by an exile, without an iota of proof, and we're supposed to believe him?"

"I say," Soranzo intervened, "he be put to torture and made to confess that he made the whole thing up."

The doge, who had been smoothing his beard as he listened, spoke up.

"Gentlemen, the accusation is too serious not to be investigated with all the means at our disposal. I propose to have the comito arrested, and to pray his lordship sopracomito Loredan," and here he intentionally changed his tone, staring at Sir Lunardo, "to come to refer to us what he knows, and after having questioned him, if it shall be the case, we will send the lad back to Zara and we'll see if he can provide us with proof of his account."

"But excuse me," someone interjected, "even if the story were true, by this time the comito will have already gone back down there to dig up the money, no?"

This was true too. The Ten fell silent, puzzled.

"That could be," the doge conceded, matter-of-factly. "But it is our duty to verify that. I ask that my proposal be put to a vote."

Outside the room, Captain Casalini took charge of Michele and led him away.

"Where are you taking me?" asked Michele, when he realized that instead of going outside they were going further and further into the labyrinth of stairways and corridors in the Ducal Palace.

"To the prison of the Lord Heads," said the captain, as though it were obvious.

Michele blanched.

"What do you mean to the prison? I have a safe conduct pass from Signor Bernardo, they told me I have been pardoned!"

"And who denies it?" Casalini rebutted. "In fact, you've been pardoned and that crime is no longer being discussed. But now you are under investigation for your revelations, and you will stay here as long as the Lords of the Council please."

Michele reeled under the blow.

"But I thought they were going to let me go to my wife!" he stammered.

"A lot of people have come through here who thought something that turned out to be wrong," the captain shut him off.

34

Sir Lunardo Michiel looked intently at his nephew, who was standing before him and trying to avoid looking him in the eye. Since the time of the voyage of the *Loredana*, the sopracomito had filled out a bit, and the shadow of a beard now covered his adolescent pimples. Sir Lunardo had never expected much of him, and he hadn't been very surprised when, upon his return from his first command, his nephew had refused to accept another. Now, however, he was considering him from a new perspective. If he had actually done what that galleyman recounted, he thought with admiration, he had been extremely resourceful in getting himself out of a tough situation, and then in hiding the truth all of this time; we'll make something of him yet.

"So," he began, clearing his throat, "do you know why I've had you called here."

"Yessir," Loredan replied, still avoiding his gaze.

"Tomorrow you will appear before the Ten to report on your voyage of two years ago. I don't want any surprises, is that clear?"

Loredan opened his mouth to speak and then closed it again.

"When I say I don't want any surprises, I hope you understand me," Sir Lunardo insisted.

"Signor uncle, I must tell you the truth. It's true that," Loredan began, but Sir Lunardo stopped him with a brusque gesture.

"Signor nephew," he then continued, standing up from his chair and going over to stand in front of him, "I don't want to hear talk of truth, I don't want to hear talk of anything. On that voyage, nothing happened at all, am I right?"

For the first time, Loredan hinted at a slight grin.

"If that's what Signor Uncle says."

Again, Michiel looked at him intently.

"That's what I say and I hope that's what your comito is also going to say. He was arrested this morning, before I could manage to find him and speak to him. So, it all depends on him."

"That carrion!" exclaimed Loredan, his eyes riled with animosity. "If he really found that money and kept it for himself . . ."

"Shut up!" Michiel ordered. "I don't want to hear anything about it, do you understand? As far as you know, the comito didn't do a damn thing; it's all an invention of that rotten scalawag. And let's hope he doesn't let anything slip out. Then," he added, lowering his voice, "when this business is over and done with, we'll settle accounts with him too."

"If they put him on the rope, he'll talk," Loredan objected, glumly.

Michiel shook his head.

"Before they start with torture, they'll send that other one to the island, to verify his story. I want to hope that your comito has used his time well, and that down there . . . Enough, that's all I'm going to say. If, as I believe, that scoundrel returns without having found a thing, then he'll be the one who's put on the rope first. And you'll see, he'll confess that he made up the whole thing. He'll confess and then some," he repeated, pleased with himself.

Loredan laughed.

"But that's not all," Michiel resumed, going back to sit down. "Tomorrow you'll be questioned and you'll have to know how to respond to all their questions. Let's see. The two oarsmen who the scoundrel says were killed after they'd stolen the gold, what actually happened to them?"

"I can't remember every last oarsmen," Loredan rebutted haughtily. "They'll have deserted on Candia." Sir Lunardi sighed.

"Actually, in this case you'd better make yourself remember because they can consult the ship's log from your galley. I did," he continued, "and it turns out you paid their salary until you unrigged. So you can't claim they deserted on Candia. According to your books, they returned to Venice, and it was only afterwards that they covered their tracks. It's too bad that in Venice it's not so easy to disappear. It would be better if they had deserted on Candia. If only you hadn't been so greedy; down there it's no trouble at all to disappear, but you insisted on pocketing their salary all the way to the end!"

Loredan shrugged his shoulders, ill at ease.

"As for the scoundrel, what's his name? Michele of Matteo, well, how is it that he got the idea to make up this whole story? The Ten will certainly ask you that. Did you perhaps do him some wrong?"

"That's out of the question. I didn't even know who he was," the nephew puffed.

His uncle looked at him with disapproval.

"Actually, you'll be a lot better off if you know," he reproved him. "I'd say there was at least one occasion for which this . . . beggar got it into his head to have some resentment toward you. What do I know? Maybe one time you slapped him to punish some insolence of his, maybe you put him in chains, and the poor wretch, to avenge himself, invented this entire story out of whole cloth."

This time Loredan got it.

"Yes, come to think of it, I remember him, it happened just like that," he confirmed, with a cunning air.

"That's the way," his uncle approved. "Remind yourself that it's your head against his."

Loredan grimaced contemptuously.

"It'll be his that rolls, don't worry Signor Uncle."

When he appeared before the Council of Ten, the comito of the *Loredana* had already spent two nights in the dungeon, and he didn't look good. Pale, with a long beard and bloodshot eyes, he stood before the doge and the Lord Heads, while the other members scrutinized him from the benches. Sir Lunardo had sat so the prisoner could see his face, and he was staring into his eyes with intention. That morning he had managed to get an anonymous note to him, hidden in a loaf of bread: "Deny everything and have no fear." The comito looked around, uncertain; but when his eyes met those of Sir Lunardo, the latter gave him an imperceptible sign, and the comito felt his courage perk up.

"Do you know why you are here?" Sir Zuanne Morosini asked him.

"No, eminence," the comito responded, hinting at a bow.

"In 1588," Morosini continued, "were you comito on the galley of lord sopracomito Andea Loredan?"

"Yes, your eminence," the comito confirmed.

"Tell us about that voyage."

Michiel made a tiny sign of assent, which did not escape the witness.

"Well, Your Serenity," the comito began, turning toward the doge and bowing still more deeply, "we went to Crete, but nothing special happened."

"Did you know the nature of Signor Loredan's mission?"

The comito kept an eye on Michiel, and saw him nod his head.

"Everyone on the galley knew, he was transporting a sack of zecchini to be delivered to the regent on Candia."

"And as far as you knew, were the zecchini delivered regularly?"

"Yes, your eminence" the comito confirmed, with a look of astonishment. What a scoundrel, Michiel thought. It's too bad we'll have to get rid of him, with a man like that you could do some things. And, who knows, maybe it won't actually be necessary to eliminate him. We'll close one eye, and keep him tied to us forever. Ten thousand zecchini! What gall!

Reassured by the mute communication he was maintaining with Michiel, the comito was steadily more confident. All I have to do is deny everything, and I'll get out of this clean, he convinced himself. Certainly, if I knew why they arrested me, and who it was that ratted on me, it would be a lot easier. But I'll get out of it, and then I'll find out who it was that talked, and I'll make him pay. He'll meet the same end as those three, he thought, with a thrill of pleasure. He was thinking of the three harquebusiers who had helped him kill the two lads and hide the gold. The next summer, when they went back to the island with a boat to dig it up, he poisoned all three of them on the return voyage and threw them overboard. Now he was a rich man, even if he couldn't let it be known and had to settle for depositing the gold a little at a time, in different banks. Just wait till I get out of here, he thought again, and then I'll get my revenge.

The questioning dragged on for a while, with no real outcome. When the comito was dismissed, and the police took him back to the dungeon, the Ten looked each other in the face.

"How clear can you get?" Sir Lunardo Michiel burst out. "Yesterday you heard signor sopracomito Loredan, and today this gentleman. That other scalawag made the whole thing up, that's all there is to it. And if it were up to me I'd put him to the rope immediately to make him confess."

"I agree," interjected Sir Giambattista Soranzo; then he

interrupted himself because he noticed he had a flea pestering him and started rummaging through his beard to look for it.

Sir Zuanne Morosini looked at the doge, who sighed.

"First of all we'll send a mission to verify whether or not the money is hidden where the galleyman says. We cannot fail to do that. And then we'll see," Cicogna concluded, standing up to signal that the hearing was adjourned.

"Here, this is it," exclaimed Michele; and deep inside he breathed a big sign of relief. Virgin Mary, he thought, has granted me her grace.

It was almost evening, and the fusta, having left Zara before dawn, had spent the whole day tacking through the Dalmatian archipelago, trying to take advantage of the westerly wind to avoid wearing out the oarsmen. Michele had realized that there were a lot more islands than he remembered, and after a while he started to get desperate, fearing that he wouldn't be able to find the right one. As points of reference he had the unusual profile of the mountains on the mainland, an isolated bell tower on a promontory, a thicket of maritime pines on the tip of the island; all these signals were imprinted in his mind, but he was still gripped by the fear of not finding them. As soon as they left Zara the pilot of the fusta, on instructions from Captain Casalini, had questioned him in detail, but in the end he just shook his head; he couldn't make heads or tails of that story; those islands had so many bell towers and promontories it was impossible to tell them apart. Casalini, not pleased, took the pilot aside.

"Keep in mind that the lords of the Council of Ten would be very pleased if this island were to be found," he told him in a low voice.

The pilot, a veteran from Istria whose chin was covered by a bristly white beard, bowed respectfully.

"Of course! But it's the lad who's got to find it, I can only take the fusta where he tells me to go and hope he remembers, and that he doesn't make us run aground."

"Make us run aground? It's your job to make sure that doesn't happen," Casalini exclaimed.

"You certainly can't expect me to know the sounding depth of the entire archipelago," the pilot rebutted, offended; and the captain, his patience worn thin, let it drop.

Michele had almost given up hope when he saw the bell tower; darkness was coming on quickly and the haze was hiding the crest of the mountains.

"Stop! Stop!" he cried out; and running up to the bow he sharpened his gaze on the islands nearby. On the tip of one of them a thicket of pine trees was rapidly blending into the nearly black sky behind it.

"That's the island, that one's it," he repeated with relief, while Casalini, having run to his side, ordered the pilot to come about.

"By now it's dark, we'll wait till tomorrow to go ashore," the captain decided; but Michele, impatient, shook his head.

"When it happened it was already dark. I saw the place in the dark, by the light of the moon, I'm sure I can find it better at night than during the day. Let's go ashore now, I pray you."

A half hour later the fusta's tender was in the water, powered by six rowers, and carrying Michele, the captain, two harquebusiers, and two sailors with shovels and picks.

"Not here," said Michele. "Up ahead there's a beach, that's where we went ashore."

After rounding a promontory, he recognized the inlet where the *Loredana* had dropped anchor on that unforgettable night. The boat came to a halt a few steps from the shoreline. The rowers jumped in the water and pulled the boat onto dry land.

"Don't try to pull one over on me, or I'll order them to shoot," the captain warned, "And you, light your fuses!" he ordered the harquebusiers.

Michele took a look around. He was trying to find the stream where they had filled the first water casks, but he couldn't find it. Overcome with anxiety, he started running back and forth on the beach, sinking down to his ankles in the sand.

"What are you doing?" asked the captain, in a threatening tone.

"Just a minute?" Michele implored him. "Ah, it's gone dry!" he exclaimed. His bare feet had tripped over the stones that marked the bed of what back then had been a muddy stream. "We're almost there, it's up this way," he said, feeling good again.

Puffing testily, the captain, the soldiers, and the sailors followed him up over the dunes into the thicket. Michele was scared to death at what might happen to him if he failed to find his way, but the events of that night were so impressed in his memory that he had no trouble getting oriented. In just a few minutes they came to the clearing where the two lads had been killed.

"This is it," Michele whispered; somehow it didn't seem right to speak loudly. "That is," he corrected himself, "the gold is not here, they buried it a little further on. I'll show you."

The murderers had buried the sack at the foot of a dead tree with gnarled branches that stood out against the sky: they needed a place that was easy to find too. The sailors gave Michele one of the shovels, and the three of them started digging.

For a while nobody said anything. The silence was broken only by the shovelfuls of sand piling up at their backs. When the hole started getting deep, however, the sailors started to grumble.

"Are you sure this is where it is?" one of them finally asked, stopping his digging.

"I'm dead sure!" Michele replied. But even he was starting to get nervous. For the first time he realized that the comito and his accomplices had had plenty of time to come and get their treasure, after the *Loredana* had come back to Venice to unrig, almost two years ago. By now, the hole was really deep; that night, the murderers hadn't dug for that long.

"There's nothing here," another sailor said; and he stopped digging too.

"They must have come back to get it," Michele admitted, drying the sweat off his forehead.

"I suppose," said Casalini. Michele looked at him to try to figure out what he was thinking but the captain's face was inscrutable.

"We've come for nothing," the captain added tersely, and he turned to leave. At that point Michele got an idea.

"Wait a minute! I know where they buried the two lads! And they certainly didn't dig them up. Let's go look for them; it's right near here!"

"I was charged to come here and look for the gold," the captain replied, shaking his head.

"But I have to prove that I told the truth! And the proof is there!" Michele insisted.

Captain Casalini thought about it. It was an annoyance and a waste of time, but if the question came out later on he would be reprimanded for not having exhausted all the possibilities.

"All right" he gave in. "Show us where we have to look."

With a shovel over his shoulder, Michele walked off through the bushes, followed by the grumbling sailors. Luckily he found the clearing pretty quickly, and immediately started digging.

"Move it, get to work," the captain ordered, when he reached them.

The sailors shoveled listlessly but Michele knew that this time his head was at stake. He shoveled so energetically that after just a few minutes he hit an obstacle.

"I think I've found them," he announced. The captain and

the harquebusiers came over to look, and the sailors started digging with more zeal. A minute later a shriveled hand popped out of the sand. One of the soldiers jumped back and they all made the sign of the cross.

"They're really here," said Michele, relieved and saddened at the same time. A few minutes later the two bodies were out in the open. The sand had kept them from decomposing, turning them into mummies. They were not a very beautiful sight, especially their faces with their mouths still open to make their last cry, their eyes empty, and just a few remaining hairs, sticking to their temples. The captain put his handkerchief over his mouth, bent over them and did a quick search; but there wasn't anything under their ragged clothes, and they didn't even have their purses around their necks.

"All right, we've found them," he said, getting back up. "Now we bury them again, there's nothing else to do. But I will report to the Lord Heads that as far as these two are concerned you told the truth."

The captain hurriedly recited a prayer, while the men took off their hats; then the bodies were thrown back in the grave and recovered with sand. Michele, fighting back the tears, remembered Marco and Giulio as he had known them when they were alive; naïve and full of expectations. I think you two have saved my life, he thought.

"That's the way it is, eh?" said the doge Pasquale Cicogna, shifting in his chair.

"Yes, Your Serenity, confirmed Casalini, standing before him.

"Fine. Well, you did well to have them dug up, captain. You may go, we will call you again if we need to."

Casalini left with a deep bow, and the doge leaned his elbows on the table, brought his fists together, put his chin on them, and began to reflect. In front of him on a silver tray there was a small carafe, also silver, filled with wine, with a crystal goblet and a porcelain bowl of candied fruit, but His Serenity took no interest in them.

"So, let's see," he began to reason in a low voice. "The gold is gone, and that's a fact. If it were only for that, the matter would be closed for good. The word of the magnificent Loredan, and of his comito, against that of a convicted galley-man. Game over."

Discontent, he drummed his fingers on the top of the table.

"On the other hand, there are the two cadavers, which could confirm his story. But who is interested in seeing it confirmed? Wouldn't it be better not to talk about it anymore? Loredan delivered the money, he did not harm the Republic. As for the comito, he can be dealt with without making a lot of noise . . ."

He was still absorbed in these meditations when an usher knocked on the door and announced that Sir Lunardo Michiel had arrived.

"Show him in," Cicogna ordered.

Sir Lunardo came in, bowed, and sat on the bench indicated by the doge, under the large portrait showing Cicogna kneeling in church, on a bench covered by a sumptuous Turkish carpet, while a crowd of women with their hands joined in prayer, prepared themselves to receive communion from the hands of the priest. There had been doges who were friends of the Church, others who were indifferent, and others who were even hostile, but Sir Lunardo knew that Cicogna was among the friends; in any event, the doge, in large part, owed him his election, a surprise result after some fifty-three ballots, during which there had even been fisticuffs. The Cicognas were not a powerful family, and Pasquale was greatly in need of allies.

"Listen," said the doge, smoothing his beard. "You know that matter regarding your nephew? Well, Capatin Casalini has returned, and they didn't find the gold."

"I knew it," exclaimed Michiel, triumphant.

"But there's a complication," the doge went on. "They found two cadavers, exactly as the galleyman had said."

Sir Lunardo reflected a moment.

"That doesn't mean anything!" he replied, with self-assurance. "As far as we know, he could have murdered them himself. On the contrary, that's certainly the case. We'll make him confess," he added, with a flash of cruelty in his eyes.

"That could be," the doge admitted. "But, according to the log of your nephew's galley, those two remained in service until it was unrigged."

Sir Lunardo made a contrite face.

"My nephew acted foolishly, I know. But he's not the first sopracomito who has forgotten to denounce the disappearance of an oarsman or two, while continuing to pocket their salaries. It won't happen again. At the same time," he added, his face brightening, "who can say if the bodies were actually theirs? Maybe that rascal killed two islanders to rob them, and then he made up the rest of it."

"Right, I hadn't thought of that; it could be a solution," the doge approved, relieved. "That's surely the way it is. I'm sure the Ten will agree to that tomorrow, you'll see. A piece of candy?"

Sir Lunardo fished out an orange wedge and started chewing on it.

"Naturally," Cicogna resumed, "you will make your nephew understand that from now on . . . "

"You needn't even say it," Michiel interrupted him. "And as for the comito?"

"We'll talk about that in the Council of Ten," said the doge, giving him a meaningful look.

The other nodded.

"I'm very grateful to you and I will remember this," he said briefly.

"I know. Go, now."

Left alone, the doge poured himself a glass of wine, drank, then put a piece of candy in his mouth and started to suck it.

The usher knocked on the door again, and announced Master Zuanne Morosini.

"Welcome, Sir Zuanne," Cicogna said, courteously. In a few words he informed him too about the result of the investigation, and outlined how he planned to direct the debate at the meeting of the Ten.

"I imagine you too will agree," he concluded. "At this time, the Republic doesn't need any scandal, and you have always been the first to say that."

Sir Zuanne remained silent for a bit. The outcome of the investigation carried out on the island, he thought, was the worst one possible. If the gold had been found, it would have been evident that Loredan had lied, and the Ten would have done their duty by demonstrating that nobody was exempt from their justice. If nothing had been found, the galleyman could have been hanged to punish him for his lies and the case closed. This way, there was still a modicum of doubt.

"Surely it would be better if the magnificent Loredan could clear himself of all suspicion," he grumbled.

"From now on," said the doge dryly, "the magnificent Loredan will tend to his own private affairs. And actually, I think his uncle will be advising him to go overseas for a while."

"And the galleyman?"

"He'll be hanged, naturally," replied the doge. "With him out of the way, nobody will have anything to object to."

Morosini pondered. That man was under the protection of the Bernardos, and he had already saved him once. But that had happened before this whole incredible story about theft and assassination had come out. He certainly couldn't continue looking out for that rascal, who would be much better off if he disappeared, instead of bothering him again.

"We will do as Your Serenity wishes," he said in the end.

"Bravo, Sir Zuanne, I will remember this," exclaimed the doge, satisfied. "And you'll see that Sir Lunardo will remember it as well. The two of you are pillars of the Republic, I'm very happy to see you back on peaceful terms again."

But when he left Morosini couldn't bring himself to feel content. Despite everything, the galleyman had made a good impression on him, and he was almost inclined to think that he had told the truth. But after all, what is the truth, when such important interests are in play? The doge and Michiel were asking him for a favor, and they would pay their debt to him. No doubt, the lad was going to end up very badly. Oh, well, Sir Zuanne thought, shrugging his shoulders. Too bad for him, that's his problem. He should have found the gold.

35

M orosini had just returned home when a visit from Lady Clarice was announced. He was tired, and would have preferred to get some rest, but he did not want to do her the discourtesy of not receiving her. Clarice came into the room, a splendor of jewels and youth, her blond hair laced with a string of pearls. With her entered a breath of perfume that his sensitive patrician's nose breathed in with involuntary pleasure.

"I have come to speak frankly with my husband's friend," Lady Clarice declared when they had exhausted the formalities.

Master Zuanne gestured courteously and waited expectantly.

"I know that the galley which brought Lippomano back to Venice also had on board the man for whom my husband, some time ago, had requested a pardon. I also know that the man had an extraordinary story to tell."

Morosini frowned.

"And how do you know that?" he asked, a little too abruptly.

"Sir!" Donna Clarice was astonished. "Captain Casalini brought me back a bundle of letters from my husband. When he realized that the man who had presented himself to him was the same man whose case we had taken on, Sir Lorenzo obviously wrote to me to advise me that he was sending him back to Venice."

"Quite right," Morosini agreed.

"All the more so," Lady Clarice continued, looking him in

the eye, "given that the man had put himself at risk by coming here to recount what he knew, and my husband, although he had issued him a safe conduct pass, preferred that I be informed."

This time Morosini didn't say anything.

"And apparently he was right, because as soon as the young man arrived in Venice he was arrested, despite the safe conduct signed by my husband."

"Signora, he was not arrested for his conviction; for that he had been pardoned, and the safe conduct issued by Sir Lorenzo served to guarantee him that the order of banishment had been annulled. He was detained to allow us to verify his story."

Clarice did not let him finish.

"The way I see it," she exclaimed, shaking her blond curls, "if the banishment had been annulled there was no need for a safe conduct, and if my husband issued him one, it was precisely for the purpose of avoiding what happened, and to allow him to come to my house to thank me for what I did for him, and to see his wife again, whom he has not seen for over two years."

What a woman's way to reason, Morosini thought, irritated. But he certainly had no desire to argue with Lady Clarice, who was sitting there next to him, beautiful as she was, with just the slightest hint of the curve of her breasts emerging from her décolleté.

"That's not quite so, Signora" he limited himself to saying, courteously.

"Ah no? Well," Lady Clarice replied, haughtily, "I can see what regard our Lords of the Signory have for the signature of my husband, our bailo in Constantinople, and do not doubt that I will inform him of the situation."

Master Zuanne took alarm at this. The alliance with the Bernardos, born the instant that Sir Lorenzo had come to him

to ask for the famous pardon, and consolidated by his appointment to Constantinople, was an important piece of the strategy
with which he was patiently constructing his party, in prepara-
tion for his upcoming election to the dogeship.

"Signora," he tried to explain, "things could not have been
handled differently; that is the procedure that is always applied
in these cases. It is too important to keep the interested parties in
custody when such a delicate investigation is being conducted."

Lady Clarice looked at him maliciously.

"The magnificent Loredan, however, was not placed in custody."

She also knows that he's involved in this, thought Master
Zuanne. That clueless pushover of a husband has told her
everything!

Before Morosini could recover from the blow, Lady Clarice
leaned forward, and put her hand familiarly on his knee.

"Master Zuanne," she said, looking at him with her eyes
flashing, "now, however, the investigation is finished. Captain
Casalini has come back. What are you waiting for to release my
man?"

"Not so fast, Signora" Morosini grumbled, looking away.
"We have to consider what Captain Casalini found."

"Why? What did he find?" Lady Clarice pressed him; then
she laughed. "What a face you made, Master Zuanne! Don't be
afraid, I don't want to extort a state secret from you, and then
perhaps denounce you to the Lord Inquisitors! The soldiers
and sailors who were with the captain saw everything, and it's
not hard to get them to talk. I know that the gold was not
found, but the cadavers yes, and they are the proof that my
man told the truth!" she concluded, triumphant.

Morosini shook his head.

"Let's not be so quick to call it proof. There could be a very
different explanation."

Lady Clarice stared at him, serious now.

"Master Zuanne, let's put our cards on the table, is that all right with you? I have spoken about this matter with my father-in-law, we have talked about it at length."

That was a lie: Master Alvise would never have dreamed of discussing affairs of state with his daughter-in-law. But Clarice had blurted it out so convincingly that Master Zuanne, despite all of his long experience, didn't think even for a moment that the woman was leading him by the nose.

"Milord father-in-law says that he would not be surprised if the Ten, given that there is no sure proof, should decide to keep the whole thing quiet. He says the Loredans have a lot of friends, even among the Ten. Now, Master Zuanne, I couldn't care less about the magnificent Loredan, but I don't want my man to be the scapegoat. Because he surely will be the scapegoat if the Ten decide not to believe his story."

Morosini pursed his lips and refrained from speaking.

"I can see quite well that's how things stand," Lady Clarice sighed. "You don't want to believe him. But those two cadavers, how do you explain them?"

"He could have killed them himself," Morosini let slip. Lady Clarice turned red with rage.

"Oh yes? I'm amazed at you Master Zuanne, I wouldn't have believed it was so easy to lead you by the nose."

"Signora!" the nobleman exclaimed, squeezing the arms of his chair.

"Yes, lead you by the nose! Who talked you into believing this nonsense! Tell me this. If that lad had really killed two people on that island, and all the rest of the story was made up by him, why in he world would he ever have come back to tell the whole story, and take the police with him right to the spot, when he knew perfectly well the gold wasn't there? Tell me that now, if you think you're capable of it!"

Morosini was about to answer but then he was left speechless. Right, why? Up till now that objection hadn't come to mind, and he didn't know how to respond to it. Clarice saw that he was dumbfounded and she pressed him.

"You can see for yourself that it's not possible! No, Master Zuanne, there's just one possible explanation, that the lad is telling the truth, and that the sopracomito Loredan let himself be robbed of the money the Republic had entrusted to him, and to avoid having to repay it out of his own pocket he boarded the felucca, with the risk of provoking an incident with the Grand Turk, and now the Ten are ready to put the whole thing to rest and send an innocent man to his death!"

"That's enough, Signora," Morsini rebutted, looking around in alarm. "These are state secrets, and they must not leave the chamber of the Ten."

Clarice laughed in his face.

"Master Zuanne! What state secret! I know it, my husband knows it, because I've written him everything, my father-in-law knows it, the whole house of Bernardo knows it, and I'm telling you that tomorrow all of Venice will know it!"

Master Zuanne trembled.

"Signora, you can't think . . ." he stammered, livid. But all of a sudden Clarice was glowing with a warm smile, and she moved still closer to him, taking one of his hairy hands between her smooth, slender ones.

"Master Zuanne," she said softly, "I didn't come here to argue. The house of Bernardo is happy about the friendship between you and my husband, and we are ready to maintain it. And my brothers too, as you well know, count for something in Venice, and they too are friends of the house of Morosini, and we will be even better friends, if you should will it."

Master Zuanne abruptly rose to his feet and went to the window. As he watched the water flickering in the Grand Canal, he heard Clarice move her chair. Although he had turned his back to her, her perfume told him that the woman was standing behind him.

"What you ask of me is not so easy," he said in a muted voice.

Clarice, unseen, conceded herself a victory smile.

"I know," she murmured in his ear. "But you can pull it off."

Obstinate, Morosini said nothing.

"I take it as a commitment, Master Zuanne," Clarice pressed him. "Do you see my gondola down there?"

At the embarcadero of Palazzo Morosini, a gondola adorned with the red and silver crest of the Bernardo family was bobbing up and down on the water.

"I came here in my father-in-law's gondola," Clarice said innocently. "Everyone knows that I've been here. And now, with your permission, I'm going to Ca' Pesaro to tell my brothers that at tomorrow's meeting of the Ten, Master Zuanne Morosini will not permit an innocent man to be condemned to death to save the head of Signor Loredan."

His head buzzing, Master Zuanne tried to think. One thing was damned clear to him: he had to choose. Before Lady Clarice's arrival, on one side of the scale there was a big favor done for Sir Lunardo Michiel and the doge, and on the other side there was nothing. Now, however, on the other side there were the Bernardos and the Pesaros, and the scales were just about even. But above all there was his fear of Lady Clarice. That woman was really capable of spreading it around that the Ten had covered up a huge scandal to avoid a conviction for a nephew of one of the Council. That, Master Zuanne understood all too well, was the crucial point. The power of the Ten had been under attack for a while now, and just two years ago it had been heavily reduced, depriving the Council of a whole range of policy decisions which it had long been accustomed to making at the expense of the Senate. Among the patricians, as Morosini well knew, many would have looked favorably on a further reduction of its powers, especially if it were justified by accusations concerning the partiality and private corruption of its components. Master Zuanne trembled again. One of the scales noisily banged on the ground, while the other rose into the air. There's nothing to be done, he decided. I have to return immediately to the palace and explain to Cicogna that we were wrong about everything; and that tomorrow, if Sir Lunardo tries to defend his nephew, so much the worse for him.

"You have won, Signora," he declared, turning around. "Master Alvise can be proud of his pupil."

The door swung open, squeaking on its hinges, and Michele, who was sitting on the straw, jumped to his feet. Against the light streaming through the opening he could see the outline of the figure of Captain Casalini, and behind him that of the jailor.

"Come out," said the captain, grumpily.

Michele walked toward him.

"They're letting you out," Casalini announced to him, when he had him right in front of him.

"How do you mean?" Michele stammered.

"They're putting you out! They believed your story, even though the gold was never found. Come on, get your things."

"I don't have anything," Michele replied, nodding at the empty cell. The captain shrugged his shoulders.

"You're lucky, things worked out for you," he added, as he accompanied him along the underground passage that led to the exit. "There was a time when I wouldn't have bet a cent on you saving your skin."

He came to the door and the jailor opened it with a big bunch of keys. Outside, the sun was shining and Michele, no longer used to the blinding sunlight, closed his eyes until they were slits.

"But can I go wherever I want?" he asked.

The captain came out alongside him.

"Apparently, you've got some friends in high places," he said, enigmatically.

"Me?" Michele thrust his eyes open. Then he remembered, "I had a safe conduct from Signor Lorenzo Bernardo." The captain gave him a meaningful look.

"There, that's what I mean. They've ordered me to accompany you to Palazzo Bernardo, and to deliver you to the wife of Signor Lorenzo. I don't know anything else and I don't want to," he concluded.

"But . . . here?" Michele asked, unable to find the words. The captain, after so many years on the job, understood immediately.

"Don't worry, they'll summon you again, they'll put everything on the record, and maybe they'll give you some prize. What did you do for work?"

"I was a mason."

"Master or apprentice?"

"My father was a master mason," Michele replied proudly.

"All right," Casalini observed. "In my opinion they'll order the guild to accept you as a master. Come on now, let's get going, Palazzo Bernardo is quite a ways from here."

In the same moment that Michele was emerging from the jailhouse door, Sir Lunardo Michiel, livid, was leaving the same palace from another secondary entrance. The meeting of the Ten had gone so differently from what he had expected that he still couldn't quite understand what happened. When the doge presented the case in terms that were the opposite of those agreed on just the day before, Sir Lunardo had started shifting in his seat, trying to get his attention, but Cicogna, lost in his beard, had succeeded in avoiding him. He'd had to stand up and intervene, to remind everybody that they were measuring the word of beggar against that of a Loredan, but by then the dye had been cast. Several of them were delighted to have the chance to cross him, and the vote couldn't have gone any worse. As he climbed aboard his gondola and gave the order to take him home, Sir Lunardo was so upset that he didn't notice the boat that was docking just a few steps away, and the four near-easterners who were getting off it, accompanied by a ceremonious secretary. As Michiel's gondola made its way out into the Grand Canal, the four looked around with curiosity. Then they walked off slowly toward the main entrance to the palace.

"This is truly incredible," the doge grumbled, putting back on the table the papers he had been examining. The Lord Heads of the Ten, who were with him in his private chambers, agreed, their faces grim. Cicogna turned to Master Zuanne.

"Someone might think this was all contrived by Providence," he said, forcing a smile.

Yes, Morosini thought, it's easy for you to say that now. But I know how hard I had to struggle to convince you last night. In any event, whether it was Providence or His Majesty Chance, it is indeed strange that this delegation has arrived at just the right time.

"At this point," the doge resumed, "it seems we have no choice. Those two reckless fools put the Republic at risk, and we cannot avoid making an example of them."

Everyone assented, gravely.

"Peace is too important to allow us to pardon those who threaten its survival, even though having to take certain measures is always painful," the doge insisted.

Those present assented again, exchanging knowing glances.

"Are we all agreed? Then let's go," Cicogna sighed, standing up.

A little later, sopracomito Loredan entered the chamber of the Council of Ten. A captain of the police followed close behind him. The sudden summons worried him a little; the evening before his uncle had reassured him that the affair would have a favorable outcome, even more so now that the galleyman had come back from the island without finding the gold, and he certainly hadn't expected he would be sent for at his palace so suddenly. On entering the room he winced; standing in a corner, handcuffed, was his comito. He looked worn out and could hardly stand up. The sopracomito looked around trying to find Michiel, but Sir Lunardo wasn't there. An ugly premonition sent a chill down his spine.

"Master Andrea Loredan, come forward," someone commanded. The sopracomito went to plant himself in front of the table. The doge looked at him, caressing his beard.

"Andrea Loredan," said Morosini, "you have lied to this most excellent Council. You allowed yourself to be robbed of money entrusted to you by the Republic, and then you denied it."

"But that's not true!" Loredan shouted.

"It's useless to deny it now, your comito has confessed everything," Morosini interrupted him, nodding toward the man standing in the corner. The sopracomito, alarmed, turned to look at him, but the other avoided his gaze.

"He lies!" Loredan cried out. "I delivered the money!"

Sir Zuanne glared at him coldly.

"That's true. And in order to deliver it you boarded a felucca, you robbed the merchants that it was carrying, and to hide your crime you had the crew thrown overboard."

"That's not true!" Loredan repeated, desperately.

Sir Zuanne exchanged glances with the doge and then nodded to the guards. A secret door opened and through it came the group of near-easterners who had gotten off the boat a few hours before. The first in line was a Turk dressed in brocade, with a pair of impressive mustachios, a club in hand, and an enormous white turban; he came forward with his head held high, an impassive expression, and without looking at anyone. He was followed by two attendants, they too in sumptuous garb, but with slightly smaller turbans, and no club. Last came a modestly dressed Levantine with a small yellow turban. He looked around anxiously, and on seeing Loredan he flinched; then he saw the comito in the corner, and hurriedly said something in the ear of the first to enter. A dragoman came over to the two of them, exchanged some words with both, and then translated for the benefit of the Ten.

"They are the ones. He recognizes them."

Sir Zuanne looked at Loredan.

"You believed that all the witnesses had drowned, but that's not right. One of the merchants that you robbed managed to free himself from the ropes, grabbed on to the wreckage of the felucca, and stayed in the water until the next day, when a brigantine came by and rescued him. It took a long time for his story to reach Constantinople, and for the Great Lord to order the opening of an investigation. Now, however, it has all come to light, and the magnificent chaush Mustafà is here to ask for reparations. By a strange coincidence, or perhaps," he interrupted himself to look to the heavens, "by the will of Divine Providence, he has arrived this very morning, in time to allow us to do justice."

Beside himself, Loredan broke out in a sweat.

"The Republic cannot tolerate that its friendship with the Great Lord be put at risk by irresponsible and criminal behavior," Morosini continued, inexorable. "Tell the magnificent Mustafà," he added, addressed to the dragoman, "that these miserable wretches will be delivered to him, and the he can take them to Constantinople so they can be given the punishment they deserve."

The chaush made a slight bow, then proudly launched into a long speech in Turkish, to which the dragoman listened attentively, preparing to translate. Loredan's legs were shaking, and the captain who was standing next to him had to hold him up. To do so he leaned in closer to him. He wasn't a nice man and on occasions like this he liked to amuse himself.

"The pole," he whispered maliciously in Loredan's ear.

"It's not true, I can't believe it!" Bianca exclaimed joyously.

"Yes it is, believe me. He'll be here shortly, you've got just enough time to get dressed," Lady Clarice said.

Astounded, Bianca looked at her apron.

"Shall I put on my Sunday dress?" Bianca asked timidly.

"You mean you need me to tell you that? Go on, Run!" exclaimed Clarice, laughing.

When Bianca came back to her, she looked her over from head to toe.

"That's fine," she decreed. "But why aren't you wearing your gold chain?"

Bianca hesitated, embarrassed.

"Giacomo gave it to me," she mumbled. Clarice laughed.

"And those earrings, didn't he give you those too?"

Bianca, proud, shook her head no.

"Those I sold! And I redeemed the ones from my wedding, the ones my husband gave me," she said, gliding her fingers over the gold circles hanging from her lobes.

"Good for you," Clarice remarked. "But the chain, listen to me, Bianca, if you don't wear it today you'll never wear it again. Or did you sell that too?"

Bianca blushed.

"Truthfully no," she admitted. "It's so beautiful!"

Clarice smiled.

"Well then, wear it. You'll tell your husband that it was given to you by your mistress."

"A gift like that!" Bianca objected. "He'll never believe it." Clarice turned serious.

"A gift like that you richly deserved, for the way you helped me to give birth. And actually, I want to give it to you now."

Bianca shook her head, now she too was serious.

"You've already given me a gift, Signora. You've brought Michele back to me."

"Oh yes? Well, that's not enough," Clarice shot back. "Go get the chain."

Bianca ran off, without having understood what it was her mistress wanted to do. When she came back with the chain in hand, Clarice had opened a jewel box and was rummaging through the jewels.

"Here it is," she decided, pulling out another chain and looking at it against the light from the window. It wasn't, naturally, the heavily bejeweled one that Sir Lorenzo had given her after the baby was born; but it was still much heavier and more expensive than Bianca's.

"Now Bianca, you have to make a small sacrifice, so you won't ever have to feel remorse. Your chain is truly lovely, but I'm going to take it for myself. And you take this one, and you'll be able to tell your husband where it came from, without worrying about betraying yourself.

Bianca, her eyes glimmering, passed the jewel around her neck.

"Have a look at yourself!" her mistress ordered, pointing at the mirror. Bianca obeyed; then she knelt at her feet, radiant, and kissed her hands.

"Now go, go down to wait for him in the garden, I can tell he's just about to arrive," said Clarice. Bianca gathered up her skirt, so she wouldn't trip, and ran off. Clarice stayed for a minute lost in reverie. Then she left the room, walked through a number of hallways, and stopped in front of a window that looked out on the garden. She saw Bianca rush outside and come to a halt, because there was nobody there. But an instant later the footman also came out of the house, crossed the garden dragging his feet, and disappeared into the vegetable garden. Clarice saw Bianca tormenting her fingers, then smiled on seeing her go over to the fountain, rinse out her mouth and spit. It took a while for the footman to reappear at the other end of the garden; behind him was Michele, who was looking all around in wonder. Bianca took a few steps toward him, unsure of herself at first, and then, when she saw him recognize her and open his arms out wide, she ran.

GLOSSARY

Aga: in Turkish, chief, commandant.

amain: with all one's might, at full force, or at full speed. Rowing amain or *all'arrancata* refers to a command requiring oarsman to use all of their strength to propel the galley at the maximum possible speed.

asper: a small silver coin circulating in the eastern Mediterranean from the 12th to 17th centuries.

bachelor: a volunteer in service on a galley as a sailor and, if needed, as a soldier.

bailo: ambassador of the Republic of Venice at the court of Constantinople.

bey: in Turkish, master, lord.

beylerbey: governor of one of the provinces of the Ottoman Empire.

buonavoglia: oarsman who voluntarily signs on part of the crew of a galley.

caulker: in shipbuilding a worker specialized in rendering boats waterproof by applying tarred oakum to the slits between the boards of the hull and then sealing it with a layer of tar and pitch.

cavallotto: silver coin engraved with a horse and minted in several cities of northren Italy in the fifteenth and sixteenth centuries.

chaush: (Turkish) a special envoy of the Sultan of the Ottoman Empire.

comito: first officer on a galley in charge of maneuvering the sails and all services performed by sailors.

corsair: a swift pirate ship authorized by a government to attack ships of an enemy state.

dervish (from the Persian dervish, "pauper"): member of a Muslim religious order noted for devotional exercises (as bodily movements leading to a trance).

dragoman: interpreter between Europeans and peoples of the Near East, with various official functions depending on rank.

felucca: a narrow, fast lateen-rigged sailing vessel mainly in the Mediterranean area.

fusta: a narrow, light and fast ship with shallow draft, powered by both oars and sail; in essence a small galley. It typically had 12 to 18 two-man rowing benches on each side, a single mast with a lateen (triangular) sail, and usually carried two or three guns.

galley: a large low ship propelled by sails and oars and used in the Meiterranean for war and trading. The narrow galley, used for war, was five meters wide and forty meters long, had three masts and twenty-four or twenty-six benches of rowers on each side. It carried several pieces of artillery and about three hundred men between oarsmen, soldiers, and sailors. Convicts or slaves sentenced to serve as oarsmen on a galley were called *gallioti* or galleymen.

galliot: a small swift galley with one lateen sail, one cannon, and as many as twenty-three oars per side.

Grand Vizier: the chief minister of the Sultan, holder of the imperial seal.

Great Lord: the Sultan of Turkey.

hajj: a pilgrimage to Mecca.

hajji: one who has made a pilgrimage to Mecca.

janissary: a soldier in an elite corps of Turkish troops organized in the late 14th century.

kapudan pasha: grand admiral, head of the naval forces of the Ottoman Empire.

marchetto: (from the name of St. Mark, patron of Venice) popular name for the *soldo*, a coin worth one twentieth (five cents) of a Venetian lira. The coin was engraved with the effigy of St. Mark.

parone: (Venetian) related to Italian *padrone* or master. An officer on a Venetian galley in charge of the oarsmen and subordinate to the comito and sopracomito. On Genoese and other galleys the role of the parone was performed by the *aguzzino* or galley-sergeant.

pianiero (or vogavanti): on the benches of Venetian galleys, the oarsmen closet to the internal corsia or lane, who holds the end of the oar. The middle position on the bench is occupied by the *postizzo* and the position closest to the sea is occupied by the *terzicchio*.

Porte (or Sublime Porte): the government of the Ottoman Empire.

postizzo: see pianiero.

privateering: war conducted by private ships (corsairs), commissioned to cruise against the commerce or warships of an enemy state.

qadì: a judge with jurisdiction over religious or criminal matters in the Ottoman Empire .

rais: captain of a ship of the Ottoman Empire.

sanjak: administrative subdivision of the Ottoman Empire.

sanjak-bey: governor of a sanjak.

Savio Grande: (Great Sage) the highest ranking member of the *collegio* or the steering committee of the Venetian senate.

scudo/i: name given to various gold and silver coins, minted in Venice or Florence, originally engraved with a shield or *scudo*.

sestiere: one of the six districts or neighborhoods of the city of Venice: Cannareggio, Castello, Dorsoduro, San Marco, San Polo, and Santa Croce.

Slavonian: A native of Slavonia, a historical region of Croatia between the Drava and Sava rivers. Originally part of the Roman province of Pannonia, it became a Slavic state in the seventh century. In Venice, the "Riva degli Schiavoni" (Slavonian waterfront) takes its name from the Slavonian sailors of the Eastern Adriatic who docked their boats there and carried on commercial activities.

soldo: an old Venetian coin worth five cents.

sopracomito: commander of a galley. In the Venetian Republic the posiiton was attributed only to noblemen.

spahì: in the Ottoman Empire, a soldier belonging to a permanent corps of cavalry, compensated with the attribution of a fief (*timar*).

terzicchio: see pianiero.

yali: Turkish, literally "seashore, beach," a house or mansion constructed at immediate waterside (almost exclusively seaside) in Constantinople and usually built with an architectural concept that takes into account the characteristics of the coastal location. They line the waters of the Bosporus in an alternation of docks, gangways, gardens, and orchards.

Zara: (from the Arabic az-zahr or "dye") a game that consists in throwing three dice onto a gaming-table. The winner must declare out loud, before throwing the dice, the total points that will show on the top face of the three dice when they come to stop.

zecchino/i: name given to the Venetian gold ducat in the mid-sixteenth century.

About the Author

Alessandro Barbero is the author of *The Battle: A New History of Waterloo* (Walker & Co., 2005), *Charlemagne: Father of a Continent*, and *Master Pyle's Bella Vita and Other People's Wars*, winner of the Strega Prize for Fiction. He is a renowned historian whose two-volume history of the Battle of Lepanto is considered to be the definitive text on the subject. He teaches Medieval History at the University of Eastern Piedmont in Vercelli, Italy.